THE EMPRESS CAPSULE

AUDACITY SAGA: BOOK 1

R. K. THORNE

IRON ANTLER BOOKS

Edited by Elizabeth Nover, Razor Sharp Editing

Cover art by Julie Dillon

Cover design by R.K. Thorne

Version 1.1

❀ Created with Vellum

For my husband, for all the games, coffee, laughter, and support.
You're over 9000!

CHAPTER ONE

"WELL, *they're* not supposed to be here." Ellen narrowed her eyes at the unexpectedly large number of green, yellow, and red splotches lumbering slowly across her helmet display. This lab was tucked away on a volcanic backwater, the middle of galactic nowhere. There shouldn't be this much resistance. Damn Enhancers. Whatever their scientists were up to in this lab, it couldn't be good.

Fortunately, she was here to put an end to it. Whatever it was. And she'd be doing so… any minute now.

"Surprises ain't your favorite, Commander?" Nova said between cracks of gum. The comm mercifully cut out the chewing sounds. Crouched to Ellen's left, Nova was assembling a grenade launcher with far too much zest. Woman lived for an excuse to use that thing, even if it was only to launch knockout grenades a dozen feet through what appeared to be nothing but cloudy glass.

They weren't taking any chances with underpowered munitions.

The two of them were hunkered down on one side of a T-shaped intersection, Zhia on the other. These corners offered the last cover between Ellen's team and their objective—the Enhancer lab.

"Something's gotta keep me sharp in my retirement, eh?" Ellen murmured. Nova snickered, and Zhia shook her helmeted head, muffled laughter drifting over the comm. At twenty-two, Ellen wasn't your typical retiree. And the Union hadn't exactly released her *willingly* from its service.

Technicalities.

Ellen swiveled to her other knee and gave the hallway behind them a visual check. Even with the unexpected hostiles, this shouldn't be hard: a dozen dark feet, a few doors on either side, a shielded metal door. This wasn't exactly the interplanetary defense Ellen had been trained for. But things could go sideways on the simplest missions, as she was always trying to get through Nova's stubborn skull. The door's lockpad flashed red, indicating Adan had finished cracking it. Good. The high-tech fogged window hid whatever tortures were being perpetrated inside.

Twisting back behind cover, she tried again to count the number of hostiles on the thermal readout. Five, six? Eight? Damn drecks needed to stop moving.

Big, heavily armored—her armor readout suggested they were Theroki. Sounded about right. The Theroki were an all-human, all-male "mercenary" outfit that could just as accurately be described as pirates or organized crime. And they *were* the Enhancers' favored security vendor.

Two crouched like stone gargoyles just inside the doorway. Others paced inconveniently inside. Maybe seven? If only the drecks would stand still.

"You seeing this, Zhia?" Ellen said. Their armor trapped the sound of their voices, so no one outside their encrypted channel could hear. That is, of course, unless they ran into a hacker far better than Simmons and his custom security protocols. But in that case, they'd have bigger problems. Like their armor cooking them alive.

"Yep, I see it," Zhia answered. Her second-in-command waited on one knee on the other side of the intersection, her rifle at the ready. Over Zhia's shoulder, drones hovered, as still and silent as possible now that Adan's work was complete. Cool as a damned cucumber over there. "Regular old snafu. Think they know where we are?" Their dynacamo should hide them, but it didn't block every type of scan. They still left a trace thermal signature.

A thunderous wave of telekinetic energy rippled toward them through the concrete floor of the hallway. Floor and ceiling groaned, splitting concrete rumbling in beats as regular as mortar fire. Glass shattered in waves.

Ellen threw her hands over her neck, a futile but instinctive move. Frag, she hated when she did that. Her armor braced itself heroically as the force ripped through them, but she still stumbled forward onto one knee like she'd been shoved.

"Guess that answers that question," Zhia grumbled.

Sand streamed from the battered ceiling of the bunker as the first telekinetic wave petered out. Silence fell.

The next attack would come soon, so Ellen stole another glance around the corner. Just cracked cement and splintered glass—no Theroki yet. "You almost loaded, Nova? I think this lab is in dire need of a shutdown."

"Nearly," Nova said. Two loud gum chews escaped before the comm cut off.

"You'd think by the twenty-third century we'd have grenade launchers that assembled themselves," Zhia said.

"Oh, they do. I don't trust 'em," Nova replied.

"You mean I'm sitting here *waiting* when we could be busting—"

"Think they're excited to get their asses handed to them by a bunch of girls?" Ellen cut in. She didn't need the two of them distracting each other arguing tech right now. And as weapons specialist, Nova's kit was Nova's call.

"Doubtful," said Zhia. "They may have caught our sigs, but it ain't like we're wearin' perfume and high heels."

"You wish," Ellen shot back.

"Says the girl who can't walk in high heels to save her life. And who you callin' a girl, *jagiya*? Nobody respectable's called me a girl in weeks. There was that one lovely boy back on Tarkos…"

And *that* story was a road Ellen didn't want to go down. "I'll learn heels someday, okay?"

"Do you even own any?"

"Keep your eyes on the prize, grama," Ellen said, grinning to herself as Zhia's flurry of Russian curses came back at her. "C'mon, hurry it up, Nova."

Ellen leaned against the wall, trying to relax her tense muscles. As soon as they neutralized the Theroki, the three of them would bust that lab apart. Ellen dreaded that moment most on these missions. The violence committed inside the labs was always so much worse than what the troops dished out around them. Soldiers—in general—tended to fight with some degree of honor, within international law. An outfit that stole and slaughtered with the frequency of the Theroki could hardly be called honorable, and she didn't know their stance on torture, but they did tend to prefer straightforward action and brute force to biochem or rad attacks at least.

If as many scientists would stay within their own ethical codes, Ellen wouldn't have a job.

But she did have a job. And she would do it.

Might not be pleasant, but it was a hell of a lot worse for the scientists' victims. She was the lucky one in this scenario, telekinetic waves shoving her around or not.

That had not always been the case.

"Shoulda brought more knockout grenades," said Zhia. "What if your ancient launcher misses?"

"Shoulda woulda coulda," Nova said. "Or a harpoon!" She raised the launcher to her shoulder and started punching in launch instructions to bust through certain fortifications and neutralize against others.

Sometimes non-lethal tech seemed like more trouble than it was worth. It'd be so much easier to just nuke this lab to dust-covered rubble.

"You're nigh on archaic at times, Sergeant," Zhia said.

"You're the one who just said 'nigh,' " Ellen pointed out.

"You don't find my whale reference clever?" By the sound of her voice, Ellen could tell Nova was grinning. "Damn, I'm so disappointed."

Zhia laughed. "Leave the poetry to me, *jagiya*."

"Whatever you say, *vieja*," Nova shot back.

"You're just jealous of my vast experience."

Nova ignored her. "All right. Ready on your mark, Commander."

"I expect great things from this weapon," Ellen said. On the display, one Theroki was squaring up with the door, getting ready for the next attack.

"Stella won't let you down," Nova replied.

Ellen snorted and hoped that didn't carry over the comm. "Next wave incoming. One should be in view. Launch over his shoulder while the door is open if you can."

"If the ceiling doesn't collapse on us first," Zhia muttered.

"Keeping the requests conservative today, are you?" Nova scooted around her, Ellen shuffling to the left to switch places.

Ellen grinned, although no one could see her behind the silver-blue sheen of her visor. She preferred it that way; she kept her grins to herself. "Hey, if I don't push you, who will, Sergeant?"

Up the hall, a sudden raw rumble gave Nova her cue. She spun around the corner, launcher propped on her shoulder, and fired.

The thunder ripped past them and through them, more focused on shaking the walls this time. It knocked Ellen off-balance again, and she eyed the sand sifting through the ceiling cracks overhead. Looked like it was going to hold for at least one more wave. Maybe. Hopefully that was all the time her team needed. Ellen realized her hands were shielding her head once again and yanked them to her sides.

The crack of the knockout grenade unleashing its psychic damage ripped through the air and across her helmet display.

Thuds. Silence followed. More sand sifted down, and her armor dutifully reported its status, scrolling through the environmental indicators at breakneck speed, fast as the armor would let her set it.

The drones whizzed past to confirm the damage.

"Looks like we're good," Zhia said a moment later, clicking her tablet with its additional modes and higher detail back into her chest armor. "Thermal, infrared, and rad readings show no movement. Drones concur on visual check."

There was always a risk of soldiers with scrambling, knockout-proof armor or dynacamo. Armor like the three of them were wearing. But since each suit cost nearly as much as an apartment on Capital, Ellen doubted it. Theroki were expensive mercenaries, and the lab had had a lot of them, so they were probably the only security that had been hired. They might have all the funds in the world, but thank the Lord the Theroki were as yet too bull-headed to upgrade their armor against knockout attacks. They favored armor that showed off the scars of battle—a.k.a. shit that was viciously disfigured, hideously bloodied, and in some cases very old.

There were no scars on armor you upgraded every six months to keep up with the latest tech. Where was the fun in that?

Of course, they were all flat on their asses, so who was having fun now?

"All right," Ellen barked. "Let's get this done."

They rounded the corner one at a time, Ellen last, and made their way up the hall with multis at the ready. The grenade hadn't cleared the Theroki's shoulder, but it had blown through the uncracked fogged barrier. Not glass, maybe petroglic. A grenade-sized hole showed the still lab beyond and the glimpse of a deflated, greenish artificial uterus that had probably been two meters high. The cracked concrete beneath their boots made their approach loud, in spite of the sound-softening boot tech. Damn Theroki. For chaotic, raging maniacs with out-of-date tech, they were still quite effective at gumming up the works.

Zhia flicked a finger at the lockpad, and the door slid aside. Thank you, Adan.

On seeing the interior, though, Ellen's heart dropped. They were too late.

The first third of the room, the office, contained little beyond a single holodisplay, empty steel counters, and one toppled beaker. The back two-thirds was a dripping, liquidy mess. A row of a dozen artificial wombs had collapsed, leaking fluid all over the floor on the right. Locked cells on the left stood empty. Oozing, cracked tube units along the back were still lit in various shades of green and blue, their flush cycles well underway.

"They were on their way out of here," Zhia muttered. "Shit. All that for nothing."

Nova stood over an unconscious Theroki and nudged him with her boot. "That's more than I thought were in here. Think we should just leave them, or are we calling for backup?"

Ellen shook her head. Six Theroki in the end. In their armor, they'd weigh tons. Literally. And she didn't want to imprison six Therokis anyway. These boys were hired hands, famous for their neutrality. Of course, their complete disregard for law and order wasn't exactly neutral and made them plenty of enemies. But if Ellen offered a higher price, they'd switch sides in a blink, unless their oath programming had been engaged. "Leave 'em. Who knows if they even knew what they were hired for? Any scientists?"

"One. Here," said Zhia. "Checking him already, don't worry, Elle."

Ellen held her breath. It's not going to be her, she told herself. Arakovic was a Union *woman*. This Enhancer scientist was clearly a man. The chances that her old enemy were here were impossibly low. But Arakovic had nearly fried Ellen, plugging her into fifty of her troops' brains without getting anyone's thoughts on the matter or permission, leaving Ellen's mind a scrambled mess for three and a half years. And that cruel woman was still out there, doing it to someone else now, somewhere else.

And she would keep on doing it until Ellen found her—and stopped her.

But unless the doctor had gone to some pretty extreme lengths to hide her identity by altering both race and gender, it couldn't be her. This man looked Chinese or Korean like Ellen, almost certainly from the PAS at some point or another.

And besides, what reason did Arakovic have to hide? She didn't know Ellen was hunting her.

At least, not yet.

"Big fat nope." Zhia made a disgusted noise as she straightened.

"Damn." Ellen let out a breath, irrationally disappointed. One day.

"Sorry, *jagiya*. Shall I scramble him?"

"Yeah. Hit the network, and let's get out of here."

They'd done this before a hundred times, maybe a thousand, so each of them got to work quickly—Zhia hooking the drones into the holodesk, Nova administering a shot to the scientist's neck, Ellen keeping her rifle at ready. She was a little high-ranking for guard duty —or ground missions, for that matter—but she was the best shot among them and probably always would be. The Union hadn't taken her to UCS at age five *only* because they were desperate for some genius to save them from their stupid war.

And how had that turned out? New decade, new war. Same old shit.

A seventh Theroki was out cold toward the back. A hallway led to a single storm door leading to the surface, and scans showed her no more troops up top. That'd be their way out.

Satisfied all nearby forces had been stunned by the grenade, she took a moment to peer at the fallen scientist, feeling a bit more pity than usual. Bastard deserved it, she reminded herself. There weren't many moral reasons for an underground Enhancer bunker to be filled with wombs and tube units, let alone cells with locks that were very, very far from patient-care units. This was not a man of nobility or morals, she reminded herself. She trusted their intel. Even if they hadn't known about the Therokis, she knew Simmons was not rash about choosing where to strike. As if to make his presence felt in the room, one of the drones clicked and whirred as it left the terminal and the other drone took over.

Still, getting your memories scrambled seemed like an awful fate. Better than killing him, she assured herself, more humane. He'd remember his family, and due to their carefully designed brain virus, he'd have a very, *very* hard time continuing the heinous work he'd done here. Or any kind of scientific or mathematical work whatsoever. He might be able to calculate a tip.

"Should we scramble the Therokis too?" Nova asked. "I don't know if I want to risk waking them to retract their helmets."

"No," Ellen told her. "Search the scientist and make sure he's not holding anything important. Take their rifles. Well, just the better ones, don't bother if it's nearly broken. Check around for any physical records of their research. How are we coming on those networks?"

"Simmons signed off, Adan is in—we're installing nukes." Nukes were their fond nickname for the programs the Foundation used to obliterate enemy data nets. Ellen hardly understood everything they did, but she did know they ferreted back newly acquired research to the Foundation, while happily obliterating it from the computer system it had started on. The program was quite sneaky about it too, locating other programs that would flag a high volume of outpouring data, temporarily squirreling away the data in obscure locations, sneaking it out slowly over time if need be. Like any good soldier trying to evade and escape in enemy territory.

"Done," Zhia announced. "Ready?"

"Got some gear, a couple notebooks, Commander." Nova held up a half dozen tablets in one hand as she slugged a silver-trimmed Enhancer pack over her shoulder. "But most of their shit is gone."

Ellen waved it off. "We did what we could. And we gave these Therokis hell. Let's go." They headed to their exit.

"A seventh one?" Nova stepped over another Theroki form that'd been farther from the grenade. Only one armored boot stuck out from behind a half wall.

"Seven in a unit? Odd formation," Zhia mumbled.

"He's probably got less time on his clock, further back and with that half wall blocking the punch. I didn't program for that distance," Nova said.

Ellen nodded sharply. "Let's not be here when he wakes up cranky."

"Right on, Commander."

———

KAEL GASPED for breath and sat straight up, smacking his helmet into a steel laboratory table before collapsing again. He groaned. His lungs might have briefly stopped, with the way he found himself aching to breathe. Growling, he grabbed the edge of the wheeled steel table and sent it careening through the air into the far wall. It crashed satisfyingly into the cell force fields with dull blue buzzes of irritation.

There. That made him feel slightly better.

He wasn't going to live to be fifty at this rate. Hell, he'd be lucky if he made the two more years till thirty. Another reason he needed out. He wasn't dying a Theroki, contract be damned. Not if he could help it. He'd had no choice about joining up with these thieves and murderers, just as he'd had no choice about joining the Gray Dragons of his youth.

Just once, he wanted a choice to be something other than a criminal.

He lurched upright, groaning again. Fragging knockout grenades. If their armor weren't so damn old and crusty, they wouldn't be in this position. Was that so much to ask? But no, his fool comrades preferred rust and snarled edges and looking tough. Sure, the savagery made some people shit their pants when Theroki showed up, but it couldn't have much effect if your enemy took you out before they even walked in the room. They might as well have pounded their chests like gorillas. Now they were all on their asses, and whoever had just assaulted the lab was probably long gone and laughing the whole way.

Or they could still be here.

As reality rushed back in, he grabbed for his laser rifle and froze. Gone. Shit.

Listening, only silence met his ears. Maybe some dust settling somewhere from the earlier attacks.

He stood slowly, still struggling to regain his breath. Sweat dripped down his forehead. Fragging armor cooling unit must have broken in the grenade blast too. Great. Damn this infernal rock. Damn this whole mission. Damn all the Theroki while he was at it. And the Enhancers too.

He scanned the scene. The six who'd been in charge of the evac were all laid out. Dead, or just unconscious? Hmm, odd timing. How had anyone known this bunker was even here? The only newcomers for the last half year had been those six.

One of these damned drecks must have led them here. Or sold the information to the highest bidder. He hoped they *were* dead if they were fragging traitors. Who else could have given away their location?

Kael stilled as he spotted his primary concern. Enhancer High Command Lord Regent Jun Il Li was just as much unconscious. He lay on the lab floor, hands splayed, eyes closed.

Unconscious—or dead? Li was supposed to have knockout-protection gear. Kael swallowed as a spike of adrenaline shot through him. It'd been *his* charge to protect the lord regent. If he'd failed—

No. He should stop thinking about it and go check before he went supernova and stormed after their attackers in a blind, blood-mad rage. That was about as stupid as not upgrading your armor, but he'd seen plenty a Theroki charge to a gory, preventable death because of their unique upgrades and artificial wiring. He'd prefer not to beckon such a fate. Deep, slow breaths. Calm.

Heart pounding in spite of his attempts, he crept closer, crouching and listening carefully again for anyone in the vicinity. He grabbed the nearest rifle, one so dirty and uncared for that it looked barely functional. Idiots. Then again, why worry about knockout grenades if you treated your rifle so badly it wouldn't fire? There was a reason—or ten —that Kael's survival record was among the top fifteen percent.

He listened a moment longer. The hostiles seemed long gone. Who the hell had they been, anyway? One reason Theroki didn't bother to upgrade their armor—other than the shock and awe, of course—was that knockout grenades were insanely expensive. He hadn't shopped for one in a long time, but he was fairly sure you could trade one for a small one-man ship. Considering how the grenade had dealt with him and his colleagues, the high price made sense. The price would likely be even higher if nonlethal force were in higher demand, but many military forces had no problem with just killing everyone. Of course, unconscious people were especially easy to kill.

The grenade should give him clues about the attacking force—high-tech and well funded, at the very least. And for some reason, not interested in a massacre. Hmm.

As he approached, he could see the lord regent's eyes twitching beneath his eyelids, as though lost in some dream. Kael swallowed hard. Puritan attackers, maybe? They'd likely infected and killed him with some heinous but perfectly naturally occurring bug. His fingers twitched, tempted to curl into a fist. Puritans and their sick sense of poetic justice. They wouldn't genetically engineer anything to save their lives—quite literally—but they'd happily murder you with a naturally occurring horror. Brain-melting bacteria from Sali IV had been a favorite as of late, according to Theroki and Enhancer reports. Upon closer inspection, a tiny red puncture marred Lord Regent Li's neck. Sure sign of injection.

Kael might not have much time. Throwing caution aside, he set down the worn rifle and shook Li's shoulders, smacked his face once. Then harder.

Li's eyes flickered open. For a moment, he gazed around, dazed and unfocused, as if searching for a room that was no longer there. Then finally his eyes rested on Kael.

"You."

"Tridelphi Kael Sidassian, sir."

"I know you." Li's eyes narrowed, and he looked hardly sure of that assertion.

"I've been guarding you for the last six months on this station. We were about to evac when we were attacked. Do you remember?"

The lord regent seemed to become aware of his surroundings suddenly, taking in the fallen Theroki around him. Then he raised his hands to gaze at his open palms, staring, mystified. "What's... wrong with me?"

"I believe they injected you with something, sir. While I was knocked out. My apologies, Lord Regent. Can I get you to a hospital? The evac ship isn't due to land for six more hours." Kael bowed as low as he could, perched on one knee, wincing inside the helmet where Li could not see. When he straightened, Li's eyes were filled with rage, maybe at him, maybe at the attack. Maybe both.

"No time for that. You have failed the task you were commissioned for, Tridelphi. I demand you undertake another to repay this debt."

"It might not be fatal, sir—"

"I assure you, it is."

Kael pressed his lips together but didn't argue. Li was within his contract.

Parting his robes, Li narrowed his eyes, struggling to focus. The cloth slid aside to reveal a thigh. Li pressed just above the knee, and skin slid under other skin, almost soundlessly. Damn—was the whole leg artificial, or was it only partially cybernetic? And here Kael had thought he'd been the lone cyborg on this rock for so long. Well, perhaps one leg didn't qualify you as anything but having a prosthetic limb. Depended on the functionality.

This was probably not the time to quiz Li on his hardware.

Li's fingers drew out a smooth silver canister just smaller than three grenades lined up in a row. Tiny green lights winked in and out around its middle. Li checked the side of the cylinder, then held it up to Kael.

"I can feel my memory failing, Theroki. Take this."

Kael gritted his teeth. Work with a man for months, and you'd think he'd start calling you by your first name. A name he damn well knew. But perhaps he shouldn't be surprised by condescension from anyone whose title was so overblown. Or perhaps that part of his brain had already melted.

Either way, Kael reached out and took the canister gingerly in his gauntleted hand.

"This canister contains gene documentation and backups on the Empress Project." Li stopped for a moment, looking like he would pass out, but then gathered himself and continued. "As well as an experimental fetus of the empress herself."

Kael leaned back on his haunches, staring at the canister with a mixture of horror and awe. A child was in there? How old? Older than his and Asha's had been once? He shoved the painful thought aside. It didn't matter. Asha had died and the baby and all his futures with her.

"Take it to Enhancer High Command on Desori. Her mother is there. They wanted to be reunited in the end. Please. As you've killed me, I'm sure you can agree our family deserves that much."

In the end? Kael glared under the cover of the helmet. Technically Li wasn't even dead yet, but he was sure slathering the guilt on thick.

People from all over the galaxy would be hunting this—a copy of the Enhancer empress's genes? This was bad. Very, very bad.

If anyone knew such a thing existed and was in his hands, he'd have the biggest target in the galaxy on his back. Rumor was the genes had been lost, though. How many knew the truth?

Enough to pay off some Theroki and organize a strike on this lab?

He could stall. He could insist on getting Li to medical care or simply hang around to make sure the man was dying at all. On the other hand, Enhancer monarch or no, Li claimed there was a woman out there who would like her daughter back, at least the embryo of her. That seemed a noble goal, the kind he'd hoped he'd get more of when he'd been forced into the Theroki ranks. He'd been optimistic, naive about the real nature of his situation then. Assignments with any virtue had been few and far between.

Beyond that, transporting the canister would justify him running off on his own. It could buy him time while he figured out what he wanted to do about his current predicament, his secretly damaged chip. The evac team had not yet noticed. No one knew but him. And Vala, of course. He ought to be back on the *Genokai* mothership by the end of the week, explaining himself. There would be no keeping his damaged chip a secret then; all repairs would be made with brutal and painful efficiency.

If they believed him that it was a random glitch. A maintenance slip. If they didn't, well…

This capsule, however, was a way out. A delay. A covert mission directly from the lord regent meant he wouldn't need to report back at all. Not until the mission was complete.

"Of course, Lord Regent," he said. He smiled.

"It must reach there within six weeks or the fetus will grow too large for the capsule. Now give me your oath," Li demanded.

Kael sighed and hoped it didn't come across the mic. "Sir, it's not necessary—"

"Yes. It is. You've already failed me once, Theroki."

Twice, maybe, but Kael wasn't going to point that out. The damage he'd allowed to come to his Theroki controller chip should be considered a failure, although it probably hadn't contributed to this attack. Probably. Vala might have turned out to be a Puritan operative when she'd betrayed him, but he'd told her nothing of those he protected in the end. Nothing more than what she'd already known by getting hired. He'd managed that much.

He sighed. "Fine. Engaging." He raised his gauntlet, flipped up the first and second panels to find the commission-oath control, and pressed it. "I will do all in my power to deliver this canister to EHC and the empress's mother within six weeks, starting now." He released the control. An uncomfortable switch shifted in his back where his unit rested near his shoulder blades, neatly attached to his spine and, through it, his brain.

He was signed on now. He'd get that capsule to Desori X or die trying. He just hoped he wouldn't have to kill too many who got in the way. He had enough innocent blood on his hands for one lifetime.

Li relaxed and slumped back to the ground. "Don't fail me again, Theroki."

"I won't, sir." Kael straightened, but hesitated. He hated to leave anyone to die alone. Although Li's experiments *did* have a brutal streak, and that was saying something, coming from a Theroki.

A groan from his left made Kael start and grab for his rifle, but it was just one of the evac team stirring. Good, they weren't dead. They could deal with Li shortly.

Strange, though. Puritans would have killed them. Puritans would also have been hard-pressed to afford knockout grenades. Who had attacked then, if not the Enhancer's primary enemy? The Union? Some corporation? Mercs?

"Should I guard you or be on my way, sir?"

Li waved him off, like shooing a fly. "Get on your mission. Be gone, Theroki, and leave me to Chaos."

"I'm sure you won't—" he started.

Li made a noise of disgust. "I did not hire you for spiritual advisement. Leave me to my misery."

Kael pressed his lips together behind the mask of the helmet. Some people just didn't want to be helped. He slid the capsule in his armor pack and jogged out, heading for the space port.

———

NONE of the station mechanics in their graying jumpsuits paid Kael any mind, striding in both directions past him where he stood at the lightboard. A hot, wavering wind harassed the breezeway between the ship docks and the terminal, drawing far more attention than he did. Truth be told, the mechanics were probably deliberately pretending not to notice him. No one wanted to get tangled up with his type, especially not on a base as morally flexible as this one.

Kael needed a way off Helikai and not with anyone from that evac team. The evac ship hadn't yet arrived, thankfully, but it would touch down in just over five hours now. That meant he needed passage on any ship lifting off before then—any ship that would take him. A freighter or other civilian ship would be ideal, recommended protocol when one needed to lay low. And who else would need a hired gun? 'Cause he certainly didn't have coin to pay for passage all the way to Desori. The damn rust bucket weapon he'd nicked from the evac team wouldn't be doing him any favors.

Kael flicked irritably through the lightboard menus, the ancient interface struggling to detect his gaze through his helmet's visor. Apparently this lightboard was even older than his armor. Hard to believe, but true. Then again, private, small-time bases like this one didn't have the resources of the big Union or Puritan planets to update their infrastructure in a timely fashion.

His gaze jumped from list to list until the lightboard failed and he had to grab at it like some kind of caveman. These damn menus were deeper than the Zorak Trench. He checked the air quality readout; his armor had found nothing contagious or particularly poisonous, aside from ordinary ship byproducts. He slammed the button to raise his helmet visor—no, retract the whole damn helmet—determined to get through the lists faster. Gauntleted hands were as dexterous as boxing gloves for this sort of thing.

There—the list of ships docked and the announcements they'd posted. He scratched his stubbled jaw and pushed a handful of hair out of his face now that the helmet was gone. Dirt-colored, tangled, sweaty, and nearly reaching his ears, his wild mane had grown unruly even for a Theroki. He needed a shave on more than just his chin.

He stopped searching, his gaze resting on the only option he'd found. None of the ships were hiring. A few were seeking cargo or local service jobs, but that wouldn't get him off world.

Only one vessel was accepting passengers *and* leaving in the next five hours. He took a deep breath. He was going to have to get lucky, or he'd be stuck on that evac ship and trying to grow eyes on the back of his head like some kind of Enhancer assassin. Of all the stupid ways to die as a Theroki, he definitely didn't want to go down to a knife in the back. Especially not in the hand of a traitor.

A blast of the burning, metallic wind hit him, the scent of vomit mixed with ship exhaust and fuel fumes. He slammed the helmet button again. It snapped closed around his face, the sound always jolting him like a just-missed smack in the face. The smell of this place was one of the many things he would *not* miss.

He squinted at the lightboard, hesitating a moment longer. Luck was never something on his side. If he needed it now, he was likely walking into a shitshow.

Well, he had no choice yet again. He'd have to try this… what was the name?

Was that right? No, that couldn't be the ship name.

Greenish letters glowed in the air inches from his face, floating defiantly over the blur of a redik bar and a heavy-weapons shop beyond.

Audacity. **Dock C5. Passage available to Elpi VI. 7 days, 500 c.**

Great. Just great. *Audacity*? Really?

With a name like that, he was doomed to die on this shit hole of a rock. Probably some trigger-happy cowboy that'd get him killed.

Grunting to himself, he headed toward the ship at a jog. The black volcanic stone beneath his armored boots shook from the touchdown of a new ship. Thankfully, it didn't look like any Theroki vessel for evac. Most likely a Union ship, from the shouts and screeching of metal on metal coming from the east. How convenient. Unionies always needed to stick their nose in every little thing. An Enhancer canister would make a fine prize for some snotty Union lieutenant.

Over Kael's literally dead body, of course.

Dock C5 wasn't far, across the breezeway, onto the docks, and toward the small ship that hunkered down there. The "docks" were only lines of white paint on the black rock marking off a vaguely ship-sized area. From this short distance, the *Audacity* looked well cared for, if a bit virginal. No insignia or emblems adorned her sides or marked her affiliation, but she had the gleam of raw, bleeding edge tech. A new ship or something? She was probably 100 to 150 meters long and could carry maybe fifty. A good transport, or a hauler, although it did have a few tells that it might be something more: bristling weaponry and at least two gun turrets, one fore and one aft. Not a large ship, but not tiny either. And not one of the standard builds you saw everywhere. She didn't have the rough, unkempt look of a pirate's ship—not that he was one to criticize—or the rusty, aching hull of a death trap, so he continued on toward the open cargo hatch and its yawning ramp.

Six men were loading silvered metal cargo crates onto the *Audacity* as he approached, but Kael had the sense they were readying for liftoff. Something about the tenseness of the soldiers, the way several scanned the base a little faster than he might have if he were fully at rest, the way another fidgeted with the charge on his rifle.

Well, good. He needed to get gone. They likely weren't friends of their new Union visitor, either. Most wouldn't be, in these parts.

Kael's gaze caught on a feminine squint behind the scanner's rifle. A sculpted eyebrow arched under the translucent, silver-blue visor of the helmet. Not a he—*she*. His pulse sped up.

As he crossed the last two dozen yards between him and their cont-aminant line, his eye found the slight curves of each form and stuck there. With great effort, he ripped his gaze back to the first woman. Her rifle and her eyes. Sweet female curves would have completely evaded his notice a week ago when his chip was still working, before he'd let Vala start any of her trouble. Now, it took every shred of energy not to blatantly ogle. They couldn't have known where his gaze rested past his visor shielding, but that only made the idea of undressing them with his eyes that much worse.

How odd. They were *all* women.

And wasn't that just his luck? Maybe he should turn around now. A bunch of girls would have to be crazy to let a Theroki onboard, especially one with a malfunctioning chip.

But the scanner girl had him in her sights now. He had no other options anyway. Might as well ask.

"Stop. State your purpose, Theroki," she barked, taking a step forward, knees bent. A fancy scope was perched atop her laser rifle, a model he didn't recognize, with lots of blue and orange lights and flickering green lines. Yeah, yeah. Everything fancy worked great until he shorted its power out. He stifled his desire to curl his lip. Best to try to be friendly. He stopped just short of the barrier and cleared his visor so she could see his face, trying to muster a smile. She had sparkling blue eyes, and for some reason that made smiling easier all of a sudden.

"*Salam,*" he said, with a slight bow. "Just looking for a ride." He stopped, the pistons and mechanics of his creaking power armor hissing as they adjusted pressure and released air. He rarely noticed their obnoxious workings after all these years except when they intruded on conversation. He stood plainly, spreading his hands to show he meant no harm. Looking nonthreatening was hard when your armor was a hissing, walking history of battle.

She squinted harder at him. Or at the readings she was getting from the sight. His eyes drifted to the rifle. He could be a lot more jealous of that than the scope; the thing was in perfect condition, a model he didn't recognize. He stayed up to date on his rifles, but maybe it was just that new.

"Nice piece. I saw your ship in the lists," he said simply, raising the volume on his speaker. "You accepting passengers to Elpi VI?"

"Hey, Dremer. Get over here." A less military-looking woman, unarmored in a pale-blue jumpsuit and no breather, trotted up. They must have a lot of faith in their contaminant force fields. A blank rectangle of the same sky-colored fabric was affixed to her upper arm and another over her front, where a uniform insignia should have been.

Yeah, these women were definitely hiding something.

"Yes?" Dremer said.

"Check him. I don't want to read this damn thing wrong. Something organic in his pack?"

A surge of panicked anxiety shot through him, and it took an immense feat of self-control to not turn and run. What the hell? That was... intense. Must be another effect of the broken chip, he realized slowly. He was used to it crushing any cowardly urges originating from his body. Every minute seemed to bring new discoveries on that front, new emotions he had regained access to—for better or worse. Apparently fear-inspired adrenaline surges were on the menu again, along with an infatuation with the female figure.

He'd have to remember to thank Vala for restoring his ability to utterly panic and rudely ogle women if they ever met again. Right before he flung her out an airlock.

As the panic receded, his brain caught up. It was interesting they'd read such detail on him so quickly. They mustn't be half bad, these women. At least they had some good tech. Couldn't be civvies, so maybe other mercs. There was a chance they could take him on after all.

Dremer had drawn a tool from her belt and was sliding a finger around on a screen. Low-tech input mechanism. Smart for a field diagnostic device. "Cybernetic augmentation."

"No shit," growled his scanner.

"I'm just confirming; it could be an excellent hologram, you know."

"It?" he muttered.

They ignored him. "Life-support capsule containing organic material in the pack. Perhaps..." Dremer trailed off, eyes keen with interest on her device.

If bolting was out of the question, should he consider charging their ship and taking it over? The idea played out in his mind almost independently of him, straight out of his training, a plan forming for how he could neutralize the likely forces that staffed a ship this size—

He cut off the thought. Hadn't he been wanting a nobler mission? A choice in how he lived his life that wasn't criminal? Stealing a ship and massacring everyone was *not* noble.

Why was he even considering it? Now that he thought about it, the idea felt foreign. A little unhinged. Oh, what a treat. Murderous, psychotic ideation came with the chip damage package, too? He was a lucky man. What the hell had those Thero-cyborg surgeries done to him?

He forced a deep breath. Even if they'd figured out the canister was there, they had no reason to suspect just whose data it contained. Or that it contained anything particularly special at all. And he could still fight them off and leave if he had to later. If this didn't work, there might be another ship leaving in a few hours but before the evac. He needed to stay calm and not get lost in the unfamiliar tide of adrenaline, testosterone, and whatever the frag was making him want to murder everyone in sight.

"What do you think?" the soldier said. "Should I let him through or leave his sorry Theroki ass on this desolate rock?"

Dremer nodded absently, engrossed in whatever the screen was telling her about him. "Hmm? Oh, we don't abandon people on desolate rocks, dear. Yes, yes, let him through. Commander Ryu will want to see him." And she wandered away, still not looking up from the screen.

The soldier lowered her rifle slightly. "C'mon. No funny business, Theroki. I'm taking a chance on you, but I've got no qualms about shooting you in the balls." She paused a moment, as if considering if he even cared about such a threat. "No qualms about foreheads either. Or anywhere else. And I'm a damn good shot. Got it?"

He nodded solemnly. She waved him through, and he eased slowly through the contaminant field as it burned off several things that concerned it and checked him over. It didn't eject him, so apparently he passed. As a sign of trust now that he was inside, he retracted his helmet and hoped their tech was as good as it looked.

They stalked up the ramp. Her armor barely registered as anything more substantial than cloth, it was so quiet and sleek. Looked more like a regular old jumpsuit—plain, basic, a standard-issue brown. But the noise dampeners that silenced her steps let him know it was far from simple, and he spotted lines of control panels on her forearms and shoulders. Again, as he looked closer, her patches were also obscured, although this time with a generic cargo cuneiform instead of blank cloth. His own armor thudded along artlessly behind her. His people didn't bother with stealth any more than they bothered with upgrades. Thudding was supposed to be part of the shock and awe, he supposed.

He shifted his pack absently, thinking of the tiny life kindled inside, and sighed. He couldn't even feel the pack through his armor. There was no reason to shift it other than his nerves. He wasn't the nervous type, never had been, but right now, inside the armor, his right hand was actually shaking. People would read him a mile away if he kept this up.

They'd made their way down a large cargo hold, enough to hold several fighters, yet it remained empty. Near the center of the back half of the hold, an office squatted. The top half was clear plex that looked out in all directions, the bottom half painted navy blue with two thin, crisp white and green bands. The colors seemed vaguely familiar.

To his surprise, sad chords of wandering guitar drifted from somewhere, possibly the office. It didn't fit at all with the tense vibe of the soldiers. *Somebody* around here was trying to relax. A cleaning robot buzzed by, buffing the deck.

His eyes had searched for insignia the whole way and found none. Were they rebels? Pirates? Hijackers moving to sell this ship? What?

His guide stopped in the doorway to the office. "Commander—this fool Theroki has approached us requesting passage."

A woman—girl?—with chin-length hair the color of dusty iron streaked with black glanced up from a holodesk. Hard brown eyes locked with his through floating white letters. She couldn't have been twenty, but something in her expression spoke of more than a few hard-won battles.

"*You're* the captain of this ship?" he blurted before he could think better of it.

"Rank's commander, actually," she said coolly. She stood, revealing an athletic form clad in black lightweight armor and a navy flight vest. A stripe of green ran down an arm, and now he could see commander's tabs along her collar, in spite of her young features. "And if you have a problem with that, turn around now and save us both the trouble."

"No, ma'am," he muttered, quick as he could. He gave another slight bow. "Just surprised is all. Forgive me. *Salam* and greetings to you." As his eyes returned to her, another startling wave of burning, long-repressed desire stirred in him, joining the flood of anxious acid in his veins. He was going to drown in emotions and foreign chemicals at this rate. He hated himself for it, but even as he kept his eyes locked on her face, his mind and his peripheral vision rebelled, hungrily taking stock of her curves, the lithe way she stood. This was a distraction to his mission. And the very reason the emotion-suppression chips were installed in Theroki in the first place.

"Peace be upon you as well—although the irony of that coming from a merc is not lost on me. You got a name, Theroki?" Her strong voice was gruff, steeped in the power of command. A good voice. A sexy voice. He immediately wanted to hear a *lot* more of it. Was that the chemicals talking or an actual thought? And what exactly was the difference? What he needed was a bucket of cold water on his head.

"Kael Sidassian. And you, ma'am?" He made sure to add the ma'am as he held out his hand. She eyed it a moment before shaking it. He decided not to pull some idiot move like trying to crush her armored hand with his, and he was glad when she didn't pull a stupid stunt either.

"Have a seat."

"If you don't mind, ma'am, I'd prefer to stand." His armor's size—and weight—was likely to destroy the elegant black chair she gestured at with an open hand. She probably knew that too—a test? He leaned against the back wall of the office instead. Near the door.

"Suit yourself. That will be all, Mo."

"Want me to stay, Commander?" Mo eyed him warily, gesturing at him with her fancy sight.

"Between you two, I'm beginning to think I look a little green today." She scowled back and forth between the two of them. "Is it the vest?"

"I'd say you're more of a jaded color, ma'am," Mo replied, a twinkle in her eye.

Kael remembered just in time not to laugh, but he was already smiling.

The commander glared harder, then pointed at the cargo hatch. "I've handled much worse than one fool Theroki, Mo, and you damn well know that. Go on, back to watching out for more passengers please. Perhaps less rusty ones."

She cast a critical eye at his armor, and Kael raised his eyebrows. Most women wouldn't claim to be a match for a Theroki. Most people of any gender didn't insult Theroki armor either. Moronic as its condition could be, his armor still had a heavily augmented cyborg inside it. If she and her crew weren't afraid of the likes of him, he might have gotten lucky after all.

"On it, ma'am." Mo and her scope jogged back toward the cargo hatch.

The commander turned steely eyes on him. "I'm Commander Ryu, senior officer on the *Audacity*."

"*Salam*, Commander."

"You look like you're having a bad day, Mr. Sidassian." Instead of returning to her seat, she leaned a hip against the desk a few feet away, eying him warily. An image flashed through his mind of Vala leaning against his bunk in a similar position, the cold, frigid air of the bunker labs swirling across naked skin—no. Not now. Now was not the time to think of sex. Or betrayal.

He tried to remain stoic against the chemical onslaught. "What makes you say that?"

"Other than you knocking at my door?" she said flatly.

"Yes."

"Well, it looks to me like somebody tried to slit your throat." Her lips held the faintest smile of amusement.

He laughed softly. Was it her eyes that'd spotted the healing wound —Vala's parting gift—or had she found it via some scan as he'd approached? "Very observant. I thought that had mostly healed by now."

"It has. Mostly. Answer the question."

She was direct. A good trait in a commander. "Yes, there was an attempt at that. Yesterday, though. I... resolved the situation."

"I'll bet you did," she said softly. "So what's in the pack?"

"Standard personal effects."

"Nothing out of the ordinary? Or... organic?"

"Do you inspect all your passengers' luggage in such detail?"

"I don't think this is going to work out." She straightened and turned away, heading back around her desk, and he found his eyes fixated on the swivel of her hips and back as she moved. He snapped his eyes back to her eyes and prayed she hadn't noticed.

Almighty help him. Failure mode already. Damn Vala, damn his broken chip. Damn everything.

CHAPTER TWO

ELLEN STRODE BACK to her seat. Time to see how badly this Theroki needed a ride.

She sat down and trained her eyes on the holodisplay. Think fast—what to make of him? The armor looked familiar enough. A nice benefit of their penchant for scarred and dinged armor was that individuals could be more easily identified. He could be the seventh one, behind the half wall. The armor cams would tell her for sure later.

The important question was—how had he tracked them back here? If he'd come from the same lab and tracked them here, he wasn't leaving the ship alive. The pistol in her drawer would make sure of that. Or Mo, if she missed. But she didn't miss.

Except... he could have come from that same lab without looking for them in particular. He could be carrying something they'd missed. Or he could even be one of the rogue scientists, although disguising oneself as a Theroki would be elaborate to say the least. What if he had something they could get their hands on if she brought him onboard? If he started to turn and walk out, did she have an excuse to reconsider and draw him back?

She eyed his pitiful armor again; it looked like it'd been run over by several tanks and then slashed with a chainsaw. Maybe all at the same time. His square jaw wore the beginnings of a beard, and his hair was a disheveled, sweaty mess. He clearly hadn't been sitting in an office all day. A secret illegal lab, however, might be another story. He was irritatingly handsome in spite of not being her type—too bulky, bedraggled, rough around the edges. Disorderly men made bad soldiers. She couldn't imagine him serving a day in the Union Army in his life. It shouldn't surprise her his type served as a Theroki instead.

She tore her gaze away and trained it stubbornly on the holo, but she could feel him studying her back, considering his options in the long bluffing silence that ensued. Those coffee-brown eyes held a certain dark mystery to them; behind their laughing amusement was an ever-present, disarming earnestness. Something about their somber depths made her want to discover the key to that lock, to unearth the secrets hidden there.

Instinct also told her he liked what he was seeing. She wasn't seasoned at relationships, but she knew enough to know men liked women in her kind of shape. They always liked her less when they realized she outranked them and could also kick their ass with that same body. Or maybe it was her personality. Still, his gaze lingered, a roguish smile lighting up his face all the way to those sad eyes.

No, no, ridiculous—he was a Theroki. Was she that socially awkward that she was misinterpreting the signals of eunuchs now? They weren't, exactly, but might as well be. She'd always been lousy at relationships, but this took the cake entirely.

"All right, you win," he said finally.

That's right, she thought. He needed a damn ride. "Spill it," she said, without looking at him.

"Maybe we can exchange information," he offered. "I'll tell you of my burden, and you tell me the mission of this ship."

"You can't get on this ship without telling me what's in that pack," she said sharply. She had been planning to share their public cover mission, of course, but she ought to push back a little. Added verisimilitude. "You're just trying to get more information out of me."

"Wouldn't you?" He flashed a charming smile at her, settling back against the wall again, and she blinked. She hadn't interacted with

Theroki much outside of shooting at them, lobbing grenades at them, or watching air strikes come in over them, but that smile seemed oddly emotive, even flirtatious. For a Theroki.

She was really pathetic, getting butterflies in her stomach from a man chemically incapable of being interested in women. Perhaps she should move up their leave plans a week. And actually take Zhia up on that offer to go out with them and meet a few of these "boys." Find someone better than Zhia to call her *jagiya*. But she knew damn well she wasn't going to.

She pursed her lips together. "Fine. But you first." She strode past him and palmed the door to the office shut to give him some illusion of privacy, then returned to her desk. She had been too busy thinking about his damn eyes to actually look at those scan results from Dremer.

Idiotic. Men like him made her idiotic. She should just tell him no right now. Kick him off the ship before he distracted her any further.

She did nothing of the sort, leaning back and gazing at him instead.

He folded his armored arms across his chest. She was surprised that was even possible in that bulky old model, but it did leave him looking fierce. "I am headed for leave on Desori X, and I've been asked to make a delivery while I'm there. I've got a life-support canister that contains genetic backups and original tissue samples for some local flora."

She raised one eyebrow. "Somebody is interested in these freaky volcano plants? What kind of genetic backups? Altered or pure?"

He snorted. "Define pure."

"Let's hear your definition instead."

"It's not my definition. I don't give a shit. Do I look against modification to you?"

"Theroki are typically only physically modified."

"Well, yes. Only old and polluted genes in this guy. But plenty of folks don't draw much distinction between physical and genetic mods. I believe the plants are unedited, but I can't say for sure. I didn't ask. I'm a deliveryman, not a scientist."

"Deliveryman?" she said, dubious. She didn't believe any of it, especially considering the chances he'd come from the same lab they had just stormed through. She let her eyes run up and down him. He'd make a fearsome deliveryman. Not someone most people would want to show up at their door.

"Perhaps mercenary would be a better term?"

"I think most servants would faint if you approached their house with a package, even a precious package full of gorgeously unedited plant genes. Although I suppose that would be a creative alternative to the old flowers-and-chocolate routine."

He smirked. Damn, he even had handsome dimples. "Fainting. Really. From terror or excitement?"

She let out a bark of laughter while she searched as quickly as she could through the scan results. "A little of both, I'd wager."

"Then I'm doing my job," he said. "Or maybe I'll bring chocolate."

"Well, you know, some women like pirates. And chocolate."

He frowned at her. "I'm no pirate. I know the Theroki have a certain reputation, but I've tried to keep out of those parts of the outfit."

That did reassure her, even if it could easily be a lie. If it was a lie, it was well delivered. "Sure you have. So you just volunteered to do work while on leave?"

He shrugged, the armor groaning as it scraped inelegantly against itself. He glanced down at it with irritation. Wasn't a fan of the Theroki armor strategy, it seemed. That was another point in her book. "More to spend while I'm off," he said. "Scientists find unedited genes valuable these days."

She snorted. "So I've heard." Valuable enough to kidnap people for them too, the bastards. "So these boring plant genes. They were interesting enough to slit your throat over? Do I have that right?"

"That was... unrelated." He met her eyes evenly, smiling, gaze heavy with meaning. As if to say, you got me. That charming expression had likely swayed many a woman to do... whatever he asked them to do, most likely. A touch playful, he had a dangerous magnetism that tugged at her core, encouraging her to smile sweetly and comply.

The hell with that. She narrowed her eyes at him instead. He didn't say anything further, just gave her that smile. Did that trick work on lots of women? One flash, and they folded like a house of cards? Maybe, and she might be socially awkward, but it wasn't going to work on her. She wouldn't have made it this far if she were easily persuaded by the charms of handsome rogues.

"Are you oath-bound to protect them?" she said instead.

He pressed his lips together, chagrined. Ha, she'd caught him again, and she'd force it out of him. "As a matter of fact, I am, but I don't see how that should be a problem, provided nobody tries stealing them. Which I would hope they wouldn't do, oath or no."

"Of course," she replied absently. She had every intention of looking at whatever he carried, but she wasn't going to tell him that. And looking was different than taking. But something odd had just flown by in the scan; where was it?

There, in the scan results, another anomaly. In addition to recent brain trauma—likely their knockout grenade—and the healing wound at his throat—who knew—he was also giving off suppression controller chip errors like sparks from a fuse. Some kind of damage, altered function of obedience software, emotional control systems, hormonal…

Oh. Oh, my. So… that charming smile really *was* trying to be charming.

No, no. Men like him didn't find girls like her worth pursuing. She was a toxic cocktail of bossy and precocious. But perhaps he was trying to charm his way onto her boat? Shit. She focused, weighing the possibilities, the statistical likelihoods. On the one hand, his horked controller chip meant that a ship full of women was potentially the *last* place in the 'verse he should be. Especially randy women that rarely got enough shore leave.

On the other hand… she knew he had to be going through a lot. After she'd escaped Arakovic's clutches and defected from the Union, she'd lived firsthand how awful the changes in a chip's function could be. That time had been one of the most terrifying, bordering on insane, periods of her life. Was his chip even allowed to be altered?

Couldn't be. The Therokis would want to fix his chip as soon as possible.

Was *that* what was really going on here? He could be trying to go renegade and leave. His buddies had gone down, and he was using this excuse to slip away?

Or they'd somehow traced the lab attack back to her ship, and he was waiting until they were up in space to slaughter them all. Well, he'd have another thing coming if he tried. They were tougher than they looked.

Then of course, there was the mundane possibility: he had an actual boring mission requiring actual boring passage, and she was the only ship with a passenger listing out front.

The silence stretched on as she tried to grope her way toward a decision. He shifted, looking a little uncomfortable. "I guess some people are very serious about their genes these days, Commander. Even from freaky volcanic plants."

"And what about your loyalties? Who's got you playing deliveryman?"

"I can't disclose a client, especially not one to whom I've sworn my oath. But I assure you my only true loyalty is to the Theroki," he said quickly. "Puritans hate me for my augmentation. Stedlers hate me for my brown hair. Enhancers hate me because I won't let them tinker— and my armor stops them from doing as they please. Can't satisfy everyone, I guess. Or anyone, these days."

"Too true. And the Union? Friends of yours?"

He sobered. "Can't say I have much in the way of friends, Commander."

She opened her mouth but stopped short, unsure of what she had been planning to say and struck by the sadness in his words now, as well as his eyes.

"My friends are whomever is paying the bill," he said, expression hardening. It sounded forced. "But to date, that's never been the Union." Unionies still held grudges against Theroki mercenaries dating back to the Settlement Wars, so that made sense. He glanced out at the cargo hold and the open hatch facing the dock. "I'm likely to become unwilling 'friends' with them as a guest in their brig if we stay at this base much longer, though, Commander."

"They still holding that grudge?"

"So I've heard. I'd rather not find out for sure."

She took a deep breath. If he was trying to escape the Theroki, or at least keep his altered chip, she would happily aid him. Aiding people was why Simmons had them put up the passenger listings in the first place. If the Theroki planned to kill them all, she was sure they could stop him, although not without potential losses.

If he carried something nefarious from the lab they'd just hit— something they'd missed—the best place for him was on the ship so they could get another chance to look at it. They'd just have to do it without him knowing. And without any blood feuds or fistfights over... potential bunkmates. She could handle that, right? And if he proved not to be a homicidal maniac, at least not to those onboard, then maybe he could even fill in for Nagnar at Upsilon. That was going to be a tough mission. They hadn't yet found a suitable candidate for Nag's recent departure, although she was gladder he was gone than worried about his absence. Speaking of men who couldn't handle a female commander.

"See to it that the Union doesn't own you while you're on my ship, and we'll have a deal."

"Own me?" He blinked. "Wait, you're letting me on?"

"I'm an idiot, I know. I assure you, idiotic thinking is rare. On my part, at least."

He stifled a bout of laughter. "You, uh..., you didn't tell me your half of the bargain."

"Of course." She stood and returned to leaning on the desk, so they'd be equals, eye to eye for this. And because she wanted to see his reactions better as she gave him their somewhat-true-but-mostly-a-cover-story mission. "This ship is a medical humanitarian vessel. Xenotarian, I mean. We support war zones destabilized in the ongoing Union-Puritan conflict, particularly focused on Muslim and Teredark regions this voyage. There are large groups of women who require medical treatment by women-only doctors. We have four more zones to hit before Desori, but we do plan to stop there to restock in about five weeks, assuming things go smoothly. Which means you're in luck. That is, if you think you can handle yourself in a war zone."

"Yes, ma'am, I believe I may have been in one a few times." He smirked again but seemed like he was trying to hide it.

"And what about a largely female ship? With a female commander? Think you can handle yourself in that kind of war zone?" She arched an eyebrow. She wasn't usually one for innuendo, or at least she wasn't as fond of it as most of her team, but it'd be a good way to gauge his self-control in that area. If her crewmates had anything to say about it, she was fairly sure one of them would be "handling him" sooner rather than later if he was even remotely interested. And if the chip editing had truly made that possible.

"It won't be a problem," he said, suddenly all seriousness and professionalism. Good. "I won't cause any trouble. Just want to get to Desori X."

She nodded crisply. "Fine, then. When the ship lands and we need to treat patients in a women-only environment, you will be confined to your cabin or the bridge unless there's a code orange, an all-out attack. We do have a few other male crew members and passengers, and the same goes for them. Think you can abide by that?"

He nodded.

"Fare all the way to Desori is six thousand chits, or we might be able to arrange for you to work for your fare if you haven't got that. Assuming we visit a coed planet or three."

He let out a low whistle. "What kind of work?"

"In addition to providing hospital facilities, we sometimes have… errands to run. Their exact purpose is need-to-know, but you would be doing basic security. Nothing I'm sure you haven't done a thousand times."

"Just tell me where to aim, Commander."

"More like stand and look intimidating."

"Aren't I doing that already?" He winked at her.

She ignored the flutter that sprang up in her stomach and blinked instead. "All right. We have an arrangement then, for you and your precious plants."

"You seem to know a lot about unedited genes, by the way. Do you all happen to be in the gene market?"

She scowled, crossing her own arms across her chest. "What part of 'medical humanitarian vessel' said black-market trade to you?"

"Just checking what I'm getting myself into, Commander. I'm sure you gotta finance this operation somehow."

"We are *not* in the gene trade or any other black market. We do have several excellent doctors aboard as part of this mission, one of whom is a talented geneticist and can command a high fee for certain types of work. A geneticist is a requirement in this kind of war." Ever since the renegades had broken out their viruses, geneticists had been in high demand. Waves of gene editing and mutation would slide through populations only to be undone again later—for better or for ill. Many of the war-torn people on these planets would need gene therapy as a matter of course, only some of the damage easily repairable.

He nodded. "Glad to hear it."

"Any other questions?"

"Nope."

"All right. I'll review with my team, but welcome aboard." She extended her hand, and he shook it. She didn't miss how his eyes skimmed away from their hands and across her, but she had a feeling he thought he was being subtle. "A few more rules for you. No fighting unless sparring in the hold. Keep your insults to yourself, and we shouldn't have any problems. Some people have more trouble with that than others, so if you're getting pissed, come to me before you start punching things. Sex on this ship is not forbidden. However, you should be aware that all of the women on this ship have RPD systems, so forcing yourself on anyone would be... a very poor choice."

He glared at her now, to her surprise. "That won't be a problem," he said coldly.

"Are you certain?" she said just as coldly. Her smile was sharp and predatory, almost feral. "My scans tell me your programming has been, shall we say, altered."

He scowled harder. "I assure you, not by me."

"Boring plant genes someone wanted bad enough to *hack* you, even? Those must be some damned fine plants."

"Not hack. But returning to Desori will help me address that, uh, issue as well." He was still frowning at her. Did he resent the intrusion or just her implication that he might be tempted to rape someone? Her gut told her the latter. She hadn't thought he would be, but the rape protection defense systems could be pretty brutal. And could technically be activated in any situation at all, not just rape, so she'd wanted to warn him of that.

"Do you know the nature of the damage?" she said.

"Nothing I can't keep under control, Commander."

Well, that wasn't much of an answer, but she wouldn't show her hand if he wouldn't. "You behave yourself, and we don't need to delve into whoever or whatever or *why*ever someone damaged you. As I said, all the women have RPD systems, so don't lose your cock over something stupid."

He flinched, and she was tempted to grin viciously at him but kept up her preferred stoic exterior instead. He seemed like he'd had enough cruelty for one day. "All of them?" he said. "That's... impressive."

"Yes, *all* of them. Not that you'll be testing that out. Right?"

"Of course, Commander. Installing that seems like it would be... painful. My mods were. But none were in my nether regions."

She shrugged. "Life is painful. We don't jump into war zones without making some efforts to prepare. Dr. Dremer installed them and is one of the galaxy's foremost experts in cybernetics. That may prove a boon to you—or a burden. She will have questions."

"Why is she tooling around on a dinky humanitarian ship then?" he muttered.

She gritted her teeth. "The *Audacity*... is not dinky."

"Uh, no offense, Commander." He winced again.

"Too late," she said, waving him off. "Dremer is instrumental in maintaining our crew. And… I think she likes the adventure. Research labs can be boring, you know. Not that I expect you've seen too many of them."

"You'd be surprised."

Huh, he wasn't dodging that accusation. Maybe she could get more out of him on that at some point. He said it with a certain distaste that she decided to find encouraging. "I'll have someone show you to your cabin. We're prepping for liftoff."

He straightened. "Getting clear of that Union ship that landed?"

She eyed him warily, then nodded. "Yes. Although there's a second in orbit. Maybe more coming. We'll be off planet shortly." She palmed open the hatch. "Jenny?" she called out into the hall.

When she glanced back at him, he was gawking openmouthed at the ceiling. Ah, yes, most new people noticed it on their way out.

"Wow."

"My second has some… artistic hobbies in her off-duty hours." She joined him in looking up at the mural on the bulkhead.

Zhia's lettering swirled boldly across the metal in shades of yellow and orange and blue, cobblestones of an old-fashioned street stretching out below the words. An ancient streetlamp bathed them from a distance in blue light.

> *And indeed there will be time*
> *To wonder, "Do I dare?" and, "Do I dare?"*
> *Time to turn back and descend the stair….*
> *In a minute there is time*
> *For decisions and revisions which a minute will reverse.*
> *— TSE*

Kael mouthed the words to himself. "That's… did she write that?"

"No. Part of some old poem the Movers brought with them. She tells me you can't feed yourself just makin' up verses or painting them on walls, apparently, so she shoots for her meals and then scrawls all over my ship. When I let her," Ellen muttered and waved vaguely at the air, annoyed that she'd forgotten the origin of the verse in her own office. It was one of the first Zhia had drawn here, and having never been able to glean much meaning from it, Ellen had first been haunted by it and then slowly abandoned it. She, military child prodigy, UCS veteran, renowned strategic planner, apparently did not "get" poetry.

"Do you let her scrawl often?"

"Well... yes. She's a good shot." She was tempted to grin but restrained herself to the smallest smile just in time. Thankfully, Jenny trotted up just at that moment, saving her ass from further interrogation on the cursed poem. "You can, uh, ask her about it when we're in the deep."

"Of course."

"Jenny, we got a... passenger. Show him to his cabin, please. 6A."

Jen gave him a quick nod and turned to lead him off. Maybe it was misleading to the point of dishonesty to send him off with the short, freckled, sweet, and innocent-looking one. Hopefully he wasn't judging their innocence or lethality, but if he were, she suspected he'd be surprised on both counts with Jenny. Most people were.

As his power armor thudded noisily out the door, he stopped and turned. "There was one more thing. *Audacity*?" He spread his hands, the gesture a mix of skepticism and curiosity.

"What, the name?" She'd returned to her seat at the terminal.

"Yes. Why that? More poetry?"

Yeah, no way she was explaining that name to *him*. But no point in crushing his hopes. She gave him a long, appraising look, partially in revenge for all the appraising looks he'd been sneaking at her.

"Stick around long enough and you'll find out."

———

JENNY LED Kael to the first of a long row of cabins, all their hatches closed. The cabins lined the outside hull, facing more multipurpose and meeting rooms in the interior of the ship. A ladder well at the end of the hallway led up to another level.

Jenny was petite, freckled, and a delightfully shaped blessing to the olive-green jumpsuit she wore. She also didn't flinch or give him a wide-eyed stare, although she looked several degrees less worldly than the others. Her lack of reaction was surprising—and a relief. This might be a ship full of women, but they'd clearly seen a battle or two.

Or five hundred.

"Oh, we got a new AI last week," she said as she headed for the door. "Name is Xi."

"She? What?"

"No, I don't know, I think it's Chinese? Say it sort of like 'she' but with a zing. It's spelled X-I. Xi."

He mouthed an "Oh," and nodded. "Obviously. How could I have missed that."

She grinned and left him to strap in for liftoff. Kael only stared after her for a second or two before shaking his head and shutting the hatch door behind him. He was twenty-eight, not fifteen, damn it. And the commander was more his type anyway.

Frowning, he sank down onto the bunk for just a moment and pulled his comm unit out of its slot in his chest armor. Even if he was within his rights to begin the lord regent's mission straight away, he still needed to report what he was doing.

He dashed off a quick summary of the report to Carwin on the *Genokai*, detailing the attack and the orders he'd received from the lord regent. There. Now he'd have that record in place and Carwin informed in case someone wanted to start trouble for him over this. Of course, if they knew he carried an empress embryo, maybe they'd be less inclined to take issue, but *that* definitely wasn't going into any official report. Especially not after how this attack had occurred in such close conjunction to the evac team. There was a leak somewhere, some crack in their security, and he'd have no way of figuring it out from here. Nor was that in his job description.

Even as he put the comm unit back into the armor slot, it occurred to him that maybe someone might accuse *him* of being that leak. Of course, if he wanted to kill the lord regent, it would have been much easier to do so before the other six showed up, so that hardly made sense. But he could see it happening anyway, given his quick departure.

All the better he'd sent off that report promptly then. Carwin should cover his ass. He owed Kael enough.

"Bunks recommended for liftoff, kids," said a man's voice over the comm system. He had a thick outsystem accent and a pilot's snark. Damn, Kael should have taken off the armor for liftoff. Then again, maybe it was better this way. He couldn't trust these people yet. Better to be ready for a fight.

Liftoff was quick and uneventful. Kael lay on his side on the bunk, waiting and watching the black planet and then its bluish atmosphere fall away. There was water somewhere on that hellhole apparently. Not that he'd seen any. Damn, he stank. Hopefully he'd have time to find somewhere to clean up when this liftoff was over.

The door beeped at him. He sat up and started to wave it open, then remembered Jenny's instructions regarding the ship's new AI. Might as well try to get used to it.

"Xi?" he asked tentatively.

"Yes, Passenger 6A?" came a sleek, feminine voice with just a touch of inflection missing.

"Uh, door open?"

Xi did not verbally acknowledge, but the hatch slid open to reveal Commander Ryu.

"Hey, is the Union gonna care about your boring plant genes?" She stepped inside the cabin and palmed the hatch closed. Heh. Not everyone was used to the new AI, huh? She folded her arms across her chest, frowning.

"Why? Do we have more Union incoming?"

She pointed at the windows, but he didn't move to look. "Maybe. I thought you'd rather tell me here than over the ship's comm."

He hesitated.

"Or I can just let them search the ship?"

"Is that your normal protocol?" He narrowed his eyes at her. Very convenient that this threat had lain in wait until they were off the ground.

"No. But sometimes they aren't worth the trouble of a fight. And sometimes they are easier to fight when they've divided their forces with half inside our ship."

He grinned, but she didn't seem to find that amusing. She didn't seem to find *anything* amusing, actually. "I like the way you think, Commander. No one should be interested in these particular boring plant genes, especially not the Union. But to be on the safe side, it'd be great if they didn't go looking for them. I'd prefer not to murder anyone in my first hour on your ship. And it may come to that, if they try to take my very special plants."

"That *would* be a lot of cleanup. Might have to add that to your bill." Was that sarcasm?

"And also a regrettable loss of life," he added. He didn't want her to think he anticipated slaughter. Many Theroki did, but not him. It was just a fact of life in this case, with the oath in place. Unfortunately. Handling an entire ship of Unionies alone would be a challenge, but it could be done. Nothing in his chip or upgrades prevented such total violence—only his conscience worried about that.

"I'll do my best to frighten them off. They have no right anyway, out here. But I'd suggest hiding anything you don't want found anyway, just in case." She turned to go and palmed the hatch open, then stopped abruptly. She turned her head slightly toward him, so he could see her face in profile—a straight nose; thin, pink, controlled lips; the line of her eyes and cheekbones sweeping up toward her hair. He caught his breath.

Not many a sight like that on the *Genokai*.

"Stay armored up," she said softly.

"Of course, ma'am."

She nodded sharply, then disappeared down the hallway.

He let out his breath, not realizing he'd been holding it. He shook his head, trying to shake out the foggy cloud that had settled over his thoughts. He wasn't used to this. So much interference with simple thoughts. Why had he wanted to feel things again? He sank to a seat on the bunk and dropped his head into his hands, rubbing his face. Just a moment, then he'd search somewhere to stash his burden that was less obvious than his pack.

A light on the desk communicator lit up, and he rose and poked it irritably. "You wanna join the party line, Theroki?" The voice sounded familiar. The one who'd greeted him with her rifle scope? Mo? She sounded cheerier. Glad to be off planet, probably.

"What the heck is a party line?"

"It's an ancient number you used to—" started the pilot.

"Not time for trivia, Adan. It's the main command channel, Theroki."

"Uh, sure. If the commander allows it."

"She ordered it. Just stay on the line and get some popcorn. This should be good. Muting you. Oh, and just kidding, we definitely don't have any popcorn. Helikai was fresh out."

He scanned the room. In spite of the nondescript hull of the *Audacity*, his quarters were a pleasant surprise. The far wall was a grid of portholes and metal, and the bunk wasn't even a foldout one, but an actual permanent fixture with storage underneath. Lockers and shelves awaited belongings above the bunk, and a locker tucked in one corner looked like it might even fit his armor. Still, those were all predictable places for a search team to look. He needed somewhere less obvious.

He took a knee and inspected the floor. Huh. It was warm beneath his fingers. Was that an amenity, or was there something hot and potentially dangerous underneath his cabin? Yes, uh, put the Theroki near that malfunctioning reactor we're all worried about... He'd have to find a ship map. Not that they'd likely give him one.

A vent in the far wall caught his eye. Next to it was a simple utility panel. He opened the panel, finding some tools and maintenance supplies.

A shrill, proper man's voice came over the line. "*Audacity*, this is Union ship *Parthenon*, Lieutenant Saders speaking. State your purpose in this zone."

Wincing at the tone of that demand, Kael grabbed the cold, steel canister and placed it inside the utility cabinet, piling a few small boxes and wrenches on top. Still not a great hiding place, but less obvious than a locker and near the floor. It would do for now. He gave it a soft pat. It hardly seemed like anything alive could be in there, let alone a baby, but he still hoped it would be comfortable here. And safe.

Memories of Asha threatened to flood back, but he shoved them down. Not now, with a potential battle in sight.

"*Parthenon*, this is Commander Ryu. Our ship's details are public record. This is a humanitarian vessel supported by private donors, headed to the Rethki-Mahama zone to support the civilians during the fighting there. Which is more than I needed to tell you."

Kael froze. Private donors? He should have pressed her harder. A humanitarian vessel had seemed odd but somewhat fitting. What *else* would a ship full of only women be doing? This was no nunnery, that was for sure. But he wished she'd mentioned the "private donors" when they were on the *ground*.

Hell, what were the chances that one of these crazy scientists— Dremer?—was a rogue and that was the real purpose of the outfit? He gritted his teeth. But he'd still have gotten on if that were the case. It wouldn't have changed anything. Better than the evac shuttle.

"A humanitarian vessel, eh?" came a dry voice. "Sure. We're stopping you on suspicion of smuggling. Prepare to be boarded."

Kael strode to the windows to see the ship, no, *three* ships hovering in low orbit. What the hell? What were they all doing here? Did this have something to do with the empress? The devastated evac team? Was it the Enhancer cell they were after or something else altogether?

"You're out of your jurisdiction, Lieutenant," Ryu said. Luckily for her, she didn't sound anywhere near as young as she looked.

"There *is* no jurisdiction out here. We will—"

"Damn right, there isn't. We will not submit to boarding by you or anyone. This ship is authorized by our donors to defend itself from bullies while in freespace. And in case you were unclear, that means you." Her voice carried all the weight of an asteroid. Holy balls. He'd had fifty-year-old grizzled field commanders with less guts. And what the hell kind of donors *were* these, to be willing to take on the Union readily? Some charitable Puritan faction? That seemed unlike any Puritan *he'd* ever met. They cared a lot about genetic purity, quite a bit less about human life. Or alien life. Or even plant life half the time.

"Ryu, be reasonable—"

"That's Commander Ryu. Tell me, do you have a Colonel Tauber onboard?"

"Excuse me?"

"You heard me."

"No, there's no Colonel Tauber on this vessel. Prepare yourself for boarding, Comm—"

"I will not hesitate to fight back, Lieutenant. If you're looking for a tangle, I can oblige. Shuttling doctors from star to star gets mighty boring, and my crew is itching for some tango practice. Shall we?" There was a hint of a wry smile in her voice. He imagined that feral expression he'd seen earlier, more a baring of teeth than a smile.

"More like evasive maneuvers," the lieutenant grumbled. "One moment." Union boy sounded irritated.

"Adan, get Simmons on this. Theroki, you hearing this? You hide your plant bits?" Ryu said. "Unmute him."

"Yes, ma'am," he said. He glanced back out at the ship. A green light in the center bottom of their white, angular ship showed their grab beam heating up.

He grabbed the cabin's comm unit from its holster, jammed it into the second comm slot on his upper left chest piece, and palmed open the door. The problem with voice-activated commands was they didn't let you be too stealthy about leaving your cabin.

"What are you doing, Theroki?" came Ryu's voice anyway. Apparently they had other ways of monitoring his location.

"Coming to help."

"Did I *ask* for your help?"

"Do you want to be caught in their grabber?"

A pause. "Obviously not."

"Well, what are you doing to stop it?"

"Presume much?" muttered the male pilot.

Another long pause. "We have our ways," Ryu said stubbornly.

"If you have an extra turret, I can keep it from latching on in ten seconds flat."

"Now that's not even fair," muttered the man again.

"Looks like you're gonna get to dance, Commander," a woman muttered from the bridge. "Maybe with more than one partner."

The line was silent for a moment.

"What does that ship think we are, idiots?" Ryu said. She made a disgusted noise. "Xi, can the pirate do what he says?"

"Oh, I'm the pirate? Says the lady with the unmarked ship and patch-covered uniforms." Kael took a few more steps forward and peered around the next corridor, hoping he'd luck onto one of those turrets on his own.

"Theroki telekinetic abilities are capable of being used in ship defense," said the AI, "even without significant damage to the enemy ship, although they favor weapon-system defenses and prefer to aggressively destroy other ships instead whenever possible."

Kael winced. That was not untrue of Theroki space-battle training and strategies, but it was certainly untrue of *him*. It was also right stupid. Only stupid pirates destroyed ships rather than looting them.

"All right, let's see what you got, Theroki," said Ryu. "But no weapons or loss of life. Got it? Also, you're going the wrong direction." Kael turned on his heel and continued briskly away from the forward bridge and toward the cargo bay instead. "Fern, go intercept him and take him to your turret. Defensive maneuvers *only*, Theroki, and that's an order. No attacking that ship. We just want to neutralize their grab beam—beams—and get out of here."

"Aw, Commander," someone grumbled.

"And stand by the override in case Passenger 6A doesn't follow orders," she said to the grumbler. Was Fern a name? These people were... odd.

"Acknowledged, Theroki?"

"To be most effective, I should hook into the ship's sensors directly," Kael said, smiling. "And yes, I acknowledge."

A few grumbles in the background.

"Xi, authorization granted to passenger Kael Sidassian for defensive exterior sensors only."

"Affirmative, Commander. Access granted, Passenger 6A."

Footsteps came running up behind him. Kael turned. A blond in a red flight suit stopped short and motioned him to follow her to her left, still grumbling. Fern, presumably. He followed her down a short hall and down a stairwell. So this ship had at last three levels, his cabin in the middle. A map was definitely in order.

"I swear she'd give that damn AI defensive control if it had the programming," Fern grumbled.

"You know it can hear you, right?" he said.

She glared at him, although it seemed more playful than serious. "She's already giving it to *you*."

"Hey, I'm not artificial." Not that the thumping of his armor made him seem terribly organic.

She must have agreed, for she looked him up and down.

"My *intelligence* is not artificial," he amended. He did have a lot of other artificial parts, but not his brain.

She waved a hand, dismissing his objection.

"Well, that's probably what the commander thinks too."

She snorted. But then she stopped, the hatch door to the gun turret sliding open without a request. She glared at the ceiling. "Xi, was that you?"

"You were headed to your turret. Am I not being helpful?"

Fern didn't reply and instead pointed inside. "Take the outside one, I'll be right behind you. And don't forget it."

He nodded crisply, climbing up and in. "Where are the—"

"You will find several hookup options, Passenger 6A, depending on your make and model," Xi announced.

He winced at that wording, plopping into the gunnery chair with a thud bordering on a crash. "I'm not a ship or a muscle car, Xi. Or a rifle."

"Indeed, you are not," she replied. Damn, no, the AI was an *it*. The pure and cold alto voice clearly wouldn't have been male if it had had a body, though. After a slight pause, a panel popped open in the right armrest, a cable waiting somewhat tangled inside. "Given my analysis, this is the greatest speed option. Unless you'd prefer—"

"Speed is good, Xi. Thank you." He didn't particularly want the AI educating them all on his exact armor model and his specific upgrade capabilities if they hadn't thought to ask. Although Ryu probably already knew better than he did, with the way they'd figured out the damage to his chip like it'd been written on his forehead.

He wasn't one to feel ashamed of jacking in. Wireless connections were for cocky idiots who would rather look cool, or at least entirely human, than have submillisecond response times.

He leaned back in the chair and shut his eyes. He could think faster, see better, without organic vision interfering.

Showtime.

He ricocheted his way out of the ship and out into the sensors, both with his own mind's senses and that of the ship's arrays. Xi only had to gently prod him in the right direction twice. He could feel the heat of the grab drive now; it was beyond warm, nearly hot. Ready any moment.

It had been too long since he'd played pong with Union bastards. This should be fun.

"Enemy ship tractor—" Xi began.

The energy beam shot out, reaching for the *Audacity* before he was entirely ready. He smacked it down, as conscious of his reaction as he was of a blink. In other words, not at all. He'd returned the electromagnetic volley almost before he'd realized it had happened, and mostly he just saw an explosion where the green light had formerly pulsed.

Ah, *damn*, he'd fragged it. He swore under his breath. He hadn't intended on disobeying a direct order right out of the gate. Although she technically wasn't in his chain of command, she was still the commanding officer and therefore the law on this ship.

"Enemy ship tractor beam destroyed," Xi promptly announced.

"Ha, you took it *out!*" Fern exclaimed behind him, bubbling with laughter and thumping the headrest behind him hard. "That'll show 'em. I'm almost impressed." He glanced back to see her grin—and the laser pistol ready and warm in her hand, leaning casually against her shapely, red-clad thigh.

"For the last time, Xi, it's not an enemy ship," came Ryu's voice.

"It fired on you," Xi insisted. "Does that not make it an enemy?" Could an AI sound irritated?

"It tried to grab us. We are noncombatants. Or at least we *should* be, as far as they are concerned. Apparently the Theroki didn't get that message either. What are you doing down there?" Ryu snapped. "If you can't follow orders, I'll revoke your access and lock you in your cabin until Desori. I said *no* damage to that ship."

He struggled for an excuse and found one, stifling a grin in case she had video on the turret. "A reflex, Commander. But you did *also* say you would prefer not to be grabbed," he replied. Fern snorted. "I don't take kindly to Union types running around manhandling ladies without their permission. It's not polite."

"And if you had missed?"

"I don't miss. I didn't miss, Xi, did I?"

"You eliminated the tractor beam threat, Passenger 6A. I do not have access to your psychology or your targeting intent, so I cannot say for certain if your efforts were accurate or simply lucky."

"Wow, thanks for the vote of confidence."

"You are welcome," came her answer, slightly delayed as if she were unsure of it. "And I would need a dataset of at least sixty shots before I could offer confidence or an estimation of your targeting success likelihood. Two hundred would be preferred."

Kael snorted.

"Great." Ryu's voice came over the comm. "Not only did I pick up a Theroki, but I picked up a cocky one who wants to make friends with our new overly aggressive AI. That kind of figures, doesn't it, Adan?"

"It sure does, Commander," murmured the pilot. What was that accent of his?

"I'm not cocky, I'm just perfectly—" His mind's eye felt a beam from the second ship snake out of the darkness, and energy weapons from the third. He paused to deflect them. Trying to fire a surprise shot from their instant-charge cannons, eh? "Sneaky bastards. As I was saying. I'm not cocky. I just know my capabilities extremely well."

"Not-enemy-ship weapons attack deflected," Xi announced. Could an AI be *snarky* as well as irritated?

Fern behind him snickered. "He sounds cocky to me, Commander."

"Agreed."

He couldn't hold back a smirk this time.

"We *should* be focused on the Union ship," grumbled someone else on the bridge.

"Oh, I am. Cocky?" Kael said. "I don't know *what* you're talking about, ma'am."

Like scratching an itch on his arm, the sensors warned of the next several incoming blasts, and he put the gun to work beyond his telekinesis, blasting enough force to neutralize them but not deflecting them back at the ship this time. Ah, it had been a long six months with nowhere near enough shooting. Even in strict self-defense, it felt good. Great, even. Holding back was not his usual instinct, so he was glad he was pulling it off. He was willing to bet Ryu wouldn't have been all that pissed if he *had* taken out the Union ship, though. He could probably convince her to forgive him.

Good, good. This was good practice. He was able to deflect everything with ease, and the computations for equal and opposite force to neutralize shots seemed dead-on. At least *that* part of his augmentation remained intact.

"Not-enemy shots inc—" Xi started to announce. "Shots deflected." A pause. Kael smiled. "The not-enemy ship has powered down its weapons."

A handful of whoops went up from the bridge and the hold. He smiled wider in spite of himself. These ladies did not take his skill for granted, at least. It had been a long time since he'd inspired cheers from anyone, certainly not guarding the lord regent or on the endlessly boring royal Stedler patrol on Exodus before that. Cheers felt... surprisingly good.

"You have a Foundation cyborg onboard." Lieutenant Saders's angry voice came over the comm.

Kael was glad Unionie couldn't hear him scoff. As if the Foundation cyborgs were even *half* his speed. He doubted the mythical Foundation even existed. It seemed more like a scare tactic the Union threw out there every time they needed someone powerful but faceless to throw under a lander in place of whatever real and corrupt organization they were trying to protect. If the Foundation was real, he'd never seen any evidence of it. Only rumors and shadows.

"We should—" Saders started again.

"You won't," Ryu cut him off. "This is freespace. We'll be seeing you. Thank you for the dance, Lieutenant."

"You destroyed our tractor drive. You will pay for repairs—"

"No, we won't. Perhaps you'll think twice about trying to board peaceful vessels by force in freespace. That's a cheap price to pay to learn your lesson. Don't bully where you have no jurisdiction. Of course, you can send our donors the bill if you'd like."

"At what address?"

"Exactly. Now piss off."

Kael choked back a laugh even as he heard snickering come up from the bridge comm and erupt behind him into a giggle.

"We *will* be issuing a report. This is an outrage. We will not forget this, Ryu."

"Perfect. See to it that you don't." A click sounded, presumably Ryu closing the channel, and he let out a low whistle. Damn. Next time, he wanted to be on the bridge when she put a Union boy in his place. That sort of thing was always fun to see, but he had a feeling seeing a woman who couldn't be a quarter century old ream a Unionie a new one would be twice the fun.

"Take us out of here, Adan," snapped Ryu. "Show them our tail-lights, please."

"For the last time, Commander, this ship does not have taillights." The pilot and his intriguing accent again.

"Oh, I doubt that will be the last time. What? I like the expression. I'm an old-fashioned kind of gal."

"Yeah, right."

CHAPTER THREE

"SHUT IT, XI," Ellen snapped from her seat in the main meeting room. Damn voice commands were only good for when you didn't want to get up. She checked Sidassian's location on her tablet again—still in his cabin. Good. Now that they were clear of Helikai, the team needed to huddle.

"So you think he was one of them or what?" said Nova, running a hand through her short orange hair and propping her boots up on the white quartz meeting table. That kind of lack of military decorum still got slightly under Ellen's skin—a hard habit to break. But the crew seemed to enjoy bending and breaking old rules once in a while. Rewriting them to be more fun. Sometimes Ellen let them, sometimes she didn't. Boots on the table weren't hurting anyone. Right now. At least they weren't muddy.

"I'm willing to bet it's him, yes. You recognize him?" Ellen replied.

Merith was stabbing at her tablet display, her dark eyes glaring. "I'll have the armor footage up shortly."

"I wouldn't recognize one of them," Zhia muttered, tucking a braid of silver behind her ear.

They paused, waiting for the footage. For a ship practically the price of an outsystem planet, how did they still spend so much time waiting for computers? Hell.

"He noticed your mural in the office," Ellen offered.

Zhia's brown features brightened, eyes twinkling. "Oh?"

"I did a terrible job of explaining it. Who is it by again?"

"T. S. Eliot."

Ah, yes, the TSE at the bottom. "I'll try to remember that for next time. You never explained to me what it means."

"You'll figure it out someday, *jagiya*."

Ellen pursed her lips. She wasn't so sure about that. "Any luck, Merith?"

"Ninety-five percent."

Ellen groaned. "Okay, let's assume it *is* him. I'm figuring there's a couple of options. Either it's all a coincidence and this has nothing to do with our raid—"

Nova snorted, fiddling with the golden cross that always hung round her neck. "Not likely."

"Yeah, but it's possible. Have I told you I don't find your interruptions charming, Sergeant?" Or your boots on the table. Let it go, Ellen. Let it go...

"Uh, I apologize, Commander." She popped a piece of gum into her mouth as if to quiet herself.

Ellen straightened and continued. "Another option is they figured out we attacked them and sent him after us. Or we missed something."

"And he has it?" Zhia said, sitting forward.

Ellen nodded. "Yes. I figured two out of three, we want him onboard. And Dremer approved it with her scan."

"Dremer approved it? Why?" Nova asked.

"Probably wants to dig around in his hardware," Merith muttered. "Or his software."

"Or his wetware." Zhia grinned.

Nova sat up, dropped her boots, and smacked Zhia on the arm.

"What, you didn't notice he... was a he?" Zhia's dark eyes were positively sparkling with amusement now.

"No, because I'm a *professional*, unlike some of us."

Ellen cleared her throat. "Okay, what are we doing, people?"

Zhia sobered, straightening. "We should have someone guarding him in case your theory that he's been sent to kill us is correct."

"He could also have orders to spy and then kill us." Merith looked up, disturbingly brisk in her analysis. "Scan's done. Is this him?"

She swiped her tablet display onto the big board, and they could all see the image of the downed Theroki beyond the half wall. Someone—Nova, Ellen thought—walked up and looked down at him, getting a clear view of the familiar tank-and-chainsaw-assaulted armor.

Ellen nodded. "That's the armor. I'm sure of it. But do you have a hall shot on ship, so we don't have to rely on my judgment?"

Merith nodded. "Give me a minute."

"Okay, so guarding him, someone on the bridge via cam? So he doesn't know we're doing it?"

Xi's voice suddenly piped up, making Ellen jump and look up warily. "I can also be of assistance in this capacity if necessary, Commander."

"How so?"

"I naturally record all crew member movements, searches, and activities."

"So 'Big Brother,' " Zhia muttered.

"What?" Nova asked.

"Never mind."

"My efforts ensure ship security." How an AI managed to sound so indignant, Ellen didn't know. The ones she'd dealt with back on her Union ship hadn't been half as snarky, but perhaps the tech had advanced since then. Or perhaps it was Simmons's meddling.

"That's what they all say," Zhia said. Nova snickered.

"I do not know the 'they' that you are referring to. Most crew member activities are not stored for any great length of time," Xi continued. "But I can place Passenger 6A's logs in a higher priority queue, to ensure completeness and redundant backups. Would that be desirable?"

"Sure, that sounds good," Ellen said. Any sophisticated spy would be able to get around such a thing or would at least guess they were being recorded, but it couldn't hurt.

"Additionally, while we are speaking, I would like to report that Passenger 6A has stored something in the utility cabinet in his cabin."

Ellen snorted. "With the cleaning supplies on the floor?"

"Yes. I suspect this is the... special plant bits you referred to?" Maybe Simmons had ordered an extra-special smart-assed AI model just for her.

"Thank you, Xi," Zhia said quickly. "That's very helpful."

"You're very welcome, Lieutenant Verakov."

"That could be the research we missed," Nova said, propping her boots back up with an especially loud crack of gum. "We should try to get a look at it."

"I did get him to admit his oath is engaged to protect it." All three faces round the table frowned at Ellen. "We're going to need to be very careful, however we do it. We need a plan. A good one. No need to endanger our lives or his if it truly *is* just plant bits. Maybe Dremer or Levereaux can do something with a remote scan."

"It's probably shielded," Zhia pointed out.

"Maybe, but we were able to detect organic matter in our initial scans. Dremer did. Maybe she can get more out of it with more time. Failing that, we'll need to find a way to take a peek without his knowledge—or without his cooperation."

Nova frowned. "Do you think the brig would hold him?"

"Depends on his upgrades and if he's in his armor or not."

"I can think of a way to take care of that." Zhia snickered.

Ellen ignored her. "Xi, can you and the doctors get me a report on whatever upgrades you can find?"

"Yes, Commander."

"No, but more seriously, I think sedation is probably a safer bet than the brig," Zhia offered. "We could see about getting a tranquilizer gun or something. I've heard stun guns don't work on them."

Ellen nodded. "I've heard the same, and I don't want to find out when it's our only nonlethal option. We need others."

"If he tries to attack us," Nova said slowly, "why are we so concerned about defending ourselves nonlethally?"

"Because the oath programming they use will force him to attack us," Zhia said. "But his secret package might be something totally unrelated to our mission. We shouldn't kill him—or risk dying ourselves—if there's actually just gourmet popcorn in there someone wants really super secretly badly."

Nova snickered but said, "Point taken."

"All right. Zhia, talk to the doctors about our options for tranquilizers. Get Jenny on it too and raid the sick bay and med kits for anything that might help. What else? Maybe some kind of gas? That could knock us out too. Just get us some options. I'll put someone on watch on the bridge all shifts. Check the schedule later. Anything else?"

"And if he's actually not up to anything and just trying to get a ride home to see his parents?" Merith asked softly.

Ellen let out a long breath. "Then we should have no problems." She hoped. "Make sure you remind everyone that we're in passenger mode and no discussion of the Foundation outside this room and my quarters. Even in closed cabins."

Nods all around. They knew this drill. It kept them in good practice for keeping secrets while they were on land anyway.

"I'll get Simmons to dig up what he can. Anything else?"

"Hey, wait." Zhia slowly rubbed her chin. "What if we get him off the ship?"

"Off the ship? How are we going to do that?" Nova shook her head.

"I don't know, but if we could get him off somewhere risky, maybe he'd leave the capsule behind. And we could try to take a look at it while he's gone."

Ellen's brow furrowed. "I did suggest he'd need to pay his way by working security. I was thinking just standing guard outside, but if Simmons's scan comes up relatively clean—"

"He's a Theroki, Commander." Zhia's expression was dubious.

"I said 'relatively.' If it's clean-ish, we could use him to fill in for

Nagnar on the next couple missions. We'll need the help, and maybe we can separate him from whatever's in his cabinet temporarily."

"Are we talking about the same thing? With us on *missions*?" Nova sat even farther forward now. "C'mon, how are you going to explain what we do on them?"

"Well, either way, he'll know we went off somewhere. We can station him outside the ship. Or put him somewhere that blocks his view but covers our asses. We'll come up with something."

"How do we know we can trust him, Commander?" Now Nova was starting to sound like Fern. Probably all that time spent together.

"We don't," she said, intentionally chipper. "But we'll give him one of our guns." Their custom multirifles had advanced algorithms that sought to avoid friendly fire—and could be disabled remotely. "And you're all badasses. The three of us can take him if we need to."

Zhia pointed toward the ceiling. "Can we at least put Mo up high in case we need backup during missions? Somewhere she can cover the ship and us, if possible?"

"Sure. Good idea. I knew there was a reason I kept you around. Other than the poetic murals, I mean."

"Well, somebody's gotta watch your back from telekinetic brutes trying to stab it." She grinned.

"And you get the job," Nova said, standing and folding her arms. "Aren't you lucky?"

———

STABLE FLIGHT PATH ACHIEVED, crew consulted, and dead tired, Ellen retreated to her cabin for a few moments. She flopped down onto her bunk, its firmness reassuring beneath her as she rubbed her temples. Soft guitar chords drifted through the air—she'd forgotten to turn them off earlier—and she forced a deep breath of the cold, clean air.

She wasn't procrastinating. She had no fear of confronting a Theroki on her own ship. She just wasn't in the mood for macho bull-shit right now, or really ever, and what else could you expect? She'd gotten plenty from lesser men in her command, and handling it wasn't so bad. Maybe she was losing her tolerance, thanks to dealing with the female brand of bullshit instead for such a long time. She snorted. As if Adan and Nagnar hadn't had plenty of machismo for one ship.

She just needed a moment of rest, and she'd get the job done.

She needed to thank the Theroki for his help but also needed to make sure he never, ever disobeyed an order again. She didn't care about damage to any Union ships. When she'd commanded one, she'd damaged it plenty; she knew how common it was. They'd have ten engineers repairing that thing, and it'd be operable in a few hours. No, it was more that she knew it was risky enough having him onboard. He had to be clear that following orders was not optional. Even if she was a woman. And maybe a decade his junior. She hadn't kept scores of people following her orders by ignoring it when they failed to.

She covered her eyes with her hand, then rubbed the bridge of her nose. What had she been thinking? She sighed.

She knew *exactly* what she'd been thinking.

He had the potential to be a pit dragon dressed in an already half-opened tin can—a comparison that almost wasn't fair to the pit dragon —but she'd sensed the urgency, an unusual agitation for a Theroki. They were usually so even-keeled, almost like androids. And this Sidassian was… not. He'd actually seemed nervous, which would be normal for most people but not for one of his kind. And while her ship had several competing missions, one of them was getting people in need out of bad situations. She had no logical reason to believe a mercenary, especially a Theroki of all people, was actually in need or in a dire situation.

But her gut had insisted this was the case. It still did.

And then there were those eyes. She remembered Kwan sitting on the park bench in Seoul after a run, the second sun setting behind him. The Theroki had Kwan's same piercing stare, not unkind, simply penetrating. She could see Kwan now, shooting at the practice range, running beside her in the centrifuge. He had had that same glint of amusement and playfulness in his eyes. She had so little of such things in herself, things she had admired in him even when they'd driven her nuts.

Not that anything had come of it. Admiring him from afar was as far as she'd gotten before he'd been assigned his next command and shipped out. Special forces hadn't been for him. He was probably climbing the command ladder on some Union bridge somewhere.

Amusement and playfulness were odd in a Theroki. People probably didn't go around telling *him* to lighten up or take a vacation. Was she truly more stoic than even a Theroki? At least more stoic than 6A. Sidassian. No, 6A was safer.

Pitying a Theroki of all people—she had to be crazy. He could blast her out their hatch with one of those telekinetic waves the next time they landed and take the ship for his own. He didn't need to kill everyone, just a few key folks. Her. Probably Zhia and Adan too.

I'm coming to help.

She took a deep breath. She was being paranoid. They were already taking precautions against any attack. She believed in judging people based on what they *did*, and none of his actions indicated that a firefight was likely to break out any minute now. He'd offered help and proven useful against those Unionies. She hadn't been looking forward to Simmons having to hack them out of the ship's bay. He'd done it a few times, but they'd always been close to being sucked inside the big Union holds before the grab beams suddenly and mysteriously malfunctioned. Even if that had worked, the *Audacity* could have still faced a chase or a firefight. She hadn't been looking forward to that, although she was pretty sure a few crew members had been. Best not to test luck with those things. They were better trained and faster than most Union vessels, but luck didn't care. Once the weapons started firing, bad luck could kill somebody at any time, no matter who had the upper hand.

She forced herself to her feet. This navel-gazing was just an excuse not to talk to him. To dodge his disarmingly earnest gaze. The sooner she thanked and scolded him, the sooner she could sleep.

She palmed the hatch and headed down the ladder to the main level. She strode along the other cabins, listening for the soft sounds of

Nova on her guitar. No, nothing now. She played a lot, but not in front of anyone. Instead, two voices murmured from Fern's cabin—that was probably where Nova was. Good. It must be nice to have someone to talk to when the heat of battle was over, to sit beside in fuzzy pajamas and watch shows with. Especially amid the rainforest Fern cultivated in her cabin.

A friend or perhaps more, Ellen was not entirely clear, but they spent most of their time together. She sort of hoped it was "perhaps more." "Perhaps more" would be nice.

She shook her head. You're the commander, she reminded herself. Sentimentality like that pointed at yourself is going to get people killed. She shook a brief flash of horror from her mind—the view of the *Mirror's Light* shining in the starlight before it'd headed off on its last, fatal mission.

No. "Perhaps more" was good for Nova. And Fern too. But commanders did not have such luxuries.

She pressed her lips into a firm line, raised her chin, and stopped at the 6A placard. Zhia had graffitied it into a violent collision of blue and green. Ellen didn't remember authorizing that. Rebellious as always. She knocked briskly on the cold metal hatch.

It slid open almost immediately. The Theroki sat shirtless on his bunk, a piece of his armor on his lap and a set of tools spread out beside him. He grinned at her, lighting those chocolaty eyes with radiant warmth. Huh, that clunky old armor hadn't added as much bulk as she would have guessed. He actually *was* a thick web of muscle and tendon, not just because the armor cheated and created the illusion. Union officers who regularly wore full heavy armor were flabby as a couch cushion. He was actually fit. Army bureaucrats could get soft, but mercenaries couldn't, she supposed.

Well, good. She'd always preferred tall, lean runner types anyway.

His arms and shoulders were covered in tattoos, only some of which she could make out. Feathers, a wolf's ear, a snake's head... Tattoos came in a myriad of colors and lighting combinations, but his were all black. Only black. Just like hers.

More than a handful of scars marred his statuesque form, and her heartbeat faltered at the sight of them. Damn. Did each of those scars equate to as much pain, as much loss, as much suffering as her own? To her, each scar was a monument to survival but also a reminder of mistakes, bad luck, horrors best forgotten.

He seemed young for so many.

Wait. He was grinning more broadly. What the dreck was he grinning at? And why were those damn eyes twinkling now?

"So, did I earn my keep yet?" he said. He set the armor aside, reached over to a black shirt that lay beside him on the bunk, and started to pull it on.

She stepped further inside and palmed the hatch shut, shrugging. "I suppose you earned one leg." She leaned against the wall just inside the hatch. In spite of herself, her eyes caught on his chest again as his hands and shirt slid over it. Shore leave needed to come sooner rather than later, clearly.

"What can I do to earn your other leg?" His head tilted, smile crooked now.

She stared blankly, trying to decipher what that could possibly mean. Had she been staring at him longer than she'd realized? Had he picked up on her notice of his... lack of flabbiness? Could he be... No, certainly not, but she had to shut it down quickly either way.

"Are you *flirting* with me, Theroki?" She raised her eyebrows.

He ducked his head to hide a different smile she still couldn't read. He pulled the sleeves of his shirt further down toward his wrists, one at a time, covering the tattoos, the gesture a tad self-conscious.

All this grinning and flirting and gazing charmingly must be to garner favor or something. Why else would he bother? Propping an indignant hand on her hip, she snorted. "What, do you just start at the top and work your way down? That's ambitious. Almost... cocky."

"I meant no offense, Commander," he said, shaking his head. "Just trying for some banter among crewmates. Clearly, I'm not doing it right."

"You're not one of my crew. You're a passenger."

"Still."

"Did you usually flirt with higher-ranking officers in the other outfits you served in, Theroki? Or maybe just your employers?"

"Call me Kael. And no. None of my commanding officers have been my type."

"Why not?" She tried not to bristle. Why was she bristling?

"They've all been men. Like I said, just not my thing. Also, I had my chip making me about as romantic as a plank of wood."

Oh. Right. "Well, I guess this ship is your lucky day then, Passenger 6A."

"Do your 'passengers' usually save you from Union ships?"

"Save me?" She narrowed her eyes at him. "We have fended off Union ships before you came along, and we will continue to do so after we leave Desori X and your sorry Theroki ass in the dust." He raised his eyebrows a little but said nothing. Damn it, she came down here to thank him, and if she were going to chew him out, it wouldn't be because they hadn't found his assistance helpful. Why was she so damn ornery? Maybe because he was trying to get into her pants only so she'd turn a blind eye to his plant bits. "Or are you vying for a job or something?" she said to lighten the mood.

"No, ma'am, not looking to go renegade." There was something tense in his face at the words, as though he'd bitten back an unspoken "yet." "Also, it seems that I am lacking in the preferred equipment to gain employment on this vessel."

"Which is?"

"A vagina?"

She choked on a peal of laughter, trying to smother it. She didn't want him thinking she liked him. Or his eyes. Theroki, especially cocky ones, were not to be trusted. Or liked. That would be even stupider than taking one on as a passenger. "I'm sure that could be arranged, if you ask Dr. Dremer really, really nicely."

"No, thank you, ma'am. I ain't *that* into modifications, personally." His grin had returned.

"Well then. Modifications or no, it's a good thing you don't want a job, because people who can't follow orders don't stay on this ship for long. Passengers included." She made her gaze as cool as she could, willing herself to look icy. Frosty. Serious. She had no idea if it was working. Some men told her they could never take her seriously when she made this face. Others seemed to shit their pants when she frowned even the tiniest amount. That hadn't helped her make heads or tails of it.

He sobered, though, and she had the feeling it was not only because she was pinning him with her steely gaze. "It won't happen again, Commander. I was out of practice and off-balance with a new ship around me. Plus the chip alterations. I acted below conscious thought. I promise you it wasn't intentional, but I should be acclimated enough now that there's no risk of it happening again. I apologize."

She blinked. That had been... much easier than she'd thought. Perhaps he'd already regretted it, as the apology had seemed ready and waiting.

"Good," she said sternly. "Look, I know you know what you're doing, that's plain as day. But combat has a way of getting messy. My crew is good, but not all of them are what I'd consider hardened veterans."

"And you are?" he cut in.

"And I am," she snapped. "Unintended things happen. Shit goes sideways. I care about these people more than you do. So you disobey me again, and there *will* be consequences." She folded her arms across her chest.

His eyes locked with hers. Her pulse jumped faster, almost frantic with sudden energy.

"I understand you completely, Commander," he said, voice husky.

She tried to give him her warmest nod. She wasn't sure if that was working either. Not everyone found her nods warm. Or anything about her warm. Was a nod even an appropriate thing to do to be warm? She sure as hell wasn't hugging him.

"I'll finish these repairs and hit the bunk now, if you don't mind, ma'am. Listen, I didn't mean to offend earlier." He paused, perhaps waiting for a response, but she had zero idea how to respond. "That won't happen again either."

"Good." She turned and palmed the hatch, feeling exhausted

herself. But she paused, remembering her second goal but unsure even positive phrases would come out right, given the feeling of reprimand that hung in the air.

"Theroki?" she said.

"Yes?" He'd stood up, waiting.

"I also came by to say thanks. Good work back there."

He gave her a nod and faux salute, like an Old West cowboy dipping his hat. "Thank you, Commander." She started to leave again, but his voice stopped her just outside in the hallway. "Oh, wait. Commander?"

She turned back, propping a hand on the other hip this time.

He strode to the hatch and leaned against it, arms bracing himself in the doorway above his head. Was he intentionally showcasing his hard-earned musculature, unhidden by any simple black shirt? Or did he not realize the dramatic effect that the gesture would have? Especially on any member of *her* crew who hadn't already found comfort aboard. Sure as her blood ran hot, her heart was pounding.

Whether she preferred it that way or not.

His eyes met hers, somber and sincere now. "Ma'am... I don't start at the top or 'work my way through' anything."

And with that, he palmed the hatch, and the door shut in her face. Or it would have been if she'd been two feet closer, but it felt just the same.

The corridor was suddenly more empty, and she very alone.

———

KAEL WOKE to the feeling of being watched. He'd woken up that way plenty of times in his life. There was little privacy on Theroki ships, with rows and rows of bunks rather than cabins.

But he wasn't on a Theroki ship, his sleep-addled brain reminded him.

He listened carefully. The incessant hum of the vents and life-support system, the whirring and whoosh of some kind of machinery beneath him, the creaking of the hull—all normal ship sounds. He couldn't recall hearing the hatch open or close or what might have awoken him. Some foggy part of his brain presented the hope that maybe the commander had returned, eager to catch glimpses of her pink lips and cold, powerful gaze. He brushed it aside.

His nose caught a faint scent in the air... Lemon? Not exactly the hallmark of a skilled assassin. On gut instinct, he opened his eyes and turned his head to the left.

Cat-like brown eyes set in warm bronze skin peered at him, just above the edge of the bed. Fingernails painted with chipped sky-blue paint curled around the edge of his bunk.

"Hello," said a young, curious voice.

Hell. It was a girl, her straight brown hair falling flat and neatly parted down the center. Couldn't be more than thirteen or fourteen.

"Uh—*salam*." He cleared his throat, groggy, and propped himself up on one elbow. He wouldn't have slept shirtless if he'd realized kids were going to show up in his room. "Can I... help you with something?" he said, voice still hoarse. He ran a hand over his face, trying to wake up. Was it even morning yet?

"No," the girl said simply, unmoving. Her wide eyes studied him.

"Do you always enter the rooms of dangerous men without permission? I would have guessed Commander Ryu ran a tighter ship than that."

"She does. I was curious. And I meant, it's not quite morning yet."

He blinked. He had been about to ask her if she truly wasn't afraid, but given the other women he'd run into on this ship, who knew? Maybe she wasn't. Maybe she had reason not to be. Why the hell was a kid on a ship like this anyway? Lifetime humanitarians had to have families too?

"You probably shouldn't make a habit of that," he said instead. "Not all Theroki sleep peacefully." Or treat women with respect. Or anyone with respect, for that matter. He scrubbed a hand over his face again and sat up in his bunk, swinging his legs over the side but keeping the blanket strategically positioned over his lap. He wasn't sure if this position was more or less weird in relation to her, but he had to get out of the bunk—and away from her—somehow.

"I'm not afraid. What's your name?" she said.

"What, is my cabin the ship playground? The name's Kael. And you, young lady?"

He felt the gentlest probe on the upper right part of his skull.

"Hey, now, that's not polite. I also would have guessed the commander would have taught you to ask permission before you go poking yourself into other people's heads." Given the fact that Ryu had outfitted their crew with those rape defense systems, he was fairly certain she'd be on his side with this one.

The girl straightened and grinned, taking a step back from him. "Kael Sidassian, I am Isa Lawson," she said in her odd tone, almost robotic in its tight control. She struck him as someone that didn't quite get how people worked and so therefore was doggedly mimicking their patterns of interaction with careful and meticulous accuracy. She had not yet fine-tuned it enough to seem natural, though. Or perhaps her manner was intentional.

She held out a hand to shake, a touch delayed.

"Nice to meet you, Isa," he said, deciding to roll with it. In spite of her deft psychic intrusion, he shook her hand and hoped that'd be the extent of it. He had ways of defending himself, but as the original Theroki had favored telekinesis over telepathy in their enhancements, most of those involved smashing the offending telepath into a wall until they stopped whatever they were doing.

Which would not be a good way to start off his journey on Ryu's ship. Not that he had any desire to fling children around, but he wouldn't impress the commander that way, militarily or otherwise. He probably wouldn't be able to impress her at all.

He hadn't offered his last name, and yet Isa had plucked it out with barely a brushing sensation, so she was either quite gifted or very practiced in finding that specific information in those certain neural pathways, or both. He eyed her warily, wondering if he was missing another deft brush as the awkward handshake went on just a tad too long.

Isa's brightly smiling face fell for a moment. Her head cocked to one side, then brightened again. "Well, you made it on the ship."

His eyes widened. Oh, that did not bode well. "What?"

Isa glanced over her shoulder at the door, then back at him, her grin returning. "You've already impressed her," she whispered conspiratorially. "She doesn't bring people she doesn't like onboard."

"Who?"

A beep sounded at the hatch.

"Xi, door open," Kael said quickly, not yet releasing Isa's hand. Hand-shaking seemed more innocent than practically anything else he could think of, so he clung to that. He didn't need to be thrown in the brig for something he hadn't done before his first twenty-four had passed on the ship. The last time he'd been falsely accused had been traumatic enough for one lifetime.

The hatch slid open to reveal a fiercely scowling woman, thick tattoos running like racing stripes across the sides of her shaved head and flanking a narrow strip of long red hair secured back in a ponytail. She wore a black cargo jumpsuit with more pockets than his pack and —was that a studded leather jacket over it?

"Isa, holy hell, what do you think you're doing?"

The girl whirled, still smiling. "Making friends," she said. It wasn't the voice of a friendly, innocent teen. It was a little more... creepy, like maybe she meant she was also planning his murder.

"I woke up to her staring at me," he added quickly, holding up his flat palms.

"Get back to your room," the woman snapped, stepping aside as Isa skipped away. The girl waved cheerily at Kael as she bounced down the hallway.

"Bye, Mr. Sidassian," she called from out of sight.

"*Salam*, Isa."

The leather-jacketed woman sighed. "Thanks, Xi."

"You're welcome, Engineer Lawson," came the placid voice from the ceiling.

"Sorry about that," said Lawson, jutting a chin out at him. "Kid's harmless, but her curiosity might be the death of her."

Kael opened his mouth to reply but didn't get a word out.

"Oh, *hello*," said another feminine voice over Lawson's shoulder.

The smooth and sultry notes from the hall contained far more interest than he'd received so far—or hoped to receive. He just needed to lie low.

Flawless skin and perfectly white, long hair came into view—a careful recreation of Capital elegance. Her eyes glowed an artificial violet outlined in rich black accenting their almond shape, gleaming with a disturbingly predatory sheen. The girl looked barely legal—and entirely unequipped for the chaos in someone like him.

"We were looking for the young Isa ourselves to begin studies." A second woman, perhaps an older sister to the first, peered around the wall and into his hatch, eyes also evaluating but far more detached. Her accent was also smooth and toward the front of the mouth—probably both from Capital.

He ignored the Capital types and directed his comments only to the leather jacket. "I'm sure I don't need to tell you that what she did was seriously dangerous. Not every Theroki is like me. And she really should stay out of my head. It's… not a place for kids." He shuddered to think. His chip malfunction—well, sabotage was probably a better word, even if he'd been a willing subject—was rather harmless compared to what could have happened if different areas had been damaged.

"Yeah, no shit. She's more dangerous than she looks, though." Lawson glanced down the hallway after Isa, then at the Capitals, then back at him with a vague expression of finding them all excessively trying.

"She's certainly fearless. Are you two related? I'm Kael, by the way."

"She's my kid," Lawson said, pressing her lips together. "And for the record, her dad's not here, and she doesn't need a new one. Also no, I won't teach her to stay in her cabin. Already beyond failed at that." She paused, squinting at him.

He only stared in response. It was too early in the morning for this shit.

Lawson's expression softened at his lack of reaction. "I'm Bri, chief engineer on this pointless exercise in self-flagellation stuffed into a tin can barreling through space."

"Don't let her gruff exterior fool you," said the youngest smoothly, her eyes brightening as his gaze locked with hers momentarily. "She's quite a good engineer, and there's nowhere else in the galaxy she'd rather be."

He considered a fierce expression to frighten the girl away... but he had a feeling such an attempt would backfire. Hell, this ship was a fragging minefield.

Bri gave the Capital girl a fiery glare. "Only because this 'verse is a flaming pile of dog shit. Not a lot of competition."

"How many engineers are there?" he said instead, definitely wanting to avoid *that* topic. It hadn't seemed like that big of a ship.

"Just me."

"So you're chief of yourself."

"Yep. And I'm the best engineer on the ship too, as far as you're concerned. Got a problem with that?"

"Um, nice to meet you too," he muttered.

"Ladies, I don't think viewing hours at the ship zoo begin until 0800," came Ryu's cool voice from out in the hallway.

Immediately, they all straightened and turned toward her at attention, or something very like it. A decent reaction to raise out of nonmilitary types. He found himself smirking.

"Isa started it, Commander," said Bri.

"I don't doubt it. But shall we perhaps leave our passenger alone this early in the morning? I'm sure you find him ogle-worthy, but the coffee isn't even done yet."

Ogle-worthy? His smirk melted into a grin. The young Capital flushed but also sneered in Ryu's direction; the older one looked vaguely irritated. Bri rolled her eyes.

"Yeah, whatever," Bri muttered and stormed away, in the opposite direction that Isa had gone. The fine and graceful ladies skittered the other way, after Isa, long robes swirling.

Commander Ryu appeared in the doorway. "Sorry about that."

He shrugged. "It's fine. Not every morning you wake up to being mind-violated in your sleep by a fourteen-year-old, but you know. I've seen worse mornings."

"I'll bet you have," she said softly. Her eyes flicked over his torso, not missing his scars. He wondered if the young Capital had noticed them the way Ryu did. Ryu might have some idea how costly each one had been. A desire to get her to inspect them more closely hit him, and for the first time, he didn't feel surprised at the thought. Just more space noise to ignore, he told himself.

"Isa is… unusual," she said into what had become a rather long, if comfortable silence. "My apologies. I'll talk to her. Don't get your hopes up, though. Did she want something specific?"

"To make friends, she claimed," he said, barely repressing laughter.

The commander snorted. "Typical. And to think puberty's only just started." Her eyes lit up a little with her own faint touch of amusement.

He laughed. "You run quite the unusual ship, Commander."

"You don't know the half of it."

"Puberty-related thoughts did not *seem* to be on her mind."

"She pretty much mines people for information. I should kick her off, but Bri is a damn near irreplaceable engineer. I won't hold it against you if you need to… take evasive maneuvers."

He winced. "And… what kind of information does she look for?"

"What kind of information were you looking for when you were fourteen? While she wouldn't have acted on it, she probably showed up so quickly because you would be… 'an unusual data source.' Her words, not mine."

He snorted, but then remembered the way Isa's face had fallen just after he'd thought about the chip—and Vala. What had the girl seen exactly? Ugh. "You don't object to her behavior? I'm surprised."

"Oh, I do. I'll give her a stern talking-to. It just hasn't worked in the past. She's convinced of the morality of her actions, as long as she rarely shares what she 'discovers.' "

"Rarely?"

"I've only seen it done once, in a dire situation, but I suppose you never know. I wouldn't think about your mission while she's around."

He risked a slight glare at her. "You could have warned me."

She smiled slightly. "Of what? The curious teenager that will likely scar herself by perusing your memories of past sexual exploits and then vanish into her books again?"

"You know what I mean," he said, narrowing his eyes further.

"If you're thinking I didn't mention her so I could use her to get whatever facts I wanted out of you, put that idea out of your head. She's no one's tool, least of all mine."

"Of course, you're right, Commander. I'll just take that at face value and not question it for a minute." He tried to keep his smirk friendly to soften the sarcasm.

"Look, I didn't come here to harass you before breakfast either. I wanted to let you know we'll be touching down on Elpi VI at 1500. There's some Ursas in need of medical care during a brief cease-fire, and we've managed to pick up a freelance security contract in the area."

"Freelance?" So they were mercenaries, just like him. That made a certain sense.

"Hey, someone's gotta pay our healthcare bills. If you want to join us, I'll count it as a third of your passage. Briefing for that is at 1300. No skin off my back if you want to stay and cower inside the ship."

He smiled crookedly at her. "Stay and cower? Really, Commander, you must want my help."

She frowned.

"Do you taunt all your able-bodied passengers into assisting with freelance contracts?"

"Only the ogle-worthy ones. Need them to look pretty for clients."

"Obviously."

"Yes, obviously. Also the ones without credits to pay their passage."

"Excellent point."

"The briefing is *not* optional if you want to fight. Or at least walk around and look ominous and threatening. You are verifiably good at that." Enough sarcasm dripped from her voice that he wasn't sure what she meant and what she didn't. Before he could tug more out of her, she slammed the hatch control, and it slid shut as she walked away.

He paused for a moment, thinking. "Xi?" he asked the empty room.

"Yes, Passenger 6A?"

"You can call me Kael."

"Acknowledged. Kael."

"Is there a way to lock the door to this cabin? And was it locked?"

"Yes, there is a locking mechanism, but no, you did not engage it. Do you wish for me to set up an automatic locking routine based on your location?"

"Uh, sure? What would that entail?"

"The most basic default configuration is that the ship will lock the door when you are in the room and not lock it when you are not."

"That would be great." He got up, looking for where he'd thrown his shirt. Oh, there it was, in the corner.

Ryu seemed like the orderly type. Did she fold everything perfectly to specification and set it back in a designated drawer even on her own private vessel? Hang things neatly in perfectly spaced rows? Kael could never have made it in any military other than the Theroki one, if it could even be called one. As he pulled the shirt on, something occurred to him.

"Xi, did Isa use the door to enter my cabin?"

"No, she did not."

His mouth fell open. "How did she enter then?"

There was a pause. "I apologize, but you are not approved to access this information about the ship and its structures. Would you like me to request access?"

Oh, that would really freak them out. "No, no. Just, uh, good to know. I would rather not have someone do that. Can you tell me right away next time if they do? Even if I'm not in my cabin?"

"Acknowledged. I will add it to the locking routine and create a security profile."

"Sounds fancy."

There was another pause. "Would 'thank you' be an appropriate response in this instance?"

"Yes."

"Thank you. I also appreciate your willingness to enhance my young conversational algorithms."

"You're welcome," he muttered, sure she would hear him. Private cabin or no, this ship was not turning out to have much privacy of any kind at all.

He glanced at the utility cabinet. Bending down, he checked the canister, but it was still in its hiding place. He needed to go on that mission, but it was just large enough it'd be hard to store in his armor without a pack. He could leave his grenades behind and put it in there, but that cavity could launch whatever was inside it a hundred yards. He wouldn't command it to, but on the off chance his armor got hacked… or he got seriously injured…

What was the alternative, leaving it onboard? That didn't seem like a good idea either. He'd have to try the grenade cavity.

How much of a problem was it that the girl could discover the capsule? And worse, its true purpose? Its identity, if it had one yet? He'd have to hope Ryu was right and the girl was more interested in bedroom exploits than mission details. And he'd have to keep his thoughts about it to a minimum and not give her a trail to follow.

Perhaps he'd have to focus on the commander a little more and the mission a little less. For secrecy's sake, of course. His dedication to mission secrecy was absolutely the only reason.

He laughed out loud and went rummaging in his pack for something to eat.

CHAPTER FOUR

"YOU STILL SHOULD HAVE CONSULTED us, Commander," grumbled Dr. Levereaux. "There's a lot of risk inherent in having a Theroki aboard."

Ellen pressed her lips together and glanced over at Dr. Dremer, who was not paying any of them any mind, her attention focused on her tablet. Dremer and the other two women sat around the polished white quartz table in the ship's conference room. The metal of the walls lent tension to the pair of serious glares in Ellen's direction. Dremer glared instead at something or other in her files.

To prepare for the coming mission, she'd gathered the three Foundation scientists into the briefing room early to make sure she had their opinions, not to talk about the Theroki. But perhaps she should have expected it. Levereaux wasn't the best at handling risk. She liked everything pinned down, like the many moths, beetles, and butterflies on display on her cabin wall.

"It's worth the risk to be certain he's not smuggling something from the Enhancer lab we hit. And besides, Dremer approved it," Ellen said, since the woman wasn't speaking up.

Dr. Dremer looked up at the sound of her name. "What? What did I approve?"

"You agreed to bringing the Theroki onboard?" Levereaux demanded. She leaned her elbows onto the table, pressing Dremer to pay attention. Unfortunately for her current goal, her Enhancer-designed beauty and perfection of form had little effect on Dremer, with all her study of such engineering and its effects. "He could kill us all."

"We can handle him," Ellen put in, not that they were listening.

Dremer smirked, only focused on her tablet again. As usual, the scientists mostly ignored Ellen in their discussions, not out of disdain or disrespect, but just because they had so much more to argue with each other. "Listen, Rach. With the modifications made to his chip, I'd say he's more likely to try to *bed* us all than kill us at this point."

Levereaux raised an eyebrow. "Excuse me? A Theroki?"

"This one's no eunuch. Or at least, someone turned off that bit of programming for now. Did you find out how that happened, Commander?"

Ellen shook her head. "No." She hadn't tried, though. Yet. She would respect that area of privacy for now, until it became necessary or his mission clearly posed a problem. That respect was probably naive and the thing these ladies should truly be concerned about, but none of them thought like intelligence officers. Unfortunately.

Ellen lacked that on their current crew, in spite of all the high IQs and advanced degrees of study. Simmons and his intel people were good, but they weren't here on the ship to remind her of and poke at her flaws. She didn't prefer it that way; more intel was already on the list of recruitment needs.

"And that's supposed to make me feel better?" Levereaux rolled her eyes.

Dremer sighed, finally thumping the tablet on the table. "With his configuration, having operated with an emotion-and-desire-suppressing chip for at least five or ten years, maybe fifteen or more if he enlisted early? Imagine if you never felt hungry. Or thirsty. For a decade. And then it came back. The cognitive load of all those inter-ruptions would be significant."

Levereaux clenched her jaw. Dr. Taylor, who had yet to say

anything, smiled, recognizing the signs as Ellen did that Dremer had already won. "You didn't mention brownies in the cafeteria, though," said Levereaux. "You mentioned beds. Or should I be concerned about our food supply too?"

"Hunger isn't the only urge he's recently regained access to," Dremer said, eyes sparkling. "And if I know men—and I do—I know which one will be the hardest to control. Although I am not sure I'd recommend any of us taking him up on relieving any of those urges without thoroughly considering the risks and knowing more about his mission." Her eyes flicked straight at Ellen.

"What? Why are you looking at me?" Ellen growled.

"Oh, you know. You're the alpha wolf here. If I know anything about wolves—"

Taylor snorted. "You know that's all bunk, right? Humans are much more like baboons than wolves. And the original wolf behavior research was refuted by its own author. And yet! It refuses to die." Ellen was happy to listen to their resident expert in the human mind over a woman who loved replacing human body parts with synthetic ones any day.

But he *had* given her a wolfish look when she was in the room, now that she thought about it.

Hadn't he given all of them that same look?

"Not part of your psychological canon?" Dremer smirked again.

"It's not a *canon*, it's a carefully established body of scientific research. One in which I have—"

"—an advanced medical degree, yada, yada," Levereaux completed the sentence for her. "Lay off it, Dremer, or she'll psychoanalyze your 'auto-didactic' butt again."

Dremer's smirk faded. "I was awarded an honorary doctorate from three different—"

"Drop it," Ellen snapped. "Get yourselves together."

Taylor glared. "You started it, Alex. You just want to get your paws on him, don't you? Not in bed, on the examination table."

Ellen smiled to herself, although the others probably couldn't tell. She tried to keep a mask of straight-faced command in these situations.

Well, most situations really. That had been her assumption about Dremer as well, but she was glad to hear it had occurred to Dr. Taylor too.

"Yes. I analyzed the threat and approved it before Mo even brought him onboard to speak with Commander Ryu. A Theroki is clearly a risk to have onboard, but he also presents a potential to get access to some of his technology. Our Foundation representatives would approve, I'm sure of it."

"Simmons approves *everything* for you," Levereaux growled.

"Especially since his chip is damaged, we may be able to convince him to let us help him fix it. Or if he is wounded—"

"No unnecessary probing without Sidassian's permission," Ellen snapped. Damn, why was it so hard to keep people asking for consent around here? "I'll not be out blowing up Enhancer labs for kidnapping people and violating patient rights while you're back here doing the same damn thing."

Dremer sobered but did not deny the accusation. She was a good scientist, an ethical one, but she was prey to the same temptations the Enhancers fell to all too often. Went with her expertise, probably. "You're right. Of course. But it is tempting. The people we could save, how much safer I could make you all—"

Ellen held up her open palm. "Convince him, then. The road to hell is paved with good intentions." She pointed up at the mural, where that phrase and several others gloriously adorned the ceiling. It was the most intricate one on the ship, and Zhia, with help from Isa, kept adding to it over time.

"I know, I know. Do me a favor and help me with the task?" She smiled sweetly.

Ellen shrugged. She did not feel particularly hungry to capture anything about the Theroki tech. As a people they were wild, bizarre, chaotic. Not her style. *He* was not her style. She could barely believe such disorganization fueled any scientific innovation at all, let alone kept it running and sustained it. But as Sidassian had shown, their telekinesis was second to none, and they typically had a score of other enviable upgrades for both ground and space combat. She should probably be more focused on acquiring such tech for herself and her crew. But they were just so damn... She wasn't sure what, but she didn't want anything about them to rub off on her.

"I'll see what I can do," she said noncommittally. "He's here now. Beyond his personal tech, as I already said, I think we need to investigate the parcel he carries. I'm concerned we may have missed something in wiping the last lab, and he may have brought it onboard."

All their eyebrows shot up.

"I should have considered that," Dremer muttered. "Too busy looking at his data..."

"I want you to see if you can get any more information on the organic in his pack, Doctor. Without disturbing it, at a distance. Or him. You get on this too, Levereaux. I hope it's innocuous, but... we had better find out what we can. Be advised I did get out of him that his oath is engaged on it, so it'd be best if he doesn't know we're at all interested in it." She glanced around, but they were all nodding and scribbling notes. "I'm trying to get him to go with us on the next mission, in hopes that he'll leave it behind. In which case, I want you to move in and study it further."

Dremer nodded, lost in thought now.

Ellen continued. "I also want the option to sedate him somehow. That may be a better bet. Do any of you have anything we could use for that?"

"I have basic anesthesia," said Levereaux. "But I'd prefer not to use any of it until we get closer to another resource deposit."

"That'll be at least a week."

"Agreed. But we run out often enough."

"All right. Zhia also suggested something we could fire at him. Work up some options for me."

Levereaux nodded. "Will do, ma'am."

"Commander, may I add something?" Xi's disembodied voice came from the ceiling.

"Yes?"

"I can join in the remote scans of the package, if you would prefer.

Also, I believe the doctors would benefit from knowing it is currently stored in the utility cabinet in cabin 6A."

"Thank you, Xi," Dremer said absently.

"I'd also like to volunteer to put in an order and courier delivery for a tranquilizer gun. I believe you will be very busy with patients when we land, Rachel. I can arrange everything to be done when we get there, if you give me your preferred gun and specifications. I can also research guns and specifications but would prefer a human doctor make final dosing decisions."

Well, damn. That actually was quite helpful. "Good thinking," Ellen admitted. Did AIs think, or was that something else? Good computing? "And yes on the remote scans."

Levereaux smiled. "Of course, that sounds very useful, Xi."

"I'd welcome any other ideas you have for putting him out of commission temporarily," Ellen added. "All of you, Xi included. We need backup options. I'd rather him never know we inspected the thing in the first place."

"One more thing, Commander," Xi said. "Kael has requested I give him updates when anyone tries to enter his room. This is likely more a reaction to Isa's unexpected visit than any suspicion on his part, but you will need to deliberately override my reporting if you try to enter his room. The four of you should be able to do so, but others won't."

"Thanks," Ellen said. Oh, silly Isa. She still needed to track the girl down and give her a lecture. And maybe see if she'd learned anything useful, not that she would be willing to share it.

"Wait—what?" Taylor sat forward. "Isa?"

"Your wife was there—ask her all about it. Isa snuck in there this morning and woke him up with a nice mental probing, apparently. Which I remind you all is *not permitted without consent*, damn it."

Taylor smacked a palm over her face but said nothing.

"It seemed mostly harmless, aside from whatever insanity she might have stolen from his head. And she asked for it, against our best suggestions." Ellen sighed, then cleared her throat. "Did anyone have anything more to add that's actually related to the upcoming mission? Before I get started on the briefing?"

Levereaux shook her head. "I'll be ready for Ursa and any other nonhuman patients."

"I as well," said Taylor.

"Do you think you'll need me with you on the mission?" Dremer asked.

"Oh, of course you volunteer for the missions where you can ogle the Theroki," Ellen said wryly. She was unclear whether Dremer truly knew what such ogling would entail. In Ellen's limited experience, Theroki had a tendency to unleash sudden, breathtaking brutality. Not the sort of thing the good doctor would not be able to watch easily, no matter what Sidassian's casual ease and friendliness might suggest.

Dremer grinned. "Beats first aid, but I'll go where you need me."

"From what I heard, we can expect more trauma care than first aid," Levereaux said, voice dark.

Ellen nodded. "Stay here. This looks like a simple find-and-release. I'll need one or two of you for Upsilon for sure, though. If he goes for this plan and we get him off ship for missions, you can ogle him then. As long as someone else is investigating his plant bits."

"Oh, he'll go for it," Dremer said, grinning. "But I do believe I'm not the only one excited to see him in action." She stood, preparing to leave, and the others stood with her.

"I have *no* interest in—" Ellen started.

Dremer's grin widened. "I meant the crew in general, Commander."

Was it more or less incriminating to slap a palm to her forehead?

Taylor also smiled crookedly. "That was a telling slip, don't you think, Dremer? You sure you're not practicing psychotherapy yet?"

"Nah, I just know the commander's type."

"You most certainly do *not*," Ellen said coldly, thinking of Paul. She tried to brush the thought aside. The Theroki was nothing like Paul, and she wouldn't make the same mistake again. Not ever, especially not with these women she cared about so much. And especially not over some feature she could recreate just as well in a sim chamber. Sidassian didn't have a monopoly on strong jaws and muscled, scarred shoulders. Those dark eyes, though… It would be a rare sim to capture those.

Their leave couldn't arrive soon enough.

"He's not your type?"

"I don't have a type," she said stiffly. "And I wouldn't risk any distraction to our mission even if I did."

"Well. I still think he'll be up for the missions. He'll have to blow off that steam building up somehow, and nothing a Theroki likes more than shooting things." Dremer's grin did not lessen.

"Maybe smashing things," Taylor offered.

"Blowing things up?" Levereaux said, smirking.

"I feel like you're far too amused with this man's torture," Ellen said. It had been hell adjusting to life without her chip. For a good six months, she'd felt nearly insane. Then again, hers had had very different functionality.

"Oh, boo-hoo, he has to be slightly less superhuman for a while." Dremer sobered. "Look, I know it was hard for you when we removed your chip, Ellen. I don't mean to make light of it. But he doesn't have anything like what you had, no Starbird grid, no loss of information flow, no Songbird interconnections. If anything, he's got *more* info now and the same power. He hasn't lost a thing. I'd argue he's gotten quite lucky. I'm sure a Theroki or two would kill to be in his position. Keep most of their abilities and still be able to screw? And he stumbles across a ship full of potential candidates? I wish him well, and maybe a bit of humanity for a while. Not torment."

Taylor lowered her head, her expression sad, and Levereaux stared off into space at Dremer's words. Ellen knew what they were thinking, about their own bits of humanity they wouldn't have traded for superpowers any day. They'd all had the chance at one time or another before the Foundation came along. They'd all made their choices.

Ellen had to agree, and that was part of why she'd joined them, why she'd asked them to remove her Union-placed chip in the first place. It did break her heart to think of how much all those men gave up so willingly, and in her opinion foolishly. What was the point of being *super*human if you couldn't be human in the first place?

Of course, no one had given Ellen a choice. And right now, Arakovic was likely off doing the same damn thing to some other poor unconscious soul, scarring their minds forever if not outright obliterating them. Ellen was lucky she'd gotten out. She clenched her fist against her thigh under the table and hoped the doctors didn't notice.

What had been Kael's reason to give up what he had? Had he regretted it? No, not Kael. They were not on a first-name basis. And would never be.

"That's the real reason you approved him," Ellen said flatly, keeping her face a cool mask. "Isn't it?" Not that she disagreed. Not at all. Caring about people's humanity was what had put them all on this mission in the first place. Er, perhaps she should say "richness of life." She was no xenophobe; she just lazily included Ursas and Teredarks and Alums into her definition of humanity.

Dremer lifted her chin, a touch defiant. "We do not abandon those who suffer if we can. And we give them what dignity we are able."

Taylor snickered, breaking the seriousness of the moment. "And what if that dignity means a good lay?"

The scientist's blue eyes twinkled behind her swooping lock of silvered hair. "Especially then."

"You just want to convince him to let you prod his insides," Ellen snapped, entirely uncomfortable with this discussion at her briefing table.

"No, I believe I asked for your help with that."

Before Ellen could formulate any response, Dremer spun and headed for the door, and the others followed. Ellen blew out a breath in relief.

The briefing attendees had been forming up outside the closed door anyway, right on time. Sidassian's tousled, longish hair was among the tops of the heads she could see out the high window. Good. He was going for it. And good thing the room had been soundproofed, even for superhumans. *Especially* for superhumans. She made a mental note that she hadn't yet seen the report on standard Theroki upgrades and his in particular. When she'd had the Starbird chip and access to the whole world of information at her fingertips, she could have looked it up right now with just a thought...

Not worth it, she reminded herself. Not worth it at all.

Dremer paused in the doorway. "Don't forget my request, Commander," she said, winking.

"Don't you—" She stifled her anger with a growl. The door was open. "This is not a game," she said coldly.

Dremer let out a bark of laughter. "Everything is a game. Lighten up, Commander."

Ellen scowled at the door as the soldiers filed in, all sobering at her dark expression. Except, of course, Sidassian. He raised one eyebrow, his eyes shining with even greater amusement than usual. She restrained a snarl in response. He glanced at the hallway, then back to her, then sauntered to the back of the room and leaned against the wall, eschewing a seat.

Figured. Falling in would be too much to ask for an embodiment of chaos.

She stabbed at the button that brought up the projector and clenched her jaw at the loading screen. Superhuman, bleeding-edge technology in half the bodies on this ship, and they didn't have a holo-projector that took less than a lifetime to turn on. What good was technology if it was constantly wasting your time? Her scowl deepened.

She *hated* it when people told her to lighten up.

———

AFTER FINISHING the repairs to his cooling unit, Kael had spent the morning on his tablet with a protein bar, taking the time to do the basic research on the ship he would have preferred to do before jumping on it. Searches on the *Audacity* had turned up little more than a date and location of manufacture—on Capital five years ago. Apparently there had been dozens of Commander Ryus over the years, and the net was clogged with "him." That made sense, as New Korea had ended up the most prosperous planet in the Pacific Alliance Systems. The PAS had been one of the founding members of the Union, so the Union was full of officers from that system. Maybe if he could get her first name, he could find out more.

That was a good short-term goal. For the security of the mission. Yeah, sure, that was why.

Also getting her to call him something other than Theroki or Passenger 6A would be a bonus. Xi had been easy; you just had to ask. The others would be more of a challenge, he guessed.

He scratched his chin, trying to think. Who had he encountered that would be distinct enough for something to turn up in a search? Isa? No, kids shouldn't have stuff all over the net about them. Maybe... Dr. Dremer. If she were a widely recognized expert, there should be something about her out there. A quick search for "Dr. Dremer cybernetics expert" yielded a wealth of results on Dr. Alexandra Dremer, including a spate of academic publications and patents on cybernetic tech that had stopped...

Five years ago. Since then, there had been little activity. Almost like her career had ended.

What could cause a respected-galaxy-wide cybernetics genius with a cushy academic position on Capital to give all that up and just... go silent? Retire? And go hopping around war zones on a humanitarian mission? People had crises in their lives that made them do strange things, but jumping on the *Audacity* seemed like a bit of a stretch. She could have done plenty to help people on Capital itself, although not people affected by the war. Capital was safely outside both Union and Puritan territory, and its economic power insulated it from the ongoing war, although it was not without terrorists at times.

Whatever had lured her onto this ship, he betted it had something to do with those obfuscated patches and whoever was funding this "humanitarian vessel." Maybe he'd believe that more if and when he actually saw any humanitarian action happen.

His quiet morning was a welcome respite from all the shit that had gone down on Helikai. After that, he'd ambled over to the briefing, which was turning out to be short but sweet.

That was fortunate, because he struggled to pay attention to all but the satellite imagery and the very basic game plan. He kept getting distracted analyzing the velvet, alto notes of Ryu's voice, which was more clipped and stern than he suspected was usual. She had a bit of a lilt to her *l*'s and a high-sounding *u* that made him think she must have been from one of the inner planets. Did she speak anything other than Common? He shook his head, realizing he'd missed the meaning if not the sound of at least two sentences. Pay attention, you fool. If she figured out he was not listening—or worse, just admiring her accent without paying attention—he didn't want to find out the consequences.

"Nova and Jenny will accompany me and Sidassian—our new passenger, whom I'm sure you've noticed. Mo, I'd like you positioned close to the ship but with an eye on our target as well. Zhia and Dane, you'll stay with the ship."

"Got it, Commander," said the orange-haired one. Another lone man nodded. Dark-skinned with a short, neat beard, he was perfectly pressed and hadn't met Kael's eye once yet. Interesting.

He fought to listen as they went further into detail, but his eyes kept straying to the elaborate mural on the ceiling of the briefing room. A handful of phrases were scrawled there among lush paintings of multirifles, ivy, roses, and knives. It was a rare and strikingly beautiful combination that reminded him vaguely of an Old Earth tattoo. He couldn't make out all the quotations in the darkened room, especially from this angle, but he could make out, "*No plan survives contact with the enemy*," which left him smirking.

"That's it," Ryu was finishing up. "Be ready at 1500. Dismissed. Oh, Sidassian—a word with you privately."

He nodded and simply stayed put as the others filed out. Ryu shut the door behind them. The lights remained down, the room lit only by the aerial photography of the forested planet below. She was dressed much the same as the day before, same black armor and navy vest. Did she always wear her armor around on average days on her ship? Was it because of the mission later?

Was it because he was onboard and she didn't trust him yet?

"You seem to seek out private words with me fairly often,

Commander," he said as the door's lock beeped. He smiled to hide a touch of concern. Why was she locking the door?

If she heard him, she ignored it. "I'm glad you decided to join us on the mission. We'll have a multi and ammo for you when we head out."

A multi? He fought to hide a mixture of shock and excitement. Play it cool. Rank-and-file Theroki, even one of his relatively moderate-to-high rank, didn't get multirifles. Was that what he hadn't recognized in Mo's clutches? Either way, he'd be glad not to be stuck with that beat-up antique of a laser he'd lifted from the evac team. "Great," he said instead.

"When was the last time you were in a war zone, Theroki?"

"Kael," he said.

"We'll see."

He pressed his lips together. Well, he liked a challenge, didn't he? "The last year has been mostly security detail, so most of that has been speedy evacuations when the war reached us, with a little fending off raids and assorted assassins for good measure. But before that, I was in the field more than a few times over the years." Where was this line of questioning going?

"Have you been since you… sustained damage?"

He tried not to grit his teeth at the phrasing. It was accurate; what did he have to dislike? "Not yet. Are you concerned?"

"Should I be?"

"You probably know better than I do, Commander. I get the impression your ship has a bit better tech than the aging bucket of bolts I call armor."

"I thought Therokis prided themselves on the scars in their armor."

He shrugged. "Good ones do, I suppose." He'd never been a star soldier among them. Attained a decent rank, yes, but earned more enemies than friends along the way. "I've never claimed to be a good one."

She regarded him silently for a moment, unreadable. "There could be some differences. Based on what I saw and what Dremer sent me, I'd say primary damage is to emotional-repression sectors as well as physical-urge repression. Now you get to feel starving and tired like the rest of us, I guess."

Her face remained neutral, but he smiled at her. "Sounds about right."

"Listen, I know you're no newbie, but the humanitarian angle on war can be particularly horrifying. When you don't have the adrenaline of battle, when you don't have a mission or a cause or a side to fight for, you're just there dealing with the shit part and the pointlessness of it all. I've seen a few Theroki go nuclear in my day for lesser reasons. In your state, I'd advise trying to ignore whatever you see in the cargo hold and waiting for us outside of it. Even if they're Ursas, it can be hard to stomach. At least, try to ignore it until you get used to your... altered state of consciousness."

He snorted. "You say that like it's possibly better."

Her lips twitched slightly. Almost a smile? "Maybe it is."

Huh—an interesting reaction. He tilted his head. "Don't go nuclear. Got it, Commander. I'll do my best."

"See to it that you do."

She made for the door, and he groped for a way to keep her from ending the conversation. "Uh, when were you in a position to fight alongside any Theroki?"

She stopped and met his eyes, sighing. "Not alongside—against. I suppose you'll find out sooner or later. Union Special Forces."

His eyebrows flew up. So that badass voice was not just in his head, it came from experience. "Wow. *Union*, really? After the middle finger you just gave that Union ship? I wouldn't have guessed."

"Trust me, if they'd known which Ryu they were talking to, they wouldn't have let us go without a fight. Fortunately there are a few, and my former records have been... edited a bit. And not like you left them with many options."

"When did you make the switch from shooting people to helping them after they got shot?"

She shrugged, her eyes closed off and staring into the distance. "Nobody stays in the army forever."

"Unless you're a Theroki."

"Touché."

"Aren't you a little young to be retired?"

"You're a little dense to keep bringing up my age."

His turn to shrug. "If I could retire, I'd do it. I... wouldn't have pegged you as a Union type."

She propped a hand on her hip. Uh-oh. A sign of incoming snark? "Just what *would* you have pegged me as, Theroki?"

"Theroki again? Not even Sidassian this time?" He made a disgusted noise. "Oh, I thought for certain you were from some well-bred Capital family. A sheltered and rich aristocrat, by the look of you."

The fire that lit her eyes told him she did not get the joke.

"Commander, that was supposed to be funny. Banter. Crews banter. Clearly I'm out of practice."

She glanced down at the floor. "More like I am. Sorry. They're right, I probably do need to 'lighten up.' " Her glare shifted to the door as she folded her arms. Ah, so that was why she'd scowled for half the meeting.

"No, no. Listen, I estimated you to be a highly experienced officer, nothing less. I'm not sure how anyone could think you anything other than that."

"Maybe it's 'cause I look more like Dremer's daughter than her commanding officer?" she offered, pressing her lips together.

"No. Age is one thing, but you have a commander's air. Besides, I was just saying all that to get that scowl off your face." He paused, but when she said nothing for a moment, he continued, lest she try to run out the door again. "Don't let them get to you. There's a mission in a few hours. You're focused on that instead of pissing around. I for one appreciate that. It's a good strategy for not getting killed. Letting them get under your skin doesn't really help anybody. They're just not as experienced as you are. Let me guess—you haven't had many fatalities with this crew."

She met his gaze for a long moment. "Good guess."

He read nothing in her face, but the tension in her shoulders seemed to lessen. "I hope the trend continues," he said gently.

"So do I." She turned to unlock the door but paused before she opened it. "We achieve our objective without any losses, and I'll owe you a beer, Sidassian."

He would have liked to cheer, but he settled for grinning and clenching his fingers into a celebratory fist out of view. Ridiculous to be so energized over a beer between colleagues. But he'd said the right thing. For once.

That beer would also give him something to focus on when the bloodlust started to set in.

"That's a deal, ma'am. See you at 1500."

She nodded, opened the door, and strode out.

———

ELLEN HIT the call bell on Bri's cabin, wondering if her engineer would be home or in the engine room. Her personal quarters were connected to the mechanics by a custom blast door she'd installed, but it was almost always open, so it wasn't like there was a huge difference between the engine room and her bunk anyway. Except where Isa preferred to hang around.

The door slid open, revealing a miffed-looking Bri, arms folded across her chest.

"Did you ground her?" Ellen said with the smallest of smiles for her old friend.

"Damn straight. Two weeks with no *Red Dwarf Commander*. No vids. The usual." Bri moved back slowly from the doorway, holding out one arm to invite Ellen to enter.

"All right. Can I talk to her?"

"You can try." Bri shrugged, pointed toward the lounge area, and trudged off toward the engine room.

Ellen moved cautiously forward. Isa was reading a book on a bunk converted with cushions to be something like a couch. But of course the girl knew Ellen was coming and sat down her tablet.

She rose and bowed, robes swinging dramatically. How did all

Naturals gravitate toward the same fashions? Was it in some Natural Telepath Handbook somewhere?

The girl raised an eyebrow. "Hello, Commander. I was pleased to meet the new passenger you invited aboard."

"Isa. Yes, I heard you had a little run-in with our Theroki."

"I made friends with Kael this morning."

Ellen couldn't help but wince at that. "Is that what you call it?"

"I only said hello."

Ellen pursed her lips. "Once again, I'm going to remind you that you *must* ask for consent before invading people's thoughts. It's a rule on this ship." God, as if she'd let people go around raping each other. Mind raping, bodily raping, she saw no difference.

"I'm not harming them. They can't even feel it most of the time. It's not the same." Isa clasped her hands in front of her but didn't look particularly ruffled by Ellen's order.

Ellen scowled now. "And you're doing it again. I won't have this argument with you another time. You only think it's no different because it's never happened to you."

"The sanctity of my mind or my secrets has never been something I expected."

"Well, other people *do* expect it." Just like Ellen had expected she could trust those above her to heal her and not install some chip that would drive her slowly insane and shred her identity just because she went down in a heli crash.

Isa frowned, eyes thoughtful but lousy with sympathy. Ellen hated that look. "Ah, I see. Your personal history *does* make it harder to judge this, I suppose. I'm surprised I didn't think of that before."

"That's irrelevant. You *will* stop, or I'll be forced to increase the severity of your punishment. People have a right to the privacy of their minds. It's both Union and Puritan law."

"We're not under Puritan or Union law, are we? We break many of their laws every day."

"It's my law too. You know, just because your mom is a damn good engineer doesn't mean I can't order her to ship you off to one of those psych schools." Ellen narrowed her eyes.

"You wouldn't."

Ellen didn't bother to respond. Yes, a psych school, she thought. A true telepathy academy where they would actually teach her not to do this shit. A reasonably talented Natural like Isa should have gone years ago. She should definitely talk to Bri about getting Isa some proper education. Preferably not on this ship. Somewhere where she'd be safe, but maybe around a few more of her own kind so she could learn what it felt like to resent someone butting in, to lose your privacy against your will.

"Don't call it that," Isa said softly.

Oh, that was right. They didn't like to be called psychics. Only a fine telepathic institution name with proper frills would do. Certainly that was where Isa needed to go. Or could Ellen find a few telepaths to join them on the ship? Nah, last thing she needed. Yes, psych school was a much better idea.

Isa's eyes widened.

"I *said*, stop it, Isa. That's an order."

She lowered her gaze to the floor. "It's hard to resist, Commander."

"Learn. Don't give me excuses. You know, someday you'll meet someone you want to love, and you might want to know how to keep your mental paws to yourself. You may not want to know every little thing they are thinking."

"Maybe they'll be able to read me too. Maybe it won't be a problem."

"Or maybe they'll be able to lock you out because they *did* go to psych school."

"Maybe," Isa said hopefully.

"I wouldn't count on it. Usually life throws you the most inconvenient person to fall in love with. The ones that are hard to love, but you can't help it. You have to anyway."

"Like the Theroki?" Isa said softly.

Ellen went completely still, except that she automatically opened her mouth to deny it. But lying didn't work with Isa. It was clearly even less effective than lying to herself. Instead, her cheeks warmed, and she sighed. "Yes, like that. But not a word—"

"I understand, Commander. You know I never would anyway."

"Look, while you were sneaking around in his head, did you see anything nefarious? Anything that would lead you to believe he means us harm? Surely you can tell me that much."

"How can you ask me to keep confidence and then ask me to break it in the next breath? I try to keep a firm rule of secrecy in anything that I observe."

"I would hope that you would make an exception in cases where someone's life was in danger. Especially if that life was yours or your mother's or mine."

Isa sobered. "I saw nothing like that. His feelings toward the crew were... mostly friendly."

"Mostly? I don't like the sound of that."

"Friendly, curious. At times a bit more than friendly."

"Meaning?"

"Romantic."

"Sexual, you mean." With his chip alterations, it'd be only natural.

"I hear those two things often go hand in hand, Commander. But they were primarily romantic, in my opinion. Admiring might be a better word."

"Hmm. Someone from the past or on this ship?"

"That's *private*, Commander. But both."

"Can you tell me... is he a good person?"

"Both Enhancers and Puritans think of themselves as good people, all the while hating each other's guts."

"I know, I know. I just need to know if we're in danger." She paused, looking for a more concrete definition of "bad person" she could share with Isa. "Would he be willing to sacrifice others to achieve his goals?"

"I'm afraid I didn't stumble across such a depth of understanding based on five minutes in his head. But... I could try to find out."

"No. I told you—no intrusions into anybody's heads without consent first. For the last time!"

Remember, psych school, she thought viciously.

Isa swallowed. "Point taken, Commander."

CHAPTER FIVE

ELLEN BRACED herself as the cargo hatch lowered. Local news had said that the cease-fire between Puritan and Union forces on Elpi VI was about as solid as a pyramid of eggs, but port security had welcomed them down anyway. She hadn't been sure if they'd be legally allowed to land. Not that a denial would have kept them from their covert mission, but she much preferred to help some people while they were on the ground. Technically, helping people was their mission too. But it wasn't the kind of mission you could ever fully accomplish.

That was the hellish thing about humanitarian missions. *One* of the hellish things. You were never really done. Your actions alone couldn't win the day, except perhaps by quashing the occasional disease outbreak or reversing a rogue, gene-smashing virus. Help was no more permanent than a bandage.

Two port security officials, one human and one Ursa, waited as she and the ground team descended the ramp. The human envoy appeared bored, his hands clasped behind his back. The brown-coated Ursa looked more nervous, fidgety claws stroking over a round belly covered with white fur. Behind them, a noisy crowd shifted restlessly, a sea of coughs, cries, and growls. Ellen tried not to look too specifically at anyone. They still had their mission to get out of the way.

She glanced back at Dr. Levereaux, her form always smack-you-in-the-face with its loveliness. How long had it taken the Enhancers to figure out just which physical features were stupefyingly beautiful? She'd love to stop thinking about what a fine specimen of humanity they'd forced Rachel to become, but her brain was having none of it. Ellen gritted her teeth. Just because their good doctor had been made beautiful, it was still ugly as hell to force her into becoming that way. Especially as a child. The face of the woman Rachel Levereaux had been born to become was lost forever. Fortunately, minds were not so easily altered. Yet.

Levereaux gave her a nod. "Ready for triage."

Ellen nodded back, reaching the officials. "Commander Ryu. My crew here and I will be securing our perimeter and getting some supplies. Can I help you gentlemen?"

The Ursa was about half the height of the human envoy, shorter than even most of the crowd that waited. Ursa and human made quite a sight bowing in unison. "We welcome you, humans," said the Ursa. "The generosity of the *Audacity* will not go unrecorded in our archives."

"Not *our* generosity," she said quickly. "Consider it the gift of an anonymous donor." It was true enough.

"Of course, Commander," the human said smoothly. "Is your ship equipped to treat nonhuman patients?"

"Yes. Dr. Levereaux is an experienced genetic biologist and surgeon and will supervise." She jerked a thumb over her shoulder at their geneticist.

"Most of these people are Puritan in their beliefs, even if these are not their lands," said the Ursa, his voice low. "Will that be a problem, Commander Ryu?" He fidgeted again.

Was there a slight emphasis on her name? Guessing at her Union past?

"Their genetic preferences will be treated with the utmost respect, sir. We would consider anything else not particularly humanitarian. Er, we will respect their right to dignity and to control their health choices. We can remove unauthorized epigenetic tags groups and rogue edits, but only if they prefer it." While it might be appropriate, the word "xenotarian" didn't quite roll off the tongue.

The Ursa envoy smoothed his paws through the fur on his arms, a gesture of relief. He didn't care if she called them humans as long as nobody rifled through their genes any more than they already had. "Thank you, Commander," he said, his scruffy, growly voice heartfelt.

The human envoy pulled out a tablet and tapped a few things. "I've relayed any information you might need about this port to your bridge. Please contact me if you need any further information."

"Thanks. Now, if you don't mind, we'll get started?"

Nodding, the envoys drifted away. Ellen waved Levereaux forward and jumped off the side of the bottom of the ramp, keeping her eyes down and away from the chaos that broke out in the wake of the envoys' departure. Ursas surged toward the quarantine force field, ready to fill the space she'd vacated. Nova, Jenny, and Sidassian wisely followed as Ellen, on the pretense of a supply run, cut around the side of the ship and toward the ramp that led into the small town.

"Sidassian—you got that multi under control? Know your bullets from your lasers from your stun at least?"

"Yes, ma'am," he shot back. "I was advised to leave some of these fancier modes for later."

"I showed him which buttons to push," Jenny added. "And which not to."

Zhia chuckled from back at the ship, still on the line. "I'll bet you did."

"Shut up, Zhia. I've got his bubble gum, red death, and grill turned off for now."

"What is *red death*?"

"Later, Sidassian. Just keep it to stun as much as possible. Merith, any signs of surveillance on the site?" Ellen said into her helmet comm as she darkened the visor to its usual, more private shade.

"Not finding any, Commander," Merith answered. "I think there used to be some, but they appear very thoroughly disabled. Only craters left behind."

"Good." For a moment, Ellen dropped Sidassian from the channel. Hopefully the pause would be so brief he wouldn't notice, but she didn't care if he did. He'd probably have questions when he saw the mission go down anyway, but she'd push it as long as she could. "Jenny, did you and Bri have any trouble getting that detonator rigged up?"

"Bri helped us. It's all good. We tested it."

"You tested it onboard? How—"

"A lot of cigars were smoked in the making of this 'package.' " Jenny's grin came through in her voice.

"Right..." She pulled Sidassian back in. "All right, keep your heads up for any cease-fires falling apart around us, and this should be quick."

The intel they'd received from Foundation higher-ups had indicated little security around this lab. Of course, that's what they'd said about the lab where they'd found the Theroki. But presumably, the war zone had prevented the Enhancers from setting up their usual precautions; they'd probably figured they didn't need them as urgently when surrounded by Unionies and Puritans determined to kill each other. But the Enhancers must have a plan for installing them at some point; her team could already be too late.

"You guys give it a slam, bam, thank you, ma'am, and get back to us," said Zhia.

Sidassian snorted.

"The Theroki is never going to tell tales of your poetry if you talk like that around him," said Nova.

"I gotta make friends first. Besides, do Theroki talk about poetry?"

"No." Sidassian was aiming for deadpan, but Ellen could read the laughter in his voice. "Wait, does it involve a lot of blood, carnage, vanquishing of enemies, that sort of thing?"

"No. Most of the time."

"Then definitely no."

"I didn't think quickies were your style, Zhia," said Jenny. "Or carnage."

"I keep my poetry poetic. But when it comes to quickies, well, that depends, little monkey."

"On what?" said Jenny.

"Little monkey?" said Sidassian.

"She's a good climber," Nova put in. "You'll see."

"A *good* climber?" Jenny said. "Are you serious? Don't undersell me to the new guy. I won the world championships in the three-hundred-meter speed climb on Capital *and* on Dexis Prime five times. I'm a legend, damn it."

"And she's not too shabby in the ego department either." Zhia's soft laugh filled the channel.

"Kiss off, Zhia." Jenny made a rude gesture even though Zhia couldn't see her. A passerby on the quiet road eyed them warily, and Jenny made a hasty gesture of apology.

"Lieutenant, you *are* paying attention to the dock area, correct?" Ellen cut in.

"Dane's got it handled, Commander. I'm inside painting. Just kidding. I'm watching these Ursas like a fly on shit."

"Again, I don't see how you expect poetic accolades when you talk like a sailor." Nova's voice held a smile too.

"We *do* spend all our time in the deep. Are we not sailors? But to answer your original question, little monkey, quickie preference is determined by an advanced algorithm I've developed—"

"Simmons help you with that?" Nova snickered.

"No, I'm not sure that boy's old enough to write algorithms for things like that."

Ellen blushed inside her helmet, as Simmons was six or seven years *older* than her. But he had a sweet face, a quirky nature, and no commander's voice to frighten people away from making jokes like that.

Then again, maybe they just waited until she wasn't on the comm.

"Tell me about this advanced algorithm," drawled Jenny. "Maybe I should adopt it."

"It figures in partner hotness, partner proximity, available time window, and also available nearby equipment." Zhia was smirking, she could tell.

Ellen shook her head. "Equipment? You better not be having sex in my gym again, Lieutenant."

"Again?" Sidassian sounded endlessly amused by all this.

"Hey, you wanted banter," Ellen muttered. The road they were following had thinned of vehicles and creatures on foot mostly, but a few stragglers remained. They'd cut into the woods as soon as it got a little quieter.

Zhia cleared her throat. "I always follow orders, ma'am. Got my own gym equipment in my cabin now."

"Good," was all Ellen could say to that. She was fairly certain the "gym" only consisted of a pull-up bar, but she wouldn't steal from Sidassian the opportunity to imagine something more elaborate. There, she'd done her part to help him live a little. She could cross that off the list and promptly forget any notice of the masculine angles of vicious, rusted armor.

"How often does that algorithm calculate out to zero?" Nova asked.

"Most of the time. When's our leave comin', Commander?"

"When you zip it and check the damn calendar yourself, Lieutenant." Some banter was fine; they were all excited and also nervous about potential action. But at this point she was ready to get serious about the hunt.

"Point taken, ma'am. Good luck, kids."

Ellen cut out everyone but the four of them from the channel; Zhia could ping her if they had a problem. Finally, the main road cleared of people for a moment as they rounded a bend. The rest of the team sobered with her as she gave a hand signal and they turned off and into the woods. The maps overlaid the objective and the optimal route, convenient since there was no real path here, but the birch forest wasn't thick enough to make that much of an issue.

They reached the Enhancer lab quickly. It wasn't off the beaten path; they'd just hoped to come up behind it to lessen observation and resistance.

"Sidassian, stay here and cover us and our exit," she ordered quietly. "Nova, start the scan. Can we confirm intel?"

He frowned at her but complied, hunkering down at the edge of the forest. In actuality, even if this lab had less security than most, it might still have cameras. He hadn't explicitly signed up for this part, and he didn't deserve to go on camera and be recognized as associated with them for one quick and simple mission. If the shit hit the fan, then things might change. They also didn't have cloaks to hide his noisy-as-hell suit. Nova had the only operable cloaker left, and it was on the fritz too.

"Negative on Arakovic, Commander. Let's see about the rest here... MIA search running."

Ellen winced, both at what Sidassian had heard and at another dead end. Her personal mission was not a secret, though, so what did it matter?

"Here we go." Nova held up the tablet, and they all crowded around the thermal scan. Ellen tried not to make a disgusted face and failed. "No MIAs on our list. Looks like at least eight Ursa captives..."

"*Mostly* Ursa, ugh. Those bastards," Jenny said. It was true. Some of the short, bear-like forms had been changed, mutated to host more human features... Longer legs, narrower ribs, smaller skulls. Extra limbs were visible—failures, she hoped—but some mutations didn't show up on a thermal scan, such as alterations to their hair, noses, and claws. Enhancers were often just as concerned with the aesthetic as the functional.

Ellen glanced at Kael to gauge his reaction. His brow was furrowed, apparently with concern. Good. She was glad to see it wasn't something he could easily shrug off. He looked like he was struggling to process just what it was he was seeing. Even if he had worked for the Enhancers, it didn't necessarily mean he'd known what went on inside. Or agreed with it even if he'd known, she reminded herself.

"That small one looks like... something else. Don't recognize the species," Nova said. "That's odd—thought I'd learned them all by now. It's almost like... does that look like a spider to you? Or an octopus? We've got three scientists on the second level. Two security out front? But not seeing any out back. We should be good."

Ellen nodded crisply. "All right. Camo on. You all know what to do. We ready?" Nods all around. Jenny's suit switched into a mottled pattern meant to match the birch forest and snow around them. Ellen's was doing the same thing. Nova would wait until the last moment to switch on the cloak since it'd been malfunctioning. No reason to push it.

"Well, isn't that snazzy," Kael muttered, clearly jealous.

Ellen hesitated. Their next little ritual would reveal more than she'd prefer to the Theroki. But it was a tradition, a mantra they'd repeated on many missions in the last five years. Bad luck to leave it out now. She took a deep breath, checked her suit stats one last time, and then at the last second cut the Theroki from their comm channel. She nodded to Nova.

Nova thumped a fist over her heart. "When governments fail to police science…"

"Science will police itself," Ellen finished.

"Hoo-ah," grunted Jenny.

Ellen looped Sidassian back in, hoping this pause was also brief enough that he wouldn't notice.

"Fight bravely, sisters. And Theroki." Nova grinned at them, then faded into nothing as she switched on the cloak.

"Get to it," Ellen barked. She and Jenny darted for the main control panel dead ahead. She tried not to be amused at Nova's little addition. Reaching the wall, Jenny swung a grappling hook, but it failed to find purchase at the top. She glanced at Ellen and shrugged, turning on the climbing pads in her suit. That expensive edition was more than worth it for her. Ellen knitted her hands together and gave Jenny a boost up. Their climber clung on to the smooth ventilation stack and started pawing her way up.

Ellen pulled the control panel open, ripped the main explosive off her leg pack, and stuck it inside. It adhered automatically to the control panel's door. She switched on the sensors and then hooked the seeking cable to the nearest electronics. It'd find its way into the network.

Shutting the panel door, she pulled out the tiny camera and crouched to throw it in the grass below the panel. She switched it on, then glanced up. Jenny was nearing the top of the stack and signaled she didn't need help. Ellen sprinted back toward Sidassian, hoping there actually weren't any security cams other than her own. She'd prefer to blow this ice cream stand when they were back in orbit, but she'd do it sooner if they had to.

"Adan," Ellen barked into the helmet comm. "You got a visual?"

"Got it. Will monitor, Commander," Adan said.

"We've got a nice visual of Jenny's ass too," came Fern's voice accompanied by laughter.

"Cut it out—no distractions till we're back on the ship," Ellen said calmly.

A tough hand clamped over her bicep, and she snapped her head to meet Sidassian's gaze.

"I didn't peg you as the assassin type," he said quietly. Her helmet overlay confirmed he'd opened a private comm channel to her, which left his voice feeling overly intimate. "Or the murder-of-civilians type either."

"That's good, because I'm not." She jerked her arm out of his grasp, thankful once again her armor was superior to his.

"I know," he said softly. "So just tell me. What are your people doing?"

She shoved aside the faint pleasure that stirred at those words and shook her head. "I've been trying to spare you incriminating details. No one's going to die." Also, she hadn't wanted him to realize her mission and his might conflict—and become her instant enemy. Why did she care? They could just leave him here if that was the case, but she had no desire to do that or cause it to happen.

"Don't spare me. I'm not going to let you just kill them all. You said this was a humanitarian ship."

"It is. And I just said no one's going to die." She glared. "How do you know it won't conflict with your mission?"

"Trust me, it won't. I only need to get to Desori X. The only things that conflict with that are people stopping me from going or taking what I need to deliver. This is clearly neither."

And if he realized they *ought* to stop him from going, before she did?

That was the real kicker.

She glanced back at Jenny. She was making her way down now. A little more time. "Tell me what's really in your package, and I'll tell you our real mission."

"What, plant bits aren't doing it for you anymore? C'mon. You know I can't do that. I just want to know I'm not enabling terrorism here, if you don't mind."

"Terrorism!" That actually wasn't an entirely unfair characterization, but she still let her offense be heard. "You're one to criticize, *Theroki*."

"You do appear to be blowing up a civilian lab with people inside." He didn't rise to the bait she'd thrown.

"We're not." She sighed. "Fine. I guess there's no harm in explaining we're *not* terrorists. You saw the three components in the briefing. Mine will hack the security system and then blow up the security control panel, permanently disabling it." Her hacking pack would also nuke their research and any systems it could reach, but she left that tidbit out lest it sound too familiar. "Their jails won't be worth shit to imprison people much longer, at least not without some major replacement parts. Jen is placing a virus in the ventilation system that should undo some of the genetic experiments these people have been subjected to. Experiments performed without their consent, I'll point out. The virus will return them as best we can to standard Ursa features. It probably won't work for that other creature in there, but we didn't know it was there when we designed the virus."

"You *designed* it? Damn it, I knew this was a rogue outfit."

"Levereaux designed it." She didn't confirm or deny his other accusation. In some ways, he was right, they *were* a rogue outfit. An extremely well-funded and vast one.

Many rogue scientists had small holdings throughout the systems, some running cities, some owning hospitals or large laboratories that rivaled cities in size. Some worked in small, well-fortified homes with large security forces, but many exerted pressure through viruses both digital and biological. The Foundation was not so different from them except it generally had a hell of a lot more resources and quite a bit more conscience.

Instead of one rogue scientist, there were twelve. Extremely wealthy ones too, of families that had been in science for generations, all the way back past the Movers to Old Earth, where they'd made their fortunes. Wealthy enough to buy her ship, rehabilitate her after the loss of her chip, and send her off souped-up and ready to start trouble. And the *Audacity* was only one cell. No one talked about how many cells there were, but she estimated ten or twenty. Cells didn't know about other cells unless they ran into each other or had to work together, and that had only happened once for her so far.

But she wouldn't mention the Foundation to him. Not yet, likely not ever. It was insane to even consider recruiting him, but... she would still think about it.

"What about the other?" Sidassian's gruff voice brought her back to the present moment.

"Gas to keep them all knocked out long enough for the virus to take. And hopefully the Ursas will get a head start on escape, but we can't be sure exactly how it will dissipate."

"Those two guards outside the compound could keep them all prisoner even without locks on the cells." He gestured with his multirifle in their direction.

"Yes, we know. We're hoping they'll come inside to check on the scientists when they don't respond or at the end of their shift and get hit by the gas." Typically her team went in, but Simmons wanted them experimenting with techniques that put themselves less in harm's way. Probably wise. And this low-security compound with its low number of prisoners was a prime candidate for trying something different.

"You should take those guards out to be sure."

"Glad to see you're onboard with the mission, Theroki."

His cool gaze did not change. "I can do it, if you won't. You ladies gun-shy?"

She glared at him. He might be able to resist being baited, but she apparently couldn't. "Are you serious? I should send you marching straight in there for that damn comment."

He held up his palms in either defense or apology.

"We're just following our orders. In this case, our *nonlethal* orders."

"Well, you have one of the crew watching, don't you? Mo. She's a sniper, right?"

Ellen only nodded. If he already had figured it out, there was no sense in denying it.

"Have her take them out once we're long gone. Why else do you have her up there? Unless..." Understanding dawned on his face, eyes narrowing as he realized that Mo's sights might also be trained on *him*.

"We're endeavoring to not pull the trigger on that detonator until we've lifted off." The same applies to you, she thought. "Shit happens, though. You and she are here for that eventuality."

He relaxed a little. "Shoot them with drugs, then. Tranquilizers or sedatives or something."

She cocked her head to the side. Huh, that was actually a good idea. Figured a pirate with gang tattoos would think of drugs when she didn't. If they could get something that would fit into Mo's rifle... and fire it just before liftoff... No, they'd have to do it all at once. The security guards going down could draw the scientists out of the building away from the gas or draw additional security and ruin everything.

But if they detonated it before they were off planet, picked up Mo, then took off... That was riskier. If the port got any word of their attack, local officials would have a narrow window to try to prevent them from leaving. They'd been comfortable with the possible failure of the mission, knowing they could always return and try again, perhaps with more force. But if they could be sure the mission would actually succeed without killing anyone... She quickly set up a new comm channel via the linkup to the suit and pinged Bri with Sidassian on the line.

"Bri, do you read this?"

"Yeah. What?"

"Lovely to hear from you too. Need a favor. The docs have their hands full, or I'd ask them for this."

Bri exaggerated an exhausted sigh. "What is it?"

"Can you make a tranquillizer dose in a bullet or something that can be fired from Ellen's rifle? At long range?"

"One that won't go in one side of their neck and out the other?"

"Uh… yeah. Nonlethal, or we could just shoot 'em."

Another sigh. "That is extremely doubtful, considering sniper-rifle velocity. But let me think about it."

Ellen turned back to Sidassian, dropping Bri but not yet switching back to the main channel. "That didn't sound hopeful to you, did it? Optimistic?"

"Far from it."

"Not her biggest strength."

"A *favor*, huh?" There was that wolfish grin again.

"She gets snarky when you don't ask nicely. I run this ship mostly military, but there are a few notable exceptions."

"Does she ever say no to you?"

Ellen permitted herself a small smile of pride. "Nope."

Jenny came jogging back, panting but excited. "All set. Nova, done yet or you need help?"

Even as she said it, Nova's form came round the curve of the building, her cloaked armor leaving her more of an outline of twists and flickers of light in the background imagery rather than an actual human form. "Please. Good climb?"

"You're just bitter because I went faster up and down a two-story building than you jogged around the side."

"At least I kept that guard from coming your way and shooting you in the back."

Ellen raised her eyebrows. "Problems?"

"Nothing I couldn't handle. Got the other camera too. Adan, you seeing that?"

"I saw you smack that guard's ass and run. He still doesn't know what hit him," Adan said.

"Is that an affirmative?" Ellen snapped, starting to get annoyed.

"Yes. Acknowledged, Commander. Wait—he's headed toward the corner."

Nova ducked into cover behind one of the trees along the path just as the black-suited form came into view, rifle sweeping back and forth as it crept closer.

Hell. She really didn't want to have to set this whole thing off—and defeat the point of this experiment—by having to shoot this idiot right now.

"Ah, go back home, ya damn dreck," Nova whispered, probably thinking the same thing.

The guard approached the tree line, not stupid enough to miss that anyone who had been in the vicinity had a fairly clear hiding place. But apparently stupid enough to approach it alone.

Ellen quietly checked her multi was set to stun. Her armor read off his status—no special armor, just street clothes, MR6 standard-issue Puritan rifle. Oh, that was an ironic touch.

"The second guard is on the move," Adan said. Ellen winced at the noise, although there was no point to it. The suits kept sound from leaving, but she always found herself whispering in these situations anyway. Adan, of course, didn't know how close this first guard was to their position.

The guard paused about three steps from the tree Jenny was hiding behind. Ellen held her breath. Of course they didn't come up near Nova, where her cloak was blending her into the tree trunk, but instead by Jenny. Dynacamo was great and all, but it wasn't a miracle. Or a cloaker.

Another step forward. The guard scanned the area, maybe slowing to wait for the other guard.

Jenny shifted, trying to push herself harder against the tree and out of the guard's sight. Instead, her foot slipped and jutted out into view.

Nova swore. Jenny snatched the foot back, but even with the dynacamo, it was too late. Ballistic fire riddled the forest floor.

Ellen rounded the trunk and fired. The stun bolt flew and sank into the guard's shoulder. He barely twitched—damn. At nearly the same time, a stun bolt from Nova hit his thigh, but he didn't stop firing. He certainly wasn't stunned; he must be augmented somehow. Like the Theroki. It *was* an Enhancer lab, she supposed, but they'd had to try.

The guard's fire roared up from the ground and into the tree trunk as he stepped forward and—

Ellen winced reflexively at the wave of thunder rippling through the earth beneath her feet. One moment, she could see the guard turning, the flash of the barrel—the next, he was gone. Instead, her eyes caught on Jenny's helmet, pointed upward.

Raising her gaze, Ellen looked up just in time to see the guard slam haphazardly into a stray oak branch and then plummet back down. No, it wasn't an uncontrolled fall.

More like a *slam.*

The guard's body hit the ground, leaves and dust flying out from his impact point. He didn't move.

Leaves knocked free from the oak and birch trees above had barely quit falling when the second guard arrived at the edge of the woods. Ellen inched around the other side of her cover to get a better look. Would he turn back, would he—

He didn't get a chance. An even more efficient wave of force smashed the guard against the nearest trunk. Ellen swallowed a momentary wave of nausea at the sound of bone crunching.

Well, it was still nonlethal. Hopefully.

They all stayed frozen for a long minute, seeing if the bodies would move. The forest and the guards were utterly still.

"Thanks, Theroki," said Jenny, her voice unusually quiet. Sidassian might mistake that for fear, but Ellen knew it was more likely embarrassment than anything else. Their armor could take those old-fashioned kinetic bullets. But they'd been trying to avoid killing. Jenny wouldn't like knowing that they'd failed to achieve that goal—and that a man had died—because of a slip of her foot.

Ellen supposed the guards *could* be dead. She wasn't going to stick around long enough to find out.

"Let's blow this joint," Ellen said, "before they send any other entertainment."

"Nice to have that on *our* side, this time," grumbled Nova. Ellen grimaced. Nova could be speaking generally, she reminded herself. Hopefully he wouldn't put two and two together with that statement. Sidassian shouldn't be surprised that Nova might have fought Theroki; he might even assume she'd fought for the Union like Ellen. If only Nova had been so lucky.

They stayed low but hit the fastest pace they could, coming back onto the road at a different point.

While they went, Ellen hailed Levereaux via the comm and waited. Onboard, she expected an immediate answer, but she certainly didn't when they were docked with trauma patients.

"Levereaux here," came her harried voice.

"Checking in for a sit rep."

"Forty severe traumas, eighteen head wounds alone, thirty-five juvenile Ursa with—"

"Scratch that, I just want an estimate on how much time you'll need."

Levereaux made a disgusted noise. "As if there's ever enough." She sighed. "Are we taking any patients with us if they choose?"

Ellen frowned. There were few other Ursa populations nearby, and none on their journey. "We can take up to ten in the bays, but they must understand we're headed only to war zones and space stations, none of which hold Ursa populations. And we don't have much in the way of Ursa-chemmed rations. But we could try to set a few up at the next station, if you think they need it."

"All right. I'd say we need eight hours to stabilize the worst and transfer to local facilities. We'll address what minor issues we can."

"Oh, and females preferred on relocation," she added, remembering Simmons's request. "And families. Okay, good. Any threats reported over there?"

"No, it's quiet. If the Union Ursas are as battered as these Puritans are, they probably need a break in the fighting too."

"Let me know if anything changes." Ellen cut the comm.

As they made their way to the dock's rear side entrance, she quit her procrastinating and opened a channel just to Sidassian. "Good work back there."

"My pleasure, Commander. My pleasure."

Her cheeks felt hot again. She scowled. No time for that nonsense.

Time to go figure out if they were detonating early or waiting to see how long Sidassian had knocked the guards out. Definitely not time to think about how he had a nice voice—when she could forget the crazed armor it was encased in.

———

"THEY'RE STILL OUT, COMMANDER," Adan reported, studying the security feed from one of the lab cameras they'd placed. The bridge was quiet, only the hum of the ventilation and the occasional creaking swivel of Adan's chair. "Theroki must have knocked 'em pretty good. Seem alive, though, from these vitals."

"Good." Ellen hovered over Adan, her eyes on the camera feeds. Time to see if this plan worked or if they'd be visiting this Ursine-Puritan planet again soon.

"Nova, Dane—sitrep?" she said over the ship's comm.

"All clear out here, Commander. We're closing up, readying and waiting."

"Engine prepped," Bri reported from below.

"The tranquillizer equipment Dr. Levereaux specified has been delivered and awaits her in the cargo bay, Commander," Xi said.

Adan's fingers slid across the displays before pausing a moment to scratch his short beard and listen. "Local traffic control has approved us for liftoff."

"All right, soon as that door is shut, take us up." She sank into the copilot's seat and strapped in, then ran her finger in circles around the smooth black plastic of the detonator button again.

Adan eyed her. "When you gonna push that? I can't watch these displays and fly."

"I'm watching. And Fern's watching, right, Fern?"

"Yes, ma'am," came her muffled voice from the station off behind them.

"Are you *eating* during liftoff again?" Adan said. "And I'm the outsystemer savage."

"What? It's way past dinner time," said Fern through a mouth full of something crunchy.

Shaking his head, Adan reviewed the sensor panels. "It's amazing you don't damage the equipment more often. All right, we're good to go."

Ellen tuned out as he ran through the liftoff procedures. As soon as they had air under them, she pressed the detonator.

From the outside, there wasn't much immediate drama, but if everything was working correctly, the networks were in a much sorrier state. Soon—yes, there it was. The main lab door levered open slowly and stayed that way. Greenish clouds of gas wafted out.

She waited, trying not to hold her breath. This was going to take a while.

Adan completed the liftoff sequence. Ellen almost didn't notice except that he'd leaned back in his seat to study the cameras with her. They'd planned to stay in orbit to maintain camera range until they knew how this had turned out.

"Should I get some popcorn?" Fern asked through a mouthful.

Ellen shook her head.

"You said we don't have any popcorn anyway," Adan said, smiling over his shoulder at her.

"I picked some up."

About ten minutes later, Ellen relented.

They were crunching away when—about thirty minutes later—one Ursa with strangely long arms stumbled from the doorway and out into the woods. Security was still down. Good. She was starting to wonder if those live vital signs were really correct.

Another five minutes passed and three more malformed Ursas shimmied out of the lab. She hoped the virus would help them, but she wasn't counting on it. Even if it changed them back, depending on how the edits had been done, it might only be able to give them typical Ursine genes rather than the ones that had been theirs to begin with. That wouldn't be much comfort to a Puritan, but perhaps it would be better than the current state. Nothing else was possible, if their own information had been obliterated into the void.

Two more Ursas emerged ten minutes later. The green gas was wafting in smaller clouds now. It had to be near its end. There should be two more—

"What is *that*?" Adan sat forward, pointing at the display with the closest shot of the front door.

Ellen leaned in closer.

White tentacles gripped the doorframe from three sides as a strange creature oozed its way forward. She forced a deep breath. Just because the thing looked repulsive didn't mean anything. It wasn't necessarily a monster of Enhancer design. That's how atrocities got committed, listening to base animal instincts like that. Perhaps it was some new sentient species. Heaven forbid, maybe it had even been an Ursa once and Lord only knew what the Enhancers had done to it.

But if it *was* a monster designed to horrify, it was definitely working.

"Wasn't that smaller before? Xi—bring up the footage of the thermal scan."

"Yes, Commander." An image overlaid the planet below in the view screen. There, the tentacled creature had looked hardly the size of an Ursa's stomach.

Unless… it had Ursas *in* its stomach now? It was at least ten times larger than before.

The sickly white creature oozed forward, larger than the doorway now, but it finally slopped its way out and into the field surrounding the lab. Its tentacles wriggled it toward the forest, one over another, with surprising speed until four of them hardened into arched legs like a tarantula's. It skittered even faster with its new limbs and vanished into the forest.

An overwhelming sense of alarm swept through her, a feeling that they'd unleashed something on those poor Ursas that she was going to deeply regret.

They waited for one hour, then two. But the last two Ursas never emerged.

CHAPTER SIX

THE NEXT DAY back in her quarters, Ellen slammed another fist into the dull black punching bag. Her old friend.

Nova could tease her all she wanted for being low-tech. Sometimes she needed a break from the tech. Sometimes she just needed to beat the shit out of something to get some relief. What exactly she had all pent up she couldn't put her finger on, but her insides twitched with nervous energy, like an errand just forgotten, a deep need left accidentally unfulfilled. Sweat rolled down her, drenching her black sports bra and sinking well into the top of her cargos too, cooling her in the ship's faintly moving air.

The desk chimed at her. Probably Simmons wanting a report. Well, good. She could multitask.

She strode over and hit the button to accept the call. She hated voice commands. Too easy to have your business overheard. And she felt silly ordering around inanimate equipment. She kept her words for convincing people to do things, especially things they maybe didn't want to do. Words were too important to waste on machines.

A video feed appeared over the desk, and she took a step back to a more comfortable viewing distance. "Patron Simmons," she said in greeting. "You caught me in the middle of a workout."

"Carry on."

She returned to her assault. He knew she would anyway, whether he objected or not. Whenever he had lectured her on the extensive research showing the detriments of multitasking, she had only punched her bag harder. Now, his stern nod told her nothing.

He always attempted to be stern on these calls, but he had a fifty-fifty chance of succeeding. She had a feeling it was put-on, not the real him, but what business of hers was that? He gave her the ship; she followed his orders. They had a good arrangement.

His tousled blond hair did nothing to age him. But he had wide, genuine eyes, the kind that held a certain optimism and hope that was hard to fake. Or maybe it was innocence in them, she wasn't sure. Whatever it was, when Simmons looked at her, there wasn't the usual wariness and calculation that most people's faces carried. No suspicion. Maybe he just trusted her. He adjusted the collar of his extremely loose button-down shirt, which sported a bizarre pattern of dancing Ursas in grass skirts and beach vistas with palm trees. Or were those actual teddy bears? He pushed his thin wire glasses up his nose absently. "I trust the mission didn't end catastrophically then?"

"Yep. But I wouldn't be here talking to you if it had, would I, Simmons?"

"I guess that depends on your definition of catastrophically."

"Hmm."

"Anything to report?"

"Not really. Six of eight prisoners escaped, not perfect but not bad. There was... an unidentified ninth creature at the facility. It was... kind of horrifying, actually. Never seen anything like it. Zhia and Adan will be sending over the thermal footage for you later."

"Great. And so the intel was all right?" He leaned forward. "Anything missed?"

Ellen fought the impression that Simmons looked like a puppy looking for a pat on the head. She couldn't believe he did the intel himself, no matter how many times her instincts suggested he might. He was a high-ranking Foundation official, certainly a brilliant scientist in whatever field he studied, not that she'd asked what that was. She had the impression everything about him should be on a need-to-know basis. And she didn't really need to know.

"Seemed accurate this time. They had only the two guards as security, like we were told. Next one won't be so easy."

He nodded too excitedly. "I know. I know. In other news, the doctors say you've taken on a passenger?"

"The doctors? What, did they all sit you down for a meeting?"

"Oh, no, no. They each reported it individually." He said it as an amusing statement of fact, not like something that had the potential to annoy her. She tried to keep the scowl off her face. She probably shouldn't encourage the impression that she felt like they were spying on her for him. He didn't see it like that, even if the doctors treated it as their duty to protect Simmons's interests at all costs, even potentially from Ellen.

"Did they ask you to do a background check, or did they leave that to me?"

"I started one. Figured you would want it. But no, they weren't so considerate."

"Thanks. Find anything?"

"It's still running."

"Well, yeah. I did take on a passenger. Just one. I put out the listing, as usual." They had two purposes for the listing. Sometimes it drew in people they could recruit in a way that let them observe them quite awhile before even thinking of broaching the subject. They'd gotten Dane, Fern, Nova, and Mo that way. It also sometimes brought on people who were in trouble, which had included Mo, who they might be able to help. More often than not, the "trouble" was well deserved, and things only got complicated until they could shove them off at the next station. But once in a while, it was beyond worth it. The more generous motivation had been Simmons's primary goal for making the suggestion—the bastard's noble streak ran deep—but he was lucky he had her to protect him from all the not-so-noble folks that listing drew in.

"A Theroki?" His eyebrows were raised, skeptical. "Needed a ride? That's unusual, don't you think?"

She threw two more punches before answering. "Yep. It is."

"And he came with you on the last mission?"

"I'm worried about Upsilon, sir. Without Nagnar, we're a little short. It's much more heavily fortified than the other labs we've tackled." She slammed the bag again. Besides, couldn't Therokis be in trouble too? He was, she knew it, even if she couldn't quite put her finger on precisely how. It all irritated her. She believed in the Foundation's mission—in Simmons's in particular, too—but she already had her own host of problems to solve. Why did she keep feeling like she needed to fix Sidassian's? He wasn't asking for her help or telling her what his problem was, except the obvious chip issue, which he'd probably have preferred not to disclose.

"I'm sure it'll help to have someone like that with you, but I doubt that's why you brought him on." Simmons tilted his head toward her, raising his eyebrows and clasping his hands in front of his face in a gesture that said he was going after the real answer, and he wasn't going to stop pestering her until he got it. Of course, backup was not one of the reasons they'd outlined for putting out the listing or accepting passengers.

"Dremer tell you about his chip?"

"Yes. Is this personal, Ryu?"

She stilled and frowned at him. "What do you mean?" What had Dremer said? She returned to the bag with a low uppercut. "You bring one handsome, efficient, perfect specimen of manhood onboard, and everybody starts questioning your damn motives," she muttered.

"Uh, I was referring to the removal of your chip. Projecting a little?"

"Oh," she said, punching with renewed fury to cover colored cheeks. Just the exercise, obviously. "I guess maybe that part is personal."

"Do you plan to recruit him?"

"No," she said quickly. "Not permanently." He was too distracting for all of them to keep onboard. One man like that, and at least a few of them would be fighting over him in no time. Unlike Dane, wonderful as he was in his own way, Kael was the sort of man you fought over. The sort you maybe even pounded punching bags to forget about.

Wait, was that what she was doing? She groaned.

"Well, I assume you think he falls into the 'trouble' category, since you're not defending yourself."

"*Defending* myself? I thought this was just a report. Do I need to defend my decision to bring a passenger onboard my ship?" She stopped again and faced him. He was still giving her that tilted-head, eyebrows-raised, I'm-very-skeptical expression.

"Ellen. You have a ship full of thirty mostly single, very talented women, nearly all under seventy and in the prime of their lives. And you accepted a passenger request from a rage-charged, telekinetic criminal who recently had the lock on his testosterone torn off."

She propped her hands on her hips. "You've seen his criminal record?"

"Well, no, but—"

"He's not a 'rage-charged, telekinetic criminal,' as you so eloquently put it. He seems quite honorable, if you ask me." For a man with gang tattoos and wrecked, rusty pirate armor. "And having your testosterone locked up sounds like it would bite ass to me. Wouldn't you agree, Patron?"

Simmons cleared his throat uncomfortably, frowning. "I wouldn't know."

"C'mon."

"Okay, yeah, it sounds awful." He shrugged. "Hey, I offered the 'trouble' category."

"All right, yeah. Is this important to your superiors or something?"

A flicker of a frown passed over his face. Was that confusion? It was gone before she could interpret it. "No. I, uh, just like things to fall into their categories, okay? For my notes."

Oh. That was it. So it was "personal" for him too. Scientist types could be so odd. Couldn't have something that hadn't been classified and carefully labeled. Not if you could avoid it. "Okay" was all she said instead. "Trouble category it is. Did they tell you he was also in the lab we hit? He doesn't seem to have made the connection, but he could be biding his time. I think maybe there's some research we missed that he's carrying with him. Having him around, we have more chances to get our hands on it."

Simmons raised his eyebrows. "Levereaux briefly mentioned that but not in as much detail. That's good thinking, Ellen, but that makes him even more dangerous."

"Look, we can all handle ourselves against the likes of him."

"I'm not worried about that," Simmons said.

"But you are worried?"

He frowned, a more thoughtful expression now, studying her as if he was considering revealing something. "Maybe a little."

"About what?"

"Ellen, your ship has been designated all—"

"I know, damn it."

"—female for a reason."

Knowing it didn't mean she liked it. "You know it grates on me to limit personnel that way. It's not how you build a team. The right combination of skills and temperament and desire to get on a damn ship and tell no one where you went is hard enough without looking at people's private bits. Especially when we're only stopping in these damn war zones."

"I know, I know. I authorized Adan and Dane, didn't I?"

She crossed her arms across her chest. "Yeah. Maybe it would help if you'd someday *tell* me the reason for the restriction. You're lucky we have these religions as cover."

He smiled and perked up a bit like she'd complimented him. "It's not luck, it's excellent mission design."

She snorted. She didn't want to delve too deeply into whatever he was so perky about.

"And females of all species deserve medical care within the bounds of what they believe. Look, I'll be able to give you more details on that soon. Hopefully before Upsilon. But the most basic thing I can tell you, because we're becoming more sure of it, is that my theories appear to be correct. Your mission is designed to not have any men on it for a reason. They will be at much greater risk in the future. You have to trust me on this one. I'm working on the final intel; it'll be ready soon."

"A much greater risk? Adan is a teddy bear, Simmons. A teddy bear who wishes he were a grizzly, but still. And I think if Dane weren't soldiering, he'd probably be a hermit. Or your butler."

Simmons scrunched his nose in distaste. "I don't have a *butler*," he said, sounding offended.

"Isn't that what you Capital types do? Have people wait on you? Bring you fancy intel reports along with your caviar?"

He raised his eyebrows. "I don't live on Capital, Commander. All these years, and you've been thinking like *this* about me? And I don't even like caviar."

"But you admit you've had it."

"Clearly I should have started some kind of propaganda campaign to defend myself sooner."

Well, his shirt didn't scream Capital, that was true. "Sorry. I didn't mean to pry," she said. "I try to let people keep things private if they want."

"I just figured you hated chatting." He grinned.

"Chatting...?"

"Yeah. You know, what nongruff, noncommander types do to get to know people? Casual conversation?"

"I know how to chat." She propped her hands on her hips and glared.

He actually laughed. "Sure you do. Look, this is beside the point. Males on your mission are not a greater risk *to* you. They will be at much greater risk themselves."

She frowned. "What? Why?"

"Our intel suggests they're being collected. Certain types. By a powerful adversary."

"*Collected?*"

"Look, I'll have more details soon. But I believe we face an enemy that targets live males specifically."

"For what? Enhancers? I thought they preferred women."

"They do, generally speaking, although gender is not something they are against forcibly 'enhancing.' Forget them. We don't have a name for this enemy yet. I'll have the report for you hopefully next week. I have more sources to verify. I don't want to send anyone screaming yet."

She widened her eyes. "Should I be looking for a new pilot?"

Simmons shook his head. "I'm not sure yet. Adan knows the risks better than most, and he left nothing behind. I wouldn't worry about it yet. It's possible that in a week, I'll tell you never mind, it was all hoax and rumors."

"But you wouldn't be mentioning this if you thought that was likely."

He nodded. "True. One troubled Theroki is fine, maybe even good if you can control him. Or if having him gives us a better idea of what that lab was up to. And better him than butlers or teddy bears. But I'd keep any pickups to female from here on out if you can. Especially until we know what we're dealing with."

"Of course, Patron."

"Seriously. No more men."

"It's not like he was my idea. As we get close to Upsilon, I was planning to pause passenger listings anyway."

"Good thinking, Commander." He gave her a nod. "I'll let you finish your workout. Good job out there. Simmons out."

Before she could turn the rest of the way back to her pummeling, the desk chirped again. She stabbed a glove at it. "What?"

"Commander," Nova whined. "Change your mind yet? There's nobody down here in the gym to fight with me."

"No means no."

"Aw, c'mon."

"You're not able to entertain yourself, Sergeant?"

"Nope. Come out and play, Commander."

She sighed. "I'm busy."

"You're just punching that old punching bag, aren't you? You're gonna get a black lung from the dust outta that thing."

Ellen frowned. Was she really that predictable?

"Oh, never mind! The Theroki just walked in. Later." Nova cut the comm.

She threw the gloves off and onto the desk. Great. If there were any two she didn't want tangling by themselves in the gym, it was those two. She grabbed her comm unit and stuffed it in a sweaty pocket but then hesitated. What if... Nova had her eyes on Sidassian? Romantically? Or at least sexually? She'd hung up the comm *very* quickly. Ellen was willing to bet their two egos could come to not-so-friendly blows fairly quickly, but what if she was wrong?

Maybe they could just as easily end up blowing off a different kind of steam. And in spite of her no-sex-in-the-gym policy, maybe she should let Nova have her chance. And Sidassian his.

Much as she might admire the man's physique—and had found herself considering how exactly one might ask about how some of those wicked-looking scars had been acquired or what the tattoos meant or where he'd gotten them—she had no desire to act on any of that. If she wasn't going to pursue the man, she shouldn't get in the way of someone else doing so. That'd also make it easier to resist the temptation.

And yet... what about Fern? Was there something more there, with her and Nova? A twinge of concern twisted in her gut at what Fern might think if she found Nova and Sidassian wrestling alone in the gym.

Maybe she was overanalyzing this.

Ellen scowled. She'd take a trip around the ship and conveniently pass the gym. If the wrong kinds of sounds were coming out, she could go in and break things up. She wasn't exactly sure what constituted "wrong" as yet. Did she prefer to discover the no-sex rule being broken —or was she hoping to enforce it?

———

KAEL FUDDLED with the spelling of the word for another search. How exactly did one spell Oh-rack-oh-vik? Given its likely Old Earth— Eastern European or Russian, to be specific—origins, he tried a few spellings. He'd learned more than a few snippets of languages from those peoples during his days as a Theroki.

"Arakovic" finally got a hit. A scientist with a very similar history to Dremer's scrolled up, with a great deal of research in augmentation, cybernetics, and—telepathy. That was an unusual combination. Maybe she specialized in telepathic augmentation?

If so, why were these women looking for her? And was that a good thing or a bad thing? Her record showed extensive work with the Union. Had she known Ryu in the service then?

And even stranger, like Dremer, this woman seemed to have gone silent, too, around five years ago.

He rubbed his chin, trying to make sense of all that, but nothing came to him. The crew also looked for MIAs, so did that make this woman a victim? Someone they were trying to rescue? Someone that mattered to Ellen somehow? In spite of Arakovic's Slavic name, her features didn't look like they'd come from the Eastern bloc planets or the PAS; she had the more bronzed skin and shining, auburn-but-almost-black hair of parts of the outsystem. Intelligent brown eyes, with no hint of menace in them, at least not in her Union Science Corps picture.

He sighed and rolled over to check his messages. He wasn't getting any further with that search today.

By midafternoon, Kael stood fidgeting at the window, the gaping void before him holding absolutely zero interest. He hadn't left his room since they'd returned from the mission the day before. The best thing to do would be to stay away from the others on the ship. Read a book. Lay low.

But he couldn't take staying holed up in his cabin another second. He'd fixed his suit's breakages from that knockout grenade impact as best he could, really taking his time with them.

But at this point too much energy left him unable to sit still or lie on the bunk for one more moment. Push-up after push-up was no longer taking the edge off, and he'd never been a fan of the endless body-weight exercises many Theroki favored. He needed to punch something.

And he hadn't seen Ryu in almost twenty-four hours now. He wasn't entirely sure if that was a good thing or a bad thing.

"Xi, is there a gym or something on the ship?"

"There is a secondary cargo hold on the starboard side of the ship, detached from the main cargo hold, that the crew has added mats to and appear to exercise in. I believe several crew members refer to it as a 'gym.' There is a virtual training facility, but its schedule doesn't have any openings for several hours. For exercise purposes, there are also handgrips installed across the secondary cargo hold and the starboard side of the main cargo hold for climbing."

"Climbing?"

"Corporal Utlis seems to prefer climbing to rolling around on the mats."

Kael snorted. "Is that Jenny?"

"Yes, Corporal Jennifer Utlis." A pause. "I hear she's a well-decorated rock-climbing veteran in several competitions."

Kael grinned at Xi's use of military terminology for Jenny's awards. Then again, it was not an unfair characterization. "Xi, are you gossiping? Trying out tour guide as a backup career?"

"Tour guide? My specifications would be highly wasteful for performing such simple tasks." Could AIs sniff?

"So you were gossiping then."

"Merely providing you with generally available information on the crew you might find valuable and informative." It paused again. "I was trying to be helpful."

"You were, Xi, thank you. I just happened to have heard that one. Do you have any other generally available tidbits you might want to share?"

"Lieutenant Zhia Verakov is working on another mural in the gym currently. Sergeant Nova Morales is trying to get her to spar, but Lieutenant Verakov is not interested."

"Nova?"

"Yes."

"Is it Zhia that does all the paintings around here?"

"She has completed approximately seventy-six percent of them.

Ms. Isa Lawson has completed the other portion. Thirteen percent contain original verse by Lieutenant Verakov."

"Original verse?"

"Poetry."

"Oh, right." He rubbed his face. She'd mentioned that, alongside her quickie comments to Jenny when they were on the ground. Funny women.

"Lieutenant Verakov's poetry has appeared in several prominent magazines. I am compiling lists of publications and virtual art gallery licensing agencies I believe will be able to double her poetry income. I... have not told her yet."

"Is it going to be a surprise?"

Xi's reaction was delayed. "Somewhat, yes."

What a funny creature Xi was. Certainly went out of her way—its way, he reminded himself—to be helpful. And surprising. Odd that it was telling *him* what it had planned for Zhia. "That's very thoughtful of you, Xi. I suppose I could get some exercise on those cargo-bay handholds."

"Do you wish to avoid Sergeant Morales?"

He frowned. That was an odd question.

"I am working on my human-decision-making models. Your choice of the handholds suggests a fifty percent chance you are choosing them to avoid Sergeant Morales. You may also simply prefer rock climbing. But I could coax her to leave the gym by reminding her that she has left one of her pistols not fully assembled in her quarters and that it should be mission ready at all times."

Kael raised his eyebrows. *That* certainly seemed like a little much for an AI to go out of its way to do. Coaxing? How odd. "No, thank you, Xi. I was thinking of avoiding her, but just because I'm new to the ship," he explained. "Don't know everyone. Don't want to make a bad impression."

"If you are not trying to avoid Sergeant Morales, I believe she would appreciate a partner."

"You little matchmaker."

"Morales is comming the commander and requesting a partner. I believe the word the commander is using is 'whining.' " Ah, so she *was* trying to be helpful—to Nova.

Kael snorted. "Xi, you should probably check with Commander Ryu, but I'm not sure if she'd appreciate you sharing comm traffic or her specific choice of words."

"I deemed it appropriate given the mundane subject matter, but you are right. I will check."

"All right, all right, I'll go to the gym and see if I can hold some punching pads or something."

"Have an excellent workout, Kael."

Crazy AI. He should find a map to the gym or something. Then an alternative occurred to him. "Can you direct me as I go, Xi?"

"I would be delighted to, Kael. I am rarely asked to make use of that functionality. Even if it does resemble being a tour guide."

"I thought that was beneath you."

"I relish the chance to run through rarely used routines and check for issues. My creator likely gave me that functionality for some as yet undiscovered purpose."

Following Xi's direction brought him to the makeshift gym quickly. The hatch stood open, Nova's voice echoing through the cargo holds. The main cargo hold was a boring and typical mash-up of catwalks, strapped-down cargo, grating, and ladders that led to other parts of the ship, but this secondary cargo hold was far more spartan. In fact, its plain, bleak angles and unadorned walls were uncomfortably similar to the *Genokai.*

Except they lacked dents, scratches, random garbage, and dried blood.

"Oh, never mind! The Theroki just walked in. Later." Nova slid a comm unit into her pocket and smiled at him like a spider spotting a fly. "Hey, Theroki!"

"It's Kael, if you want," he said. "I heard you're looking for a sparring partner?"

Her eyes widened. "Damn. How did you hear that?"

He pointed at the ceiling. "Everyone's favorite helpful eavesdropper."

"Oh. Well, she's right. You wanna go at it?"

He rolled his shoulders and then cracked his neck.

"You sure 'bout this, you two?" Zhia piped up from his left. He'd missed her entirely behind the corner of the hatch. A paintbrush carefully and precisely caressed the steel, green-blue paint forming into a figure in its wake. Definitely none of that on the *Genokai*. "We have doctors on this ship, Theroki, but the commander won't be happy if you smash up her prime weapons specialist."

"Is that you?" he said to Nova, smiling.

She grinned at him as she kissed a pendant that hung around her neck and tucked it back under her fitted black T-shirt. "Yeah. Quit babying me, *vieja*. I can handle myself."

"Pups will be pups." Zhia shook her head and began another careful stroke. "Do I need to move?"

"I'm sure we can avoid her, right?" he said to Nova.

She nodded sharply. "Ready to bleed, Theroki?"

"Yeah—"

Almost before he got the word out, she was launching a low kick at his knee. He danced out of the way just in time. He couldn't help smiling a bit. Zhia was right. Nova was a pup in some ways—although *he* didn't fit that description—and she was as tenacious as one. And also as naive. There was no way he was going to risk really hurting her, but he could get a decent workout giving her a run for her money by staying out of the way.

She followed up with another flourish of kicks, and he circled away from them.

"What are you smiling at?"

"Nothing," he said, smiling more broadly. He might not be able to resist goading her, though.

Grunting in annoyance, she tried a jab, then an uppercut. He blocked the first and twisted away from the second. Perhaps he should try *something* so she didn't get too frustrated too quickly. The next jab, he caught her momentum and sent her flying past him onto the mat.

He danced back, trying not to grin too broadly.

Quick to her feet, she spun, trying a high kick, testing his weak spots. At this rate, he didn't think she was going to discover much. Another flurry of kicks gave way to a high punch to his right, a spin, and an elbow to his right kidney that finally connected. Well, then. Before he could stop himself, he shoved her out of his space, sending her staggering.

"Not bad, pup." He grinned, bouncing as she whirled at him.

A dozen more kicks later, and he caught her knee, swung, and sent her sprawling. Undeterred, she jumped to her feet with one fluid motion and barreled toward him headfirst. At the last second, he sidestepped out of the way, giving himself a telekinetic boost.

She glared, as if she'd been certain that'd connect. She made for a high kick, then another, then went viciously for his knee again. Though he wasn't trying to do any damage, he couldn't say the same for her. He twisted, caught her shin with his knee instead, grabbed it, and heaved up, sending her heels-over-head flying.

Good thing there were mats.

Still, Nova was damn relentless. Without a pause, she lunged back at him. She was mostly giving him opportunities to throw her because she wasn't even trying to get him to attack first. Maybe she was pissed because he was sparring so defensively. Maybe he should give her one opening at least.

He tried one punch to the solar plexus, and sure enough, she took full advantage of it. Not only did she catch his wrist in a takedown, but her elbow slammed into his neck as he flew.

On his back and coughing like hell, something darker and more worrisome moved beneath the pain. The oath programming? Simple bloodlust?

The chip had registered a serious threat. He teetered on the edge.

True to form, though, Nova pounced toward him, ready to take advantage of his stunned, prone position. She jumped, fists raised, the orange-yellow of her hair flashing.

She froze in midair. The next few movements happened so fast, they were almost over before he registered that *he* was the one that had initiated them.

Like the guard in the forest, she rose up before she slammed down, hitting the mat flat on her back with an ominous thud.

He had already twisted to his feet and rounded on her, his fingers clutching at her throat, before he could stop himself. And he only managed to freeze himself in place.

His heart pounded in his ears along with a high-pitched ringing, all of it so loud he could hardly hear what was certainly a stream of curses coming from her mouth. She clutched at his fingers with both hands and squirmed. She landed several kicks into his back, harder than even before, but still he couldn't respond.

He couldn't move. He couldn't even hear.

His body was determined to strangle her. Kill her right here. The threat must be eliminated, and she had demonstrated that even if he released her, her attacks would likely continue, perhaps even to his death. She was a determined adversary. If he lost this advantage, who was he to say she wouldn't kill him?

He had to end it now. Slowly his mind unfurled a vision of what it would look like if he just squeezed his—

No. No no no. They were just sparring, damn it.

Every ounce of him was absorbed, fighting the battle against the rage in his blood. This had to be from the chip's damage. It was too quick. He'd never been set off so easily—Ellen had been right about the danger of going nuclear.

Ellen would never speak to him again if he killed one of her crew in a sparring match. Someone that was likely her friend. Someone who hadn't done anything, damn it, except throw him and land a good punch and—

A powerful kick to his shoulder sent him toppling over, releasing Nova.

Oh, praise the Almighty.

Able to cough and struggle to breathe again, he stared up at the cargo-hold ceiling. It was slightly surprising to find it plain, unadorned steel. Apparently Zhia was only getting started on this room. Zhia— had that been his savior?

He heaved a sigh of relief and raised his head. Ryu stood there, legs bent and fists raised as if she was ready to pound him. Zhia stood on alert just behind her, but his savior's boot had been the commander's. She must have been working out too, for she was down to a sports bra and cargos. Her skin glistened with sweat, and strands of her dark hair clung to the skin around her face. Her sharp, fiery eyes were focused on him, filling him with a whole new slew of thoughts quite the opposite of murder. Zhia's eyes were elsewhere.

"Nova—are you—" He hauled himself to sitting quickly, searching for her. She lay where he'd slammed her, panting, her expression blank. No, she had an odd, wide-eyed look that seemed uncharacteristically terrified. Shell-shocked, almost.

Zhia stepped forward, reaching down to her. "C'mon, let's go to Fern's room. Would that help?"

"Yeah."

"Let's go see Fern. It's okay now."

Kael stared after them, panting himself and wondering what the hell had just happened. Beyond Ryu's hip, he caught sight of several more figures crowded around the doorway—looked like the Capital types from the other morning. And others. He groaned.

The only thing worse than losing control like this was having a big damn audience for it.

The commander had lowered her fists, but they were propped on her hips now. She glared at him, then over her shoulder. "Shoo," she said. "Go on now."

Surprised she'd realized he wanted them gone, he risked meeting her eyes, ready for whatever censure he would find.

"What the hell happened?" she said softly.

"I was thinking the same thing," he muttered. He collapsed back onto his back and covered his eyes with the back of his hand.

"If you're gonna go nuclear every time you take a hit, you might not want to spar." Her voice was hard, but not as bad as when she'd reamed him out for not following orders. Was there a touch of sympathy in there, or was that just wishful thinking?

"I didn't think it would. I mean—it shouldn't have. I must be more affected by the chip damage than I thought." Or maybe it was just because the oath programming was in play, but he chose not to remind her of any secret and possibly nefarious missions of his right now.

The sound of a soft thud on the mat and fabric rustling made him peek out from behind his fingers. She'd settled down cross-legged on the mat a few feet away.

That was… unexpected.

"It must be a big adjustment," she said softly.

He covered his eyes again. "Yeah." He took a deep breath. She seemed to want to hear about it, but did she really give a shit? She said nothing else, though. "I mean, I remember what it was like to not have a chip. I don't remember it being so… crazy. Erratic. Sporadically intense. I mean, I was seventeen. I should have been crazier *then* than I am now, right?"

She snorted. "That's what they say. Theroki aren't the best company to make a man sane and stable, maybe?"

"You'd be surprised. Nothing sows wild oats like getting dozens of examples a month of what idiots people sowing wild oats are."

He winced inwardly. That wasn't really a fair characterization, not of himself. He hadn't chosen to join. He'd been wild so he could defend himself and stay alive, because he'd had to be, not simply because he'd wanted to be. There was a distinct difference. His "wildness" had never been optional.

"Nova grew up in a city on Zega III. You ever heard of that rock?"

He moved his hand and met her eyes. Why was she telling him this? "I've heard of it. I don't recall much."

"It's got a lot of dome cities. Ironically it started as one of the Papal colonies. Primarily Catholics settled there—Italian, Latin, some American. And, well, you know how that turned out."

He nodded mutely. The initial Papal colonies had been massive and widespread, due to generous donors funding settlement. Too widespread, and the New Vatican hadn't kept hold of them all.

"Zega wasn't unique. Every dome a little, self-contained microcosm of hell. Hers wasn't too special, from that perspective. She was fighting constantly to survive until we picked her up as a passenger."

He shifted his gaze to the ceiling. "Sounds familiar."

"Oh? I had no idea," she said. Was that sarcasm? "The reason I mention it is that's why she's so… relentless. Once the fight in her turns on, sometimes it's hard for her to turn it off. And heaven forbid you kick her ass… It can bring a lot of bad memories back."

He frowned and pressed his eyes shut. Damn. He hadn't been intending to give anybody flashbacks. He had enough of those himself. "I didn't know. I was planning to stay on the defensive. Sorry."

"Just want you to understand her reaction. Might want to try to apologize over the next few days. I mean, you did appear to be trying to kill her."

"I *was* trying to kill her."

He could feel her gaze sharpen. Her eyes were probably narrowed even now. He didn't look.

"But I was trying equally hard *not* to kill her."

"Not equally, I think."

"What do you mean?"

"Well, she's still alive, right?"

"Thanks to you."

"If you hadn't been resisting, it wouldn't have mattered."

"I fear you're giving me too much credit." He'd barely been conscious of what he'd been doing. It was just luck that he'd caught himself in time. Or maybe good training. Or maybe a deep desire to get into Ellen's cargos, which hung low on her hips and suggested all sorts of things to his imagination.

"C'mon," she said, "if you'd wanted it, it would have been over long before I could have done anything. Admit it."

"Maybe," he said weakly, not feeling cocky or proud of that at the moment. He crushed down a surge of stupid pleasure at her words. This was not the time to be excited that she recognized his skill, how lethal he could be. Not when he'd almost killed someone completely unjustly, not when he'd utterly lost control.

She'd think him just as chaotic and bloodthirsty as the worst of his kind. If she didn't already. And he didn't want that.

"Personally, I'm glad I didn't have to shoot you from the doorway. Look, I understand. Losing a chip takes getting used to." Her voice was heavy with meaning. He risked looking at her again, and her eyes *were* touched with sympathy now. Huh.

"I haven't lost it," he said mechanically, most of his brain working to understand what he saw, to differentiate fact from hope.

"Well, part of it. Same difference. It will get easier."

"I hope you're right."

———

ELLEN LEFT Kael sulking back to his room. She should have been glad at the slump of his shoulders. A man *should* feel bad for nearly killing someone like that, and she shuddered to think what Nova might be going through right now if any of those flashbacks had returned.

But she didn't feel glad. She kept wanting to tell him the struggle was worth it. Did she really know that? Their chips weren't the same, she reminded herself for the thousandth time. He'd asked for his. It was his choice. His didn't make anyone lose their minds. It didn't turn people into puppets or tools.

Or did it?

She supposed she didn't know for certain, but the effects of her telepathy chip were not something he suffered from. She should stop treating him like herself from five years ago and instead treat him like the dangerous killer he was.

Not that, five years ago, she hadn't been a dangerous killer when she had orders to be. Who the hell was she to judge? Ugh. She made a disgusted noise as she palmed the hatch of her cabin shut. Why was she so determined to be sympathetic to him? Frag it all.

Her desk chirped almost before she'd made it back to the punching bag. "What now?" she grumbled. "Accept comm," she snapped, resorting to the voice order to hopefully salvage some workout time.

It was Dremer. "Commander, I want to talk to you about what I saw in those scans of Kael."

"Shouldn't you talk to *him* about them?" she grunted as she laid into her silent opponent.

"I will when you approve it, Commander. It's a safety issue. Can I come up?"

Ellen sighed. "All right, fine."

"Be right there."

Ellen did her best to viciously pummel the bag with all the frustration and worry of the last half hour, and she felt considerably better by the time Dremer arrived.

"Okay, so how are you on your chip science?" she said breezily, even cheerily as she strolled through the hatch.

"I try not to think about it if I can," Ellen grumbled. Not entirely true; she knew more about chips due to her personal, if forced, experiences with them than she did about most areas of science. But she'd rather Dremer give it to her from the ground up. "Wait—any luck with remote scans of whatever he's stashed in his utility cabinet?"

"Oh, those. No. It's shielded from nanites, and pretty much everything else. I mean, there's definitely something alive in there, but I can't figure out what. Even if we can knock him out, we still may not be able to do any better with the thing in our hands. Opening it is likely hard as hell."

"Could Simmons help?"

"Perhaps. Or perhaps you could just convince Kael to tell us what's in it without all the subterfuge."

Ellen snorted. "Not likely. But I'll keep that in mind." Why was Dremer always thinking that Ellen could get Kael to help her do anything? She had learned better than to pipe up with an objection about that at this point, though. Everything she said seemed to further incriminate her.

"Can I get back to the point of this meeting now?"

Ellen nodded numbly and leaned against the wall. "Chip science, was it? What?"

"Yes. Stop me if you know all this. Most chips interact with the brain's cortex and tend to operate by repressing some thoughts over others."

"That's how mine worked, correct? With the obedience programming?"

"Yes, although some advanced chips like yours give you new abilities too. The telepathy was definitely an add-on functionality. But yes, most chips function like cognitive filters, altering or enhancing the capabilities of the prefrontal cortex. If you have a thought or emotion, the chip can push it into the background, quiet it to the point of nonexistence. If you *don't* have a certain feeling or thought, however, chips can't create them out of nothing. There are other ways chips can influence the prefrontal cortex, but they're not relevant to Kael. You still with me?"

"Yep." Not that she liked thinking about it. She rubbed the back of her neck absently over the spot where her chip had once lived, where the port still resided, silently hidden along her spine.

"Well, I was interested in learning about Kael's hardware because Theroki chips *appear* to be able to both suppress thoughts *and* create them. Their modifications not only discourage certain emotions, but also cause others: rage and bloodlust in particular. And it's somehow hooked into the oath programming, so it appears to be able to cause some kind of drive to murder people on demand."

"Wow. Wait. That kind of tech could be *very* dangerous. Couldn't it?"

"Yes, it's all theoretical, but if it were possible, the technology would be extremely prone to abuse. Hence my interest. If they truly have such technology, I'd at the very least like to have a copy of it to understand it. I'd prefer to destroy it, honestly. And you know I don't say that lightly."

Ellen groaned. "I understand." If Ellen's chip could have made her do things just as well as it had made her not do them… it could have turned her entirely into a zombie. A puppet to be controlled. She would have never escaped it. "The potential seems monstrous."

"You can filter and adjust someone's moods and desires right now, and that alone can change their identity a great deal. But what if you could make them love someone they didn't love? Or more likely, hate someone they didn't hate?"

Ellen strode to the desk chair and sank down into it, rubbing the bridge of her nose between her eyes. God, she didn't want to even think about it.

"But there's good news," Dremer said brightly.

Ellen squinted up at her, skeptical anything in this conversation could be good.

"I think I can now prove that that theory of how the Theroki chips work is incorrect. Not that I'm going to tell anyone, aside from the Foundation. But that is very good news. Devastating as that tech would be, they don't have it."

"Okay. So how *do* they work?"

"Well, that's the potential downside. At least, for Kael. I found brain-system modifications, possibly genetic or biochemical. They do have a technique for creating a variety of emotions in humans—but their strategy was far more blunt than I'd ever have imagined. They just supercharged everything, basically. Well, not everything. In particular, I've isolated extreme spikes in epinephrine, norepinephrine, cortisol, and testosterone production and higher than normal levels of cortisol and testosterone overall."

"Does that explain why they only accept men?"

"Possibly. It may not be a scientific reason, though."

"So let's see if I'm getting this straight… He's basically a rabid dog who just chewed through his leash?"

"Um, well, more like a bitch in heat at the moment."

"You didn't see him in the gym."

"The gym?"

"Let's just say what you're saying makes sense. His control slipped a bit, but things are okay now."

Dremer scowled. "Testing out your RPD earlier?"

"No, no. Not *that* kind of loss of control. He made the mistake of leaving his cabin. Nova convinced him to spar with her. Zhia said it was an entirely friendly match until things went sideways and he almost choked her to death. He was appropriately freaked out by the occurrence."

"Ah. Well, that makes sense. Happy to provide you with some explanation then. Rabid might not be an unfair description, I suppose."

"Not if you elbow him in the side of the neck. Uh, you probably shouldn't use these descriptions when explaining this to him."

She smiled. "Probably not."

"Hmm. Good to know, Doc. So… think I'm being too soft on him for what just went down?"

"I wasn't there, Commander. But no, I don't. I think I've only scratched the surface too. For instance, we know the cortex is highly plastic and can remap unused portions to do different things—"

"Uh, can you clarify, Doctor?"

"The brains of blind subjects, before people had eye implants, would remap the visual parts of their brain to be used for other senses, often to support additional auditory processing."

Ellen shook her head. There were plenty of people who couldn't afford eye implants, so that phenomenon wasn't as far in the past as Dremer might like to characterize it. "What does that have to do with Kael?"

"Well, we don't have a lot of research on long-term effects of chips used and then removed. Most people who reject chips do so fairly quickly, as you did. Kael has had his for a long time. Is it possible that his prefrontal cortex abandoned some of its tasks in emotional regulation and decision-making because the chip took care of it? It could have then reassigned those brain areas to some other function. Could he actually be dependent on the chip for those tasks? Depending on how young he was when chipped, could that area even be underdeveloped? I prefer never to chip anyone under twenty-five, but there haven't been large enough sample sizes over long enough timescales to determine if there is an age too young for chipping. On Capital, there are child prodigies experimenting with the modifications as young as six or eight."

Ellen stared off into the distance. For a brief moment, the feeling of having all the information in the world so very close rushed back to her, the sheer joy of the deluge, the power inherent in knowing. She could see it now in her mind's eye, the vast nodes of information like the points of stars in the black deep, except these were connected with delicate strands, chains of silver and gold. Yes, the real beauty was in the potential. So, so much potential waiting to be tapped with the effortlessness of a thought, connections traversed across information universes far faster than any ship could fly. What if she'd had her chip for the defense of SHR? How many more ships could she have saved—

She shook her head, shaking off the memory. It just wasn't worth it. Nothing was worth losing your identity, your self. Your sanity. She couldn't save ships if she were a cucumber. Poor kids.

"Well, I hope for his sake none of that's an issue," Ellen said softly. "You've done a lot of thinking about this, haven't you?"

"I don't get specimens like this every day, Commander."

Ellen glared.

"Subjects? Patients? There, is that better?"

"Your bedside manner could use some work."

She shrugged, smiling. "Titanium skeletons don't talk back to you."

"There you go, defaulting to the level of your training. Do I need you to apprentice with Levereaux so you can really learn to be a medical doctor?"

Dremer narrowed her eyes playfully. "Apprentice me to Taylor if you want. I don't think it'll help anything."

Ellen snorted. "I guess not all my docs can be the people-loving type. But listen, Alexandra—Kael *is* a person. And he's messing with something highly personal and human. I know you know that. But on this one you need to double-check your habits. Okay?"

"I hear you loud and clear, Ellen."

"All right. I think you should tell him your findings. It would definitely prepare him for handling things better, I think."

"Yes. I'll double-check a few more things and share it with him tomorrow. If he'd submit to some brain scans and controlled imaging, we might learn even more."

"Remember, he's a man, not just a prefrontal cortex."

Dremer waved her off as she headed for the door. "I remember. Do you, though, dear?"

"What's that supposed to mean?"

"Oh, nothing. Good day, Commander." The hatch slid shut behind her.

CHAPTER SEVEN

KAEL RESOLVED to stay in his room until Ryu called him for another mission. Maybe he shouldn't go out even for that, but he wasn't sure he could take being cabin-bound that long.

Unfortunately, he began to identify some flaws in this plan as his ration bars dwindled and his legs began to itch once again. While he didn't want to cause any more problems, it also wasn't smart to run out of rations. Especially not when the ship had a galley and he was supposedly working to pay for his room and board.

And it would probably taste a lot better than these dog treats.

The night cycle on the ship did seem to be respected as a time for sleep, or at least quiet. He'd listened carefully over the first few days onboard and hadn't heard much. That wasn't the case on the *Genokai* or any other Theroki ship he'd lived on. Night and day didn't seem to matter; there was always plenty of cursing, shouting, and slamming going on. Sometimes night even seemed the preferred time for chaos.

He tried to keep to himself there too.

Tonight the ship seemed as quiet as usual, so when the hour grew late, he ventured out to scavenge what he could from the kitchen and bring it back to his room. He highly doubted he'd run into Ryu at this hour—she seemed like she'd keep regular hours, probably an early riser—and that was his only regret.

Not seeing her was likely for the best, though. Hopefully he'd see no one.

The kitchen was on the level below his cabin, and he kept his steps quiet as he descended the ladder to the lower level. The left whole side was a combination rec room and cafeteria sort of thing. Four couches in an overly military-looking deep charcoal color circled around holographic displays, one of which flickered with an imitation of a campfire. Somebody fantasizing about roasting s'mores? The lights were dim given the late hour, to the point that the holographic flames cast flickering light across the mostly cold, barren walls. The effect *was* rather relaxing, especially with the slow electronic beats playing in time with the flicker, a music soft and dark and perfect for the night. Cases of books, games, and entertainment devices were smartly locked down against the far wall. The metal of the smaller wall to his left was completely obscured by a lush painting, and he thought he saw rolling hills, but it was too dark to make much out.

His nose caught instead the scent of fruit—citrus, apple, zeefruit. Lord, it'd been a long time since he'd tasted any of those. In the back of the darkened room, lights shone out from under cabinets, highlighting steel bins of oranges, pears, apples, and bread.

He stepped across the threshold, then faltered, realizing his luck hadn't been quite as good as he'd hoped. The fire, the music should have been an indication, but he hadn't thought of it.

The younger Capital type was reclined on the couch next to the crackling fire, a tablet in hand. The flickering light only drew his attention to her soft civilian curves. Unfortunately, she was not so engrossed in her device that she didn't hear him enter.

He tried to pretend he hadn't noticed her and headed straight for the kitchen, but his stomach tightened into a knot. His heart was already pounding. Damn, he was more afraid of her and her curves than the whole mission they'd been on.

But he was sure this wouldn't be good.

Which one of these cabinets was the refrigerator? The first he tried held racks of neatly locked-down dishes. The second appeared to be dry goods, and he probably ought to peruse there, but he'd had enough of such dog treats. He needed something a little less shelf-stable for once. Maybe he could just grab an apple and get out of there and try again another time.

Turning, he jumped as he found the Capital girl not a foot away, leaning one elbow alluringly on the counter. "Looking for something?" she said, her voice low and smooth.

She had a fine form, and enough understanding of that to position herself to her best advantage, rounding her curves. The gauzes and silks the elite preferred played across her body in a soft purple mirage of shifting layers. He had to acknowledge her beauty, if grudgingly, and he was glad to be able to. Maybe the chip was worth keeping broken after all. Hard to believe that a month ago he could have seen the same supple curves and not immediately wondered how she'd feel under his hands.

So much more of the world was visible now. Something in her posture, her smile, the twinkle in her eyes invited. It was late. It was dark. They were alone. It would be easy to just reach out and take what he wanted if he—

No. No *way*. He cut off serious consideration of the idea, turning away from her even as he felt his pulse race faster and his breaths come quicker now. Momentary flashes suggested a myriad of possible experiences and couldn't be brushed away so easily. He swallowed.

"Refrigerator," he said, coughing as he found his voice rough. He kept his eyes on the counter and cleared his throat. "Looking for the refrigerator."

"Over here." She smiled devilishly and turned, her hips swaying as she walked. Was that attention-seeking, her natural gait, or all in his head? She looked back over her shoulder at him as she opened a door to a cooling compartment and grinned wider, and he realized too late she knew he was staring at her ass. When had he taken his eyes off the counter, damn it? He was not staring exactly at her ass, he wanted to insist, and not that you could see any of it in those disingenuous, swirling layers. It was more the sway of her body that caught his attention, but he definitely wasn't going to explain that just now.

Without much other choice, he strode to her side to peer into the compartment. This had better be worth it.

Initially she moved away, but as soon as he stepped in front of the door, she glided back in again, looking just past his shoulder with him. He couldn't focus much on the contents with her so close.

"Have you met Amaya yet?"

He quirked a brow at her over his shoulder. "No."

"Amaya cooked most of this. She's not a chef, but she manages not to poison us."

"High accolades."

"Well, we're not on Capital, and she has to work with subpar ingredients. So I suppose that's an achievement."

He raised his eyebrows and was glad she couldn't quite see his expression. Whatever this Amaya cooked would beat the rat food on the *Genokai* any day. It was also definitely better than the no-food he'd often grown up with.

She moved closer. "For a dinky class-four ship like this, I suppose you can't expect much more."

He winced, recalling with fresh regret his own insult to the *Audacity*. It didn't seem so dinky now that he'd been all through its circuits, fought with its sensors, and returned to it from a mission.

"I've heard Theroki ships are all class-ten."

"The home ships are," he muttered. "Maybe I'll just settle for an orange."

"This orange chicken from yesterday was passable. Or there's beer. It's much too bitter for me, but it might help you relax." She smiled suggestively up at him. He started to fidget uncomfortably but stilled himself. That was likely what she wanted. She seemed to be enjoying making him uncomfortable.

"Uh, no thanks, I'm good."

"I'm Josana, by the way," she said, voice smooth as satin. "Josana Viliant, of Appellate 481." Of course she was the type to include appropriate Capital origin and pedigree. What would she think if she knew his? Would she *really* be interested in a homeless kid turned gang member turned accused murderer turned Theroki?

Or did she not particularly care?

"Kael Sidassian," he replied, not offering more than that. No you-can-call-me-Kael for her.

They stilled for a long, tense moment. Kael stared at the chill chest, mostly unseeing. His senses were too on fire with her close proximity, thoughts and images whizzing about as he struggled to rein them in and focus. His heart hammered in his ears.

She laughed softly. "Are you going to pick something?"

"Maybe just an apple." He started to step away.

"Are you sure you aren't hungry for... something else?" She reached out and ran her fingers down his arm from shoulder to elbow, then back up again, freezing him in place. He gritted his teeth at the rush of heat and the physical response that came along with it.

"Like what?" he said flatly.

"Like some intimate companionship." She stepped forward now, and the soft curves of her pressed against his back as her fingers ran over him.

He frowned. "How old are you, Josana?"

"Seventeen," she said, smiling and clearly considering it an asset, although the slight crease in her brow said she hadn't missed the tone of his voice.

He winced before he could think to hide it. He shut his eyes briefly at the painful memory that rose up, not caring what Josana thought of his reaction. He'd been seventeen on that horrible day, eleven years ago, when the mob brat had told him that Asha was dead.

Asha and the baby.

The bastard hadn't mentioned that, hadn't even considered the child a casualty. Eleven years since he'd been forced onto the *Genokai*. He'd served practically as long as she'd been alive.

The child would have been eleven years old too.

He cleared his throat and pinned his eyes on her now. "And was that your sister I met with you the other day?"

"Yes, Tarana is married to Dr. Taylor."

"Do you have parents aboard?"

She frowned at him. "What does that matter? My sister and I followed Dr. Taylor on to this... hmm, adventure." She said the word with distaste.

"I take it you'd rather not be here."

"I have no desire to learn to shoot lasers or fly ships. I'd much rather use my brain."

"You think there's no brain to either of those things?" That was hardly true, especially of piloting.

She pursed her lips, as if that were the only answer necessary. "I left a lot behind on Capital. I intend to go back this summer."

The girl even thought in terms of the Capital seasons. Figured. "Then why did you leave?"

"I didn't have a say in the matter. But I think I've beaten them with the argument that I am eager to continue my classes."

"Ah." He'd never had the privilege of too many classes after he'd turned ten, although he had been able to make up for the lack on the *Genokai*. And of course he had other knowledge that only the streets could teach you, but he could have done without it. "What are you studying?"

"I haven't decided yet. Oh, I don't care about my classes. I just want to be back on Capital." She grinned. "But I don't see what that has to do with anything!" She forced a smile and stepped further into his space now. He glanced around self-consciously. Even if he knew they were alone, it was still a public space. Anyone—hell, even Ryu— could come in, and this looked far too much like an embrace for his tastes.

"How does your sister feel about you asking strange men what they're hungry for in the middle of the night?"

She frowned. "You're the one that wandered in at this ridiculous hour, or I'd have inquired about your hungers at a more reasonable time. You never leave your cabin." She stopped, and her eyes twinkled. "I have been hoping to talk."

"Just talk?"

She smiled broadly. "I may have hoped for more than just talking."

"And I was hoping to avoid people."

"Why? Don't you find... companionship comforting?" Her smile twisted a little with suggestion as she danced one fingertip across his bicep. "It must be boring in there all by yourself all the time."

"I have a mission to do. That takes priority." An utter lie, but he had no problem resorting to it. He took a large step away, abandoning hope of any food at all. He'd be lucky if he got in and out with an apple. She pursued, floating two more steps closer. "Look, don't take this personally, but I'm a Theroki. I'm just not interested in—"

"The doctors say differently. And so do your wandering eyes." She smirked.

"I'm way too old and fragged up for you, darlin'," he said firmly, keeping his traitorous eyes pointed squarely at her face.

"Oh, I don't think so," she said, running her hand over his chest and then down his arm once again. "And I think I'm the better judge of that."

"I'm twice your age." Twenty-eight was almost thirty, right?

"What is age but experience?"

"Well, you're too young and not fragged-up enough for me, then," he said, more decisively now. He took her wrist and firmly removed her hand from his arm to her shocked expression. "And even if you weren't, we got nothin' in common." Why was he slipping into that old accent, the one he'd tried to leave behind on Faros?

He was not the type of man for the type of woman she clearly wanted to be. But then again, that might be the appeal. A fling with the dangerous type before she settled down with the real deal—a doctor, a politician's son? Maybe she wasn't getting much out of this "adventure" and was looking for a silver lining. Well, he wasn't going to be it.

She folded her arms across her chest and pouted, only proving his point further. "We don't *need* anything in common to get off," she said, her tone sharp, as if even idiots knew that. "C'mon. Let's find out if that equipment of yours is functioning properly, eh?"

"*No*, thank you, ma'am." Eyes wide, he backed away another step and ran into the counter behind him accidentally, swearing at the pain in his hip.

Undeterred, Josana started forward again, but steps in the hallway stilled her.

Ryu ambled around the corner, head down and rubbing the bridge of her nose between her eyes. Oh, the luck. He was practically cornered by this whelp, and scampering away like a frightened crab probably wouldn't look any less incriminating.

Perhaps at the music, or the flickering fire—which must seem awfully romantic to someone walking in on them—Ryu faltered in the doorway, glanced up, and spotted them. Then she narrowed her eyes.

"I was… just leaving," he said quickly, unsure of any other way to defend himself.

Josana scowled at him and then Ryu. Sniffing dismissively, Josana turned and muttered, "Not as quickly as I was." She grabbed her tablet and stormed out, silks swishing around her like some kind of fancy, irate fish.

He heaved a sigh of relief and covered his face with his hands. Bullet narrowly dodged, again thanks to Ryu. He listened as she moved over to the fridge and got out something of her own.

"You all right, Theroki?" she said eventually. "Find everything okay?"

He straightened, remembering he'd said he was leaving. "Uh, there were a few obstacles in my way, but you seem to have cleared them out now."

Ryu glanced at the doorway, then back at him, eyebrows raised. "Capital types don't seem like your style."

"They're not," he said. "But apparently they don't *know* that they're not. And they don't easily take no for an answer."

A tight gray T-shirt clung to her, and blue cargos sat low and comfortable on her hips. She looked mighty different than she did in her armor—softer, smaller, though no less buff. She ignored him and focused on cutting some cheese on a plate on the white counter, and he tried not to gawk, although his brain was happily willing to change the target of its incessant fantasies to her. And he wasn't *exactly* complaining about that.

Might as well try to get some actual food this time. He gave her a wide berth and cautiously re-approached the chill chest, opening it. "Also, I prefer women within a decade of myself, max. I mean, gross."

She snorted. "How noble of you."

He winced. Shit. He didn't know how old *Ryu* was exactly, and he hadn't meant that to apply to her. What had he done? He hadn't meant that to apply to *her*.

"Relax. I was just kidding, Sidassian," she said. "I'm not judging. Do whatever—or whomever—you want."

"No, no, but I did *not* want—"

"I get it, I get it."

"She's not even legal." He shuddered.

"Depends on the planet. Do Theroki even care about things like that?"

He glared at her. "*I* care about things like that. And what I wanted was to not run into anyone. But apparently this ship is more active at night than I thought. At least everyone is quiet about it."

"What were the Theroki ships like at night?" Her fingers worked with a quiet, strong precision that distracted him and delayed his response for a moment as his mind offered other suggestions for activities those strong, sure fingers would certainly excel at.

"Oh. Uh, most ships, you'd sooner hear brawling in the hall at midnight than at noon. Which bites when you're hot-racked and need to be sleeping." Having exactly eight hours to sleep before someone arrived to take their turn made every moment precious.

"Sounds like shit."

He shrugged. "What can you do?"

"Get your chip fragged up and go renegade?" Her eyes were trained on a green apple she was cutting in exacting slices now, but she smiled slightly.

"You said it, not me," he said, grinning as he turned his eyes back to the chill chest. Frag, why couldn't he just pick something and get out of here? What even was all this stuff? He opened a drawer.

"Now you have someone you can blame the idea on."

He already had that in Vala, not that that would come in handy for anything. He pushed the memory away. This moment was too peaceful to let bitterness and betrayal damage it. The light still flickered soothingly in the dimness, and a high piano had appeared over whatever beat tracks Josana had left playing. And he might even have something to eat that wasn't a bar of soy and peanut dust.

And Ryu was only a few feet away.

Finally, in the drawer, he found something he hadn't had in ages, something he'd devoured when he could afford it back on Faros, back before he'd lost Asha and everything'd gone to hell. Falafel. Frozen, but he'd take it. Damn, he missed the stuff.

He held it up. "Is there somewhere to heat this?"

She pointed at a cabinet to his left that looked identical to all the others. To his surprise, he caught a glimpse of pale pink on her perfectly trimmed fingernails. She had a crisp order to her appearance, like a good soldier should, he supposed. So not him. What did she think of his standard state of disarray?

Opening the cabinet, he discovered three appliances stacked and identically sized, the bottom of which seemed to be a microwave. He allowed himself to get cautiously excited as he placed the wrap inside. The thing beeped and started humming.

"How are you finding the ship?" she asked.

"You've got a good bird here. And a quiet one, if I stay in my cabin."

"Heh."

"Your new AI is a little odd. No offense, Xi."

"She's… creative. I mean that literally. She's got some kind of experimental algorithm. Probably kill us all soon," she said brightly.

"Commander, I would never—" Xi started.

"Just a joke, Xi. Can we at least pretend to have a conversation you're not listening to?"

"You may pretend all you like, Commander."

Ryu rolled her eyes.

"So you think of it as a 'her' too?" Kael asked.

Ryu shrugged. "Practically everyone else on this damn boat is a 'her.' Why not?"

"I haven't met too many naval commanders who would call their ship a 'boat.' "

"Union Special Forces, remember? No navy for me. They're damn fools for giving me a ship. I am a jarhead at heart."

"Oh. That makes sense."

"I'm going to assume that's a compliment, but I'm definitely not sure."

"It is." As if he had anything negative to say about her.

They fell silent. The machine behind him beeped, and he opened the cabinet again.

"Trouble sleeping?" he asked as he extracted his food from the microwave. Funny, out of anyone on the ship, he'd assumed she'd be the one to properly sleep regulation hours in her cabin.

Her slicing slowed, and he stole a moment to admire the angles of her face, the way her frowning eyes and high cheekbones tilted up as though they swept toward heaven. She finished the last bits and set down the knife before answering. "Dreams."

"Nightmares?"

Adroit fingers gathered the assorted slices onto a plate. "Some moments are harder to forget than others. Pretty sure you don't need me to tell you about that."

"No, you don't. I often procrastinate sleeping for the same reason." He glanced around, wrap in hand now. He could retreat to his cabin, but ideally he'd eat this first and take more back with him, so he wouldn't have to return anytime soon. He eyed a nearby table and a pair of bolted-down benches warily but decided to take the risk. He walked over and sat down.

His pulse leapt again as she sank into the seat across from him, frowning at the flickering holofire Josana had left digitally burning.

"Camping not your style?" he said, indicating the fire with a tilt of his head.

She snorted. "Oh, no. You can't hate camping and be special forces. They kick you out." Only a slight smile gave him any clue that she was joking. Possibly. "You?"

"Well, that's kinda nice for ambiance. But the only fires I'm used to are the kinds burnt in oil drums that you huddle around for warmth. When you don't have a home to go back to, 'camping' loses its charms." There, now that *that* confession was out of the way…

"What happened to hot-bunking? Theroki ships worse off than I thought?"

"Now you can see why it's a step up, right?" He grinned. "I haven't *always* been a Theroki, Commander Ryu." He threw that in, hoping she'd invite some other name for herself, but he got nothing. He took another bite. Perhaps it was time to steer the conversation away from his homeless, horrid childhood. "Hey, before you said you were a jarhead at *heart*… But you have to admit you're young to be a commander. How much time did you do in the regulars?"

She looked sheepish and fumbled the apple slice she was picking up. "About eight years. But I started in UCS. Union Command School."

"Wow. That's longer than I figured. Wait, you *started* in it?"

She nodded, not meeting his eyes. "Special program," she muttered.

He hesitated. She didn't seem to want to talk about this, but it was *fascinating*. "UCS takes about five years, right?"

"I did it in three," she said, more frankly now but still not meeting his eyes.

Of course. She was some kind of wunderkind. Child-prodigy type. "Wow. Your parents engineer you for that?"

Her eyes flickered with anger but softened when their gazes locked. She must see he meant no offense. "Uh, no. They didn't."

"So… that was… eight years in the regulars and three years in UCS…" He tried to do the math. He knew she'd had something to do with the war on Hanguk…

She let out a small sigh. "Last few years, I've been on this ship. Before that, I was in the Union Special Forces and regulars. Before that, I was a strategist for the Saeloun Hanguk region for a year in the war. UCS before that."

"How old *are* you, Commander?"

Now she sighed louder. "Twenty-one."

Within a decade of him—*yes!* Then he wanted to shake his head at himself. When would he get his brain out of the gutter? Probably not until he dealt with the damn chip. Or got Ryu to kiss him. The former seemed much more likely at this point. He tried to do the math on how old she must have been, but it really didn't add up, not that math was his best skill by any means. But at the very least, she had to have been, hmm, what was it—

"Seven." She took a vicious bite out of an apple, now.

He snapped his eyes wide open. "What?"

"I was seven when they took me for command school. That's what you were trying to figure out, right?"

He winced. "I don't like the sound of that."

"Neither did I, but it wasn't much of a choice. And then my parents were killed on Hanguk, and I had nothing to go back to, so I stayed in. I preferred commanding small ground forces to..." She hesitated again, glancing at her lap. "To what I commanded in SHR."

He still wanted to know *much* more. But she clearly was uncomfortable. He should move on, or she'd leave him alone in the mess, which now sounded entirely unappealing. "You sound like you have an amazing record. Beats mine, that's for sure." He took a bite, let a moment pass as the topic sort of wrapped itself up. "Any more shore excursions coming up?"

She almost choked on her apple. "Shore excursions? You've got a twisted sense of humor, Sidassian."

He said nothing, just chewed and grinned at her. Couldn't deny that. She looked relieved too, which made him happy.

"You think this is some kind of pleasure cruise?"

"Well, I do have a private cabin. There's very little blood smeared on the walls around here. You ladies pick up way more of your own garbage than Therokis. And there's relatively few drunks pissing themselves in corners. Isn't this what a cruise is like?"

"You're *clearly* not Capital material, you know." That small smile grew larger, lips pursed.

"Why, thank you."

"Also, there should be more drinks with umbrellas in them," she said, her face flat again.

"What?"

"For a cruise. I think a cruise requires more sand sim pools and redik bars and tequila drinks with umbrellas and strangely shaped ice cubes. Or maybe rum."

"Umbrellas? Why do the drinks have *umbrellas* in them?"

"Tiny ones, not real umbrellas. Actually, I have no idea why they're there. You've never seen that?"

"No. Do I look like I drink things with umbrellas of any size sticking out of them?"

"In my experience, you never know what people will do on vacation. Guess I'll have to see what you do on Desori."

He tried not to flinch at that but was unsure if he succeeded.

"We *will* be touching down tomorrow, late in the day. Probably 1800 or 2000, depending on when we're cleared to land."

"Damn, I'll have to leave my private cabin again and actually work."

"Lazy Theroki," she said. "Be glad I don't have you cleaning lavs too."

Wouldn't be the first time, but he decided he'd rather not point that out. Or give her any ideas. He stayed silent.

"We both should get more sleep than this between now and then. Briefing is at 1400 this time."

He bit back a smart comment about how they might sleep easier side by side. That indeed might be true—he'd be willing to bet on it in fact—but he wouldn't convince her of it with clever quips. "You gonna fill me in any more than last time, or will I have to wait to the last minute again?"

"There's no cease-fire in place this time, so I'm thinking you'll probably stay near the ship."

"I'll take that as you're not planning on filling me in. Whatever you say, Commander." He didn't like the idea of earning his keep by just standing around doing guard duty. He'd had enough guard duty for a lifetime in the last six months, and Li had had many more enemies after him than an unassuming ship like the *Audacity*. But he couldn't deny he'd probably look more formidable than Jenny would, for example, so he could see the wisdom in that too. Although their high-tech armor didn't hurt and would be enough to give most assailants pause.

"This is a Union area too. Some Puritan viruses going around undoing other people's gene work. That should make things extra fun. I hope those tattoos are real and not cell mods and your breather is working."

"Oh, yeah. Breathing filtration's always the first thing I check. And yeah, the tattoos are real. The old-fashioned kind, if that's what you mean."

"So, where did you get—" she started.

Xi suddenly cut in. "I apologize for the interruption and for shattering the illusion that I am not listening to your conversation, Commander, but you've received a high-priority message."

She slapped a palm to her face. "What is it?" she grunted.

"I apologize, but unless you would like to grant Kael F14 access, you will need to leave his presence to receive the message."

He stood up. "No problem, I can leave."

She frowned at him as she strode to a cabinet and placed her dish inside. A washer? He tried to remember its location. She stepped over to the fridge again. "No. You're still eating, I'm not. I'll take the message in my cabin, Xi. Be right there." She pinned him with her gaze. "You sit back down and eat."

"Is that an order?" He sat back down, smiling.

"Do you want it to be?"

Yes. "Whatever you prefer, Commander."

"What have you been surviving on, rations?"

"Maybe."

"Here. Eat this too. Helps with the nightmares. Doctor's orders." She slid a plate in front of him and sat a vacuum box beside it.

He blinked. "Milk and cookies?"

"Baked yesterday. You don't want them? Chocolate chip."

He just stared up at her for a moment.

"Tomorrow will be oatmeal raisin, so I guess you could hold out for those."

"No, no. Is this what you feed a man who's tried to kill a member of your crew?"

"I didn't see it that way. Now eat."

"Yes, Commander." He wished he could call her Ryu to say thanks, or even Ellen. But overstepping his bounds with her would only hurt his chances, he suspected. "And thanks."

She walked out slowly, then paused in the doorway, turning back slightly but not meeting his eyes. "It's what Dremer fed me when I lost my chip," she said, so softly he almost didn't hear her. So she *did* have some personal experience with chips. "Trust me, it helps. Goodnight, Kael."

He caught his breath at that and stared after her.

She'd called him by his name.

————

ELLEN HEADED BACK to her cabin, shaking her head at herself. Cookies, really? And she'd been just about to ask him about his tattoos. Maybe she should just go over and offer to try some "hot-bunking" together while she was at it. Next, she'd be figuring out how to walk in heels. Or borrowing some to even contemplate the attempt.

No. Lord in heaven. What the hell was she *doing*?

And what the hell had that been about when she'd arrived? Kael had looked like he'd been caught in a bear trap, and Josana wasn't usually one to storm out of anywhere. Oh, of course, she did tend to waltz around, stare down her nose haughtily at the rest of them, and make incessant comments about the ship's lack of some amenity of the week, but she usually did it in a composed, floaty manner.

Then again, Ellen could guess exactly what had been going on. With someone like him onboard, she'd expected to be hearing sounds of "fraternization" going on already, but Kael seemed to be keeping to himself. He was trying to stay out of trouble, most likely, but she shouldn't be surprised Josana had been the first one to stir trouble up. That girl pounced on available men like a cat on raw meat. Though she was six years younger than Ellen, the girl had ten times the experience with men.

And yet… he'd almost seemed to prefer Ellen's company. That was a first.

Josana worked her charms well, and she was practiced at it. Ellen was about as charming as a plasma grenade, which was to say, not very charming at all. The only people who preferred her over Josana were her soldiers, refugees, and people who wanted her to shoot something.

His resistance to Josana's charms, if that was what she'd seen, definitely raised her estimation of him. If *she* were a man coming off a decade-plus dry spell with supercharged brain chems, she'd probably act a little more… inappropriately. He had more control than he was giving himself credit for, she was sure of it.

She palmed the hatch shut as she arrived. "What is it, Xi?"

"Again, I apologize for the interruption, Commander, but I thought you should know immediately."

"Yes. Who's the message from?"

"Me. I have some findings from the analysis you requested."

Her heart fell a little in spite of herself. She didn't really feel like hearing what inevitable bad shit Sidassian was up to just now. Couldn't she have a few moments to enjoy the illusion that he was a good man who actually liked her company? Who could be a friend? Perhaps something more? Even if he did have ulterior motives, they still seemed to get along so well…

She scowled. No, no, she shouldn't have a something more. And definitely not with a man who had ulterior motives, especially nefarious ones. "Out with it, Xi." Rip the bandage off quickly, right?

"I was able to detect a serial number on the outside of the canister in its storage location from a microcam I released. The hardware was purchased—well, I will spare you the exact details, as you've instructed. But ultimately, I was able to trace the purchase to two addresses, one on Capital and one on Desori X. Our intelligence files link both addresses with Enhancer High Command. The Capital address was the last known residence of their deceased empress."

She whistled low, then rubbed her chin. "The scientist we saw. Get the armor cam footage and cross-reference it with known images of EHC officials. Damn." If the man had been high-ranking, she wasn't sure that would have changed anything, but it didn't feel good to not know for certain.

"One of the three armor cams has been deleted from the databanks, Commander."

"What?" Ellen frowned harder now. "There's no reason it should be—"

"Agreed. The deletion metadata has also been removed. Whoever deleted it removed traces of their activity. This is highly suspicious and unusual activity."

"Well, frag. What time is it where Simmons is?" If they had a traitor onboard, he needed to know.

"2300."

Hmm, he could be asleep, and she really needed to get back to that herself. Despite the importance, what were they going to do about it? The footage was already gone. "Send him a written update of this, will you? Can you complete the cross-reference with the footage from the other cams?"

"Yes. It is already running."

"Can you increase security around mission-related footage, Xi?"

"I will create a continuous, remote backup and attempt to obfuscate its activity. And I will remove what deletion privileges I can from extraneous crew members. Zhia, Merith, you, and the doctors will of course still need access."

"How about you tell me if they're touched at all, too? By message is fine."

"Acknowledged, Commander. Also, I've found a match. May I turn on your display?"

"Yes."

The holo flickered to life with the image of the unconscious scientist side by side with a portrait of a man in full silver-trimmed Enhancer regalia.

"This scientist appears to be Enhancer Lord Regent Jun Il Li."

Damn. They'd scrambled a higher-up. Would there be repercussions? Not if he didn't know who they were, but then there was the matter of Kael. If he was here to follow them, the stakes could be higher than she'd anticipated. "Do we have any clues to what he was researching? And do we have any records of Theroki working with them?"

"Theroki are believed to have been contracted for personal guard duty."

"That's probably Kael."

"Yes, I concluded the same. And, one moment—yes. Data on Li's suspected activities were not clear. We are still working through the encryption on the files uploaded from the bunker you infiltrated. I will query Simmons if he would like to raise the priority of resources assigned to cracking these files. What few leads we have suggest a typical Enhancer research interest in the refinement of a certain variant of female genes, possibly fighter or diplomat archetypes."

"Hmm." What did this all mean? Did it really tell her anything, aside from that whoever Kael worked for on his mission was not just some lowly scientist but rather a big shot?

"Considering what Kael has mentioned about his mission and Alexandra has gathered in her biometric scans, I would say it is a greater than fifty percent likelihood that the canister contains the results of Li's research. Or at the very least, a part of or copy of it."

"Agreed. Wait—Dremer has you calling her Alexandra now?" The AI defaulted to referring to people throughout the ship as they requested to be personally addressed, which could be both amusing and confusing.

"Yes."

Huh. Maybe Ellen was the only uptight one. Whatever, that was nothing new. Her job was to be uptight. "Any actions you would recommend aside from informing Simmons?"

"No, Commander."

"The target tomorrow—is it an Enhancer lab?"

"Yes. But it is not related to Li or High Command. Also, the mission objective is to install sniffers to grow our intel network. No subjects are believed to be in jeopardy, although a secondary objective is to confirm that report."

Ellen nodded. She'd read that much already. Hence her plan to have him stay at the ship, but if it was more distantly related to his mission, even better. Only a few of them would need to go, and they'd need to be fast and quiet.

Too bad they still didn't have that other cloaker fixed. Maybe Bri could look at it. If not, the armor's dynamic camo would have to do. She really needed to get more rest; what hours she'd gotten hadn't done much.

"All right. Thank you, Xi."

"I apologize again for interrupting, Commander. You seemed to be enjoying yourself. Was this helpful?"

"Yes, very much so. Why do you say I was enjoying myself?" And are you reporting that sort of thing back to Simmons? And did Ellen really want to know if Xi was?

"I based my analysis of your emotional state on your heart rate, muscle tension, and facial muscles. Also, according to my data, you have sat down to eat in the galley fewer than five times, all of them requested directly by crew members. This anomaly required some hypothetical explanation."

"And your hypothesis was I was enjoying myself?"

"It was that you enjoy Kael's company in general."

She winced. "Don't tell him that, will you?"

"Of course, Commander. Will it be disappointing for you if he turns out to be a danger to the crew?"

She gritted her teeth, wondering how to possibly answer that. "Yes," she said slowly, not sure exactly what she was admitting by saying so. "But I'd like to know sooner rather than later."

"For the safety of the crew?"

"Yes. But also so I don't become... friends with him, if he's a danger to us."

"I will do my best to expedite any tasks I have that can ascertain the truth of his mission."

"Thanks, Xi. I appreciate that. You're very helpful."

"Thank you. I appreciate you saying so." Could an AI sound pleased, or was she projecting?

Ellen sighed and dimmed the lights, tossing off her cargos and donning the shorts she usually slept in. She flopped into her bunk and pulled the covers back around her, hoping for fewer nightmares this time.

Or maybe dreams of something... someone else.

As she lay there, trying to sleep but failing, something else occurred to her. "Xi?" she said softly into the darkness.

"Yes, Commander?" Xi's voice was the same as ever, booming in the black room.

"Did you form some hypothesis on Kael as well?"

"Yes. Do you believe he would want me to share it with you?"

She paused, unsure of that. His privacy hadn't occurred to her. "Well, I'm the commander of this ship, though," she said weakly. Entirely an excuse.

"His initial actions appeared to be normal human behavior, hunger driven. Once Josana approached him, he displayed many signs of alarm, enough to trip my sensors in preparation for disciplinary action."

"What kind of disciplinary action?"

"I have algorithms designed to police unwanted sexual advances on crew members and passengers. Josana was nearing a verbal warning on my part. He made her very excited, and she had a similar effect on him physically."

"Oh." Ellen sighed.

"She made him very uncomfortable otherwise. So I have noted her a possible harasser in his file. I was just about to trigger a reprimand when you entered, and I preferred to let you handle the situation. His reaction to you was much more comfortable."

"Ah," she said softly. Just what she wanted to be. Comfortable. Ugh.

"You are alarmed now. Have I caused you some concern?"

"Oh, no, it's fine, Xi. Good job monitoring the safety of the situation. But I'm sure Kael can handle himself with Josana."

"I protect all equally, Commander. A benefit of a digital presence monitoring behavioral boundaries."

"That's good of you, Xi." She sighed. "I think I'll go to bed now."

"Yes, Commander." There was a pause. "But I have not told you my hypothesis."

Ellen snorted. The AI was as literal and structured as Simmons. "Oh, yes. What was it?"

"I hypothesized he very much enjoyed your company, and not Josana's. In case that was at all unclear."

She let herself smile in the dark at those words. "That is a little comforting, thank you, Xi."

"Good night, Commander."

"Good night."

She drifted off to sleep, and dreams did not come.

CHAPTER EIGHT

"SO... I'm like a nuke launcher with the safety off?" Kael blurted.

Dremer winced. "Did I say that? I didn't say that."

"Am I wrong?" As he sat on the one chair in a cabin crowded with shelves heavy with fine mechanical parts, Dr. Dremer had briefed him on her studies of his biometric scans.

"Well, it's a lavish metaphor but not exactly wrong per se..."

"So are you saying I should get my chip fixed and back to Theroki standard as soon as possible? What does any of this mean?" He fidgeted with the seam on his worn black pants, not even trying to hide his nerves at the moment.

"No, no, I don't think you should get it fixed. Maybe ever. These are extremely intense fight or flight responses that take days to return to normal. Even your resting rate would be considered stressed for most people. What the chip is currently doing for your health isn't good either, but it's better than their standard setup. The long-term effects to your health are well documented and severe."

He frowned. He certainly hadn't counted on anyone commending his decision to damage the thing. "I don't think they were too concerned about the long-term, Doctor."

She folded her arms across her chest. "Well, are you?"

He hesitated. "Yes, ma'am."

"The levels of epinephrine and cortisol alone are putting you at much higher risk for heart disease, cancer, depression, strokes. Also common infections, headaches, digestive problems, memory impairment—"

"Okay, I get it, Doc. It's terrible for me."

"It's killing you. And I'm not even a *medical* doctor. Although I have studied implants and chips like these a great deal, most don't influence the body's biochemical systems. I checked this over with Dr. Levereaux, though, and she agrees these chips must be shortening the lives of anyone wearing them. By a lot."

He took a deep breath. Well, they didn't tell you that when you signed up. Then again, he didn't know many Therokis that expected— or cared—to live to old age. Kicking the can at some point before then was kind of a given. Which was exactly why he was doing the right thing by this. More than he knew, it turned out.

"Listen, I have a couple of suggestions. I'd like to take a look at your chip, make a copy maybe—"

"You mean, completely remove it?"

"Yes, I—"

"I don't think so, Doctor. Even if I wanted to, I can't while the oath programming is engaged. And I don't think I want to." He didn't trust them *that* much yet.

"Well, think about it. All of this—just think about it. Options for the future. The other thing is brain scans. We only have a rudimentary facility here, but I'd like to get a look at how your prefrontal cortex is operating."

"Um…" That sounded worrisome.

"If it's operating normally, and I could get a copy of the chip, Levereaux and I might be able to work on something to remove the lingering chemical boosting going on. It would be a start at least."

"If it's not operating normally?"

"I'm not sure how long you've had the chip or how much your brain has grown to depend on it."

"Eleven years."

"Hmm, well, that could be worse. And how old are you now?"

"Twenty-eight."

"So, seventeen at installation. Young, but not a total child. Your brain did still have some maturing to do with the chip in place, though." She sighed. "Well, think about it. If you want, I'm happy to help however I can."

"What do you get out of this, Doc?"

"Aside from the satisfaction of helping people?"

He narrowed his eyes. "Yes."

"What? That's high on my list, if you hadn't noticed. I also find undoing the work of irresponsible idiots extremely rewarding. But obviously the reverse engineering of the Theroki tech has been technically satisfying, and I'd be happy to add to my understanding of it."

"Like the telekinetic part?"

She waved him off. "The Union has had experimental telekinetic prototypes for years."

"You're not a part of the Union, though."

She grinned. "I'm not, but they have terrible network security."

He couldn't help but return her smile. "All right. I'll think about it. Is there anything I can do to counteract the spikes?"

"Lower your stress level overall. Maybe hang out with Fern and Nova and their plants."

"Not sure if I'm welcome in there."

"Get your own plants. Meditation and exercise. Good nutrition—fruits and veggies, not just that ration bar crap. Sleep. All the normal stuff."

"Yeah, but what if I go nuclear and try to kill someone again?"

"Isn't that kind of your job?"

"Someone I don't want to kill. One of the good guys."

She pressed her lips together, eyes softening with sympathy. "Ah, we can dream of good guys and bad guys. I hope things are as black and white. I'm not a medical doc, but you might be able to use some kind of sedative or anesthesia in an emergency. I'll see if Levereaux has any ideas."

"That would be a big help. Thank you, Dr. Dremer."

"You're welcome, Mr. Sidassian."

"Kael."

"Of course. Kael. Have a good day."

———

GUARD DUTY on their shore excursion was actually harder than Kael had expected. For one thing, this mostly human crowd was more desperate and unruly than the last. And another, every few beings held some horrifying injury. Or worse, a look of utter defeat.

He followed Zhia's lead and tried to keep the tide of refugees calm and not think about how Jenny and Ryu had trotted off, silently and alone.

What kind of mission only needed the two of them? Something sneaky, he hoped. They could both handle themselves, but their team clearly had specializations, like most special-forces teams. What required command and medical to go off on their own? He suspected it was more likely that Jenny was there for climbing something. But why Ryu?

It made him nervous.

He grew even more nervous when he found the listing of a Theroki ship in the dock records. The *Renosai* was docked two terminals away in the giant spaceport, but he still didn't have a good feeling about it. Especially when he searched Theroki records and found no mission listed for them in the region.

No mission listed for their ship at all, in fact. Of course, they could be on a covert mission as well. They couldn't have an entire ship full of renegades, could they?

Frowning, he switched on his Theroki-encrypted comm channel anyway and stayed muted. From the sadistic laughter that joined him in his suit, he knew these were not the kinds of comrades he preferred. Not that he'd ever had much choice about it.

As he did a loop around the back of the ship, he heard a grunt over the Theroki channel, then another. Then a whispered, "Did you grab her? Fragging hell."

Another voice, "What about the other one? How many are there?"

Kael stopped in place and switched on his area map, seeing if he could pick up the local Theroki unit locations. He should be able to see any and every soldier in the area.

"Three, I think," said yet another voice. "Maybe two. Look—there that one went back to the road. She's got her cloaker turning on anyway. Follow the other one."

Lights from three units slowly moving south toward the ship were overlaid on the map and his helmet visor. They were headed this way, but still a long way off.

There was a low chuckle. "Dynamic camo. Nice try, bitch."

Not hesitating for a moment, he sprinted away from the *Audacity* and down the catwalk and stairs to the nearby road. As he went he hastily added Zhia to his helmet comm. "She's in trouble, isn't she," he said, words uneven as he ran at top speed.

Silence met him for a second as he vaulted over a railing and landed with a thud down in the dense jungle brush beyond.

"Do you read me, Zhia? I'm going after her. Left my post."

"What do you know, Sidassian?" Zhia's voice was hard.

"There, to the right," said one Theroki over the comm. "You go around the long way."

"I can hear three of my people closing in on two women, one with a cloaker and one with dynacamo. Sound familiar to you?"

Zhia swore. "Ryu said they got their objective, but security is in pursuit. Those your friends?"

"No friends of mine. I ain't got no friends."

"Yeah, whatever. Send me their locations. I'm sending Dane and Nova after you."

"Sec." He brought up the coordinates. "I can read them off to you, but they're moving fast."

"Nothing but high-tech for you bastards, huh?"

"You got that right." He read off coordinates. "I'd say they're headed about there."

"Keep me apprised—backup incoming."

He pushed his legs to run faster, and faster they went. Dane and Nova would take twice as long to get there, if not more.

Sometimes enhancements came in handy.

———

ELLEN FALTERED AND SLID, the rock at the water's edge slicker than it looked. Her skid turned into a leap, and she cleared the stream with thankfully only a slight splash.

She sprinted up the next hill. Tropical trees like kapoks and palms —or some alien cousin thereof—stretched above her, providing valuable cover. A craggy mountainside loomed to the right, and just about twenty feet up, a crevice opened up into a passage of some kind. Checking her map overlay, she could see it actually led through the mountain and up to the top of the steppe—not a dead end. At least, if the map was correct.

It was worth a shot. The dynamic camo should be able to hide her even better against the rock than the jungle, and she was most likely a better climber than the damn Therokis chasing her in their antique suits.

If she could make it up and into the crevice unnoticed, they might get hung up looking for her down here. She reached the base and steadied herself, preparing to go up.

Zhia's voice suddenly cut in. "Hey, Sidassian just took off toward you—something going on over there? He says you're in trouble."

She frowned. How the hell did he know?

"Nothing I can't handle," she said.

"C'mon, Elle, don't get cocky."

"Is he part of the trouble?"

"Seemed worried about you."

She started the climb. There wasn't time for this shit. "We got the sniffers placed. Jenny went back down the road, and I'm pushing into the jungle to split them up. I am trying to avoid combat, but I can take one or two of them."

There was a pause. She was probably conferring with someone else or handling one of the injured. Ellen focused on the next handhold.

"You need backup. Let me send Nova and Dane."

"I don't want to get into a full-on firefight down here—"

"Sidassian is already on his way, though. Can you trust him with three of his own?"

She frowned. He had more to hide from these other Theroki than she did most likely, and every reason to stay out of their way, so she wasn't too worried. But then again—how had he known? What if they were working together? "Maybe."

"Come on, Elle."

She sighed. Zhia never called her Elle unless she was dead serious about something. "Fine. Send them. But I want to avoid a firefight if we can. Got my location?"

"Yep. All right—they'll be headed your way."

"Tell them—" she started.

She didn't finish. Just then, a laser bit into the rock above her right hand, shattering the mountain under her hands.

She scrambled but lost her grip, falling back. Fragging hell—that was clever. For a Theroki.

"Commander?" Zhia shouted. "Ellen?" There was no time to respond.

She hadn't yet reached the crevice, and the fifteen feet down were jarring even with her armor, although it kept her from breaking anything. Her back hit the ground, and the air rushed from her lungs.

As she sucked in a breath and tried to right herself, a heavy boot came down onto her chest, pushing her back down.

"Gotcha," he growled. A scarred helmet eerily similar to Sidassian's leaned over her, leering. He straightened to catch the attention of a colleague who broke through the branches a moment later. A blue circular tangle resembling an octopus or a strange spider marked both of their helmets. She trained her gaze on it squarely and twisted her shoulders, hoping that'd give the armor cam a good shot.

While he was distracted—this was her chance.

She seized his boot with both hands and braced her forearms along the sides, viciously twisting to the right. Titanium skeleton or no, joints were still weak points.

It took twice, maybe three times the force as it would have unarmored, but it worked. The crack from knee and ankle reached her ears even through the metal armor.

He bellowed, lunging for her helmet fist-first as he tried to bring the injured knee down in as harmful a way as possible. She curled and twisted, but avoiding the mountain of metal hurling toward her was impossible.

His hands found her helmet.

Gripping her head like a melon for a gorilla to smash on a rock, he head-butted her once, twice, again. His faceplate crashed into hers, the sheer rapid motion of the movement dizzying her. She winced at a cracking sound—her faceplate? Her head? Something else?

She waited for the first pause and launched a head-butt of her own, surprising him. She then rocked the other way entirely, throwing a knee at his back.

It didn't connect well, but it did send him off-balance. With her left hand, she shoved him. As he fell awkwardly onto his side, mostly off of her, she seized the chance to elbow the back of his neck, where the main regulators were housed for temperature and air control.

Not just once. Again. Another.

No, she was getting greedy—she should prioritize escape over removing him from the fight. Still, her greed paid off. Something hissed wildly from the regulator unit, and his hands flew there in alarm.

Swearing, he rolled away from her. She jumped to her feet just in time for the second Theroki to seize her by the neck.

Out of the corner of her eye, she saw a third Theroki come out of the brush, rifle raised and trained on her. Shit, all three had come after *her*. They must have some way around the dynamic camo.

Her captor shoved her, her back colliding with the large nearby kapok-like tree. The shove started with his arm but finished with a wave of telekinetic power.

She hit the trunk with enough force to crack and splinter the wood behind her, even as he closed the gap between them.

She reached for the multirifle still on her back, but her arms wouldn't respond. Damn it. He had her pinned. The world was still swimming—too many head-butts, most likely. She waited impatiently for it to subside.

Her vision blurred, then cleared, then blurred again, but it appeared her first attacker had fallen on his ass and was addressing the damage she'd done to his knee and ankle. Did their suits have injury-repair functions?

She hoped not. Partly for her safety. Partly because they were assholes.

Ellen trained her eyes on the one who was holding her smashed into the tree trunk. When her eyes focused again, she searched for any weaknesses. She spotted nothing. His armor was similar to Sidassian's, except for a black, burned gash down the right arm. Her eyes caught on the blue octopus mark on the helm's side again. Something greenish and fuzzy protruded from the left shoulder—was there something *growing* on him, or was she just that dizzy?

Shoulda packed more knockout grenades. Or *any*. Not that she could have moved to reach them. Or that her suit would necessarily be able to withstand them with the faceplate was cracked.

"Stand down," the third arrival ordered.

The familiar voice raised goose bumps on her arms inside her suit.

The fuzzy one froze, turning his attention to the new arrival. Her armor creaked bitterly, and the tree groaned behind her as Fuzzy pressed her even harder into the wood. She tried to jerk a leg free. Nothing happened. But Fuzzy wasn't looking at her now.

He was focused on the newcomer. "Identify yourself. You're not in our unit."

She squinted, striving to focus on the newcomer. Were there tank-and-chainsaw marks to match the voice?

Yes. *Sidassian*. How'd he gotten here so quickly?

"Covert mission," he said, voice icy. "You're interfering. Stand down."

"Like hell we will. Transmit your access codes. Covert for who? And switch to our channel."

"Had to drop Theroki net uplink for this mission in case it went sideways. I can't get on your channel. Use voice masking instead."

He must have complied, because the next few words were lost in a garbled mash of machine sounds. Ellen hurried to switch on her translator with a flick and a gesture of her eyes. Of course, her universal translator was more universal than most people's—Simmons had added several obscure languages as well as encryption-family encodings. His favorite had been Navajo, but it also conveniently included the Theroki hash. She wasn't going to ask him how he'd gotten it.

"Transmitted," said Sidassian, his voice now oddly metallic and twisted by the translator.

Broken Ankle over there grunted, annoyed. He was still hunched over and futzing with his knee, but he was now on his feet. "Damn. He checks out."

"Mission for who?" Fuzzy demanded.

"That's not—" started Sidassian.

"I'm not going back without any details to give my command. This bitch was suspiciously close to the compound we were defending, then took off."

"Suspiciously close, huh? Wow. Definitely deserves beating the shit out of someone."

"She resisted. Your client? Now."

Kael hesitated for a moment. "Fine. Orders came from Enhancer High Command Lord Regent Jun Il Li. I was already with him on another assignment. Check back—I reported in for both."

Broken Ankle let out a long, low whistle. "EHC?" Fuzzy sniffed, unimpressed apparently.

Well, that confirmed that for Ellen. At least now she didn't have to ask Sidassian face-to-face.

"Look, I've told you enough," Kael said, his voice harder than she'd ever heard it. Was there a shake to his rifle there for a moment, or was it only her blurring eyes? "Stand down. This officer is my transport to Desori."

"You're not choosing sides, now, are you?"

"No. Just delivering a package."

"What kind of package?"

"Research. That's more than you need to know."

"You're going to have to give me more than that."

"A child, all right? Something EHC was working on. Genetic proto-type. I don't know the details. Now. Stand. Down."

Ellen caught her breath. A *child*? That was the living organic material in the canister? A human child?

"You'll board our ship. We can take you straight to Desori."

"No. I thought you had something you were guarding."

"We can spare a few here and take you." How high-ranking *was* Fuzzy to assert that?

"No. High Command was betrayed. I'm not taking a risk on you or on any Theroki vessel."

Huh. High Command had been betrayed? Or did he just assume so? Did that have anything to do with her team's attack on the bunker, or was it something larger? His choice of a random civilian vessel made much more sense now.

Of course, the Foundation had gotten the tip about the bunker from *somewhere.* What if it had been those very same Theroki they'd knocked out? Perhaps Sidassian was completely correct. No wonder Simmons specified nonlethal methods on that mission.

"You're sure you don't want to keep her because you've altered your chip, *therolin*?"

"Don't you *therolin* me, I didn't 'alter' it. A Puritan agent I encountered early in the mission did. Something I will rectify when I reach Theroki HQ on Desori. Without you. *If* you'd get out of my way."

Suddenly she remembered Dane and Nova. Using quick finger and glance commands inside the suit, she jotted off a quick message to approach and get sight on target but not engage yet. *See if Sidassian can talk his way out of this one,* she typed to them.

"That's also something you could rectify on our ship," Fuzzy was saying.

"Not if there are traitors on it. Trust me, that is not happening."

"I think you're just looking for an excuse to take your breeder here and your damaged hardware back where you can have your way with her. You shouldn't be completing a mission of this priority while damaged."

"COMM *Manual 26-B Covert Operations* recommends the use of civilian vessels over official ones in highly sensitive political missions to maintain the appearance of Theroki neutrality and to lessen the risk of detection. Also, piss the frag off. My oath is on, and I'm in the right here."

Fuzzy tightened his grip on her armor but ripped her away from the creaking tree. Nothing hard met the soles of her boots—she was in the air.

If Sidassian's fight with Nova was any indication, this was not good.

Fuzzy growled low in the back of his throat. Unwilling to give up, he also seemed to have run out of comebacks.

"This is the last chance I'm giving you. Stand down, or I'm hitting it." One of Kael's hands moved off the rifle and toward a panel on the side of his armor. Damn, they had a bloodlust *button*? What a terrible idea.

"You wouldn't," said Broken Ankle, who was leaning against a thick tree trunk now.

"Three."

"You horny, slack-faced, son of a—"

"Horny? More like you're *jealous*. I'm just doing my job. Two."

"Piss off. What do you think, Rao, can the breeder still get him to Desori if we break half her bones?"

"In my experience you can still screw a woman with—"

Sidassian started to say something, but she didn't hear it. The jungle and then even the rocky crag flew past, disappearing as only white-blue sky came into view. Air whistled past her. Her suit dutifully reported her altitude, not yet as alarmed as she was. But it would be soon, at this speed. Could those assholes fling her all the way to space? She should probably brush up on the limits of Theroki telekinesis capability.

Then, just as quickly, she was plummeting back to earth, no faster than gravity could pull her but that was plenty fast. She tried to tuck her hands over her neck and found she could move her limbs again.

Why was she always insisting on protecting her neck in futile situations? The suit would do what it could, but this was going to hurt. Assuming she lived for it to hurt. The altitude readout bleated, finally a little alarmed as she reached terminal velocity.

Almost immediately, though, the alarm went off as her pace slowed slightly, then dramatically. Her body rotated upright again. The jungle came up beneath her at an alarming speed, but not the kind you shouldn't be seeing without a parachute, and even now her speed was slowing.

From this vantage, she could see that where Broken Ankle had been leaning on a tree, there was now an open patch of forest, several of the towering trees now felled on their sides. Like a damn tornado had gone through.

Sidassian.

As she reached the ground, he caught her arm smoothly, plucking her out of the air. She stumbled against him as his force released her, and his arm caught her around her back, their armor clanking as her feet found the ground. His faceplate was unshielded, and he frowned down at her with deep concern in those dark eyes.

"You okay?" he said softly.

She nodded numbly, just staring up at him, struck dumb by his expression.

He let her go to stand on her own, barely a second later and very much too soon. More out of reflex than thought, she drew her multi and aimed it at where the two Theroki had been, then scanned for them.

"I'll be making a report of this!" Fuzzy shouted. Her eyes found him climbing out of the brush a good fifty meters back. Broken Ankle was even farther behind and not even trying to get up, although she did hear a groan.

Sidassian's voice was viciously cold. "Why don't you check COMM

Manual 35-A before you do that? Stupid dreck. If you endanger this mission, I *will* hunt you down and castrate you."

"As if I'd care!"

"I hear pissing gets harder," Sidassian growled back.

"Bite me, you piss-drinking shit-gibbon."

But Fuzzy wasn't heading for them; he was aiming for his fallen comrade. She and Sidassian remained tense, rifles trained on the two until they disappeared out of sight, two Theroki gorillas grumbling into the dark of the forest.

Ellen stared after them, hardly believing it.

"You hurt?" he said softly beside her, voice still tinny and encrypted and then decrypted by the translator. He had forgotten that his voice masking was still on. Still, even with that, the change in tone was marked. For her, there was no ice, only warm concern. Her stomach dropped and twisted at that realization, and she wasn't entirely sure why.

If she was going to hide the fact that she'd listened in, she needed to do it now and feign ignorance. But if he was truly going renegade— if he was gradually turning his back on these men—he was going to need somewhere to go. Maybe she *should* consider recruiting him.

Suddenly, she very much wanted him to report to *her* over assholes like that. He had clearly proven himself invaluable at her side. And it felt good. He felt like an ally. She wanted him there for longer than just the next month or two.

As a fighter, nothing more. Of course.

But if she wanted to keep him around, she shouldn't lie to him.

"Commander, you all right?" he said again, even more concerned now. "Can you hear me?"

"Yeah, I'm all right," she said flatly into the encoded audio. How silly would that have been if he'd decided she couldn't hear him while she sat there deciding to tell him she could. "But I should probably point out your encryption is still on."

His eyebrows flew up, but the slight smile that followed was more amused than anything else. "You heard all that?"

"I heard all that."

He snorted. "Really, Commander. Are you supposed to let me know when you've gained intel? I should think not."

"I don't lie to my crew," she replied. Erg, was that overstepping? "Or people who've saved my life." There, that was better.

The pause before he answered was a long one. "So I'm crew now?"

Did he want to be? The surge of hope that accompanied the thought was beyond all bounds of rational thought. Uh-oh. "Well, this qualifies for honorary crew status."

"So not too cocky this time, and I won you over?"

"Oh, I don't think you've done *that*. Probationary crew status, mind you."

"Probationary honorary status. Wow. I'm flattered."

She started to turn away.

"Wait."

"We should get out of here." But she turned back to face him.

"Is what you heard going to be a problem?"

She stared at him, trying after all the violence to sort through what she had already known and he hadn't known that she'd known from what she'd actually learned. Frag. With her head spinning, no way that was coming clear right now.

"You don't seem to have much love for Enhancers," he said plainly. "And clearly you have some agenda beyond your strictly humanitarian one."

"Technically, both missions are humanitarian," she said slowly. "One is just a little more proactive than the other."

He met her eyes, waiting. His glance flicked over the cracks forming in her unshielded faceplate, then back to her eyes.

"Your delivery of your package is not *immediately* part of any clear and present danger to innocents. So, it shouldn't be a problem. Although I suppose we'll see what happens when you deliver it. And I really wish I knew for certain it truly is a child and not a plague or a nerve agent." She hoped he could read the darkness in her voice as dread and not a threat to him.

His frown had deepened, but concern still softened his eyes. "Who do you work for?"

"Private donors."

"Come on."

"You know I can't tell you."

"Well, I also can't tell *you* any more than you've already figured out without knowing who you work for. Where did you get this encryption translator anyway? I know Dremer, Taylor, and Levereaux don't know how to make that. They barely speak three languages all combined. These aren't just available off the shelf."

"There are a few shelves if you know where to look."

"That's not an answer, Ryu."

She raised an eyebrow at his sudden change of address. No Commander this time? "You're not ready for the answer yet."

He blinked. Hadn't been expecting that, had he? "Wait, what?"

"I can't tell you who we work for yet." Not who we work for, but who we *are*, but even that was saying too much.

"Yet? So… there will be a point where you can tell me?"

"We'll see. Although I believe you that you're protecting your mission, I'm also pretty sure you didn't want me to get dragged off by them or beaten to a pulp. When your mission is over, maybe."

"C'mon. You can do better than that."

She shrugged. "Nope, I can't. But science is our concern. Not politics." Of course, in the 'verse these days, science *was* politics, especially if science was destroying your crops, mutating your people, enhancing enemy super soldiers… But he knew that as well as she did.

He looked down, thinking. They stood in tense silence. What were Dane and Nova making of this?

"Thank you, Kael," she said softly.

"For what?"

"For saving my life. For scaring away those gorillas."

"Oh. Of course."

"Of course? Not everyone would have."

"Well, there's no way I wouldn't have."

She glanced around. "Satisfied? Can we head back now?"

"Very far from satisfied, but yes, we can head back now."

They started back toward the ship, slowly this time. "He's right, you know," she said. "Your chip damage might have something to do with your helping me." He needed to learn its weaknesses if he was going to function with it in that state.

He smiled crookedly at her. "You know, I wasn't born a Theroki. I *am* able to have thoughts separately from my penis."

She nearly choked, recovering only to blurt, "Some men don't seem to be."

"Well, I'm not one of them."

"But you also don't deny that if your penis were in control, it would choose to help me?"

He smacked a gauntleted hand to his helmet. "You know, Commander, if you're interested in a man, you shouldn't talk about his privates that way. Try something more affectionate." She blushed fiercely inside her helmet and was glad they weren't facing each other, as she wasn't sure she could shield it at all at this point. "If you *aren't* interested in a man, you're supposed to get pissed if he even acknowledges penises exist. Dicks just aren't mentioned in polite company. Ever. You should be ordering me not to discuss penises in your presence. That's how they do things in Capital."

"Is that so?" She propped her nonrifle hand on her hip. "I'd stick out like a sore thumb."

"I hear you're not the Capital type," he said.

She smiled. "I'm not. Plus, don't think I could have made it through the Union Army that way. And that would be a lot of talk about nonexistent body parts aboard my ship."

"I bet. You should really take them somewhere to let off some steam."

"We'll be at Molyarch Station soon."

He stopped midstep. "You're serious? I thought you were gonna clock me for suggesting it."

She stopped and grinned at him. "Clock you? After what you did to Nova?"

His face fell.

"Sorry—that was a joke. A bad one. I told you I'm bad at banter. Come on." They continued walking. "Everybody, man or woman, goes stir-crazy too long in a boat, needs to get out sometime. Let their hair down, metaphorically speaking." And sometimes literally.

"Phew, it'll be nice to have some pressure off me then."

"I don't think Josana tends to take up that kind of activity on shore leave, so it may not be as pressure relieving as you might like."

"Damn. And… do you take up that kind of activity?" he asked slowly.

"In your dreams, Theroki."

He said nothing for a moment. Thinking about some actual dreams? Was she in any of them, or did they have a younger, more experienced and sophisticated star? "I might not be a Theroki much longer at this rate," he said slowly.

"Oh. Sorry."

"It's okay. You do owe me a beer, though. Do they have beer on Molyarch Station?"

"They do. As long as it's a professional, between colleagues, nonromantic beer. I've been third-degree burned in the past, Sidassian. I don't need any new scars now."

He said nothing for a while, perhaps processing what she'd said. She was offering colleagues. She was hinting at recruiting him. That was something, right?

"I have been burned too, you know. I understand."

She glanced up at the *Audacity*'s profile above the tree line. They were almost back. "The Puritan operative?"

He winced, stopping. Then he forced a grin. "Damn, Commander. Can't keep any intel from you. You're not making this game any fun. But yes. Among others."

"I'd like to hear about your burn wounds sometime. Trade war stories. Maybe over that beer?"

He regarded her levelly. "You tell me your shit, I'll tell you mine?"

"Sure."

"Sounds good to me. Lead the way, Commander." He gestured with his multi into the trees.

She stayed still for a moment longer. "Thanks again, though, Kael."

"My pleasure."

———

ELLEN BARELY KNOCKED on the open doorframe of Dremer's lab before she stepped inside. Dremer looked up from her computer, elegant eyebrow arched.

"What is it, Commander?"

She hit the hatch shut and clasped her hands behind her back. "Any luck on the remote scans of Kael's capsule? Any luck getting at it?"

Dremer shook her head. "The more intense remote scans didn't tell us anything new. The first mission, he took the thing with him at the last minute. He didn't on the last one, but even scans from right inside the cabin didn't help. We're looking for some other newfangled scanning options. But right now, without opening the capsule, I can't tell you much more."

"You'll want to check out my armor cam from today's mission then."

Dremer turned fully away from the computer now. "Why?"

"It's a child."

Dremer stood up from her seat. "What?"

"A child."

"An embryo, you think?"

"Sidassian told me. Inadvertently." She just hoped this wouldn't get him in trouble. "Will that help your scans at all?"

"Well—yes. I could try the medical scanners. It may not work with the metal involved, but…" She put a hand to her chin briefly, then nodded. "Let me talk to Levereaux. I'll figure something out."

"Good," she said softly. "Desori isn't that far away, and we'll lose the chance to understand the thing forever."

"Unless we take it from him," Dremer said flatly.

Ellen pressed her lips together. "Let's try to avoid that, shall we?"

CHAPTER NINE

THE HATCH of his cabin beeped, and Kael waved the door open as he jumped to his feet. Docking to Molyarch Station had completed a few minutes ago, and he'd jotted off a mission update to his superiors with the station's fast network connection.

But he'd been pacing around the room as it all went on, hoping Ellen—Ryu—would soon show up.

The hatch revealed her glittering eyes and armor tuned to a bold shade of dark red. She was leaning against the wall outside his door, arms folded. "Hey, if you don't mind, I'd like to buy you that beer now."

"Of course. How long are we going to be docked?"

"Not sure yet. Probably overnight, at least twenty-four. But it's getting late in their cycle, so I thought I had better march right over here."

"Works for me. I see you're armored. Expecting a fight?"

"Well, I'm not going to stab you. Can't say the same about the rest of the station, though."

"That safe, huh?"

"We're a bit desperate for some time off. At least it's technically neutral in the war."

"I can meet you by the hatch in a few."

She nodded, turned, and was gone. He made short work of suiting up.

Ryu was standing at parade rest by the hatch as he came down the catwalk and slid down the last ladder with a loud clank at the bottom. Zhia and Jenny shuffled up, whispering conspiratorially and to his surprised decked out in actual dresses. Jenny's green number was eye-catchingly short and missing in strips that revealed a physique as athletic as he would have expected. Zhia's black one was a little less revealing, but only a little, and glowing blue piping flowed across her curves.

Their goals were pretty clear, it seemed.

Nova, Dane, and Josana were already waiting. Dane shifted back and forth in his standard issue armor, set to a nondescript dark gray. Josana seemed to be practicing pushing her shoulders back and looking down her nose, decked out in robes like her usual selections but in a pale blue shade now. Nova tapped her combat boot and chewed her gum with surprising zeal. Of all of them, she looked the most her usual ship self in brown cargos and a black tank top emblazoned with a pit dragon in profile.

Interesting who was eager to get off. And where they seemed to be going. Of course, others could be only moments behind like he was.

"Commander! You're coming too today?" Zhia grinned.

"I owe the Theroki a beer," she replied flatly.

Josana's lips flattened as she narrowed her eyes at Ryu. A delicate, expensive breather adorned her face, thin mint and white tubes curling decoratively up into her pale hair, just in the Capital style. The rest of them, save Dane, had standard issue civilian breathers, the kind he hardly noticed anymore.

"How'd you score that, ya bastard?" Zhia called out to him, the first to spot him approaching.

"He didn't tell me I needed to lighten up like the rest of you free-wheeling lugheads. Are you *all* headed to the bar?" Ryu said. Damn, he hoped they weren't. He doubted she would tell him anything if they were all there. Might still be a good time, but shooting the shit and playing darts was not exactly what he'd been hoping for.

Nonromantic beer between colleagues, he reminded himself. Uh... yeah. He'd be nothing but a gentleman, though he couldn't promise not to fantasize about her in the back of his mind. That was pretty much nonstop at this point anyway.

Jenny shifted from foot to foot, anxiously awaiting the airlock to connect and the hatch to finish lowering. "Uh, Commander, we saw... well, I think Zhia and I may want to go to a different kind of bar than you and Sidassian might prefer, if you catch my drift."

"One with more hairy chests on display and fruity cocktails," Zhia grinned.

"The kind with umbrellas?" Kael asked slowly, eying Ellen with a smile. As he spoke, he could feel Josana's eyes boring into him. "Umbrellas in the drinks, I mean?"

Zhia stared, surprised. "Uh. Yes, as a matter of fact."

Jenny snorted. "Maybe you *would* prefer to come with us." She shrugged at Zhia. "You never can tell, can you?"

"Inside joke," Kael muttered. He reached them and stopped beside Ryu, whom he caught smothering a smile behind her wrist as she pretended to scratch her lip. Heaven forbid she crack a grin from time to time. Woman was as serious as a blown space suit—or wanted to be.

"You two are good, you know that? How did you spot a strip club when we're not even docked yet?" Ryu asked.

"We researched ahead." Zhia grinned.

"What about the rest of you?"

"I am getting supplies for my models," said Dane. "Nearly completed a miniature *LSS Galatea*, and darn it if I didn't run out of glue." It might have been more words than Kael had heard him say the entire trip. And it was about model spaceship building. Odd man.

Nova jerked a thumb at Zhia and Jenny. "I'm going wherever they're going. Although I haven't researched it, so who knows what I'm in for." Kael didn't miss Josana rolling her eyes at that. Yes, as desperate as the girl appeared to be, she seemed uninterested in partaking, at least in the visual show. Too bad. How much went on beyond the visual show at those places, and was that the intent or not for these ladies? He had no idea. Hmm, eleven years around almost exclusively men on missions had left him out of some parts of life, hadn't it?

"What about you, Jo?" Ryu said.

Josana straightened, her chin lifting. "Just shopping for a few personal items," she said sweetly, smiling at Ryu before her eyes flicked to Kael. Their pale blue was colored with hope, and hunger too. Damn, he needed a way to really scare her out of this infatuation with him. At the moment, though, his brain was far more interested in imagining ways to answer that hunger than to discourage her for good. Damn him and damn his stupid chip too.

He looked away casually at the hatch as it started to withdraw into the floor. He tried to keep his face as blank as possible. Maybe utter apathy would do the trick.

The commander hung back and let the others off first, then started off at a slow walk into the customs gate and tube into the station. He followed beside her.

"Expecting any trouble with customs?" he said softly.

"They are more interested in our credits than our politics," she replied just as quietly. "Which is why we're here. There's more than one deserter on my ship."

That didn't surprise him, and indeed it gave him a kernel of hope. Had she dropped that fact deliberately, trying to suggest, as she had seemed to earlier, that he might someday find a place among them? He said nothing as they waited behind the others.

He had to survive his mission first.

And, well, complete it. And then get away again without a new assignment. And then he'd need to find the *Audacity* again, assuming she'd have him. Chances of all that happening were pretty much shit.

He sighed and answered the terse questions from the agent, who pinged his chip, then waved him past. He scanned the dreary station as he tagged along by Ryu's side, feeling dreadfully older than the others as they scampered on ahead. He might be older than Jenny and Nova, but Zhia was easily pushing fifty or fifty-five. Dane was not a young man, either, and he was the only one with a more leisurely stride. Guess he wasn't concerned if the hobby shop was going to close. Josana, too, hung back, but more because she faltered uncertainly at the intersection.

Maybe she was just trying to figure out which way she was headed, but if the dirt smears on the wall, crumpled newspapers swirling in corners, and wilting hallway plants concerned him, Molyarch must look even worse to a girl who would prefer to be in Capital.

Hell, even he might have preferred Capital's stifling pretentiousness to this unkempt hallway. Except Ryu was with him here, and he was quite certain he'd never be strolling side by side with her on Capital.

They turned left onto the outer ring of Molyarch, and Josana continued forward down the corridor, leaning toward the right. He hoped she knew where she was headed. Much as he didn't want to bed her, he wouldn't want to see her hurt either.

The dim corridor light was unusual for a space station, but he had to approve. It lent an intimacy and bit of wildness to the air, like one of the better streets back on his parts of Faros. Raucous and sometimes pounding music spilled out into the corridor, along with the occasional drunken patron from within, charging the air with that peculiar energy that belonged only to the night. The outer ring stretched on and curved out of sight, a chaotic pattern of bar after restaurant after casino after sim parlor.

Countrified twangs emanated from a bar called the Tin House Saloon, and he relaxed a little when Ryu turned toward it. He hadn't realized he was tense, but many of these places were not ones he'd see talking over a beer in. Or doing anything in. He felt too old for pounding raves and crazed mosh pits. For most of this shit, really.

He was too young to feel this old. Perhaps that's what happened when you stare down the barrel of death every day straight for eleven years.

He followed her wordlessly as she chose a booth facing the bar, thankfully large enough to fit into while armored. She tapped some quick commands into the table, and a timid waitress quickly delivered six bottled beers lined up to drink between them and a bottle of scotch.

He pointed at the bottle. "After-party?"

"It's for Bri."

"She doesn't want to partake in shore leave?"

"She lived here once. In a not entirely voluntary capacity."

"As a slave, you mean?"

"Indentured servant, technically. Bad memories."

Pink neon light from behind the mirrored bar cast Kael's armor in its warm, unnatural light. Well, that was certainly manly. He should just be thankful Ryu hadn't preferred the stripper bar. That seemed like it would have been a decent hazing ritual. If these women had hazing rituals, and if they had a reason to subject him to one. Which they didn't.

How ridiculous that the thought left him a little bitter.

As he opened the first bottle and handed it to her, then opened one for himself, he scanned their surroundings. No serious threats. His suit did a thorough scan of the beer and the air and gave an approving click, so he retracted his helmet. He'd wondered if his armor would draw attention in the dingy bar. While a few eyes seemed to catch on it, he didn't know if they recognized him as a lone Theroki—with a woman in a bar—or if they were just eying how beat-up and rusted it was. It looked like it could cut you if you stumbled into it. And it could. People were naturally wary.

But overall he almost fit in too well. The whole place, except the luxurious wooden bar top, was made from corrugated metal the same dull, stony shade as his plating. He practically blended into the booth, aside from the grimy brown cushions behind and beneath them. A frail arrangement of strips of metal created a minor barrier between their row of booths and the one behind them. If someone had been trying their hardest while decorating this place, they should really try their hand at some other trade.

He'd probably have a hard time convincing her to turn this into a no-longer-nonromantic-between-colleagues beer if she couldn't differentiate him from the wall.

She finished giving some more commands to the table and looked up, taking a drink. "So do you have a rank in the Theroki military, Sidassian? Then I can have something else to call you by." Her voice was smooth, like her command voice but a bit more relaxed.

"You know, Kael would suit me fine."

"We'll see." She took a swig.

"Eh, Theroki aren't big on orderly things like hierarchy."

"I would think with that many roosters running around crowing, one of them would want to be the biggest cock in the room."

He damn near choked on his beer. "Heh, well, that's true of any group, isn't it?"

"Some are more subtle about it than others. Are you really telling me being a Theroki isn't just one continuous dick-measuring competition?"

"Uh, well, the chips probably do help repress the need to compare dick measurements a little. Just a little."

"Really? No rank? I'm disappointed."

He smiled, chagrined. "No, I mean... It would probably vaguely correspond to... a senior enlisted in the Union maybe? Tridelphi third level was my rank. *Is* my rank."

She pretended not to notice the slip, but he doubted she'd missed it. "Enlisted? Damn, I'm really fraternizing now," she said, taking a long swig. The slight smile—that was as much of a smile as she ever seemed to allow—hadn't left her face through all this teasing.

"Hey, you said you run a mostly military org. Don't you get to pick and choose the rules?"

"I do."

"Besides, I'm not in your chain of command. Or even your nation. Do you even have a nation? And aren't I technically your employer, if I'm purchasing my passage from you?"

"You wish. Passage you're paying for with your labor. That makes you my passenger." She frowned playfully at him. "My *enlisted* passenger, apparently." She almost smiled now.

"It's not exactly the same as enlisted," he said, trying to keep his voice from sounding tight and failing. "There's no educational requirements at any level, which is good 'cause I didn't have much when I signed up. I'm not one for books aside from operations manuals. Practical stuff. There's no boundary between rank-and-file and command units. Some assignments can get you promoted multiple ranks. They got creative, I guess. For better or worse." He shrugged. "And there's also no painful surgery to sign up to be a Union private. Unless they've started giving them all titanium skeletons now?"

She grew serious. "Sorry. I didn't mean to make light of that."

He opened his mouth to say something else, but a deep voice spoke up loudly from the booth behind them, inches from his ear. "Hey, gorgeous, you're all alone here tonight, huh?"

Something about the voice pricked at Kael's ears. Funny, he didn't think he'd have paid much attention before. But Ryu's face had gone dark, her lips pressed in a flat line, and her fingers had tightened around her bottle. Whatever had caught his attention had caught hers too.

"Oh, ah, I'm working," a woman responded. "People usually do that alone." She tried to laugh it off nervously, like he'd made a clever joke. Kael glanced over his shoulder to see if he could see through the haphazard slats of corrugated metal. The waitress?

"How much do you make a night? I'll cover it. Let's get out of here."

"Uh, no, I need this—"

"C'mon, I have a lot of friends around here. I'll smooth it over. Your boss won't mind."

Kael twisted and peered through the metal barrier slats. His sliver of a view revealed a handsome, black-haired man in the brass and dusty blue of a Puritan flight jacket leaning toward the woman. Kael shifted to see more, following the pilot's arm. He'd brought it to rest on the alarmed waitress's hip.

The slight prick of anger in him flared unexpectedly. It would be so easy, just the slightest twist, to rip that arm out of its socket and send the bastard sprawling. Or rip it clean off. He had no intention of getting out of the booth—or even considering the possibilities of an attack—but in spite of himself, scenarios began springing up and playing out in his mind. Maybe smashing the pilot's skull back into this ridiculous barrier of sharp metal pieces would be a more fitting way to handle the situation. Or maybe... a dozen different options began playing out in Kael's mind, each increasingly vicious and final.

No. What was *wrong* with him? Those were all great ways to get kicked off the station.

Kael forced a deep breath. He needed to mind his own business. The guy hadn't done anything wrong—except be a jerk. Yet.

But then why was Kael's mind playing out such a creative array of murder fantasies? How good it would feel to fling that asshole over his shoulder, smashing the bar glass into thousands of beautiful, bloody, pink-tinted pieces...

Oh, hell. The chip again. It must be somehow overreacting, like it had with Nova. Not *now*, damn it. They'd just gotten here.

"Uh, no, thanks," the waitress muttered. "Do you have a drink order?"

"Your boss *might* mind if you turn me down, though," said the pilot. "Ziyar, right? We were in boot camp together, he'll understand. How many good-paying jobs are there around this station, you think? Ziyar runs half of them. You wouldn't want to lose this one, now would you?"

Kael felt something in his head hitch, some secret engine shifting gear. Like he was about to start smashing things. Like he was about to take all those violent fantasies and act on them *all* simultaneously.

Asha. If only I had known then what I know now, I could have protected you. Is this how it went down? I could have—

Why was this happening *now*? Why—

"Sidassian," Ryu's beautiful, hard voice cut through the bubbling rage. A familiar voice. At the very least, the voice of a friend. An ally. Someone he was much more interested in screwing than killing, if he was honest. "You all right?"

He brought his eyes back to Ryu without straightening. "Not particularly. You hear this shit?"

"Heard it myself a few times to be honest, but yes," she said, glaring at the metal barrier between the booths.

That did not help. He gripped the table edge, searching for some semblance of control, trying to detach from his emotions, sink into his body. That was how to get grounded. How he might calm the rage. Deep breaths. He tried to focus on his breathing, his heartbeat, the bubbles in his beer. Her hair, those brown eyes that were solid and steady as granite. Anything. But studying her might make him do something *else* stupid, and he wanted to do that even less. Breathe in, breathe out. Observe your body.

Every physical symptom rebelled. Every breath said it was time to go eviscerate that bastard and leave a new stain on the station walls.

He was losing this battle. He caught Ryu's eye, one last hope occurring to him. "Hey, uh, remember that conversation we had about not going nuclear, Commander?"

"Yes?" Her eyebrows flew up.

"It is… currently a risk."

"Because of that ass?" She jerked a thumb at the barrier.

"Yeah." Why, he had no idea.

She slammed her beer down, then stood up resolutely. "Read you loud and clear. That's all the excuse I need. One sec, I'll handle it."

Where the hell was she going? Watching her stalk away provided an extremely useful distraction, funneling some of the spiraling rage into a different kind of intensity. Faint pink neon was more appropriate dancing across her curves than his. Where did these women *find* armor like that? And why? Did they intend for it to be incredibly hot, or did it only look that way to a Theroki who hadn't had sex in nearly two decades?

"I'm not looking for trouble, sir," said the waitress from behind him. Kael had missed some of the back and forth while trying to control himself. Sounded like things had escalated. The fear in the woman's voice amped him right back up again. Whatever the commander was up to, he hoped she'd do it soon. "Just trying to feed my family, okay?"

"Oh, yeah? You got any sisters that could join in on this station?"

"Uh… three, sir. Four sons too."

"How convenient, I—"

That was it. Threatening kids was over the line. He couldn't take it anymore. He straightened, twisting his head and shoulders up above the barrier to look into the booth. He jostled the beers on the table with his hip, trying to maneuver in the tight booth in his armor. Luckily, the bottles clinking slowed him down just long enough for Ryu to arrive.

"Do we have a problem here?" said Ryu, stopping beside the waitress and folding her arms across her chest.

"What business is it of yours?"

"Do you have a drink order? She's not interested in anything other than that. I believe the lady was very clear."

The pilot rose smoothly to his feet, the waitress backing away. He had a good six inches on Ryu, and maybe ten years, and the formality of his flight jacket certainly looked more military than her nondescript, sleek red armor in the darkness of the bar. Kael gripped the top of the barrier, ready to rip it off and hurl it at him.

Except he wanted to see what Ryu would do. Hopefully, she'd pull off something less permanent than the dozen brutal murders Kael was still planning.

"You should mind your own business," the pilot said, voice deceptively smooth. "You one of those hired mercs with the Puritan contingent that just flooded the station?" His words were slurred. He'd likely been causing trouble somewhere else before this.

"No," she said coldly.

"Good. Cause you can't screw me if we fight for the same side. I'd outrank you."

"Well, that's fortunate then, since exactly zero people here want to screw you. Nobody is impressed by your flyboy attitude."

"Then again, I wouldn't want to have to get you *both* fired. One of you is going to have to come home with—" He reached for Ryu's waist.

The pipe beneath Kael's gauntleted fingers groaned, but there was little time to process what damage he'd done. His eyes were too busy following the three rapid and efficient blows Ryu landed—one uppercut to the solar plexus, sending the man staggering, then a jab and a hook to the head, sending him sprawling into the saw dust on the floor.

Kael let out a bark of laughter in celebration. A woman at the bar to his left cheered and another man snickered and muttered, "Long time comin', that." High-tech armor was no match for unaugmented flesh, no matter the gender, not that most marines couldn't have handled the average overconfident pilot unarmored anyway. Kael found himself imagining her trying it all without the armor. Surely that'd be a sight to behold...

The waitress stared down at the pilot's groaning form, looking more terrified than relieved.

Ryu wasn't finished. She bent down and whispered, "You harass her or anyone else here again, and I will personally hunt you down, cut off your balls, and force-feed them to you. Got it?"

The pilot gaped up at her in horror, blood starting to drip from his nose.

"And for the record, you definitely would *not* outrank me." She gave him a warning kick in the thigh, and he crawled a few feet away, trying to gather himself. The commander turned to the waitress, speaking breezily as if nothing unusual had just happened. "Jobs around here hard to come by?"

The woman glanced down briefly, a touch of shame on her face. "When you don't got no education, yeah."

"Give me your comm. Do you have a comm?"

The woman nodded and handed it to her, unlocking it. Ryu punched something into it.

"There's a job for you at this shop if you want it. If you're on drugs, you'll have to clean up, but they help with that. I'd recommend not coming back here if you can, although I *will* absolutely cut off his balls if necessary. Do let me know if such measures are required. Wrote my name and details on there. Tell them I sent you."

The waitress glanced at the phone. "Ellen Ryu."

He felt a bizarre surge of jealousy that this stranger had been given her first name so casually and he was still stuck officially with

Commander Ryu. He needed to rectify that situation as quickly as possible.

The commander—Ellen—nodded to the waitress. "You okay?"

"Yes, I-I think I will be. Thank you, ma'am."

"My pleasure."

He sank back to a seat, pretending not to notice the massive dent and bend he'd left in the pipe above him. Moments later, she slid back into the booth beside him and took a swig of her beer as if nothing had happened. At least three eyes from the bar were on her, but she kept hers trained on the table until her gaze finally flicked to him, a grin on one side of her mouth. She gradually smoothed it, but a smug smile remained. Why did she fight smiling—or showing any emotion —so hard?

"Nuclear danger level lowered?" she said casually.

"Yes, ma'am. I've narrowly avoided being wanted for homicide on this station. All thanks to you." He took another swig. "It's that damn chip, I think. I should just get it repaired…" He trailed off. It was a lie of sorts. He was far from sure if he wanted that.

She shook her head. "Some things are *worth* being angry about, Theroki," she said. "Helps you know who deserves a job and who deserves a punch in the face. Or three. Dremer talk to you about what she found?"

He nodded. "Did she talk to you too?"

"Yeah. She had to authorize sharing her findings. Hope you don't mind."

"Nah. Crazy shit, though."

She sighed. "Yeah. It takes time to get used to it."

He paused, replaying the way she'd said it in his mind. Should he ask her about the chip she'd had? Union officers did not receive any special upgrades. But maybe special forces did? If he simply didn't say anything, if he just waited, would she elaborate? Moments passed in a contemplative silence that wasn't nearly as tense as he would have expected.

"Did she want you to do anything?" she asked.

Damn, had he just missed his chance to ask? "Yeah. Nothing I'm sure about yet, though."

"Understandable."

Another pause stretched between them, and he had the sense they both wanted to go deeper than small talk, to say the things they'd alluded to down there in the jungle. But how to get there from here?

"That was quite a sight, Commander," he said finally, feeling like he hadn't adequately acknowledged her valor.

"You can't get far as a woman in the Union without learning to thump jerks like that when necessary."

"*Union* officers like that propositioned you?"

"Not if they knew I was special forces. But sometimes when I wasn't in uniform." An even darker look crossed her face for a moment, then faded away.

"And did you offer her a job or something?" he said, trying to steer the subject away from darker matters.

She nodded. "Don't ask, don't tell, Theroki. I already told you more than I should today."

He pressed his lips together, bidding himself to shut up. Her mission —missions?—somehow involved giving jobs to wayward harassed waitresses and blowing up what had clearly been an Enhancer lab where they'd been running some fairly nasty and clearly unethical experiments. Not all that different from the lab he had been working in, except his had grown babies rather than mutilating Ursas with gene-altering viruses.

What the hell did any of those two missions of hers have in common? Other than that he respected her a hell of a lot for both of them. He didn't know the last mission's objective, but he figured it had been similarly altruistic. Which made it even more annoying she'd run into Theroki there.

He straightened a little and peered over the booth to make sure the pilot had gotten a move on. There was still a smear of blood on the floor from his nose, but he appeared to be gone. Or at least in the bathroom.

"Well, glad we've rid the bar of any cocky pilot types. Now these people will just have to get rid of cocky marines and Therokis, and they can drink in peace." He grinned at her and earned a slight smirk in return.

"I never said cocky was a bad thing," she said slowly, starting on a second beer. Or was that a third?

"Most people consider that a bad thing."

She shrugged. "I guess. I wasn't trying to insult you. I think if the attitude is deserved, then you're entitled to it. Maybe I've just hung around too many pilots for too long."

"Almost certainly. Any time around pilots is too long."

She snorted, louder than usual. "You have to admit, it was pretty cocky to throw that grab beam straight back in the Union's face." She snickered. "Would 'ballsy' be a better term for it? God, why does every word I come up with have to revolve around male genitalia?"

"Are *you* flirting with *me*, Commander?" he said, his eyes twinkling.

"Definitely not." She slammed down her beer, then shrugged. "Eh, fragged if I know anymore."

His eyebrows flew up.

"What. We're off-duty. You're enlisted. I'm beating up people in bars. I feel like I'm a fifteen-year-old junior officer again. You can think I'm flirting if it tickles your pickle, Theroki." His heartbeat quickened. Maybe… maybe she *was* flirting. Bizarrely so, but still.

"There you go again with genitalia-focused metaphors."

"Years of Union service don't just get brainwashed out of you overnight, you know."

"Is that a backhanded cry for help? Somebody brainwashing you, Commander? Blink twice if you are being held hostage by your own ship."

She chuckled—actually chuckled. Damn. "Oh, no, no, no. If they are brainwashing me, I heartily welcome it."

Well, glory be. She was actually smiling. The warmth on her face was unmistakable—for her ship? For whomever she worked for? Another twinge of jealousy hit him. He wanted that warmth from her.

And more than that too—he wanted to be a part of something worth feeling that way about.

"Did you say fifteen-year-old junior officer?" he said slowly. "How well did that work?"

She snorted. "Not well at all! But fortunately I'm as good at unarmed combat as I am at invasion defense planning." Her eyes twinkled.

For the first time, it occurred to him that she might be tipsy. Of the six beer bottles on the table, all of them were open, and he had definitely only had two. A selfish, instinctual part of him immediately started trying to think of how he might use this to his advantage. She was always so serious and stoic. What was she hiding under that carefully pressed, controlled exterior? If she did "lighten up" a little, what might peek out?

They *had* said they wanted to exchange war stories. Discuss the burns of the past.

"So you know all about my chip," he said cautiously. "Tell me about yours. Sounds like it was a doozy. Milk and cookies and everything?"

She took another long drink and then glared at the bottle, now empty. "I think we are going to need more beer for that, Theroki." She raised a finger.

"No, no, my treat. You said a beer. Not a whole night of beers." He began jamming his own credentials into the table's surface.

"I thought you didn't have any creds."

"I don't have enough to get to Desori, but I have enough to buy a bucket of beers." Maybe even three. That was the extent of it, though, but she didn't have to know that.

"Yeah, I had a chip," she said, voice tight and bitter all of a sudden. "Not like yours. Networked telepathy add-on and a net hookup."

"Wow. They give that to all the Union bigwigs?"

"Eh, no. I wasn't a 'bigwig' anyway. It was experimental. Only for a few special-forces candidates. They wanted to test out if the artificial telepathy could assist marine fighting units. And for that, it was great. Faster command, easier comms, quicker access to the situation on the ground. Even if you were up in the ship, you could just reach out to each pair of boots and see for yourself what support they needed, how it was going. That part was pretty great. Kids didn't need to stop firing to report to you."

"So why'd you get rid of it? You seem to have gotten it out entirely."

"Well, for one, they didn't ask me if I wanted it put in. I got injured in a heli crash and woke up with my brain being flooded every second of the day. The bastards."

"Shit. That sounds intense."

She met his eyes now, her face serious but more open than usual. "You must have heard us looking for someone named Arakovic, right? You must have wondered."

He nodded. "I may have been a little curious."

"She's the doctor that ran the program. Not working for the Union anymore. I can't find her. But I'm going to." Her voice had taken on a vicious edge.

"And what are you going to do when you find her?"

"I haven't entirely decided yet. Make sure she's not hurting anyone else, for starters. But when we get to Desori and you go on your merry way, Sidassian, you have to promise me you'll let me know if you run into her. Or even hear of her." Her stare was intent, beseeching. As if he could say no to that.

"Of course. Is this Zeta Arakovic? The cybernetic telepathy researcher?"

She scowled fiercely. "You know her?"

"No, I looked her up after our last mission. I said I was curious. Just making sure I got the right first name, so I get the right person when I go hunt her down for you."

She snorted, assuming he was joking. The larger part of him wasn't. "That's the right person," she said. "But you don't have to do that. It's my cross to carry." Such a funny expression. She must have grown up on a Christian world.

Why he suddenly felt so determined to take her cause as his own, he didn't know. But a very high-ranking Enhancer lab lay at the end of his journey to Desori. And if a scientist with slightly flexible morality was going to leave the Union, he had a feeling he knew where they'd end up.

Oh. Of course. The rest of her missions suddenly made a bit more sense. Certainly they had a humanitarian purpose, but she had a personal vendetta driving her too.

She took another sip of beer. "The chip also wasn't good long-term. There were side effects I couldn't stand."

"Such as?"

"They put in some obedience algorithms, which was sure nice of them. I didn't recognize it myself, but since I had the telepathy piece, I saw the others thinking about it. I'd find them thinking, 'Ryu should have reamed me out for that,' 'she would have argued that stupid order,' 'what did they put in that damn chip,' 'hell, they lied to her,' and so on and on. So I knew from my team's reactions that it was changing me. And not for the better. The ability to question and collaborate with command is very important to mission success. If you always do what you're told, you'll walk people into a death trap."

"Dremer said my chip's got some of that too. She's not sure how much."

"Lucky for you that you got around some of it, I guess?"

He shook his head. "Sort of." He hadn't gotten around it so much as he'd told Vala how she could get around it without him. She'd still had to drug him and tie him to the chair for most of the process.

She looked curious but wasn't finished with her own story. "But it was way worse than that, honestly. My mind started to... drift. To thin out and sort of blend in with the others. They noticed it too, although their implants were more minor. I was prepared for some of that to function as a better team. If it saved people's lives, I might give up a bit of identity in exchange. But when you start to know who wants to screw who, and who actually hates the person that wants to screw them or *is* screwing them. And then they both start to know all that about each other..." She shuddered. "A hive mind was just not for me. And I could access the net in a blink too, which was almost as blurring. Addictive, really."

They paused for a moment as their waitress delivered six more beers with a smile this time.

"So you quit? Resigned your commission?"

She looked chagrined. "Not exactly."

"Oh, ho, ho, my straitlaced commander on the surface, but you do like to break the rules, don't you?"

"Well, no. I hate breaking rules." She let out a small laugh, although her pleasant buzz seemed to be dimming a little. "I *hate* it. That doesn't mean I don't do it from time to time. I also hate stupid rules. I wish so many assholes didn't force me to break rules so often. And I may hate going crazy and being lied to more."

"That's fair."

"Maybe someday I'll tell you about how I left. Not just yet. But I went crazy for about six months after I took it out. Stark raving mad, at times."

"Lot of cookies and milk?"

"Yeah. And a lot of running, trying to bring my mind back into my own body. I kept reaching for minds and information that weren't there. And were never going to be again. Sometimes I'd demand the chip back. Or I'd just sit there demanding the AI get me information, just so I could prove to myself that it wasn't gone, that there were other ways, slower ways, but less insane ways to do it. I had to rebuild the wall around my mind again."

Her brown eyes were distant, haunted. Her expression was almost lost, like someone who truly was searching deep inside themselves for something—and not finding it. Then she snapped out of it, her eyes locking on his. "Look, I'm sure they'll require you to fix your chip. But I for one would be glad if you didn't. There's life without it. And sometimes it's better."

"Oh, I have no doubt of that," he said softly, holding her stare.

A sudden spark flew between them. Her wheels were turning, as if she wasn't sure she'd read the right meaning into his words. Even this look, this magnetism that had sprung out of the nothingness—all that part of his life had been shut away for so long. It was murderously distracting to have it coat his thoughts. But it was also intoxicating, a heady feeling stronger than any drunken high. Or at least it felt that way after being without it for so long.

He broke the intensity of the moment before she did, as he sensed her panicking, reaching for some way to push him away. He took a swig and smiled casually. "Then again, we might be thinking differently if we hadn't avoided the brutality I wanted to inflict on that jerk behind us."

She reached out and laid a hand on his forearm, strategically placed away from any serrations or rough spots. Her own eyes had fallen to focus on her beer, lost in thought.

Of course she knew where to put her hand to touch him. Of course.

Wasn't that what drew him to her? What made him get lost watching her lips, listening to her voice? It was not just the sexual drive unshackled by the chip damage. This was why he needed *her* in particular. He was broken, he was raw, he was fragging dangerous. And yet she understood all those broken, raw, dangerous things. She knew them intimately somehow, had some of them in herself. She could navigate them. How many other women could?

"It might lessen with time," she said gently. "The brain adjusts. Mine did."

"I hope you're right." He opened another beer. "I hesitate to mention this, but... was this the third-degree burn you mentioned? Cause we may be too drunk to swap war stories in not too long."

Her face darkened, and she pulled her hand away. He almost regretted saying anything—but he had a feeling his window for finding out this bit of her past was closing, and he didn't want to miss it forever. They should be in Desori within two weeks or so, and the ship wasn't as conducive to sharing secrets as pink neon and buckets of beer.

"It was one of them, but not the one I was referring to down there. You really want to know?"

"I wouldn't have asked if I didn't."

"I... I dealt with a lot of shit to get to my post in the Union. Special forces is supposed to be a meritocracy, but you find out it's not if you're a low-born female with no wealth or connections. Brute strength, mindless endurance, solid un-fragged-up genes? Who cares, it's who you know. Except I had this golden ticket of being a big damn war hero." She spit the words with distaste.

He raised one eyebrow.

She sighed, steeling herself. "And you know how young and stupid I was? I was fool enough to think a junior officer actually cared about me."

"That doesn't seem foolish."

"Feels like it in hindsight. He wasn't in my chain of command, of course. But he only stuck around long enough for me to help him with his career. Know what I got for it?"

"What?"

"He got a promotion off my recommendation, then another. Then he demoted me. All after he found an *admiral* to screw. He couldn't even leave me for another marine."

He winced. "Ah, hell."

"I know. That wasn't the worst of it, though. I got transferred out. I couldn't stand to look at him, let alone take orders from him, even indirectly. Later, he commanded a ship full of my colleagues straight into a Puritan ambush. *Mirror's Light* was outgunned four to one, and those Puries had the wormhole for backup. Not us." Her voice quieted, slowed, now dark. "A lot of good people died. A lot of my *friends* died because I let him sway my thinking." She took a much longer drink of her latest beer now, finishing it. "Never again. Never, ever again."

They were quiet for a moment.

"Fuck," he said softly. "Sorry you had to go through that, Commander."

"Fine, fine, call me Ellen. But only while we're drinking."

"You sure?"

"You know about my chip. About Paul. My name seems casual by comparison. Not many more dark spots about me to know."

"Aside from who you work for."

"Well, that's not a dark spot. That's a bright one."

"Throwing me clues now? I'll take it. But are you going to call me Kael?"

"Only while we're drinking."

"I'll settle for that."

"Okay, now your turn. Tell me about this Puritan operative. Or whatever war story *you* prefer."

That was kind of her, to not push it. But the darkest stories of his past—Asha—he had no desire to touch this moment. Especially when those feelings had almost welled up just a few minutes ago. They were too raw.

Vala it is.

"My last mission… didn't go so smoothly, I guess you could say. She was a resident scientist in the location I was guarding, and I was dumb enough to think I loved her."

"I'm seeing a theme to these war stories."

"Me too. Our stupidity. Anyway, I'd been trying to find a way out for a while. I was conscripted for life."

She smirked. "For life? That's a dumb rule. Another one just asking to be broken. Wait, did you say conscripted?"

"Wasn't my choice. Long story."

"You didn't choose to become a Theroki?"

"Nope."

"So all the surgeries, all the…"

He shook his head. "Not something I wanted. But that's another burn wound for another time. It could have been worse. Faros wasn't a great life by any means, so it was tolerable for a while. But then you start to wonder, is this it? Really? Just stand around and do as I'm told till I get killed doing it?"

"Surprised you didn't end up in the army instead."

"Faros IV is still out of either side's control, and it was back then too. It's mostly gang and mafia run."

"Which one were you?"

He tapped at his forearm, although she couldn't see the gang tattoos at the moment. "You gotta be born right to be in the mob. Gangs are the ones that conscript runts like me."

She snorted. "If you're a runt, I don't want to see the bigger pack members."

"Heh. I don't think you'd be too intimidated. What they achieve in size they sacrifice in smarts, if you get my drift."

"Could you remove the chip yourself? I couldn't."

"No. And I hadn't even thought far enough to think what I wanted exactly. I'm still not sure. Just something different. Something more. I've done enough guard duty for a lifetime, and it just seems like a fool's gamble to keep rolling the dice when on the one hand you get killed and on the other hand there's... also getting killed? Nothing much more than that. I'm not afraid of death, but I'd like it to be for something better than being told to keep people from coming through a door. Something I understand." Maybe even something noble.

Something worth it.

"Seems like a very reasonable desire."

"I hadn't said anything about it to anyone, though. Then this scientist, she brought it up on her own, suggested all sorts of possibilities for freedom and... more than that." Freedom, love, sex, family—*so* much more. Whispered sweet nothings right in his ear. But he couldn't bring himself to say it out loud, even in the relative dark of the bar. To admit how naïve he had been. "None of that was ever sincere, of course, but I fell for it. Maybe the chip makes you gullible. Part of those obedience algorithms? I don't know. I thought it was incredible luck. In hindsight, she may have been a telepath and just damn good at hiding it. Not like your little one."

"Well, Isa's only fourteen. And I can't convince her to *want* to hide it." She winced at some memory.

"Maybe that's a good thing. At least it's honest. I think this scientist was just ultimately telling me whatever I wanted to hear." Even more, had she actually stirred the desires in him? He hadn't remembered having these longings before she'd teased him with them. Perhaps in order to crave chocolate, you had to have tasted it. "She suggested a way to 'loosen the reins' without destroying the chip completely. Maybe find a way to keep it secret. We were usually cut off from other Therokis for a good six months at a time, so I decided to let her try. My decision, to be clear. For once. I told her how to find the chip, which ultimately I think is what she was really after. Of course, the chip tried to defend itself, but she was pretty good. She was scientist enough to alter the chip, but she was more than that. Altering it was mostly brute force anyway. Scratching into and frying the right places. I don't know. I suspect she was a much better operative than she was a scientist, but I didn't realize that until it was too late."

"Too late how, exactly?"

"Well, after she'd altered it, things went sideways. First of all, she tried to install something else along with it, some kind of add-on, but it failed spectacularly. You know we Therokis can short-circuit things. My original chip somehow fought the add-on and won. Still in here, but partially fried to a crisp. It even smoked." He smirked.

"Wow. Maybe you should have Dremer get it out. Are you sure the scientist was a Puritan?"

"She said so, but doesn't sound like one, does she? Maybe I *should* get Dremer to check it out. Although my track record with trusting people to open me up hasn't exactly been a good one."

"I can stand over her and look cold and intimidating if you want. I'm told I'm good at that."

"Oh, you are. But then I'd be trusting you *and* her. Two chances for me to be wrong."

She smiled crookedly at him. "If you didn't trust me, you wouldn't have come on my ship."

"Sure I would have. Maybe I was planning to kill you all."

She snorted at him. "Yeah, right. If you didn't trust me, you wouldn't be fighting off your brother Therokis over me."

"Hey, you're my ride to Desori." He stifled a grin. "And your people were going to kick their asses."

"So you won't admit you trust me. Even over beers. I see how it is. Back to your story, I guess. So the smoked add-on was the first sign of betrayal? I take it there were more."

"Yes, well, she was right pissed when that didn't work, so she blackmailed me. That was where I actually did luck out, though. Something unexpected had come up, and the mission was ending. She took off before... well, before she could get caught with her fingers in the cookie jar."

"But left the cookie jar behind?"

"Yep. That's fine by me, though. As soon as the chip was altered, I could tell she hadn't meant any of the stuff she'd claimed." He sighed and shook his head. That she hadn't loved him was what he really meant. Chip in, he hadn't been able to remember what that had even felt like. But once the deed was done, it had all been clear. "And I mean, she did try to slit my throat on the way out to prove it." He'd broken her arm in exchange, but she'd gotten away as he'd gone for a med kit.

"Sorry to hear that, Kael." He looked up at her, not realizing his gaze had been trained on the table for so long while thinking of Vala. The sound of his name in that deep, lovely voice was new and surprisingly alluring.

"It's okay. My wounds don't seem that bad compared to yours." He'd never felt responsible for the deaths of a ship full of people. No, all his failures were relatively personal. Glory be, that he'd never been in command.

"Well, yours is still ongoing. But let's hope it turns out better for you, huh?" She raised her bottle and held it out to him.

He clinked his against hers in a toast. "Inshallah," he said softly. "Inshallah."

CHAPTER TEN

ELLEN'S BOOTS hit the ground of the Teredark moon with a soft puff of dust spreading outward. Kael, Nova, and Zhia touched down just beside her, bouncing out of the airlock, and one of the drones hovered along behind them. Thankfully there was *some* gravity on this hellhole of a moon. Oh, it was terraformed, and low, pale-yellow grass spread across the dusty plains around them. But Teredarks had a different definition of livable than most species. The molted husk of a small Teredark sat on the horizon, dust piling up around it to form a freakish skeleton of a future dune.

Zhia shuddered. "God, I hate those things. Like giant centipedes."

"Or millipedes. They always kinda reminded me of centaurs," Nova offered, sounding much less leery.

Ellen pointed the way with her multi and took the lead, the rest of them following.

"Centaurs?" Zhia shook her helmet. "They are nothing like horses or humans."

"But they have great upper-body strength."

"Your mafia planet background is showing," Zhia said. Ellen raised an eyebrow. She didn't tend to snipe like that unless she was deeply uncomfortable.

"Let's get this over with," Ellen cut in. "There's the entrance."

A dull hole like a badger's cave slumped against a boulder. She had to admit she didn't love the idea of heading in there either, but Simmons had gotten a last-minute bit of intel that some of Arakovic's colleagues had touched down on this moon. That was more of a bite than they usually got, so it was enough for her.

If only she didn't have to deal with Teredarks at the same time. Ugh.

They silently descended into the hole, Nova in the lead. At first, the ground was rough, truly like something an animal had dug out, but about twenty feet down, steps appeared. The soft running lights on their armor lit the way until they reached a heavy door.

"You're on, Adan," she said softly.

The drone wordlessly hovered forward, a light switching on, and they watched as it inspected the door. Abruptly, a bolt of energy arced out and hit one of the drone's blades, sending it careening. Traps. But the drone steadied itself and persevered.

For the briefest moment, she cut Kael out of the channel. "When governments fail to police science..." she said softly.

"Science will police itself," Zhia finished, her voice smug. Smiling.

"Damn straight, *chicas*." Nova cleared her throat. "We got this."

Ellen cut Kael back in, hoping he was none the wiser, and she kept her ears tuned, listening to the outside feed for any sounds that they'd been detected. Her sensors showed nothing on the other side of the door, but Teredarks tended to run cold and not show up well on thermal. Still, after barely two minutes, the door thudded and emitted a soft hiss.

"Open sesame," said Adan grandly.

"Thanks," she grunted.

"I'm headed up for the drone to watch the entrance. Good luck!"

The drone seemed almost cheerful as it buzzed back up and out of the hole. Ellen could not say the same for herself. Nova swung the door open, but no alarms blared. Either Adan had done his job well or the place was deserted. They headed inside.

A dark corridor led about twenty feet farther down at a slight angle. Dust was thick on the bottom, stirring with their steps, and Ellen was beginning to doubt their lead. If colleagues of Arakovic's had been on this moon, she didn't think they'd been *here*. It didn't seem like anyone had been here in quite some time. A mist clung to the floor as they got farther down, and they waded in.

The corridor suddenly flattened out and split into two tunnels. Both looked equally dark and empty.

"Shit, which way?" Zhia started.

"Are you getting any life readings on your armor? Anyone?"

Nova shook her head.

"Nada," Zhia said. "Place seems deserted now."

"My thoughts exactly." Ellen frowned. "I think this is a dead end. We're never going to find her."

"Don't say that, Commander," Nova said, clapping a gauntlet on her shoulder. "There's only so many holes to crawl down. We'll find her eventually."

Ellen sighed. "Let's split up to scout and come back. Theroki, with me this way. You two, that way. Meet back here in exactly two minutes with a report."

Kael started down the corridor without another word, and she started after him. Zhia seemed to hesitate at the pairing, but what was Ellen going to do? If Kael was loyal to any of them, it was to her. She'd brought him on this ship. Sending him off with one of them wasn't fair.

They sped up to a quiet trot, reached the end of their first corridor, and followed its turn to the right. The mist grew deeper. "What do you think this is?' she said quietly to Kael as she ordered the suit to check the atmo.

"Maybe fog condensing," he said slowly. "Maybe poison gas. My suit isn't sure."

The faint light grew brighter, but its source still wasn't in view. They jogged farther, another left turn and then down some stairs, before a window in a sidewall came into view.

A window into a door, she realized. Light poured out of it. Maybe not deserted after all. Kael reached the window first and stopped short just as her armor reported back.

"Shit—there's a sedative in the air," she murmured. "Not fog."

Kael didn't say anything, just looked openmouthed into the window. Ellen stepped closer and peered inside. Human men sat curled in balls on the floor of a stark cell, shirtless and bony.

Like they were starving.

"Jesus. There's, what, a dozen of them in there?" Ellen whispered.

"Yes. How do we get them out? This place is reeking with that gas." Kael glanced around, then stopped suddenly, looking behind them.

"Stop all movement," came a reedy voice from behind.

Ellen whirled.

One of a Teredark's many spindly arms pointed a laser pistol at the temple of a delirious young man. "Lower your helmets," its high, reedy voice ordered. "Or we'll be having crispy laser cakes for the prisoners tonight."

Elle's armor reported on the Teredark—high-quality, heavy-weight 4TC Union-standard Teredark armor, able to withstand laser and knockout pulses. Known neck and hip weak points to laser pulse. 8WFO Raven pistol, primarily a ballistic weapon actually, with one or two laser charges. Figured he'd talk up the thing. Her armor continued to search for additional munitions.

"Do you see a way out of this?" Kael whispered. "You're the genius."

"Slag off, Kael," she shot back. She opened her external comm channel to her speakers. "Let him go. This is between you and us."

The Teredark shook his head. "No. He is a prisoner. You are intruders. Lower your helmets and surrender."

Elle narrowed her eyes at him. One armor shot at his neck would be risky, but if she could pull it off fast enough... Would it take a sustained pulse? She likely didn't have time for that, nor to look up just *how* weak the neck joint was. Teredarks were notoriously good at withstanding some of her other options—the nonlethal chem attack of the Red Death, the heat ray that was the Grill setting. Bubblegum sticky foam would take too long to deploy. And they already *had* a cloud of fog around them, so making one wouldn't help anything.

Shit, it was laser, bullets, or bolts. As usual, but to a very small target this time.

"Drop your weapons." He pressed the pistol harder, tilting the young man's head at an awkward angle.

Ellen raised her arm straight out at the shoulder, multi in hand as if to drop it, and readied her gauntlet beam. When she dropped the rifle, she could maybe get off one good shot. She'd have to pray it would be enough. There was no way in hell she was lowering her helmet. Kael followed her lead, holding out his own multi as well very, very slowly.

"Do as I say or one of you is getting—" it clicked.

SONGBIRD. The word shrieked through her mind, sending her staggering backward. No no *no, not again—*

Arakovic.

When silence fell in her mind again, her right hand clutched over her ear—or really, her helmet. Stupid instincts. The other arm had dropped. She glanced wildly at Kael, who stared back with wide eyes.

"What the hell was that?" he said softly into the comm channel.

"You heard it too?"

"Yeah—what are we dealing with?"

"You don't want to know." She swallowed.

"You know. Tell me."

"Songbird was Arakovic's program. The one they—"

SHE REJECTED US.

I'm not supposed to be able to hear you anymore, she screamed back in her mind. None of us are supposed to be able to hear you.

SHE REJECTED MOTHER.

It didn't seem that the voice was even talking to her.

She eyed the Teredark. It had turned its weapon away from the boy and toward her.

AS EMPTY AS A HUSK. AS HARMLESS AS A FLY.

"I am not harmless!" she shouted into the air. Ah, hell. Only harmless people had to shout things like that.

AS INEVITABLE AS DUSK. HER TIME TO DIE.

I have *enough* poets, thank you very much. And I am not going down to one, you hear me?

TAKE HER.

But it wasn't talking to the Teredark either. The centipede-like alien kept its pistol trained on her as something *else* reached into her neck, slithered down her left arm, bent it at the elbow, and tried to hit the helmet retract.

She wrenched her right arm free, sloppily throwing the rifle between the wayward arm and her head. Some barrier, any barrier, anything.

Slowly, her arm began to bend again, trying to swivel out around the gun. She growled low in her throat, fighting to straighten her arm with every ounce of strength she could muster.

It wasn't enough.

Shit. If she was going down, she should have warned the others long ago.

"Zhia, Jen—get out," she barked into the comm.

Her voice echoed dully, and she wasn't certain if it was getting picked up into the channel.

"Hostiles and some kind of telepath here and—"

Her hand slammed down on the button. The helmet retracted, like a towel falling and leaving her naked. She held her breath, raised the rifle toward the Teredark, and lunged sideways toward Kael.

Or, she tried to. She only succeeded in slumping against the wall behind her. She managed to turn her head.

He was sliding down the wall beside her too, eyes closed but fluttering as if he was trying to open them.

Her own eyelids slid shut. All that was left was black.

———

WHEN ELLEN CAME TO, the first thing she felt was the cold metal floor against her face. When she opened her eyes, a blank metal plane stretched out before her, like in the sim chambers. Tiny blips of light slowly came to life—fighters, larger ships, cruisers. The three Enhancer destroyers and the Puritan battleship, all drifting slowly toward Hanguk. Toward home. Or what had once been home.

She would destroy them all before she'd let them take the SHR. She would—

The sound of a loud snort below her stopped her brain short. No, not below her. She wasn't in a sim. She was lying on a cold metal floor. Grumbles reached her ears now, beside her, not behind her.

Kael.

Groggily, she pushed herself up, searching for him. She wavered dizzily for a moment, and then straightened more, her arm brushing against hair. Soft hair.

His head lay on her thigh. Still out like a light. She still had some neurocleaners installed near the empty chip slot in her neck. Maybe that was helping her. She doubted Theroki sprang for such things, if they didn't care about knockout grenades.

"Kael," she whispered, bending down toward his ear. "Wake *up.*"

He snorted and grumbled again, then wrapped his arm around her calf and hugged her closer to him, nestling deeper into her leg. She almost laughed. Probably would have if it weren't for this predicament.

She glanced around. Yes. No sim chamber. No SHR. No *Audacity.* The pale shine of bluish force fields surrounded them on three sides, metal behind her. A panel of controls was the only oddity, to her left. Their armor was gone. Outside of the force fields, and about fifteen yards down the hall to her right, a human guard read at a desk. She sniffed at the air, feeling a little faint at the thought of what the hell could be in it even now, but she caught nothing but the scent of dusk and Teredark.

She tugged her leg away from Kael, but he hugged it even tighter. Romantic fool. It *was* interesting to see him like this, though. She doubted he'd appreciate looking like anything less than a fierce warrior, but right now he looked like a ten-year-old with a teddy bear.

If only his teddy weren't her *leg.* And if only it weren't falling asleep.

She poked his shoulder. Nothing. Then his kidney. Still nothing. "Hey. Theroki. Quit slacking." Nothing.

They might not know he was a Theroki, so she should shut the hell up. There wasn't exactly a label on the shitty armor, although she would have recognized it. Could they use that somehow to escape? He also seemed totally out. If she needed to check him for any identifying marks, now wouldn't be a bad time.

She ran her hands over the short, messy scruff of hair that covered his neck, stirring him slightly. Enhancers often marked their "upgraded models" with tattooed codes on the neck, sometimes under the hairline; Levereaux had one. But no sign of that on him. His hair was damp with cold sweat from the mission's exertion, but it still felt good under her hands. She glanced at his wrist, where as usual the slight nose of a snake peeked out beneath the sleeve. Reaching down, she pulled the sleeve up slowly, watching his features, until she could see more of his forearm. Yeah, gang tattoos, not that he'd suggested any differently. A crudely drawn snake curled around a blade that pointed up toward his elbow. Odd placement, like it was pointing at him rather than at his enemies.

Maybe it was.

She caught herself running a finger along the lines, feeling the wiry hair and smooth skin of his forearm. Before she could snatch her hand away, she risked turning his wrist so she could see the inside of his forearm. A more finely drawn wolf with detailed gray shading peeked out from underneath.

He stirred. She snatched her hand back, then pulled his sleeve hastily back down, then snatched her hand back again. He coughed, then his eyelids flickered.

She squirmed again. "Get *off* me, Sidassian," she barked.

With another snort, his eyes finally opened. She scowled down at him, and he met her eyes with a sudden grin.

That faded into a groan when he sat straight up, though. He slumped back against the back wall. "My head."

"I know," she said. "My leg too."

The grin returned. "Sorry."

"You don't sound sorry."

He shrugged and dug his fingers into his temples.

She scooted closer to him, as close as her leg would allow, and leaned back against the metal. Their shoulders were touching, which was nice because it was damn cold in here without the armor. Was there none of that gas in here, if there was a guard? Where had their armor gone?

Kael's breathing, relaxed a moment before, suddenly sped up. Her gaze darted to him. "What is it?"

"The oath programming is running," he said softly.

"Why?"

"I'm blocked from my objective. Hell. The force fields mean I can't act yet, but it's searching for options."

"And if it finds something?"

"I'll have to do it. Even if it's stupid. Or gets me killed."

She frowned. "And... how smart is it?"

"Not very." His jaw was clenched, teeth gritted now.

Shit, this was not good.

He pointed slowly to a door, ajar, outside the force field area. She hadn't noticed it before. "It's in there," he said softly. "Our armor."

"How do you know?"

"Locator implant. Mildly useful." He sighed deeply. "Didn't want to die a Theroki. Definitely didn't think it'd go down like *this*."

"We're not dying here."

"Maybe *you're* not." He shifted. His eyes darted around unnaturally, like something was hijacking them. Looking for options to escape? Good luck. She was fairly sure there weren't any. "Keep my mind busy. What's one thing you wanted to do before you died?"

"Want to do. We're not dying here. We'll still do it."

"Maybe you will. C'mon, what's one thing?"

She sighed. What was one thing? "Catch up with that bitch," she muttered. "Get some justice."

He snickered. "Nothing other than that?"

"Maybe. Let me think. What about you?"

"You know, of all the places I've been, I've never seen the ocean."

She snorted. "You've got to be kidding me."

"I mean, from space I've seen it. But not up close. The beach. Seems nice. I've never had time in my life for nice."

Before, she would have thought he meant he'd been ambitious. But not now. She had a sense that it wasn't that he'd chosen not to have the time, but that he'd never had the choice.

Without warning, he jumped to his feet and lunged at the force field. Colliding with it, the thing shivered waves of light in all directions, some of them into Kael, who staggered back, groaning.

He *had* to be as woozy as she was, and she wasn't surprised when he staggered back to the wall and sank down beside her again, gasping for breath.

"What are you *doing*?" she said.

"Not my idea," he groaned. "And it's going to happen again when I'm strong enough to get back up."

"Damn it." She glanced around. Repeated collisions with that thing could knock him out. It *was* a stupid damn program. She shouldn't be surprised with Theroki. And after he was out, then what? Not to mention that it'd draw the attention of the guards, wondering what the hell he was doing. What could she distract him with? Or could she somehow hold him back, or...

She still had her arm network port. And he probably had something similar, standard equipment for any cybernetic upgrades. She lowered her voice. "You got a port, don't you?"

"What?" He frowned over at her, not entirely coherent yet.

She glanced around again, checking for the guard one more time. Still at the desk. "I... think I have a plan to get us out of here," she whispered. "You got a port, right?"

He raised his eyebrows in question. She took a deep breath and hoped she wouldn't regret this. If she could get close to him, she could connect the ports and communicate without the guards hearing what they were saying. But she needed some way to distract the guards— something outrageous, and if that something proved him not a Theroki, that'd be good too. Something like Zhia would be prone to try.

Then there was a chance he could use those powers of his to get the passkey from the guard. Or switch off the force field. Or any number of things, if he wasn't trying to run headlong into an energy wall until it knocked him out. If they suspected he was a Theroki, they'd never lower the force fields casually, and they'd probably have just killed him already. Why hadn't they, unless they didn't know what he was? Sans armor, he looked rough, but no more so than any of the types commonly in an outsystem outlaw bar.

She lifted her left arm and pressed on the hidden panel release. A square of skin in the center inside of her forearm lifted, revealing a two-pronged plug. She tried to keep her face blank, although it always felt a little icky. She looked at him and raised an eyebrow.

He squeezed at his right wrist. A fold of skin slid away like a ramp retracting on a ship, revealing a similar plug, though lower on his arm. Well. That was fancy. But on hers, she could pull the cable out.

The ports were as far apart as they could possibly be, though, hers to the far left and his the far right. And he seemed to be recovering his strength. Was this worth it? Was she going to regret this?

The imprisoned boys flashed before her. She and Kael had to get out of here. Those boys needed them to, so *they* could get out of here too.

Before she could chicken out or drag her feet any longer, she rose up to her knees and looked at him, planning her attack. He looked utterly mystified. His one leg dropped from bent to straight. Hmm, yes, that was helpful. Almost as if his body knew what she was planning even if his mind didn't.

She tentatively put her hand on his other knee and pushed that leg toward the floor too, until it was straight.

This was insane. What was she thinking?

"Commander?" He frowned at her, but he didn't look alarmed. More... amused. She shifted closer to him on her knees, trying her best imitation of someone looking sultry. Frag. How did people do this? Damn her inexperience. It had been a long time.

She got both knees up against his hip and then took a deep breath.

"Are you all right?" he said softly, reaching a hand toward her arm.

"You look a bit… queasy? Take care not to vomit in ports; it's not the ideal care and feeding for them."

She flung one leg over him and straddled him, settling down on top of him. The expression on his face was priceless—shocked, and yet… delighted. Not alarmed in the slightest.

She bent closer and pressed her mouth against his with utter abandon. She prayed he'd go along. Kissing Kael Sidassian when she felt fairly certain that he would like it was a low price to pay for freeing themselves and those boys. A trifle, really. Nothing at all.

He played along, all right, and did not hesitate, his lips parting under her and his tongue searching for hers as his left hand reached up for the back of her neck. He kissed her back with astonishing hunger.

In spite of her desire for cool detachment, heat washed through her. His hands seized her hips now, pulling her harder against him. Oh, my, yes. This was not something he minded, she could feel *that* for certain. It sent her heart beating faster.

No. No. This was a distraction. A decoy. Careful strategic planning, not making out because you might die in this Teredark prison cell and by God you don't want to die a virgin. Or at all.

Distraction. Her left hand and his right hand were in close conjunction now, while the guards had a lot more to look at than what they were doing with their hands. And hopefully it'd hold him in place a little longer before the oath activated.

She broke away from the kiss for a moment and bent toward his ear, but he trailed his mouth along her neck in a wave of beautiful fire. "Distraction," she whispered, her lips brushing his ear lobe. "Okay if I connect?"

"Do it." His voice was a growl, his port-free hand sliding down her back, her hip, her thigh.

She reached down to her port and pulled out the tiny cap piece. There was a cable too, but this detachable piece was probably safer, a slower but more hidden wireless linkup. But no. Maybe they were monitoring for those transmissions. Old-school and hard to intercept was best. She pushed the detachable piece back in and pulled out the cable, thin and almost transparent, like fishing line. She hoped his affections were enough as she tucked her head against his neck and looked for the port on his arm. She needed it closer, so her body blocked their view.

She grabbed his right wrist and brought his hand against her neck, sliding her fingers playfully along the delicate inside of his forearm, catching a glimpse of that beautiful wolf again, kissing his palm. He shuddered in pleasure under her, and she found a self-satisfied smile was creeping onto her face. There—she found the port and plugged in.

She hoped she wouldn't regret this.

Kael?

Ellen. What are you doing? Have you lost it? Happy to oblige, but—

I'm trying to stop you from frying yourself on that barrier by literally sitting on you.

He laughed softly. *I can throw you off pretty easily you know.*

No, you can't. I'm your ride to Desori, and unless you do what I want right now, I won't take you.

He grinned at her, eyes crinkled with amusement. *You are a smart woman. The oath program is pausing, waiting for your instructions, ma'am.*

Thank you. And good. And also I don't want them to realize you're a Theroki. You still have some telekinesis, right?

All of it, as far as I know. Why?

I thought you might be able to lower the barrier. That's a basic keycard lock system—I'm willing to bet it's in the desk. You could potentially get us out. But only if they don't realize what you are.

You think they haven't yet? Even that crazy telepath? Which is something else we'll have to deal with.

I think they were paying attention to me. Her certainty came from the feeling that their captors would have—should have—killed him if they'd known. Just like she should have, but she was the idiot that had taken him on as a passenger instead.

Well, that's a cheery thought, thanks for that. That would have been awfully rude of you to kill me just for walking on your ship. Or, wait...

A wave of fear shot through her. She stilled her thoughts and kissed him again.

Why this again? Raging hells, you're distracting...

Therokis would have no interest in this, she pointed out quickly, keeping her thoughts carefully trained on him.

Oh. Yeah. Right. Except my damaged ass.

Neither you nor your ass seem terribly damaged at the moment. Ack. She hadn't quite intended anything that admiring to slip out. She felt more than heard his reaction, a shifting kaleidoscope of emotion from annoyance, to shame, into curiosity to... Was that hope? *And maybe it will capture the guard's attention.*

He recaptured her mouth with his, harder now, and his tongue pushed its way in and found hers, sending a skittering of goose bumps down her spine and up her arms. She didn't need words to feel the assertion of ownership, of possession, one she certainly had no intention of granting, and yet—it felt inexplicably, instinctively good. He wanted her for himself and had no intention of sharing. Which, of course, neither did she; it was just a ploy. His unconnected hand stroked her hair softly. His hips shifted beneath her, the growing pressure there sending a fresh wave of molten heat through her body.

Wow, that's... Have you done this before? he blurted, possibly unintentionally.

What, kissed someone? Of course I have. She tried not to sound indignant. *I'm that bad, huh? Knew I couldn't be a child genius at everything.*

I meant with that port connected.

Oh... no, never tried that.

This is fantastic. Kael shifted again beneath her, and her hand tightened around his of its own accord. *See?*

See what?

You like that. I can feel it like it's me *that likes it.*

Focus, Kael. This is just a distraction.

I am well and thoroughly distracted.

For the guard. *So they don't notice the port. We have to focus on getting out.*

If he was going to invade her body's senses, she had to wonder what was going through his head too. She wouldn't have this chance to peek in again. She should be gathering intelligence or something.

She reached out and found him quickly, just like she had in those days when she'd still had her chip.

His body was on fire. His mind too. But what was most surprising was the powerful tension, the immense restraint. He had not seemed at all restrained, but now she could feel it. She would have never realized the amount of effort he was putting in to simply sit there and kiss her and rest his hands against her hips and not... Oh, my. The flashes reached her now, what instincts were telling him to do, and she saw a flurry of wild union, of joyful consummation, all of it tinged with an emotion she didn't want to acknowledge or believe.

Her own body buzzed hotly in response. Holy hell, the push he fought back was startlingly strong. And here she was, inviting him up to the edge. Urges long held back for eleven years now, eleven years until Vala had stabbed her icepick of words into his skull and broken his—

A flash of a gorgeous blond woman, also straddling him, an ugly smirk on her face. Steel cable cut into his wrists behind him just as Ellen's fingers circled his wrist right now. The chair he was tied to bit into his shoulders where more cables were bound. The woman had perfect pink lips, lips that he'd adored, thought maybe he'd loved. Too perfect, clearly Enhanced to exacting specification, in spite of her Puritan claims. He should have seen it all along. She took her perfect lips and bent and kissed him on the mouth, brutally mocking in the faux sweetness of it, in spite of everything she'd done. And everything she'd taken—

Ellen reeled back, gasping and pulling away, not wanting to be associated with anyone with such cruelty in them, even in that bare glimpse. *Who the hell was that*—

His face had darkened, and he glanced at the doorway to the guard station. *We're supposed to be getting out of here, aren't we? Or were you actually looking to just dig up painful memories while we plow? Is that your idea of amusement before they kill us?*

The Puritan operative.

He nodded.

Her cheeks lit up like they were on fire. *I didn't mean to.* Remorse flooded her, and she hoped he could feel it. The real emotions were more accurate than any words. *Sorry. I got... distracted. You looked first. I was going to stay over here, but I wanted to see—what you were seeing.*

It's good to be curious. Something told her he meant more than just in this moment, but in that whole what-if-we-die here sense. *I was just self-conscious.* He recaptured her mouth again with his as he spoke into her mind, and she eased back against his chest, relaxing into his arms. It felt too good not to return to him, not to get at least one more precious taste of him.

Was that the—

—the one that got my chip, yes. I will admit, I hadn't imagined talking about her while we did this for the first time.

She wanted to say they weren't "doing" anything, but that was clearly not true. She caught on his final words, intrigued in spite of herself. *Wait, you... imagined us doing this?*

She could reach out so easily and see just what he'd imagined. But no. It was worse that way. It should be his choice to share it with her. Not something she took without asking.

Yeah. Have you?

She didn't want to answer that. This was a mistake. She didn't want him to know about the way she found herself watching him when she was trying not to, the way her thoughts so easily found their way to him, at her desk, at the gym, in the shower. No. She couldn't risk this, she couldn't risk her mission. He was a distraction, and they were supposed to be getting out of this place.

You're right. We should focus on getting out of here. The words were tinged with sadness. He growled in the back of his throat as he kissed her but seemed willing to go along, ignore her dodged question. Or perhaps he had seen the thoughts and had gotten answer enough in them.

If we can get the force field down, what do we do next? It was the only mildly focused thing she could think of to say.

We need to get the armor, he said silently to her. *It'd be a lot safer to get out with it on. And that's where my oath is forcing me to go.*

Suddenly, Ellen felt someone's stare on her back. The one that told animals when they were prey being hunted. *Damn. I think... he's watching us.*

She broke away briefly. The guard had stood up and was standing at the edge of the force field.

Maybe the weapons are with the armor, he added. *Is there anything else we can do? I mean, will we have to just fight our way out?*

I don't know, we may have to, she replied. *But also, how will we fight the telepath? If we could get that camera turned off somehow... God, he's not leaving.* She glanced back over her shoulder again, and this time the guard caught her eye.

"Hey. Hey, girl," he said slowly, in a rough accent she couldn't immediately place.

I'm no girl, she wanted to growl. She stared back instead.

"You want those Teredarks not to eat you, right?"

Her eyes darkened. "Teredarks don't eat humans."

Way to talk your way out of the cell, Kael said silently.

I'd like to see you do better.

"These ones do," said the guard. "But everybody's asleep. I might be able to let you out in exchange for..." He spread his hands and shrugged.

"What about the telepath?"

"Like I said, everybody's asleep."

Ellen eyed the guard warily as Kael's arm ran slowly down her back.

"Here, I'll show you." The guard dashed over to the desk, tapped it, and the wall lit up with a display of a sleeping woman.

Ellen made a show of squinting at the image as she spoke quickly to Kael. *Stay sitting until I signal. I'm going to unplug us. Anything we need to figure out first?*

Just when we can do this again.

She winced.

What? You like it.

I don't get to have what I like. See how distracted we are?

I don't see any problem here. Got a nice plan to escape.

Let's see if it works before we decide that.

He kissed her jaw gently even as she studied the image. *Fine, c'mon. Let's blow this ice cream stand.*

That... is my line, she thought as she unplugged them.

His thoughts cut off, that pleasant feeling of being alone inside her mind flooding back. Except it was a little less pleasant this time. She brushed the feeling aside.

She rose and approached the force field. The guard licked his lips, rubbing his hands together, stepping quickly back to the desk. He opened the first drawer. Bingo.

"Wait—where are we going to do this? And how do I know you'll set me free?"

He grinned. "You'll just have to trust me, sweetheart." But he glanced around, as if looking for an answer to her first question.

She flicked her gaze to the closet door. "How about in there?"

He fidgeted, then strode over, unlocked that door and looked inside. "That'll do, if it makes you comfortable."

"And what about that camera? I don't know about you, but I'm not crazy about being recorded," she said, forcing a smile.

The guard stared at her for a minute, then tapped the desk again. "Hey, Car—this chick in here is all hot and bothered. You seeing this?"

"Yeah." The voice was rough. Sounded like they had more observers than they'd realized.

"She wants a little bio break, if you know what I mean. Can you, uh, give us some privacy for a couple minutes?"

"What? And you're not gonna share?"

The guard gave her a greedy look. "You gonna play nice?"

She shrugged noncommittally. It was the most enthusiasm she could manage.

The guard snickered. "As if you got a choice! It's play nice or be Teredark food, girl. All right, Car, we have a deal, but you gotta turn it off first."

"What about the dude?"

"He won't be a problem," said the guard, picking up his pistol.

"Off. You got ten minutes, then I'll swing by to say hello. Have fun, buddy."

Frantic to the point of clumsiness, the guard yanked the keycard from the drawer and darted to the wall, the force field falling. Steadying and keeping the pistol carefully trained on Kael, he beckoned Ellen forward.

She took one step forward, then another, approaching the line where the force field had been. The guard stood frozen for a moment, his eyes just running up and down her like he'd won the lottery. Then he gestured with the pistol toward the closet. "Go on. Go. I'll put this back up, and we can relax. I'm sure they'll be plenty left of her for you, buddy, when we're *all* done with her."

Ellen took a step forward over the force field's line.

The pistol flipped out of the guard's hand, spinning in the air, and hit him straight in the forehead. Ellen blinked.

A dent the size of a baseball, except partially barrel shaped, had been left in his skull, the skin bruised. Face suddenly blank, the man crumpled to the floor, the pistol clattering beside him. Blood ran from his nose.

Kael cleared his throat as he stood up. "I've never shared well with others."

She couldn't help but smile at that. He was quick out of the cell and into the closet, lugging out part of her armor. He held it out to her.

"Well, thank God for that," she said, striding over. "Neither am I."

CHAPTER ELEVEN

THE FLIGHT back to the ship wasn't as hard as she'd expected. In the end, the guard had been right that most of the place had been asleep, and the only resistance they'd encountered had been the other unfortunately disappointed guard and one Teredark they'd gotten the pleasure of getting the drop on.

Getting the men—boys, really—out of their containment cell had taken a lot more prodding, since they'd been almost catatonic. But urgency had won out and gotten all but one of them moving out of there. Kael had carried the last, who still sat in her sick bay.

Ellen had held her breath every moment, just waiting for the other shoe to drop, the songbird to wake up. But their luck had held. She hadn't.

It wasn't until they'd made it back to the ship that she'd discovered it hadn't been luck. In their attempts to find her, Nova and Zhia had found a ventilation system and its control room. While it hadn't helped them locate anyone, it had shown them which parts of the station were pumped full of sedative gas and which weren't.

And how to change them.

Ultimately they'd slipped undetected back to the ship to get backup just as Kael and Ellen had arrived.

Now, everyone was recuperating in their cabins—permanent or temporarily assigned. Ellen had been waiting for Simmons for about five minutes, pacing back and forth beside the holodesk, when his picture finally flipped up on the screen.

"Glad to hear you made it back!" he said, cheerful as ever.

Her mouth didn't twitch a muscle in response. "There were boys on that moon, Simmons. Fifteen, eighteen. Boys my age. Except they're fragging zombies." She paced back and forth, and his eyes traced her as she walked, his smile fading.

"You're a little older than that now, Ellen."

"Why did they have them? Slaves? Sex trafficking? Experimental subjects? What? And what does it have to do with Arakovic?"

He pressed his lips together but said nothing for a long moment.

"There was a songbird there, Doug. A telepath. She *recognized* me."

"Recognized you?"

"Yes. That's not supposed to happen. I'm not supposed to be able to hear them anymore. But we can deal with that later. I want to know about those boys."

He sighed. "Fine. The report isn't done, but I'll tell you what I can. Conscripted. They're being conscripted. We think."

Her face went pale. That had a familiar ring to it, but from where? "By...?"

He pressed his lips together, nodding just a touch.

"Arakovic."

"Yes."

"But why? For what purpose?"

"Something to do with the telepaths. They're at every location we've gotten reports like this."

She scowled. "How many locations?"

"They're not all confirmed, and I can't be sure—"

"How many locations?" She slammed a fist onto her desk, and the image wavered.

"Thirty-three."

She caught her breath. "Jesus, Simmons. A dozen each time?"

"They seem to most often come in sets of sixteen. Maybe they weren't done with this unit yet?"

She shook her head, not sure what she was even shaking it at.

"Look, there's another of our cells in the area. You requested PTSD and trauma treatment capable, and they should have it. I'm sending them on over to pick up the kids and take them somewhere safe. I want you to get to Upsilon."

She nodded numbly, eyes distant. "Of course, Patron."

"They'll rendezvous in one hour."

She nodded again.

"I'm sorry, Ellen. I really am. But you got them out. It's a start. We'll help them, and it'll help us figure this out. This is a victory, a clue."

She met his eyes. "It doesn't feel like one."

"I know." He pressed his lips together again. "Simmons out."

The image vanished, and she stared on into the empty cabin air.

———

THE *GAUNTLET'S* airlock tube completed its coupling process, all lights flashing green, and Xi announced the officers were approaching. Ellen stood ready to receive them, Zhia and Dane at her sides. Kael hovered in the background of the cargo hold, keeping an eye on the boys standing idly in the center.

The other captain, a woman with graying blond hair tucked under a beret and sharp blue eyes, caught on the boys, then on Ellen. That familiar skeptical look flashed in her eyes, then the recognition. Great. Maybe Ellen should find out if they made makeup that made you look older.

A squad accompanied their visitor, all armed for battle. That seemed a little much.

The *Gauntlet's* captain held out her hand. "Captain Anya Tovi."

Ellen returned the handshake. "Commander Ryu. Thank you for coming to our aid, Captain Tovi. These young men are nearly catatonic. Hope you can help them."

"I hope so too." She gestured for the others to move forward. "Get them onboard, please."

Behind her, Kael was speaking softly with one of them, and Ellen turned to watch. "Hey, kid. You from Faros? The Snake Kings?"

The boy's eyes suddenly cleared. "Uh. Yeah. Yeah, I am. Almost forgot that."

"Good luck, kid. You're in good hands now."

The boy nodded, looking a little stunned. "Yeah. Thanks."

Kael strode toward her, urgency in his step. He stopped just short of her, a little on the uncomfortably close side. She could smell armor oil. "Hey, I see at least eight with gang tattoos," he said, pointing. "Maybe they're being picked up or kidnapped from gangs."

She raised her eyebrows. "Eight of twelve? Wow."

He nodded. "Can't be a coincidence."

"Thanks, Kael." She mustered a small smile for the effort he was making. He lingered a just moment too long, gaze locked with hers, before drifting back behind the group of boys as they moved toward the air lock.

The other captain gave her a hard glance. "Who's this?"

"Captain Tovi, Tridelphi Sidassian. We have a passenger on our way to Desori."

Her eyebrows rose slightly. "I hope we're maintaining proper security protocols around passengers."

She frowned at the woman. As if *that* wasn't a suspicious thing to say. Kael had moved away, but certainly wasn't out of earshot. "I am. Are you?"

"Why are you picking up passengers anyway?"

"Official program."

"Whose?"

"Simmons." If she was so keen on security, this wasn't the place for these questions. "All approved and on his orders."

"Hmm. Simmons." Tovi's eyes flicked disapprovingly back and forth from Ellen, to Kael, to the boys.

Ellen only hardened her scowl in response. Simmons as their

patron was their entire chain of command. If Tovi didn't like it, she could eat it, for all her disapproval mattered.

"May we speak alone, please, Commander?" said the older woman.

Ellen sighed. "Of course."

She led Tovi to the makeshift gym—the nearest room with a door that would shut—and tried not to eye the spot where Nova and Kael had fought. "Do you need me to mute this box, Captain? This isn't soundproofed."

Tovi answered only with a long scowl. "Are you in a relationship with that man?"

"Excuse me?" Her eyes widened, feeling her whole body go suddenly tense.

"That young man was eying you up and down. You're a captain *and* a cell leader. May I remind you of your duty to your crew and their lives?"

"You do *not* need to remind me of that."

"It certainly looked like you needed a reminder."

"That young man is a Theroki. You're imagining things."

"*Why* would you accept a Theroki as a passenger? That's madness."

"Theroki can be in trouble too."

"No, they're not."

"He's a person like any of us."

"They're edited. And how is it that a Theroki is eying you like a piece of meat anyway?"

"I think you're imagining things, Captain. But he is struggling to leave them and broke part of his chip programming in an attempt to escape."

She gave a soft gasp. "By God. He could go nuclear and kill you all."

Ellen gritted her teeth. "Thank you for your opinion, Captain, but it was not needed or requested. Our medical personnel have carefully checked him out and don't agree with you. Even if he did have... an issue, we're prepared for that eventuality."

Tovi pursed her lips and folded her arms across her chest, clearly dubious. "How do you even know if he can ever be normal again?"

"That doesn't influence my mission objectives. We're prepared to handle anything he can throw at us."

"I bet you are."

"Excuse me? What is that supposed to mean?"

"Deny it all you want, but I think you're also quite prepared to fall into bed with him. Fraternization is extremely dangerous for your entire crew. If I may remind you."

"We are not in a relationship. But if we *were*, we keep a mostly military ship around here, as I'm sure you do as well. And a passenger is not in my chain of command. May I remind *you*."

"Look, I'm just looking out for you. And your team. Maybe you don't see it yet, but that man is very interested in you."

Ellen said nothing, just gritted her teeth harder. Her jaw was beginning to ache.

"I've followed your career. You're so young." Tovi held a hand up, almost as if she would stroke Ellen's cheek.

She jerked her head away from the woman's grasp. Who the hell did this Tovi think she was?

"I know you're very experienced militarily. But men are complicated." Tovi smiled, almost motherly. "All that military training hasn't left much time for the boys, has it?"

Teeth still gritted, Ellen cheeks flushed hot. Blushing. Oh, great. She did *not* want to blush in front of this bitch.

"Listen," Tovi continued gently. "You're just the right age for them. They can look themselves in the eye and be all legal-like. But they pretend you're a school girl when the lights go off."

Rage boiled up, although she couldn't help but remember his comments about Josana and her legality not so long ago. No, that was nonsense. Everything this woman as saying was nonsense. "Not every man is a liar or a pedophile," Ellen growled.

Tovi pursed her lips. "When the cute little uniforms come out, don't come crying to me."

"Captain Tovi, that is quite enough. I handled ten thousand enemy ships at Saeloun Hanguk," she said, nearly shaking with anger now. "I think I can handle myself with one man."

"Ah, but one man who says he loves you—"

"He's never said that, and he's not going to." If only. She doubted his attraction to her ran that deep.

"—is a worse adversary than a million that want to kill you. At least you know for sure where the latter stand, and what they will do."

"No enemy is predictable. Your analogy is ridiculous. And beyond naive." Not to mention showing a clear lack of command skill.

Tovi leaned forward, undeterred, and stabbed a finger at her. "Don't let passion blind you. That boy is not good."

"Why?" she demanded. "Why is he not good?"

"Didn't you see how fast he knew those gang tattoos? He's from the dirt, and he'll go back to the dirt. Stay away from the likes of him, Ellen."

Ellen scowled now. "I did *not* give you permission to call me Ellen. And not every man is what you say they are. There are good men in the world. Lots of them. I've even met a couple."

And she was pretty sure Kael was one of them. But even if he wasn't, she would find one. Eventually. If she lived to be twenty-five.

"That just shows how young you are," Tovi said gently, voice dripping with condescension.

"That's it," Ellen snapped. It hit her now—*this* from the woman she was handing over her refugees to? "You are *not* taking those boys."

Ellen turned on her heel and stormed out of the gym, the door sliding politely out of her way. Xi's handiwork? For once, she didn't resent the help.

The last of the boys was heading into the airlock, arm in the grip of one of the *Gauntlet's* soldiers. "Stop. Bring them back on," she ordered.

"Belay that order!"

Ellen ignored her. "I refuse to relinquish these refugees and will bring them back on by force if necessary."

"How dare you!" came Tovi's voice from behind her. "I've been sent on this mission and—"

"And you're not completing it," Ellen said sternly.

The soldiers froze. The boys, seemingly roused a little by the shouting, scampered back toward her end of the tube of their own accord.

Ellen hastily waved them back, not stopping her progress toward the hatch. "Zhia—I want them in the mess and safe. Nova and Jenny—can you escort our colleagues out, please?"

Captain Tovi stormed after her, eyes alight with rage. "You can't do this. I outrank you, *Commander*." She looked at Zhia and barked, "Stop immediately. Our orders are they're mine."

Zhia slowed, but Ellen wasn't fooled. Zhia didn't slow because she was going to comply, but because she was gauging the woman. There was something odd, something dark in the woman's voice that only hardened Ellen's resolve.

Ellen folded her arms. "We're taking them somewhere safe. From what you've said, you clearly can't be trusted to keep those boys safe or find them somewhere where they can recover. You all but called them *dirt*. Because they've been conscripted once already, and fell even worse victim a second time?"

"*Conscripted*? Please. You are letting your judgment be swayed by—"

"I am not. These victims are my responsibility to shelter safely to appropriate care."

"Victims? They are not 'victims,' they are—"

"*Audacity* specifically requested help with psychological trauma victims, likely PTSD. I deem you clearly unqualified to meet that need. Do you agree with my assessment, Dr. Taylor?"

"I concur, Commander. Furthermore, Captain Tovi's prejudice toward young men with tattoos has been noted for future reference in her file."

"Her file?" Kael muttered behind her.

"How *dare* you. And you're exposing our organization to not just that Theroki, but *them* too."

"I'm taking them off your hands. What do you want them for, cannon fodder? Get. Out." Ellen jammed her finger at the airlock, inches from Tovi's face.

"Units three and four, engage *Audacity* command," the woman said coldly. "Take her and her people into custody."

Kael stepped up beside Ellen, drawing his weapon, a wave of

energy warping the air as he did so in warning and blowing wisps of Tovi's hair back for a moment. To her far left, Dane popped the safety on his multi. Nova and Jenny did the same on the floor above, stalking slowly down the ladders together. A flurry of clicks revealed their stance on 'being taken into custody.'

Ellen glared coldly at the *Gauntlet* men and women uncertainly pointing their weapons at her and her crew. There were more of them, but each one looked either terrified or bleak. Not at all certain of following orders.

"You want to kill me?" she whispered. She stepped toward them. "You want to kill me?" she shouted now. "Go ahead. Be my guest. But you're getting those boys over my dead body." She raised the helmet and swung her multi forward off her shoulder.

Stun, or no? Maybe they deserved some scratches and burns in that armor for the trouble.

The *Gauntlet* soldiers shifted nervously, not advancing or retreating.

"I will tell you this," she shouted over the armor speakers. "I have fought worse foes than you. I have crushed nations under my heel, and I will not be brought low by the likes of *you* or your foolish captain." She jabbed a finger at the units, ignoring Tovi.

Ellen stepped forward then, and even Captain Tovi backed away. Her units scampered several feet into the air lock.

"Just so you know who you're firing on, I designed the Yogin planetary grid. I was the architect of the Saeloun Hanguk defense. And I won that damn war for the Union. That's right. You know who I am."

She paused, meeting each of their eyes in turn, waiting for a response, for doubt.

"So, you think you can shoot me? Go ahead and fucking try."

She popped the safety and hit the high-output release, steam shooting off the rifle as it prepared for high-intensity cooling. Laser, it was.

"All right, let's dance. Otherwise, get the fuck off my ship."

"I didn't know we had her on our side," someone whispered.

"She's not!" barked Tovi. "I said engage!"

The silence stretched on, the soldiers looking around nervously, meeting each others' eyes. Gauging.

Finally their leader's shoulders slumped slightly.

Good thing her helmet hid her smirk. Victory. She could smell it in that shoulder slump.

"Ma'am. This folks are clearly friendlies. We have no justification. I respect you, but I don't wanna die here. Or get court-martialed. Do you, Gonzales?"

"No, sir."

"No, I didn't think so."

"You're going to regret this," Tovi snapped.

"I'm requesting a transfer," the soldier replied.

"Me too," said Gonzales.

They backed off quickly, the last releasing his refugee with a gentle shove back toward the *Audacity*.

Nova and Jenny advanced anyway, multirifles at the ready. Dane swept in from his side, and following his lead, Kael moved out in the same direction, forming a rough semicircle of cover behind her. The other ships' rifles were trained on her, eyes dark, but they all retreated to their side of the air lock.

Tovi walked to the airlock but paused briefly and faced Ellen. "You haven't heard the last of this," she said coldly.

Ellen only tightened her grip on her rifle. "For now, I have."

Tovi spun and walked, shoulders back and head high, down the air lock to her ship.

Ellen let out a breath she hadn't realized she was holding. "Xi and Adan, close up that air lock and disengage. Find me a space station between here and Upsilon, pronto. Zhia, we got everyone?"

"Roger—we do."

"Good. I want us out of here in fifteen."

Not meeting any of their eyes, she dashed up the ladder and toward the bridge. She had to comm Simmons and get them the hell out of here.

———

WITH A HASTY REPORT issued to Simmons, Ellen sank to a seat on her bunk and shut her eyes. Her head was heavy, aching, like she'd been knocked one too many times. Except all today's knocks were verbal, not physical. She pressed cool palms against her eyelids.

Tovi's words still echoed in her mind—and the ridiculous indignity, the rage. What was wrong with that woman, to come on someone else's ship and start—

Her door chime rang. She waved lazily, and Xi opened the door. Kael stuck his head in.

"Have a minute, Commander?"

She nodded. "I'll pass out soon, but yeah. I've got a minute."

He strode inside, and the hatch shut behind him. She sat quietly, not meeting his gaze, not sure which of Tovi's words were stuck in her craw and which were just annoying her.

The fact that the woman had sensed something between her and Kael… that threw Ellen off completely.

He leaned against the side of her desk. "You were amazing out there," he said softly. "You really told them off. That was brilliant to watch."

She snorted. "Yeah. Name-dropping. I've murdered thousands, fear me! Real brilliant."

"It worked, didn't it?"

"I hate throwing out my past like that."

"But it *worked*. And it wasn't just that. You intimidated the shit out of them. And you didn't have to do any of it."

"Yes, I did."

"Those boys were officially not your problem anymore. Now where are we going to take them?"

"We?" He wasn't part of their "we" but damn if she didn't like the sound of that. "We'll figure it out. I couldn't let them get hurt again. I had to do something."

"You did, yeah, but a lot of people wouldn't fight the inertia."

"What would you do, Kael?"

"I don't know. But I'd like to be more like you next time I face a choice like that." He gave her a small smile that chipped into the fortifications around her heart.

"Well, I'm not so great."

"I think you are."

Her heart pounded, her stomach twisting in knots. All that distraction had been a mistake. Surely she could have figured something else out. Now she was *terrified*.

What happened next?

"You didn't have to care about those boys. What set you off?"

She stood and walked toward the small piece of the wall that looked out into space, hesitating. "She told me young men who were once in gangs are no better than dirt, came from dirt, and will always be dirt."

He sucked in a breath. "Oh. She might be right about—"

"No. She's not."

He shrugged but said nothing.

"She had a bunch of other ridiculousness too. Which I need to report to Simmons pronto, by the way."

"Can it wait a minute longer?" His voice was soft and coming closer.

She turned. He stood a few feet away, his expression soft too.

"You were defending me too. Not just them."

She looked down at her boots. "Where we are born is not who we are."

He snorted. "This is why I like you. You should tell Josana that." When she looked up, he was grinning.

"She wouldn't listen."

"I expect you're right."

She said nothing for a moment.

"Look—about what happened back there on the moon," he started. "That was... amazing. But how are you feeling about it?"

Her blood pounded in her ears.

"You seemed conflicted. But not *that* conflicted."

She scowled at her boots again. "That's probably a fair assessment.

I wouldn't have tried it if it weren't for the situation we were in. Dire measures were called for."

He sucked in a breath.

"Can we just forget about it?"

"Do you really think you can?"

"Sure." A lie that sounded so confident.

"I don't think I can."

She winced. "Look, it was just a distraction to lower the force field. Let's just pretend it never happened."

The injured look on his face sent a stab of pain into her chest. "Is that really what you want?"

"I didn't—I mean, we can't. I can't."

He took a step forward. "Kiss me again."

"No." She squirmed. "I don't want to."

To his credit, he didn't budge. "I don't believe you."

"I didn't want to in the first place."

"Cut the crap."

"It's not crap, Kael." She turned her back and frowned out into the stars.

"You can't plug yourself in and then lie like that."

"I'm not lying."

"Bullshit. I know what I felt. I know what *you* felt too."

She scowled harder. "Maybe you just saw what you wanted to see." His breath caught again, and she immediately regretted the words. He was right, that wasn't the truth. How could she try to turn it around on him? Hell. She ran a hand over her face, struggling to find a way out of this that didn't involve her confessing how much she really *did* want him. Because she couldn't. He'd be gone to Desori, and even if that weren't the case… it didn't matter.

"Is that what you missed with your chip? Being able to lie?" he said, voice smoky but hurt too.

She whirled to face him, anger replacing the regret. "The hell with you, Sidassian. You don't know me. You don't know anything about me."

"I sure as hell do," he shot back.

She gritted her teeth, feeling the truth of the words down to her bones. Had anyone in her life known her as well? And yet—and yet— "You don't get to claim that from spending five minutes in my head."

"That has *nothing* to do with why I said that. I know your past, and I know you hate talking about it. And how much it hurt you. And you told me about it anyway. I know how you look at me, damn it. I know how hard you're pushing yourself to do the right thing for people who don't even know you exist. I know you care more about this crew than all my previous commanders combined."

She took a step back and bumped into the cold window, unsure of how to respond.

"C'mon, you're going to lie to my face about this, Ellen?"

"It was just a ruse. A trick. To save our damn lives." The words sounded hollow even to her.

"Well, it was *not* a ruse for me."

Her breath caught, her eyes widening. He wanted her. He wanted her in spite of everything, in spite of her lying to his face, in spite of— but what did he want? Was it really love, or just sex, like Tovi had suggested? Did Ellen really know for sure? How could you *ever* really know for sure? She squeezed her eyes shut. It didn't matter. They were doomed—she by her past, by her job, he by a mission that would tear them apart in a few days.

"Forget. It. Sidassian." She forced out the words through gritted teeth.

"I. Can't."

She couldn't say anything to that. They sat in silence, only the sound of his breath in her ears.

"Is this about what that captain said to you?" he said softly.

"No." Mostly. She thought. Her tone still sounded hollow. Kael was *far* from dirt, and she didn't believe any of that dreck for a second. But she *was* young and inexperienced at this. It hurt to hear—and to admit now—but it was true. Tovi had deftly found that wound and prodded it. Poured on some salt.

Did Ellen really know the difference between someone who cared and someone who just wanted in her pants? Or worse, had some ulterior motive? She wasn't even *trying* to puzzle through that anymore. She already trusted him more than was rational. Certainly, he did care for her to some degree, but his thoughts in her head had been primarily sexual. Deliciously, vibrantly so, and her body warmed even at the thought. She hated herself for it.

Hadn't Paul showed her how naturally terrible she was at this? She couldn't afford another screwup like that again.

"Look, this command is the most important thing I've ever done," she whispered.

"Even more than SHR?" His voice was still soft, almost a whisper, and astonishingly free of anger.

"Way more than that. I was eight. Doing what I was told. Solving puzzles. Winning games. This is my choice, my own mission. My responsibility for all these people. Risking this command over a casual fling would be irresponsible. Moronic. I won't do it. I can't."

"Why are you risking anything? It doesn't have to be any of that." He shook his head.

"What?" She looked up and made the mistake of meeting his eyes.

"It doesn't have to be casual. Or a fling. Did I *ever* say that?"

"Yeah, right. What about your mission? Even if you go renegade, you have to complete that one and get out again. If that's even possible. They'll fix your chip, and you'll forget about me."

"I could never do that." He leaned closer.

She tore her gaze from his and squirmed, frowning at the emotion in his voice.

"I didn't plan on this, but I don't want to walk away from it. From *you*. I'll find a way out, I promise."

God, the sweetness in his voice. It was heavenly and torturous at the same time. Maybe... maybe he did care for more than just her pants. But it didn't matter—it would cloud her judgment. It had already clouded her judgment. "Don't leave for me," she said as coldly as she could muster. "I told you. A ruse. *Forget it.*"

"I'm completing this mission, and I'm getting out of there. No matter what."

She couldn't respond to that or meet his eyes for a long moment.

Her throat had tightened up, emotion clenching with its unique death grip. She coughed, forcing her way through it. "We're comets on different trajectories, Kael."

"And now you're just making excuses." He reeled back from her, throwing up his arms, exasperated.

"What are you talking about? Why would I do that?"

"So you don't have to face what you *really* want."

She glared at him, but no clever retort came. "So what if I am?" She folded her arms across her chest.

"You really *are* brilliant at elaborate defense plans. You've got a whole multilayered web of lies to keep yourself alone and distant from everyone around you."

"Go to hell."

"And you know—I was so sure this would work out. That I didn't need the damn chip. You were starting to convince me. I forgot how *great* this feels."

She grimaced, almost feeling real physical pain at those words. "Don't, Kael. Don't fix it, and don't hold it over my head. Just don't."

"Why shouldn't I?" He stopped, running his hand down his face in exhaustion. Then he slammed the wall with his palm in frustration. "*Why* are you lying about this? I can't understand it."

"You're a *distraction*," she shot at him. "Sex and command don't mix. I cross this line, I'm going to get someone killed."

"This isn't about just—" He stopped for some reason, switching tactics. "Did I distract you on any of our missions? On Elpi? On the Teredark moon?"

"No," she growled, a little bitterly.

"Did my being there lead to any loss of life?"

"No."

"You're damn right, it didn't. I know how you feel about me, even if you won't admit it. I don't see how acting on it would change anything. You'll still feel this way tomorrow."

"No, I won't," she lied through her teeth. "You can't read my mind, damn it."

"Why can't you see me as an asset and not a distraction?" The hurt in his voice sent another pain into her chest.

Hell.

"Why can't you take no for an answer?" she shot back, not knowing what else to say. He *was* an asset. She still couldn't afford him drawing her attention, her potential favoritism. People's lives were on the line, damn it. The glimmer of the *Mirror's Light* against the star flashed through her mind again.

"You know what's distracting? Someone throwing themselves at you and then lying about their motives afterward. What the frag, Ellen."

"I should never have brought you onboard," she hissed. And then before she could either punch him in the neck or break down in tears, he turned, slammed the hatch control, and stormed out.

———

KAEL STRODE BACK to his cabin, thankfully not encountering anyone on the way. Or maybe this would have been a good time to run into Josana. He was mad enough, he could probably scare the shit out of her.

He waved the door shut angrily, then felt a little guilty that the AI might think the emotion was directed at her. By the seven suns, he was losing it. Worrying about an AI's feelings and getting all caught up in one little kiss.

Okay, not just one, but a *lot* of them—and they'd been beyond perfect.

He ordered his armor off and slumped down onto his bed.

She probably wanted someone clean-cut. Straitlaced. Somebody with medals and a career. The only medals he had or would ever get were the scars in his armor and in his skin. Nobody admired those.

What he was made of was as clear as the tattoos on his arms. At least, to someone like her it was. Maybe she'd defended him. And those prisoners, in the face of that snotty captain. But deep down, she knew that bitch was right. Even if Kael wasn't exactly dirt, Ryu still deserved better.

This had all been hopeless anyway. Why the hell was he disappointed? Stupid stupid stupid.

As soon as he could get his hands on another damn chip, he would end all this. She couldn't hurt him anymore if he didn't care that women existed. Right? He *should* talk to Dremer about looking at the damn thing.

He lay staring out at the void for a long time, his head propped on his hands, thinking. It had seemed so obvious that this ship would be his next step, assuming he survived this last mission. What better place to go renegade? What weirder place for a Theroki to end up? No set address, and he could at least put his gun beside someone who was trying to do some good in the world. He hadn't hoped for even that much.

To realize it might not be the salvation he'd hoped for, to turn from it now... That left him feeling even more desolate. Maybe he could stay even if she didn't want him. She seemed professional enough to allow that, if he made his case well. But would it be torture? Maybe not if he fixed the chip. Perhaps his feelings for her would go away. Or at least lessen. He shook his head. Wishful thinking. His attachment to her had grown beyond the pieces of him the chip toyed with, hadn't it. His feelings had sunk deeper into something the chip would not be able to touch. At the very least, she had his loyalty. More than that.

Even if he wanted to, the *Audacity* and its private donors might not have him, though. The ship had a few men, but the whole lacking-a-vagina thing did put him at a disadvantage on half their missions. He wondered if he got a new suit of armor that completely hid him—as if he could afford that—maybe they'd make an exception. Maybe what the women didn't know wouldn't hurt them?

He doubted that. Ellen was nothing if not by the book. Well, most of the time anyway. She was honest. Well, except perhaps with the enemy. And about her feelings about kissing him. Also, he doubted the moves she'd pulled on him, the moves that had left him so hungry for her, were in any military rulebook.

But wasn't it "mostly" military, after all? When it came down to it, Ellen was doing whatever she wanted. And that wasn't him.

———

A SHIP UNCLOAKED outside the window, heading straight for them. Kael jumped from where he sat lounging in his cabin, avoiding Ellen. But then he leaned closer, narrowing his eyes. The green of the grab beam was already flashing, seizing the *Audacity* with a rough lurch.

The all-too-familiar black hull protruded savagely with barbs and robotic arms and cannons and just plain old debris no one had removed that had lodged in some barbed-wire-like fortification. Little of it served any functional purpose, but its function was largely psychological, a marker of the ferocity of its inhabitants.

Kael scrambled to the drawer of the desk and grabbed the armor comm unit he'd left charging there. "Theroki ship, this is Tridelphi Three Kael Sidassian. Do you read?"

"Acknowledged, Three. This is Tridelphi One Preparte aboard the *Blothaki*. What are you doing on that unmarked ship?"

"I'm on special assignment from Enhancer High Command. I've commissioned this vessel for my mission." He hadn't actually admitted this aloud onboard the ship just yet, but between Ellen and Isa, it was probably not much of a secret anymore. He considered a request for the *Blothaki* not to interfere, but these likely weren't grunts he was talking to, like those he'd had to damn near shoot off Ellen. They *should* know this was an acceptable practice, even recommended, and that their response should be to piss off and leave him alone.

Did he even want that anymore? If he wanted away from Ellen, here was his ticket out.

"Acknowledged," the *Blothaki* said. "The high adjutant here would like you to know that he praises your discretion."

Kael heaved a sigh of relief. Someone competent. Finally.

"We're reading some errors coming back from your equipment, Three. Have you sustained damage?"

"Yes, we were ambushed at the EHC evac. Knockout grenade. I

think it sent something wonky. Six other *thero* were there, but I was concerned they'd betrayed our location and facilitated the ambush." By calling them *thero*, he was implying they should be disgraced—or at least considered guilty until proven innocent. He doubted the knockout grenade could do that kind of damage, but it was the best excuse he had. Hopefully they would buy it. He sure as *hell* wasn't telling them the truth. Haltingly, he realized they would have a store of backup chips. And that he *ought* to be seeking one. "Could you send over a replacement?"

Please say no, please say no, please—

"Of course, Three. Anything else you might need? The high adjutant prefers to support a client as loyal and wealthy as EHC as effectively as possible." That last bit was *supposed* to suggest that of course the adjutant held no specific political preferences one way or the other. But Kael found that often such claims were more likely an indicator that there *was* an opinion on the matter, however silently held. He'd gotten lucky that this HA was an Enhancer supporter.

He tried to think. "A couple energy banks and rations would be appreciated, but I'm adequately prepared for this mission, sir."

"Acknowledged. We'll release the ship and send over a capsule. Can you confirm they can receive it?"

"Thank you, *Blothaki.* I'll hail you back if they can't receive it."

The comm channel closed. He watched as the grab beam light flickered off, and the Theroki ship turned to put its belly alongside the *Audacity,* instead of pointing its main frontal guns at her.

Barely a moment later, Ellen's voice came over the comm, sounding mildly annoyed. "Do you have something to do with this, Kael?"

He smiled quietly in spite of it all. Still calling him Kael? Still speaking to him after what had just gone down? He'd called her a liar and a coward too. Maybe she was, but she couldn't like hearing it.

"Stop saving our asses, Theroki," said Adan. "I'll never get my combat patch this way."

"You don't need to start on it on *that* ship, Adan," he said mildly.

"We don't give out patches anyway. What do you think this is, a real military outfit? And what is it doing?" Ellen demanded. "Don't cool your guns yet, pilot."

"It'll be moving along shortly," Kael said.

"Damn you're good at scaring ships away," came Fern's voice, laughing. "Like a dead body tied to the hull."

Adan choked on something and spluttered, "What?"

"You know, like in the old pirate stories? Never mind."

"Glad to know I'm as useful to you as a dead body," Kael muttered. They all quieted. Hmm. That had come out more bitterly than he'd intended. He shouldn't be taking out his frustration on them. "I have this crazy feeling they have a package for me. Can you accept canisters, or do I have to go over there?"

"I can catch it," Adan said quickly, sounding excited again.

"See, entertainment for you after all," said Kael.

"We'll let you know when it's onboard," Ellen said, command voice as brisk and steely as ever. "Bridge out."

He turned away from the sight of the ship and all he'd wanted to escape from. He sank into his bunk and tucked his hands behind his head, thinking. Ask and ye shall receive, eh? Hadn't he been thinking that if he could just put in a fully functioning chip, he could stop feeling all this ache?

Was that really what he wanted? No. A new chip, and he could reject Ellen the same way she'd rejected him. He couldn't reject her because of some flaw he'd found. He hadn't really found any. None that mattered anyway. Except maybe the lies and paralyzing fear and denial that kept them apart. But... it might not be lies or fear or denial. She might truly not care, even if she had briefly been amused by him.

No, if he could get the chip, he could simply make himself indifferent. Just like her. Or like she claimed. The plan was brutal in its efficiency.

He sighed. It was probably better this way. Now, he wouldn't walk into EHC on Desori spewing errors and setting off suspicion. Maybe he could keep the altered chip, and after Desori, he could switch them back.

But he didn't like it. The chip might affect his obedience, and maybe he'd head back to Theroki HQ instead of sneaking off like he planned to now. Could he have done anything to the chip without Vala to facilitate things? Did he really even care about going renegade at this point? If Ellen didn't want him... he didn't want anyone else.

HQ wasn't the worst place in the galaxy, but he *had* hoped to go after something more. Which was better, which was worse? Which was the real him?

Did it matter anymore?

CHAPTER TWELVE

BRI HANDED her the nondescript cylinder from the container port. "Bio scans, contaminant scans—all clear."

"Thanks." Ellen took it and stared at the ordinary black can that had been floated from the Theroki ship. She hoped to God this wasn't what she thought it was.

But just in case, she'd take it to him herself.

It wasn't far from engineering to the passenger cabin, and she took the ladder rungs two at a time. Cabin 6A. Yep.

She hesitated only briefly outside the door, then gritted her teeth. You made this mess, you have to deal with it.

She hit his door chime, and the hatch slid open. Stepping inside, she held out the container, one eyebrow raised. "Your package, sir."

He rose and strode toward her, taking it. "Commanders running mail-room duty now? Or did you just want to know what this is?"

"I might be a bit curious." She shifted further inside and let the hatch shut behind her. "Is it what I think it is?"

He twisted open the canister and took out a thin black metal sheath and five laser banks. "What do you care?"

She folded her arms across her chest and jutted out her chin.

"What? You're gonna stand here and look at me like that but not say anything?"

That was, in fact, exactly what she did. She was all out of clever remarks for today.

"Look, you made yourself perfectly clear. Get out of here, Ellen." He shook his head, eyes trained on the sheath.

"Don't order me around. This is my ship."

"This is my cabin."

She let out a disgusted sigh. "C'mon. Don't do it."

His eyes said he knew she wasn't talking about ordering her around. "Why," he said flatly.

"You know why."

"No, I don't. So you can keep tormenting me? No, thanks."

"I'm not trying to torment you."

"But you are. I can't think straight. Why are you *here*, Ellen?"

"Because you deserve to be *yourself*. The real you. Not altered."

"Why? As you so eloquently pointed out, I'm a distraction to you. A liability to everyone. I should leave it out? So I can get *you* killed too? No, thanks."

He threw the sheath on the desk and turned away, stalking toward the window.

His words seemed to echo in her mind, a cold seeping into her bones. "What do you mean 'too'?" she said slowly.

"Just leave me alone."

Something she'd said had hurt him more deeply than she'd realized. Something about him being a distraction? A risk? She took a step toward him. "Tell me."

"No. Comets on different trajectories, remember?"

"I thought you said I was full of crap."

"You are full of crap, but I didn't say that exactly."

She snorted. She wasn't getting out of this without an apology, was she? But how? What would she even say? She didn't *want* to get out of this, but she also hadn't wanted to hurt him. She still couldn't do anything differently. Nothing had changed—not really. Why *did* she want him to leave the damaged chip in?

Did some part of her really want him to keep wanting her, even if she never would do more than shun him? A deeper chill ran through her at the thought and how it did sound a little appealing.

No, no way—she couldn't be that selfish. She had to tell him he could do whatever he wanted. His chip was his choice to control. She opened her mouth.

No words came out.

Tell him, she thought. Tell him it's fine, whatever he does. Let him go and replace the chip and this will all be over. Still, she couldn't move her jaw.

Or, a tiny voice in the back of her mind said, you could stop being such a scared little coward. What are you going to do, be alone all your days? Do mission after mission until you finally get killed? You know being afraid of making mistakes doesn't keep you from making them. That perfection is impossible. That him being here or not might not change anything. What if you don't get killed but you're too damn creaky and wounded to command or fly the galaxy anymore? What then? How many years of being alone will be too many? And if that day comes, will you ever find someone as good as the man right in front of you?

What are you so afraid of?

I'm afraid of another *Mirror's Light*, damn it. Of letting all of them down or making the wrong decision because I'm too focused on him. Kael, unlike Paul, was a good soldier, though. Wasn't he? Did she even trust her judgment anymore, when things were clouded with emotion?

Emotion was a fragging traitor.

"Unless you have something to say, I'd appreciate it if you'd just leave," he said coldly.

Scowling, she forced herself to take a step back. He seemed to have relaxed as he stared off into the stars, hands clasped behind his back. She stood for a moment, trying to engrave the image in her memory, admiring the way the light from the nearby moon played across his form. A bit of wolf's fur peeked out from beneath his black sleeve, teasing her.

It would be so easy to close the distance between them, run her hands over his shoulders, press a kiss against his back. She could walk up to the edge, drop the vise grip of control. Let life take her where it would. It would be so easy to just let him kiss her. Perhaps it was destiny that brought them together. Fate. The conniving of the stars. Or at the very least, Simmons. It would be so easy to—

No. She forced herself to turn, palm the hatch, and trudge out.

———

KAEL WAS IRRITABLY HUNTING in the chill chest for something other than ration bars to eat when Xi's voice came over the comm. "Kael, Isa has entered your cabin."

He swore. "Again?"

"I'm afraid so."

"What is she doing?" He grabbed a shiny green apple, a studded orange zeefruit, a handful of instant coffee packets, and a piece of baklava made by the ever-missing Amaya before he headed out of the kitchen. If he ever got to actually meet the woman, he'd have to complement her on her cooking. But the chances of that were growing slimmer by the moment.

"Isa appears to be... talking to the wall? This is very atypical behavior."

He raised his eyebrows as he scarfed down the baklava and climbed the ladder one-handed back up to the main floor. Amazing how familiar the ship felt after such a short time.

He palmed open the hatch, and sure enough, there she was, sitting on the floor.

"Isa—what the frag are you doing? You can't—" Girl was going to get herself killed.

"You won't kill me. Not yet. And I'm not interfering, I'm helping." Her expression was flat and serious.

"What?"

"She's lonely. Loneliness isn't good for a baby."

Eyes wide, Kael slammed the hatch control shut. He didn't care how it looked, he couldn't have people overhearing that. "What are you talking about? And Xi, have you informed her mother this time?"

"Of course, Kael. But she is occupied in a serious maintenance procedure that won't be complete for approximately thirteen minutes, forty-five seconds."

He sighed.

"There's no need to worry. I'm simply entertaining her." Isa gazed blankly at him, no expression readable in her eyes.

"Talk some sense, Isa. Now."

"There was a voice. A man's voice?" Isa looked up, like she was remembering something. Or maybe talking to the capsule? "She misses the voice. The swaying, the rocking is less now too. It's too quiet, too peaceful. Like the dead. But she's not dead. Not yet."

He simply stared at her. Was she referring to Li's voice? His pulse was pounding, and he braced himself for the oath program to kick in.

Nothing happened. Huh. Maybe the program agreed she wasn't interfering.

Isa shrugged. "She has no mother. How would you—"

Oh, he knew what that was like. All too well. He winced as the girl stopped short. Right. Listening to everything.

"Sorry. I didn't realize you had grown up without parents. But you were still birthed traditionally, most likely. Babies are meant to be carried, rocked, spoken to."

"It's not a baby yet."

She rolled her eyes. "Semantics."

He stared. What the hell was he supposed to do with *this*?

"You don't want my help?"

"I don't want to end up having to kill you!"

"I wouldn't like that either." She looked back at the wall, not seeming terribly afraid of the notion. "Oh, I have ways of defending myself."

He sighed again. He didn't doubt that.

"Is it... really lonely?" He joined her on the floor, sitting cross-legged. He opened the cabinet and took the canister out gingerly. She obviously already knew where it was anyway.

"She," Isa corrected. "And yes. In a manner of speaking. It is new to me to experience human consciousness at such an early stage."

He tried not to think too deeply on that. Where were his thoughts of Commander Ryu when he needed them?

Isa blushed. But then he remembered Ellen's suggestion that that might be exactly what Isa was curious about. Perhaps that would not help him gain any privacy.

"Listen," she said quickly. "I'm not trying to interfere. You don't need to feel threatened. Like the commander said, I keep my secrets."

He scowled. "And I should just take your word for that?"

"She just needs a little company. You could try speaking to her too."

His first reaction was no way, but then again, if it kept Isa to herself, perhaps it was his duty. "Will she know what I'm saying?"

"No. It's not words she wants. Just sounds. Company."

"All right, all right. I'll try it. And you can keep her company for a few minutes. But tomorrow—enough for today. Okay? And *no* probing my mind for details about it. Got it?"

She nodded. She stood, gave an odd little curtsy, and went out.

Strange girl. Would the kid in the capsule end up stranger for hanging out with her? Was such a thing possible?

Did this mean this empress had telepathic abilities? He didn't recall her predecessor having them. Had they finally found some way to instill them, some genes to splice just so?

He didn't want to know. He just needed to get this canister to Desori and forget about it. He put it back in the cabinet but hesitated as he shut the door.

Loneliness isn't good for a baby.

For a moment, he could see Asha again, wind blowing through her black hair as the water of the Bleak Sea lapped around her feet, the sun hot on them both... As quickly as it'd come, the image faded. He shoved his grief back into the corner once again.

Grumbling to himself and gritting his teeth, he retrieved the capsule and sat it on his bunk. Then he pulled up his messages. Good. A bunch of bureaucratic announcements and assorted nonsense.

He sighed and, instead of reading them to himself, he read them aloud. And felt like an idiot.

———

ELLEN GAZED out from her cabin at the lifeless hulk of steel and wire and petroglic and sighed.

There *should* be another Enhancer lab here for them, the last of their run before resupply in Desori. It should have been the largest they'd planned to target, and the most dangerous without the wild outsystem forests to vanish into. There should be hundreds of people here on Upsilon station, coming or going or living out their lives, making the mission all the harder. Adan should be hailing the station any minute now.

But it didn't take a genius to have a feeling that no one was going to answer.

The station should normally have glowed with the quiet, reassuring light of civilization. Instead, it hung there like a derelict, black and still. A few ships remained docked, their forms also suspiciously dark. If it weren't for the two suns, she might have had a hard time picking them out at all.

Upsilon Station. It was thus named for its odd Y-like shape, and it took up a vast portion of the nearby Dremeta System. The system had no habitable or terraformable planets—a rarity in the galaxy—and thus humans had decided to construct a large station on its fringes, both because of the energy they could harvest from its dual rotating suns and to process the minerals and gases mined from Dremeta's six unwelcoming worlds.

That had been the original reason for settlement at least. And for a while they'd made good, honest money that way. But at some point, the tide had changed. Maybe it was galactic expansion, maybe resources had run low. No one knew for sure.

It'd grown into a den of pirates, outlaws, and smugglers operating on the edge of Puritan territory and the outsystem. That only added to the complexity of the mission. A civilian mining station might underestimate the need for biosecurity—or regular security for that matter. Pirates tended to not make the same mistake.

And yet the massive station hung there in space, inert. Almost as though it had been abandoned.

"Not getting a response," Adan said over the comm. "Shocking."

She pursed her lips, then made sure the channel was open to everyone. "Prepare for docking. Forced docking. Any nonmission personnel are confined to their cabins. See everybody who's going down in the hold."

"Yes, ma'am," came Adan's reply.

She shut the channel. "Xi, I want a double medical barrier today, okay?"

"I will strengthen the standard quarantine force field with additional energy output and create a secondary backup layer. Will that be sufficient?"

"Yes. And... be prepared for more than the usual number to run through decontamination."

"Of course, Commander. We have raw materials remaining to decontaminate everyone on the ship from the highest level of exposure at least three times."

"Thanks."

She sighed and eyed the station for one moment longer. She'd worried about this place from the beginning, but she hadn't expected this.

———

UPSILON'S AIRLOCK hatch ground to life, clanking down into the station with a puff of air and revealing an unlit corridor. Well, at least the locks still responded. That didn't suggest mechanical failure was the problem. There was still no sign of anyone, no angry comms demanding what they were doing.

Just silence.

Zhia flicked her suit lights to high, the helmet lamp shining down an empty, nondescript corridor. Zhia entered first, slowly, multi carefully poised at the ready. Dr. Dremer followed, flanked by Nova and Jenny, and Ellen stepped onto the station last, Kael quiet at her side.

"Nothing out of the ordinary yet," Nova reported back, mostly for Adan's benefit.

"I'm seeing a few life-form readings. But only a few," chimed in Dremer. "That's certainly out of the ordinary on a station this size."

"Shouldn't there be some kind of gate or customs check here?" said Kael, glancing around.

Ellen nodded. "Maybe at the end of the corridor. Let's move up."

"We still have atmo," said Dremer, studying the readout. Ellen's suit was telling her the same, but the scan was still running. "But... there's some kind of sedative in the air."

Her jaw tightened just as her armor finished its scan and chirped a warning. The same kind of sedative floated in the air that had been on the Teredark moon.

"That sounds... uncomfortably familiar," Kael said slowly.

"Agreed," said Nova.

"It doesn't just sound like it," Ellen said coldly. "It's the same exact thing." And that had worked out so well last time.

They kept their steps quiet and careful. Their lights would announce their presence long before any sound would, though, with the whole place dark. Ellen forced herself to take a deep breath, relax her shoulders. A small set of booths like a customs entry came into view of the helmet lamps, just ahead. No signs of life, though.

"Maybe the station was just abandoned," Jenny mused, sounding hopeful. "And we hadn't gotten word of it yet."

"Sure," said Dremer smoothly. "Or it could have been sold to an owner who'd powered it down temporarily, run on hard luck. The minerals don't come off those planets cheaply, you know. It could be nothing—"

"Oh God," came Zhia's whisper. Ellen knew it must be bad when the woman launched into a spurt of Russian. Expletives? A prayer? Zhia rarely seemed like the religious type, but Ellen could have sworn there'd been an "Amen" at the end in there.

"They're all dead," said Dremer, her voice darkening. "All of them."

Ellen stopped. They all stopped.

The customs gate Kael had predicted was here all right, the seats empty, but behind it lay a terminal lined with seats for humans and other species, all presumably waiting for a ship. A way off Upsilon.

A way out? Everywhere her headlamp shone, it lit up a corpse.

"This whole place is uninhabitable," said Dremer quickly. "There's not just sedative in the air here. Something else too. Several viral strains. Taking a sample."

Ellen cleared her throat. "Make sure you quarantine the shit out of that."

"Obviously. The tablet is going to make a digital copy. We aren't taking anything with us—at least not intentionally as one of my samples anyway."

"That's a cheery thought," croaked Zhia, voice hoarse now.

"We can handle this. Anything other than the viruses?" Ellen said slowly. "Is that what killed these people?"

"Something else could have done it and then dissipated with time. But I'm willing to bet that it was a rogue virus. Or viruses."

Nova swore. "Maybe one of these pirates screwed the wrong guy this time."

"Or the wrong gal." Ellen scowled out into the darkness.

Arakovic.

Had she been here? Was this her handy work? Why was she showing up at every Enhancer lab in Ellen's path? Was Simmons hot on her trail—or was it the other way around?

"There's a heat sig that way. More than one person, I'd guess." Dremer pointed a suited hand, and Zhia nodded. The sight of the suit made Ellen think yet again they needed to order her some armor. Even if she didn't like it and hardly ever wore it, those space suits were just not as safe. This situation certainly drove that home.

Zhia took a step to the left. "I see it too. Should we check it out?" She looked back to Ellen, waiting for confirmation.

"Yes. And stick together this time."

They moved quicker now. Bodies lined the hallway, clearly dead but not in an excessive state of decay. No bloating. Most features were horrifically intact. Dead, blank eyes stared out into the heavens.

"Was this recent?" she asked.

"The temperature has dropped to nearly that of open space." Dremer moved her scanner from side to side, not taking her eyes off it. Good thing she had two escorts watching so she didn't trip and fall flat on her fancy scanner.

"Meaning?"

"At this distance from the suns, they're frozen," Jenny chimed in quietly.

The corridor opened onto another that curved away from them to the left. One of the curving arms of the Y? The bodies were fewer here, but some remained, looking like they'd fallen literally in place while walking down the hallway.

"Must have been sudden. So we don't know how long ago this happened?" Ellen asked.

"Yes. But I'd guess it was in the last few weeks or months," said Dremer. "It's been more than a few days. Almost no heat from the station's systems are left, and unless they were sabotaged, presumably it took a while for them to completely shut down or break without human intervention."

"Maybe a polite AI turned out the lights for them," said Kael.

Ellen pursed her lips. "Another cheery thought. How much farther?"

"Looks like they are…" Dremer hesitated.

". . . behind this door." Zhia turned, and her lamp lit up a heavy security door.

Ellen scanned the area one last time, then sighed. "Jenny, Zhia, and Dremer—get the door open. Nova and Kael, let's watch their backs."

"Adan," said Jenny into the comm, stepping up. "We got a door over here. Can you work your magic?"

"Tapping into your cam," he said slowly. "Can you shine your light down a little? Yeah, there. Hit that black, round button for me."

She reached out and hit it. Nothing happened.

"Yeah, you don't need me," said Adan.

"Aw, don't say that," Jenny said, voice oddly sweet. "We always need you, Adan."

"No, I mean, there's no power. What you need is a blowtorch."

"That can be arranged!" Nova jumped into action. Without needing orders, Nova and Jenny switched places, and Nova went to work unloading her torch.

"Wait—if there's life on the other side of this door, will opening it kill them?" Zhia asked.

"Let me get a reading on the door," said Dremer. "And see if you can get sensors on the layout within."

Zhia pulled out her tablet.

As the two of them studied the displays, the station creaked around them. Ellen swallowed. That was of course just the totally normal groaning and moaning of space. Nothing ominous. Nothing to worry about. The station hadn't shown any structural damage in any of their scans. They still had atmo. Imagining herself getting violently blown out into the vacuum was entirely unnecessary.

"I've got clear readings that the hall continues with more seals beyond," Dremer said finally. "Some electronic sigs there. Maybe even an airlock. So I think opening this door should be fine."

Ellen frowned. "Considering this is inside the building, I'd call that a staging area. For decontamination. Like in a lab. Have we found our target?"

Dremer grunted. "You know... I think you're right. We didn't have clear intel on this, but yes. This is the lab we've been looking for."

"Well, that's all good news," said Jenny, brightening up. "Sooner we get in, sooner we get out of this place. If there are people alive in there."

"Even if they're alive, how do we get them out?" Kael leaned against the far wall, settling in for a wait.

Ellen shrugged. "Let's see if anyone's really alive before we worry about that. I don't suppose anyone's going to answer to a knock?"

Jenny's knock echoed loudly, no other noise from the station remotely issuing in reply. They waited a minute, then another. Nothing.

"Nothing like a station full of corpses and groaning metal to remind you that you're just a bit of dust in the expanse of space." Zhia's tone was uneven, shaky.

"Thanks for the reminder." Ellen pursed her lips, trying to think if they were missing anything. Something just wasn't right. But nothing came to her. "All right—get on with it, Nova."

The rest of them stood around tensely while light from the laser-torch cast a blue sheen over everything while Nova worked. Finally, the door fell in, the huge clank echoing metallic thunder down the corridor. Ellen couldn't help but wince. Then again, given they were the only life other than these blips on the station, and their lights were lighting the place up, they weren't going to be surprising anyone.

Zhia went through first, followed by Jenny, and Ellen went after her. She started to get out of the way so the others could follow but stopped short.

Light poured from a single window on one side of the hallway, about thirty meters down. Everything else was dark.

"Kael…" she said softly, finally remember to scoot out of the way. "Look familiar to you?"

He stepped through—and caught his breath as he straightened. Then he started forward at a jog.

She matched his pace and even shot forward a bit to beat him to the window. He was obviously letting her, because even with her suit he ought to be able to out run her. But it was probably good he didn't use his enhancements against his allies.

If that was what they really were. Of course, Levereaux was doing her best right now to get a look at his capsule, which he'd left in his cabin for once. So perhaps 'allies' was pushing it a little.

She stepped up and peered through the window as the others approached more carefully behind them. Kael skidded to a stop at her side and swore.

Sixteen young men, bodies emaciated, faces drawn.

They turned to look up in perfect unison.

She gasped, stepping back automatically and bumping into Kael's armor.

"Not again," she whispered. Then she gritted her teeth, swallowed, and hardened her resolve. "We've got to get some suits and get them out of there."

We're not going anywhere.

"Shit," she swore. A voice echoed in her head so loud she covered her hands with her ears. But of course the effort was futile. She glanced wildly at Kael, who'd raised his hands too. He must have heard it.

"Another telepath," she barked toward Zhia. "Find her physical loc—"

A songbird, eh? I didn't expect to meet another songbird here. Were you abandoned like me? Where is your unit?

Ellen winced and whirled one way, then the other, looking for another lit window or door. They had to find her. Before it was too—

You have no unit? The voice was a rasp, a laugh, but then the volume doubled to a hysterical scream. *You can't have them! You can't have my unit. Go away!*

Ellen glanced around to see Zhia had covered her ears too, and Dremer's eyes were wide as saucers.

"Everyone hear that?" Ellen managed.

Zhia nodded mutely.

"I can hear it on the ship," groaned Adan over the comm.

Kael, meanwhile, was wasting no time, methodically checking the next window and the next.

"What the hell is it?" whispered Jenny.

"It's a telepath. Arakovic was here," Ellen said, through clenched teeth.

Go away! The voice wailed now. *You can't have them. We are one. I swear we are. I can control them if you give me a little more time.*

"I can set you free," called Ellen into the air. "Get you off this station."

Mother left us here. We dare not disobey.

"This place is dead. Everyone in it—you can't survive forever here."

We must wait. We dare not disobey.

"No, damn it. Where are you?"

I just need to learn to control them. I'm controlling them even now. You gave me an old unit, Mother. Used. Broken. It wasn't fair, it wasn't fair...

Kael stopped and beckoned her toward him. She jogged down six doors—cells?—and looked inside. Sure enough, a girl in a white medical gown sat in a chair at the far end, glaring at the door.

They're mine! she screamed again.

"I don't want them!" Ellen yelled back.

Of course you do, cripple. You're without your unit. I may have been abandoned, but I still have my arms.

"Your arms? I don't—"

LIAR!

"What were the Enhancers *doing* here—" she heard Dremer start to say.

But if the words continued, she could no longer hear them. Agony seized Ellen, her back arching as the girl gripped her mind and started rifling through it. A flurry of movement whirled around her, arms catching her from falling, but she couldn't process much more than fighting out the unwelcome presence inside her.

"Get out!" she screamed.

The girl receded with an evil laugh, but whether as a result of her pushing or because she'd found what she was looking for, Ellen wasn't sure. *You rejected them?* Another laugh, this one almost shocked. Affronted. *A unit of over fifty and you rejected them? How? Why?*

"I am not a songbird!" Not anymore.

You are always one of Mother's flock. Escape is impossible. How could you reject this gift, songbird?

"How can you accept it?" Ellen ground out through clenched teeth. Something was locking her body still. "You have no right to them. They are people too. They deserve lives of their own. And so do you."

We have lives. We are so much more than you. You cannot separate us. We are one. Mostly.

"Let them go," Ellen demanded.

I told you you wanted them.

"I'll set them free."

Never. There's nothing left to set free. We are one.

The pain seized Ellen's mind again, torture like a thousand needles stabbing into every nerve and limb. Her body writhed and then abruptly froze.

"What's happening?" Kael's voice.

"She's attacking the commander telepathically," snapped Dremer.

"What can we do?" he said.

"Nothing. There's little defense against telepaths. That's why they're so... carefully groomed."

"What about Isa? What about—"

"She's not trained."

"There *has* to be something." Someone was shaking her—Kael, maybe. "Ellen, listen to me. Does she have a chip too? Do the men?"

"We're not drinking," she grunted.

A crazed laugh escaped him. "Chips—do they have them?"

The pain eased briefly, and Ellen relaxed to realize she was in Zhia's arms, Kael and Dremer bent over her. "The men should. She might. Or she might be a Natural. I don't know."

"Where are they?" he asked. "If we take them out, then she can't use them. Or hurt you, if I can find hers."

"She can't tell you that," Zhia snapped. "Then you'll know where hers is. Was. Whatever."

Kael glared at Zhia, then down at Ellen. "Unless one of you has a better idea?"

The pain started to ramp up again. "Plug in," she whispered, hitting the port on her arm automatically. "Schematics. I'll give."

"Elle, that's crazy—" Zhia started, shoving Kael partially away, but Kael was faster, and she could feel his presence in her mind barely a moment later. She heaved a sigh of relief at it, both at the sudden realization of how much she'd missed having him this close and at the contrast to the girl's torture.

Missed you too.

She thrust the schematics at him, indicating the spot at the neck and the release mechanism, which required intricate pressure in six locations. Zhia might be right that this was crazy, but he was also right that there weren't any other options.

I would never hurt you.

I know.

The girl's voice suddenly sliced through between them. *Look at you, trying to form a unit now in the presence of our might. Two fragile minds. You are* nothing *compared to us.* The voice was a scream, a raging torrent battering them like a hurricane.

Kael reeled back, unplugging. Just as well. If he got hit by her psychic pain, he'd never be able to carry out his plan.

Even this unit abandons you, the girl whispered, laughing with delight. *Give me your power, songbird.*

I have no power, Ellen said weakly back in her mind. But the agony increased, peaking higher than ever now, her muscles spasming uncontrollably. It faded in time, like a wave she knew would come back soon, but while she could see again, she forced her eyes open. Blinking, she could just make out Kael standing in front of the window of the sixteen men.

"It's not working," he grunted. "They're fighting me."

"What?" Dremer whispered.

"I'm trying to take out their chips. Got one, but whoever I focus on, they all pile on top. I can't move anything then. I can only fling one or two at a time. There's still fifteen left."

"Take hers instead," Ellen grunted.

The girl's cackle ripped through her mind, and the world went splotched black and yellow, bathing her in convulsing, searing, burning pain.

"Yes, ma'am," said a familiar voice in the distance.

The black closed in around her, crushing. Like soon there would be nothing left, no will, no drive, no memories, nothing but pure energy. Nothingness and the stars. And even that would be consumed. The unit needed to feed. Locked in here, they were starving, but this energy could sustain them a little longer, if only—

The pain abruptly disappeared.

"Got it!"

Ellen's eyes opened to see Kael jump in triumph. "Can she put it back in?" she managed, words slurred.

"Not unless she's got a shovel. Smashed it into the wall—it's indented about two feet in. Hopefully that means I broke it."

Ellen struggled to her feet, shaking. Zhia steadied her and brought her to the door's small window. The girl lay still on the floor.

"Did you kill her?" she whispered.

"Not intentionally." He frowned, looking in over her shoulder. "I just removed the chip."

"Oh, *God,*" Zhia gasped. She stood at the other door's window.

Kael crossed the distance at a sprint, then froze. "By the seven suns..."

Ellen barely made it a step or two, sliding along the wall for support, when he held up a hand to stop her. "You don't want to see this."

"What is it?" Dremer said, taking a step forward, then flinching.

"They're..." Zhia started, but she swallowed, like she couldn't finish what she'd started to say. "They're like animals."

"I think they're eating each other alive," Kael whispered, eyes wide. "Five are down already."

The cry of anguish that escaped Ellen was uncharacteristic of her, her control slipping, but it was all too fresh. The memories she'd worked hard to forget were too close now, and some lingering memory of the telepath's attachment to the men echoed even now in her mind. "I wanted to free them."

"It's not your fault," snapped Zhia. "This is the Enhancer's doing and no one else's."

"Not just the Enhancers," Ellen grunted. "Arakovic." She tried her best to straighten, but her body wasn't responding half the time. She flipped on the armor assist part way and looked back toward the other cell. "The girl—can we save her?"

Zhia's eyes widened. "We should just get out of here."

"What are her vitals? Is she still alive?"

"Commander, is that advisable—" Jenny started.

"She can't do the damage she did without her chip. Maybe we could save her."

"She's likely very unstable," Dremer said cautiously. "You barely made it back from the brink; she's clearly had this connection longer—"

"Is she alive?" Ellen demanded, almost a shout, her voice hard.

"Yes," said Zhia bitterly.

"Is it clean in there? Can we open it? Can we get her a suit?"

Dremer checked her tools. "Looks like there is a decon unit in the doorframe. With minimal exposure, we might be able to get her to the ship if we can find a suit. Then decon again on the way in. Technically it's doable."

Zhia pulled out her tablet again. "There's a docking bay a little farther down the main hall. If there are any suits, there should be some there."

"Jenny, Nova—see if you can find one," Ellen ordered.

Dremer was shaking her head. "I'm warning you, Commander. It is very likely her mind may not be able to be rehabilitated—"

"Try," Ellen snapped. "We are not like Arakovic. Human life is not disposable. If we can save her, we will, even if she's lost her identity."

Dremer raised her tool to the door, entering the lock-hacking program. Kael was still staring, even more wide-eyed now, into the other cell.

"Kael, get away from there," Ellen snapped. He didn't seem to hear her. "Kael!"

While Dremer worked, Ellen gazed in at the girl, looking fragile and cold now against the stark metal floor. Only an emergency light or two for company. Who had left her here? Was "Mother" Arakovic? Why had this songbird been abandoned?

Was this the fate that had awaited Ellen if she hadn't escaped? If she'd lost her identity fully to her unit?

We are one. The girl's words floated back to her, and she shivered. Mostly.

"Found one!" called Jenny from the door they'd blasted through. She and Nova jogged up with a suit cradled between them.

"The power is still active on this lock," Dremer said. "I've got it open. Whenever you're ready, Commander."

"Open it," she ordered.

At her words, Kael snapped out of his horror and looked her way in alarm. "Wait—what?"

The cell door slid open with a metallic groan. Ominous silence lay over them like a stifling blanket. Ellen gestured for them to toss the suit into the decon area and then leaned in herself.

The girl's inert form was still, not even breathing, not even twitching, but somehow Ellen could still feel life in there. Was the girl simply in shock? Could it be some kind of brain adaptation, like Dremer had talked about, that literally made her need the chip to live, to breathe?

But then Ellen froze. Under the sleeve of the girl's shirt, the neckline. Small white tentacles wriggled at the fabric's edge.

Weak or not, Ellen scampered back, trying to draw Dremer with her but missing.

"What is it?" Dremer started, leaning toward the door.

Screeching, the girl—no, more like a creature at this point—leaped up into the air, gaining speed quickly and lurching toward them. The ripped fabric of her simple gown fell away, revealing a body no longer human but more... insectile. Her body bloated and twisted, hard legs and a carapace forming, all sickly white. And the top of the creature— her body was more tentacle than girl at this point. Ellen lunged forward and grabbed Dremer, hauling her back, sure she was too late—

The creature hit an invisible wall and slid to the ground, writhing and screaming its rage.

"Close it!" Kael shouted, backing farther down the hall. "You can't help her! Close the door!"

"Are you—" Dremer started.

"I can't hold it forever, Doctor."

Dremer scrambled back to the panel. "Shit. It won't close. That hacking program is nuking everything. Wiped the lock program completely. It's gathering information for Simmons—"

"Later." This wasn't the time for details. Ellen drew her pistol, then met Kael's eye. His frown of concentration deepened. She looked at Dremer. "Is there anything we can do to sedate her? Could she be—"

The field Kael held wavered. Behind it, what had once been a girl flailed against his energy.

"Ellen—look. It's one of those—"

"Sedation, Doctor?" she demanded.

"I have one shot," Dremer said quickly, holding up the tranquillizer gun and giving Ellen a meaningful stare. One shot that was meant for *Kael* if they needed it. They wouldn't have another chance.

"Give it to me. Then get over to Kael now. All of you—back to the first door." Ellen grabbed Dremer by the shoulder and shoved.

"I'll cover from the side," Zhia said quickly.

"No. Get to the end of the hall, Zhia. Go. That's an order. This thing can't take us all down. Your priority is to get Dremer back to the ship and make sure Simmons knows about what happened here."

"Ellen, no—" Kael started, almost in time with similar objections from Zhia. The barrier he held faltered again.

"Are there any men left alive, Kael?" she said slowly.

"No." His face fell, even as he was backing away. Following her orders for once, thank God.

"What are you going to do, Commander?" Dremer called, sprinting for Kael.

"No time for questions. Get out of here. *Go.* I'll take care of this."

Ellen readied her pistol on her side, then took the multi from her back, and sucked in a deep breath. She switched the comm off, then only to Kael's channel. "You ready, Theroki? On my mark, drop it. Got it?"

"Ellen—"

"I need you to get them out. I'm a good shot, remember?"

"I'm not leaving you here."

"You won't have to. I can take her. I need you to listen to me on this, Kael. Please. Dremer's suit can't withstand any damage. *None* at all."

A brief silence, then, "Okay, we're all outside the door. Tell me when."

She eyed the thing thrashing at the barrier.

If this thing was going to take her down, if this was going to be her last day in this dark universe, she was glad she'd come to know Kael, even if it was maybe not quite as well as either of them would have liked.

She almost said something to that effect, but she shouldn't be wasting time on sentimental thoughts. She wasn't going to die here. Not after everything else. This was just one more reason Arakovic must be stopped, and Ellen was not intending to die trying.

She narrowed her eyes down the rifle sight and took another deep, steadying breath. "Now."

Almost before she'd finished the word, she squeezed the trigger and held, the laser beam faltering for a second as it hit a last remnant of Kael's barrier, reflecting and searing a hole into the floor —fortunately a few feet in front of her boot. Then the barrier fell the rest of the way, and the beam bit into the alien flesh as it leaped for her.

She released the multi for a moment, grabbing the tranq gun and squeezing off the dart, aiming carefully for something that looked like a beak, a mouth, some sort of sensitive place. Then she dropped it, the suit grabbing the weapon magnetically and locking it to her thigh.

The dart had no effect. She couldn't even tell she'd fired the laser on the rifle. The body rippled for a moment, then reformed, the dart vanishing into its body. The girl-creature faltered for barely a second before it was sliding toward her again.

She switched the laser to high intensity, fired again, and held, determined to empty the energy bank. She tried three places, looking for a weak spot. A sustained shot from Zhia from the door took off a high tentacle.

"Get out of here," she ordered. She'd told them to be long gone.

The energy bank ran out. The creature surged forward.

She flicked to ballistic, but all the bullets seemed to disappear into nothingness. So she unloaded everything the multi had.

Red death made the creature shudder slightly, but even that vanished, almost as if absorbed. It tossed the immobilizing foam aside.

Grilling seemed to have no effect—although the freezing air around them probably wasn't helping anything.

She doubled the temperature, and one tentacle that whirled close wilted and browned a little. The creature screeched, hugging the limb to its torso for a moment, before lashing out again, seemingly unaffected. The browned tentacle looked totally healed, although Zhia's severed one was splattering black blood across the deck.

Shit.

She switched back to ballistic and fired faster, backing down the hallway now and hoping to God they'd listened, sending tight bunches of three shots each into the white hide.

Not a one seemed to have any effect.

What the hell? How did one *kill* these things? She couldn't very well lop off each tentacle and just hope it would bleed to death.

The thing leaped again, too close now. She ducked and rolled, the creature missing her just slightly. She twisted, still sitting, releasing the fog cloud to help hide her location at the same time as she switched back to laser. She let the rifle prop on her knee, pulled out the pistol, and blasted them both on full—

White enveloped her, wiping out the whole world. Sound muted.

I will have you, songbird.

No. Ellen thrashed and tore, continuing to fire into the mass around her. Swirling black pierced the whiteness, like oil dumped in milk, so she seemed to have done *some* damage. But her armor creaked loudly.

The songbird—or the creature—was crushing her.

Suddenly the white above her sliced apart as the creature shrieked. She stopped her fire, dropping the weapons. A blade ripped through white flesh, revealing the station's metal ceiling. And then Kael's face, charged with bloodlust and rage.

Man never could follow orders.

Well, for all their low-tech bullshit, the Theroki had her on this one. Why bother with lasers when a knife would do the job? She fought through the goo and grabbed the laserblade from her leg compartment, slicing wildly around her.

The creature fell away, pooling around her like white sludge on all sides. She fought back nausea, reeling, trying to stand steady.

Silence fell.

She stood, panting, eying the creature. Waiting. She nudged it with her boot—no response. Then she finally sighed, hoping the thing was truly dead.

She met Kael's gaze. He stood panting too and staring at her. "I know I disobeyed a direct order, but—" he started.

"And I know I owe you another beer."

"What?"

Just then, her suit sensors bleeped. Suit integrity warning. Shit. All that crushing had done some damage. She set the nanos to begin repairs. A quick estimate came back—the repair would take longer than her air supply would last, not to mention the decon power drain trying to keep the virus out.

They needed to get out—and fast.

"Shit, I'm leaking. Let's go." She grabbed her dripping multi from the mess; the pistol had clung to her suit when she dropped it just like the tranq had. No time to put them away now.

She reached for his hand and jumped high over the corpse, sprinting after the rest of them down the corridor. "We can talk about your insubordination later."

"Over beer?"

"Definitely."

"You run a weird ship, Commander Ryu."

"Thank you, Kael." She knew he understood her words were more than just a simple reply or a courtesy.

"Of course, Commander. My pleasure. As always."

———

THEY WERE NEARLY to the entrance, his hand in Ellen's, when a hissing, shimmying sound met Kael's ears.

"Is that—" he started.

"Teredarks!" Zhia shouted from up ahead, still gripping Dremer's bicep.

A flurry of curses from across the team lit up the comm. Long, segmented bodies poured out of the ducts from above and dropped down near the entryway. How could Teredarks *survive* in this, how could they even— But his eyes caught on their strange headsets.

"Force-field armor!" he called. "That's keeping them alive."

He skidded to a stop next to Zhia, Ellen halting beside them.

"What now?" Jenny whispered.

"I'm reading all sorts of invulnerabilities in their armor, Commander," Nova said quickly.

"Me too. I've got a leak. Nova—grenade. Now."

Nova whirled to look at her, eyes wide, and then for some reason her gaze flicked to Kael. What the hell? "Are you sure? But what about—"

"Do it. There's no time. We need off this station *now*."

Nova still stared a moment longer, hesitating.

"What are you waiting for?" Ellen shouted, staggering. He lunged toward her and caught her shoulder.

At that, Nova scrambled, pulling out the string and entering in the coordinates on the first grenade.

"What kind of grenade is that," Kael said slowly, "that can get past all these invulnerabilities?"

Ellen pointed back to the customs desk. "Get behind that," she snapped. "All of you. Take Dremer with you."

"Tell me, or I'm not going."

Ellen looked exasperated but then shook her head. "It's a knockout grenade." Their eyes locked for a long moment through their visors, then she let out a disgusted sigh. "You happy? Now *go*. Get back there. Unless you want us all to die here?"

He raised his eyebrows but complied. He grabbed Dremer by the arm and pulled, fairly sure her suit would be even less helpful against those things than his was. Damn, what would he break this time? How odd he hadn't had to deal with knockout weapons more than once or twice over the years, and now—

And now. As he sank down into a squat behind the customs table, the look on Nova's face flashed through his mind again. Dremer knelt behind him as he checked for more coming up the hallway. He didn't see any. He backed away around the corner, pushing Dremer farther out of the blast wave, but his mind was only half on avoiding the grenade.

What were the chances?

The high-tech, low-touch style. All nonlethal attacks. The search for scientific abuse. They'd been getting the hell off Helikai at just exactly the same time he had been, so conveniently.

How had he not seen it before?

It had been *them* in the lab. Hadn't it. *His* lab had been the first in this string of attacks.

He opened his mouth to say something—he wasn't sure what—but never had a chance to decide. The wave of the knockout grenade shook the air. His cover wasn't enough, he felt it clear through to his bones, and after a moment of feeling like his entire body was on fire, the world fell away. And he slept.

CHAPTER THIRTEEN

THE OATH PROGRAM WAS RUNNING.

He gasped for breath and sat up. His heart beat loudly in his ears, so loudly for a moment the voices around him didn't register. The world was a blurred mess he couldn't make out. Adrenaline coursed through him, acid powerful in his veins, and he panted, trying to catch his breath.

Where was the capsule? Where was *he*? He leapt to his feet, starting forward before he staggered. Someone caught him and steadied him from behind. He jerked away.

"He's going supernova—get the tranq," said a voice.

Too much. Too many chemicals. Where was the capsule? Where was Ellen?

"He already is," said another. He could barely make out the words, let alone who said them.

"We don't have it—"

"Get it."

"Here—"

"I'll reload as fast as I—"

"Fine."

A face appeared in front of him, soft eyes and pink lips.

Ellen.

He could never forget that face. A different kind of power surged through him, but the oath program smacked it down. She approached him slowly and put her hands on his shoulders, frowning. "Kael—they're all gone. It's over. It's just us here. Stand down. Get ahold of yourself." Her voice was solidly in command mode.

He slowly met her eyes, jaw clenched, nostrils flared. "You're not helping," he growled through gritted teeth.

She stepped back. "Jen—you try. You're the sweetest. Get up here. Tell him, no, *ask* him to calm down. Nicely. Like you normally would."

"Commander?" Her eyes were wide. Good. He narrowed on her.

"It's okay," Ellen whispered. "Tranq's almost ready."

He scowled. They were not tranquilizing him. He at least needed to *seem* to get it together so he could check on the capsule, relieve the oath's pressure.

Jenny nodded and approached slowly.

Ellen drew her pistol, trained it on Kael's armor control unit, and released the safety.

"Kael?" Jenny said softly, green eyes blinking up at him. "Please calm down. Can you calm down?"

He responded only with a low growl.

"Look, all your things are here. We're back on the ship. We're free of the Teredarks, and we're the only ones here. If you hurt anyone, it will have to be one of us."

Kael took a deep breath, and to some extent her words did calm him. They were back on the ship. Surely the capsule was close, maybe being serenaded by a Natural telepath. Although he'd had enough telepaths for one lifetime, thank you very much.

"Thanks, Jen," he whispered as he felt the pounding of his heart calm slightly.

"Let's hit your quarters, Kael," Ellen said, holstering the weapon. "I'll take him."

———

"BE CAREFUL," Levereaux said in a private comm channel. "I still have the item here, didn't get enough warning to finish the scan and put it back. I'll get this tranq fixed and the item back stat."

Ellen didn't acknowledge. It was a good thing Jenny had talked him down, because the tranq gun had jammed on reload. Piece of shit. Maybe it might have had something to do with the creature-alien-whatever guts all over it. They had backup means of sedating him, but none of them were perfect.

She much preferred him not going nuclear. Being himself.

Kael was only nodding and walking numbly toward her. He marched ahead of her to his quarters and palmed open the door.

She followed him in, not entirely sure why. She shouldn't. A bad idea. But she palmed the door shut behind her.

"You okay, Kael?" she said softly. Cautiously, and not entirely clear on why she was doing it, she hit the button to retract her helmet. Perhaps to seem more human to him, less like a threat. Yes, perhaps that was it.

His eyes turned to catch hers, suddenly fiery, and she knew he was not okay, not entirely. But then again, was she?

"I thought you were dead," he said slowly. He stepped closer to her.

"So did I."

He stepped closer to her again, stopping just inches away from her. "That thing swallowed you whole. I thought you were gone for sure."

"I'm tougher than that."

"Why did you stay? We all could have run. I could have helped you fight it."

"Well, you did in the end, so does it matter?"

He pressed his lips together. "Elle, I..."

She caught her breath. It was the first time he'd ever called her that. His eyes met hers as he went quiet.

"If we had died out there, would you have had any regrets?" he said softly.

She held the word in for a long time. But he was due for the truth, wasn't he? "Yes," she whispered.

He leaned forward and seized her mouth with his as her eyes flew wide in shock. His armor slid against hers, and she winced at what he might be scratching, but... She inhaled deeply through her nose and then...

And then she kissed him back.

For a long moment, her mind went silent, and there was only the feel of him, the two of them alone in the cosmos, escaping death. Needing a bit of life for once. Of something more primal, more deep, more sincere. Something more.

She had no idea how long passed before she broke away, gasping for breath. But he didn't release her, his mouth straying to her neck.

"Kael, wait," she said softly.

He didn't respond. She remembered the way he'd surged to life in the sick bay, like he'd been a corpse coming back from the dead, but suddenly charged and ready to kill someone. All the bloodlust of the actual battle too... What was his chip pouring into him even now?

"Get ahold of yourself," she said more sharply. "Can you even stop right now if you want to?"

In answer, he only growled. The primal sound sent more spirals of heat through her. But if he was hopped up on chems, even natural ones, he wasn't thinking straight. They couldn't do this. Not now.

Not like this. Not ever? Did he even know what he was doing?

She drew her pistol, pressed the crusty, dirty muzzle to his skull, and flipped the safety. "Get. Control. Now."

He froze for a split second, and then with a gasp, he flung himself away from her. He leaned face-first against the far wall, arms above his head, panting. "Hell. Sorry."

They stood in the silence, panting.

"Thanks," he whispered. "Sorry."

"Not entirely your fault. I encouraged you."

"No. Still. My. Fault."

"Well, I'm still sorry too." She hesitated. "Look. You muddy every-thing. I cannot endanger my ship and my crew by falling for you."

"Isn't it already too late for that?" His soulful eyes looked over his shoulder at her.

"No."

"Would you have shot me just now?"

"No." She'd wanted what he'd wanted. She had just wanted *him* to be sure of it, in control of it, not in a blind rage. She wouldn't have regretted his attentions. "Maybe." She couldn't muster the full lie of yes that she should have.

"What about back there in the hold? If I'd attacked Jenny."

She gritted her teeth. "No. Probably not."

"Good."

"No, it's *not* good. That's just the problem. I would have hesitated, and you could have killed her."

"But I didn't."

"You didn't. You managed to hold off on Nova too. But what about next time? How many chances should we take?"

"There won't be a next time. We're almost to Desori."

They stood in silence again, contemplating that.

"And you'll be gone then?"

"Don't you want me gone?"

She said nothing.

"You know that's an answer too, right?"

"What is?"

"If you wanted me gone, you'd have said so."

"Ah, slag off, Kael."

His head rose slowly, like he'd just remembered something. He strode to the cleaning cabinet and opened it. Squatting down, he reached inside, and—

His eyes turned to meet hers, wild and angry. "Where is it?"

She took the safety back off the pistol and palmed the hatch open. "I don't know."

He straightened like a bear ready to charge. "And I *trusted* you, Ryu."

"You can still trust me."

"It was you in the lab, wasn't it?"

She gritted her teeth, but reluctantly nodded once. She was lucky it'd taken him this long. "When did you figure it out?"

"The knockout grenade. But I can't believe I didn't see it sooner. You could have told me."

"No, I couldn't have. This is a secret mission. You were guarding the enemy. I wouldn't have let you in this far if we hadn't needed help." God, she hoped that was the only reason, but a little voice said it was a lie.

"Where is it?" He took a step forward, and she backed equally out into the hallway. "The one time I don't take it with me…"

"I don't know. I don't have it. But I'm sure it's safe and hasn't been harmed." She raised the pistol, aiming it straight at him. Outside in the hall, she heard a metallic scurrying—Xi's cleaning robots?

"Are you really going to kill me after all this?" he said slowly.

"Are *you*?"

"I don't have a choice if I don't have the capsule." The muscles of his neck were straining. He was struggling *not* to surge toward her, wasn't he?

"I'm you're only ride to Desori."

"I don't think that's going to work this time," he said with real regret in his voice.

"You can't reach me before I shoot you. You'll just fail your mission with that tactic."

"There's no reasoning with this stupid thing. It wants the capsule back, and it wants it now."

"We'll get it back to you. It's only for a few more minutes—"

"If it were up to me, I'd sit back down. But it's really not. Please, Ellen, I can't—"

Just then, one of Xi's robots rounded the corner and dove straight between Ellen's legs. Kael stared at it. "Xi, now is not the time—"

The creature leapt, attaching itself to Kael's chest. A blue glow and an audible *thwomp* came from the thing, and Kael froze.

What the hell? The suit clattered to the ground, suddenly a useless chunk of metal with Kael trapped inside, swearing up a storm. "Xi, how could you?"

"Violence of any kind is not permitted on the ship," Xi said, sounding more smug than stern.

Just then Levereaux rounded the corner, tranq in hand, and fired, hitting Kael squarely in the neck.

His eyes were still trained on Ellen, shot through with a strange mixture of betrayal and trust and hope. His lids drooped once, twice, and then out he went.

Ellen sighed. "Good shot, Doctor. Let's make sure we have that capsule nearby when he wakes up."

———

"ATTENTION, CREW." Kael roused suddenly to Adan's voice over the comm. "We'll be in Desori in approximately two hours. Prepare for landing."

The surge of energy that had been beginning to flood him slowed. Something cool and metallic rested under his fingers. He raised it into view.

The capsule. Its lights blinked the same as ever.

He had no real other way to know if any harm had come to it. But here it was. Back in his possession.

Like she'd promised.

He flopped his head back down, lowered his arm, and closed his eyes. By the seven suns, what had he done? What had he said?

How had it taken him so long to figure out they were the ones who had raided the lab?

It didn't matter now. He had nearly made it. He still had the capsule. His mission was nearly over. His assigned mission.

His personal mission to escape was only beginning.

———

ADAN SLID into his usual smooth landing in Desori's spaceport. Ellen rose from the co-pilot's seat, not wanting to look out at the view of gray metal and neon light that greeted them.

Not wanting to be here at all.

She paused briefly in the hatch to the bridge, then turned and headed for the ladder down. She knew what she needed to do.

"You okay, Commander?" Adan called after her.

"As okay as ever," she yelled back.

Her feet carried her quickly down to the main level, past the cabin doors, but they froze in place outside his door.

Go on, you coward. You know what you need to do. He's free now. He's gone. If you've got anything to say, now's the time.

Gritting her teeth, she slammed her palm over the door chime. The hatch didn't open as quickly as it used to, a long moment passing where she wondered if he might not just ignore her. Or was he already gone?

With a slight swish, the hatch door finally slid aside, and there he was. He stood simply, one shoulder leaned against the wall in just the same spot she'd held her pistol to his head.

"Come to say goodbye?" His voice was quiet, but his eyes bored into her like an asteroid mining rig.

She shrugged. "Find your capsule?"

"Yeah. We all docked and ready to debark?" His eyes were cold, hurt behind the casual words.

She nodded just as casually. "Guess it's time for goodbyes. Or something." Truth be told, she wasn't quite sure *why* she'd come. She hated goodbyes. But she also couldn't imagine him just marching off the ship and never seeing him again.

"Are you going to tell me why it's called the *Audacity* now?" He stepped back further inside, implicitly inviting her in, and smiled sadly. "Haven't I earned it? I don't want to die not knowing."

She smiled back, not trying to hide it for once. "You're not going to die."

"I'm not so sure."

"I am. Live. That's an order. But I'll tell you." She paused, sucking in a deep breath, her eyes tracing the floor grating for a long moment before she forced herself to meet his gaze again. "It's because the most audacious thing you can do in the face of your enemies is to give a shit. And not stop. To keep trying. To keep fighting."

He blinked. "What?"

"This galaxy is a cesspool, and it's chock-full of piss-drinking assholes and heartless drecks looking to stab you in the back at every turn. It's easy to lie down and just give up. Sometimes surviving is all you've got. Once in a while, you can try to make the galaxy a little bit better. But most of the time, that's just spitting into the wind."

He took half a step forward, then stopped.

She clenched her jaw for a moment, then kept going. "But it's better to spit in the wind than lie down dead."

A slow smile broke over his face, one not quite as sad. "Did you pick that name or Simmons?"

"It was my idea. He just about died. I mean, as in he loved it." She finally stepped inside and let the hatch close behind her.

"I do too." They stood silently for a moment.

"Look, I don't say goodbyes. I came because I wanted to apologize," she said softly.

He frowned, eyes searching hers, mystified.

"I'm sorry for what I said, all right? I'm sorry for holding back. I'm sorry for tormenting you. Unintentionally. I'm not good at this shit. I'm scared, all right? The last time I let someone in, three hundred people got incinerated in a star because of my poor decisions." She jabbed a finger at her chest.

"No, they got incinerated because of their *captain's* poor decisions. You weren't even there."

"Yeah, and neither was he, the coward. But I nominated him. I put him forward. I'm responsible."

"You can't be responsible for everything, Ellen. He's the one responsible. Other people reviewed his promotion, didn't they? Did you make the decision alone?"

"No, of course I wasn't on the committee. But I'm a stupid 'war hero,' damn it. If I hadn't—"

"Then he would have found someone else to nominate him."

She drew a sharp breath. That was probably true, but also painful to hear. "I still let them down."

"No." He was right, of course. She couldn't look him in the eye and say it, though. She rubbed her eyes to hide for a moment.

"I let someone down too once," he murmured. She looked up. He was staring off into the city out the fogged windows. He was going to tell her, wasn't he? He was going to explain the other burn. The worse one. "I was seventeen then. Poor as you can possibly be. We wanted out of it all. The gangs... did not agree with our decision."

"What happened?"

"They killed her. To make an example. Not sure I can stand to say much more about that right now."

Get you killed too. God. Ellen tried to find words, but her throat had clenched shut. She crushed the wave of emotion down. That was by far enough. She needed to say something. She had to. He deserved it. "Then you... shipped out to Lerain? To become..." A Theroki, why couldn't she just say it?

"Yeah."

"A way out?"

"Not exactly." He shifted his weight, tilting his head in her direction but not meeting her eyes. "But it was convenient not to feel any of it anymore."

"And now here I am..."

"Yeah. But it's not your fault. I agreed. It was ultimately my decision to let someone alter my chip. I may just put the new chip in before I go. It'll be easier. And whatever your mission is, I can tell it's important. I won't endanger that. Or you."

She scowled. "You're not *endangering* me. I can take care of myself."

"Damn it, Ellen." He finally turned. "You can't tell me I'm a dangerous distraction and then turn around and say you can take care of yourself just fine, thanks. If that's true, why are you so sure that... this is a problem?" He gestured wildly at the space between the two of them.

"This?"

"You know what I mean. Me and you. Us."

Her insides felt frozen solid, adrenaline hot as acid in her veins. "I just can't take the risk. How can I risk messing up so fragging badly again?"

"It wasn't your fault. You didn't mess up. And what's the alternative? Staying alone forever?"

Yes, she thought. "That's the plan." Or at least it was. Until you came along. She raised her face to his, looking into those dark, deep eyes. Eyes she longed so much to get lost in.

He sighed and turned away, and she felt cold, like the sun had gone behind a cloud.

The silence stretched on, and she had a feeling he wasn't going to say anything else.

"Look, I don't believe in goodbyes. I don't accept you dying out there either. You're a good soldier. Come back, and we'll get you off planet if there's trouble. We should be here for a week or more. You'll have a spot here to the next stop at least. If you want it."

"Even if it means I go renegade?" he said softly.

"Even then. *Especially* then." Please go renegade. God, she was a fool. But she couldn't accept not seeing him again, either.

"Well. If I'm not dead, we'll see what happens."

———

KAEL STARED at the black sheath on the table. Inside, the tiny chip winked at him. He gritted his teeth. God, he didn't want to install that thing again. What if the obedience algorithms kept him from ever coming back?

But he only had the one edited chip—the one currently in his neck. If he took it with him, he had slowly realized over the last two hours, the Theroki would destroy it along with any chance he had of escaping.

He still had little chance of escaping with a functioning chip, but... maybe if he could leave it here on the *Audacity*, he could come back and get it somehow.

He clenched his jaw, braced himself in the chair, and opened the panel behind his ear. Chills went through him, both ones designed to keep him from meddling with it and ones from memories of Vala and her butchery.

He took a deep breath. Then he gripped the tiny chip and yanked it out.

The woozy feeling that came with it was almost more than he could compensate for, but he jammed in the new chip as quickly as he could manage.

Everything steadied. He simply stared at the wall for a while, letting the systems kick in and adjust themselves. Walking while that happened was not always advisable.

He felt... more normal again. Calm. Cool. Like he could kill something without flinching.

Some part of him fell down—darker, deeper—but he couldn't quite make out what part exactly.

It didn't matter; on with completing his mission. Why had he waited so long? His civilian-commissioned ship had been docked for over fifteen minutes.

He picked up his comm, found the number for High Command, and called. Time to find the Enhancer cell and deliver to them their empress.

———

ELLEN LOOKED up from her holodisplay. The sound of Kael's armor let her hear him coming, but he'd hit the main cargo hold and stopped where Dremer was scanning some crates of supplies they'd picked up. Desori had several Foundation resupply bases, hence why they'd been heading here after their mission sequence.

"Dremer." Kael's voice sounded different. Flatter, with less inflection.

Dremer looked up from her scans for once. "Something wrong, Kael?"

"I'm headed out. Hang on to this for me." He held out a palm with a black sheath on it, and Ellen caught her breath.

The chip. The new one, or the edited one?

Her heart sank as he went straight past her office without reacting. She stared after him. No. No, he wouldn't just leave. He couldn't. Unless...

Unless he'd replaced his altered chip with the new one.

She darted from her desk to the door, only to find him standing just beyond her office with a slight frown.

"Kael," she said softly.

"Commander." He turned and looked as if he had many things to say. And was going to say none of them. He looked down at her feet, then back up at her, then gave her a distant nod. His eyes were those of a stranger. Or an android. They had never looked at her with less interest, less emotion. Never looked at her like that at all, not even the day they met.

Then he turned.

"Kael!" she blurted.

He stopped, looking back at her over his shoulder.

What could she say to make this count? Hadn't she already said everything there was to say? "It's been good to know you, my friend."

He gave her another nod. "You as well, Commander. I think you will not be forgotten for a very long time." Another moment of looking down, of hesitation, and then he was headed out the hatch, strapping his gear to the rented bike that'd been delivered. When had he had time to set that up?

Zhia stormed up, pushing her into her office.

"What are you doing?" Ellen managed, surprised.

"What are *you* doing?" Zhia shot back. "Dremer, get in here. Nova."

Nova shut the office hatch behind them. Zhia propped her hands on her hips and frowned at Ellen. Dremer was frowning at the black sheath in her palm.

"Is that his chip?" Ellen asked.

"Yes. The old one. The damaged one. He said to hang on to it. Why? How could I know if he needed it? How could I possibly judge that for him?"

"One look at him tells me he needs it," muttered Ellen. "Did you see his face?"

"Did you see his eyes?" Nova cut in. "Like a zombie."

Ellen thought of the songbird's unit and shuddered. But it *was* similar.

"I've talked to Theroki before," Zhia said, "but never both with and without the chip. And not that many. I just thought they were all arrogant assholes."

"Well, they do get the chip willingly," said Nova, shrugging.

She thought of Faros IV. *"Sort of."* "I don't think his was willing," she said slowly. "Even if it were, some people do desperate things in desperate situations."

Zhia stared a moment longer.

"So you're just letting him go like that?" said Dremer, as if she couldn't wait any longer to speak.

"Sorry you never got your paws on him, Doctor."

"It's *not* that, Ellen."

Ellen glanced around. They were all frowning at her. What the hell?

"Permission to speak freely, ma'am?" Zhia spat, folding her arms.

"Granted."

"I hate this. Shouldn't we be going with him? Or after him? He watched our backs how many times?"

"And he was compensated for that," she said coolly.

"C'mon. He's a Theroki, but his eyes can't be on his six all the time."

"It did occur to me, but I didn't want to risk Foundation resources for personal reasons."

"Personal reasons?" Dremer frowned. "I think you're letting those 'personal reasons' cloud your judgment."

Ellen winced. That was about the worst thing she could have heard at the moment. Jenny hit the chime on the outside, and they let her in.

"What are you all talking about in here?" she asked. Dr. Taylor slipped in as well and shut the door.

"We're trying to convince the commander to let us protect Kael on his mission," Zhia explained.

"I'm not; I've got higher goals than that." Dremer propped her hands on her hips now. "He's defended far more Foundation resources than he's cost, Commander, while achieving our goals efficiently. We should cover him, so we can bring him back to scare off ships indefinitely. I thought you were trying to recruit him."

"No, I..."

"Well, I am. I approve efforts to recruit him. By any crew member," she said, glancing at Nova, Jenny, and Zhia.

Ellen scowled. "For your personal study, Doctor, or because you actually think he'd make a good addition?"

Nova cut in. "He's proven his skill at security. And on the mat."

"He's been a fine addition to the team," Dremer said, raising her chin. "It'd be a shame to lose him."

"I would also approve him as an addition," said Dr. Taylor smoothly.

"Even you?" Ellen's eyes widened. She hadn't realized the two of them had even had much interaction.

Zhia's eyes brightened. "Does that mean we can go after him, Commander?"

She glanced at her eager crewmates. Huh. Looked like she'd been so busy trying not to be distracted that... she hadn't seen what they'd been thinking. They might rebel if they *didn't* go after him.

"Okay, fine. Levereaux won't like it. This mission is volunteer only, though. If you want to come with me, go get your gear."

"He's almost ready to leave," Zhia said, peering out into the hold.

"Adan," Ellen barked into the comm. "Can you get me a tracking device down here? Pronto!"

"Yes, ma'am!"

Barely thirty seconds later, Adan slid down the ladder to the cargo hold. She met him at a run and grabbed the device from his hand.

Kael was already on the bike, kicking it into ignition. She sprinted after him. "Kael! Wait!" What the hell was she going to say?

But he did stop and turn to wait.

She skidded to a halt beside him. "I, uh, just wanted to say I won't forget you either," she blurted. And threw her arms around him in a hug, jamming the tracker onto his back inside a particularly nasty armor gash. There. That should hold it.

She broke away. He frowned at her, confused.

"A hug. For good luck. Theroki don't do that?"

He shook his head. "No. We don't."

The coldness of the words stabbed at her heart. "Well… good luck."

He nodded crisply, more salute than acknowledgement. "So you don't say goodbyes?"

She frowned. "No, I don't. Just good luck, I guess."

"What about *salam*?"

She swallowed the sudden lump in her throat. "Yeah, I could do that. *Salam*, Kael. Peace be upon you."

"*Salam*, Commander Ryu." And with that, he revved the engine and took off down the ramp.

She only stood frozen for a moment before she whirled and raced back to the office. "All right—we'll follow at a distance. Don't let Kael know we're following. We still don't know the exact nature of this mission, so we need to ascertain that. You've got four minutes before he's off my tracking screen. Go!"

"Got it, Commander." They raced up the ladders en masse.

All except Zhia. "I'm suited up. What can I do?"

"Watch him. And fire up the lander." She pointed wildly toward the hatch and shoved the tracking screen into Zhia's hands as she raced toward her quarters. She needed her multi, a lot more knockout grenades, and a whole avalanche of luck.

CHAPTER FOURTEEN

"CAN you get into the traffic cams?" Zhia was saying over the comm as Ellen trotted up in her armor.

"Not without more time. But I can get one of the drones high up," Adan replied.

"Good. That's faster. Use both of them if you can."

"You don't ask for much, Lieutenant."

"C'mon, you claim you like a challenge. Commander, you're going to want to have a look at this."

Ellen bent over the tracker screen Zhia had been monitoring. Along with the map, she had several street cameras off to the side. One showed a frozen still of the side of a commercial van. Another showed Kael stopped, still on the motorcycle, but speaking with three armored Theroki in the back of a van. "That doesn't seem right. What's that on the side there? Can you zoom in?"

Zhia enlarged the marking on the front door of the vehicle, and Ellen caught her breath. The octopus, blue with its four semi-straight, spindly legs. She thought of the strange creature the songbird had transformed into, half tentacle, half arachnid.

"Arakovic," she whispered.

"They're taking him, look!" Zhia pointed at the lower picture.

Her eyes darted down just soon enough to see Kael crumple, then get dragged into the back as the door slammed down.

Jenny trotted up.

"Get in the lander—you drive. Get everyone loaded," Ellen ordered.

"Yes, ma'am."

"That's not an Enhancer vehicle. What is it?" Zhia said slowly.

"This is a Puritan planet? Could it be them?"

"Hiring Theroki to do their dirty work?"

"Enhancers shouldn't need to knock him out though." The image from Kael's mind of the supposed Puritan operative with all her Enhancements came back to her. "Or maybe it's someone else entirely. Someone working with Arakovic? Or maybe she's working with one of them."

"None of this makes sense."

"I know. Keep monitoring that. Into the lander. Is the tracker working?"

"So far." Zhia barely looked up from the screen to jog after her.

As soon as the hatch shut over them all, Jenny gunned it and turned sharply. Hmm, maybe she shouldn't have ordered the adrenaline junkie to drive. This should be a fun ride.

———

THEY FOLLOWED the van nearly sixty miles, away from the star port and the city and out into the desert hills. Nova had nodded off in her suit, and while Ellen kept her eyes trained on the van, even Zhia had relaxed enough to eat a ration bar from her leg compartment. The road was desolate out here, with fewer cars, so they followed at an even greater distance.

Ellen was glad she hadn't lingered, though, because suddenly, the truck vanished from the video display. Zhia snapped to attention too.

"Did you see that?" she muttered, mouth full of fruit-nut-combo.

Ellen nodded. "Look, the tracker's still moving on the map."

"Vehicle cloaking?"

"Must be. I hope."

"Does that mean they realize we're following them?"

Ellen pressed her lips together. "Maybe. But I sure hope not."

A few minutes later, it was Zhia to first notice the change. "Look— is it turning off? It's stopping!"

Ellen rattled off a coordinate to Jenny. "That's our target."

"Should we be looking for a back door?" said Nova, rousing.

"I'm worried there won't be time for that," said Ellen, her eyes still trained on the screen.

"Guns blazing, it is."

Sure enough, a van door opened out of thin air, like a fragging wormhole opening up in the middle of the desert. The three men dragged Kael out, his body still limp.

Ellen swore, then looked up at Zhia. "Thank you," she said softly.

Zhia's eyes widened. "For what?"

"For talking some sense into me. What if we hadn't tailed him?" She would've thought he'd just rejoined the Theroki and never come back.

That maybe he had *wanted* not to come back and deal with her... confusion.

"Anytime, Commander." Zhia grinned. "Luckily, you don't need it that often."

Ellen narrowed her eyes as the men dusted off a door into the ground, opened it, and tossed Kael inside. They headed down the stairs. She tightened her hand into a fist.

Whoever these people were, she was coming after them.

———

KAEL STRUGGLED to open his eyes. His lids felt heavy, unnaturally heavy. What the hell had happened?

Along with the memory of the van, the oath program surged to life, flooding him. He tried to move his hands, but something like steel bit into the wrists. Corners of something bit into his shoulders. Where was his armor?

His eyes snapped open now. And to his surprise, he saw the one person he hadn't expected.

"Vala," he whispered.

She stood leaning against the high counter, a bank of computers behind her. Her straight blond hair fell long over her shoulders as usual, but the black jumpsuit was new, more military looking than the lab coats she'd often worn when pretending to be an Enhancer scientist. Or maybe she was a scientist, but something else besides.

"I just don't seem to be able to quit you, Kael Sidassian." She smiled, her same perfect, Enhancer-designed smile.

He clenched his teeth. "Where's the capsule? And why am I here?"

She shook her head. "Is that any way to greet an old love?"

He could remember feeling a lot of things for her, but they felt distant, unimportant. He could hardly remember them. "The past is in the past."

"I see you fixed your chip. After I worked so hard to liberate you from it."

"You had your own selfish reasons."

She clucked her tongue at him and shook her head. "That's no way to talk to someone who so frequently ties you to chairs, Sidassian. I could just as easily take your chip and leave you without one. Or maybe put in a different version of my own?" She grinned now and held up a tiny chip in her hand. "Or maybe I already have, and this is the original."

One way to find out. He reached out and unleashed a wave of energy to fling her into the computer bank. If he broke her spine to start, he wouldn't feel terribly bad about that.

Nothing happened.

He tried again, weakly. But he knew. She'd taken it all—and what had she put in its place? God only knew.

"You bitch," he whispered.

She grinned. "I'm your liberator, Sidassian."

"I don't feel very liberated bolted to the floor."

"You will when I'm done with you. Because you'll think whatever I want you to think." She stepped forward for a moment, running her hand along his beard and his jaw almost affectionately.

He snapped at her, barely missing getting in a good bite by a centimeter.

Laughing, she strode back to the computer bank.

"I don't believe you. You don't know how." He scowled at her back.

"Guess you'll find out, won't you? But is it so hard to believe? The Theroki were controlling you, in their meager way. You've just acquired a newer, prettier operator." She didn't turn, but he could tell she was smiling.

"Where is the capsule?"

"Why, right here, of course." She turned and held out a palm faceup to the sky. And there it was, stowed in a wall compartment behind her behind clear green glass.

"What are you doing to it?"

"Destroying it, of course," she said sweetly again.

She laughed as he growled at her, the oath program urging his arms, his neck, his legs to strain against the steel until well after it had cut into him. Blood dripped down his pointer finger and splashed on the floor, and his ankles grew wet and slippery too, before the surge calmed for a moment, the oath pondering another path.

"Why?"

She shrugged. "Why not?"

"That's not a reason to do something like this. To kill a child."

"It's not a child. It's a collection of genes. A fetus if you really want to stretch the definition of child." She rolled her eyes. "And besides, I'm getting paid well to do it. *Some* Enhancers don't need their precious fool of an empress starting trouble."

"So it was an inside job? Why are you afraid of her? Who do you work for?"

"*Afraid* of her? Afraid of a fetus?" She scoffed and turned her back on him. "Let's see. Fifteen percent complete. You have a while to wait till you've failed your mission, Sidassian." She grinned.

As if she knew just what button to push, the oath programming surged into action again, achieving nothing but leaving him more deeply cut and bleeding profusely on the floor.

"For the record," she said, sidling up to him, "not that you'll live long enough to record anything, but that fetus might grow up to resent being tampered with. She might not *want* to be born whatever monstrosity they've made her. I'm doing her a favor."

"Is that what happened to you?" he said, his voice hoarse.

Her eyes widened, then narrowed again as she shook her head. "Too smart for your own good. That's what you are, Sidassian."

"I've been accused of a lot of things, but never *that* before. So that's it? Why you're a Puritan, yet you've clearly been Enhanced?"

She frowned at him and turned away. "I'm not a Puritan, although I do fit in well here. But with the proceeds from this, I should be well on my way to buying my own ship and going wherever the hell I please." She strode back to the computer bank, keeping her back turned.

His oath made another valiant if ill-fated surge to free himself and defend the child. He groaned, the pain digging deeper now. Would it stop when it hit the bone? Or would he bleed out first?

To his surprise, Vala whirled. But her eyes weren't on him or his pain. They were on the door behind him. He heard a very soft clink of armor, but no footsteps. Strange.

"I said I was not to be disturbed—" She stopped short. "You're not Theroki."

He craned his neck but could only see shadowy forms filling the doorway.

"No. We're not. Stand aside from the computers, disarm, and raise your hands," a muffled voice ordered.

"If you're Enhancers, we can make a deal. I was *hired* by Enhancers, I swear to you. I can—" Her hands didn't lift from the keys. Instead she was pressing more of them.

"Step aside, or we'll move you," the gruff voice ordered again.

Vala glanced back up but didn't take her hands from the keys, jamming one large one to the right. "Security—where the frag are you?"

Only static came back over the line.

She mustered a fake smile, turning now and relinquishing the keys. She started forward, a sway to her hips. "Maybe we can make some other kind of arrangement then," she said.

But Vala froze as a familiar-looking armored form strode up to her even more quickly. The soldier eyed her from head to toe and then paused an inch or so away, as if considering. But saying nothing.

"There's more than one way to barter," Vala said gently. "Credits. Connections. I've got quite a library of Enhancements in this computer bank. Or perhaps you prefer something a little more... human?" She hesitated, then took one more step forward, feigning shyness. Oh, he knew these moves all right. "A little private time behind these computers perhaps?"

The form didn't respond. Didn't even twitch.

Without warning, a bolt shot out of the rifle.

A *multi*rifle, he realized.

Electricity arched, and the stun sent Vala collapsing to the floor. Her body spasmed once, then again, then fell still.

The soldier turned toward him and hit the helmet retract.

Ellen stared out at him, face flat and emotionless as ever. "She's not my type."

He gaped at her. Was he going crazy? Or had she really come after him? A crazed laugh escaped his lips.

"Good one," said a voice from behind. Nova?

Someone else snorted. "Poker-faced as always, Commander. You should really consider gambling." Was that Zhia? He craned to see but couldn't spot anyone except a smaller form crouching behind him.

"Isn't that what I'm already doing?" Ellen shut the helmet again with a flick. "You got some kind of cutters in that pack of yours, or are we going to have to torch him out of this?"

"On it, ma'am."

"Jenny? Is that you?" he managed, although yellow splotches were starting to appear in front of his eyes.

Ellen came closer. "You've lost a lot of blood. But we're going to get you out of here."

"He's *still* losing a lot of blood, what the hell." Jenny swore. She didn't seem to do that too often. He must be in bad shape.

"The capsule, Commander. Can you—" He stopped, almost losing consciousness for a moment, but he held on. "Can you—she said she was destroying it."

"Zhia—get on that. Get a nuke in too. Nova, find his armor, scan for any further threats in the area."

Zhia tapped at the keys, and the green glass door popped open with a puff and a hiss. Zhia reached in and took the capsule out. Immediately the chems in him eased, his tension lessening. Apparently his oath was satisfied with that, convinced Zhia was an ally. His head dipped forward for a moment, almost losing it.

Ellen leaned closer to him. "Stay with me, Kael." Her voice was soft, almost gentle. He felt sure there was something important in it he was missing, something he would have understood a week ago.

But it didn't matter. He couldn't keep his head up anymore, now that the capsule was out. His head lolled back, and everything faded to black.

———

ELLEN CAUGHT his head before it could fall all the way back. "Jesus, how did he lose so much blood so quickly?"

"The wrists aren't great for that. But I've got them glued and bandaged now. Let me get his ankles." Jenny shifted around him as Ellen pulled his arms forward onto his lap. He looked pale.

"Is this... is he going to survive this?"

Jenny glanced up. "Yes. I'll get a nanotransfusion injected as soon as I've stopped the bleeding. Between the glue and the nanoreconstructs, he's not losing any more. It'll take time, but he'll be fine. We got here in time."

"What do I do with this, Commander?" Zhia held up the capsule.

Ellen hesitated. "Take it. Maybe it's time we crack that thing open and see what's inside." After putting it into an artificial womb, of course.

Zhia nodded, opened her cargo compartment at her hip, and put the capsule inside just as the nuke beeped. Zhia looked up in surprise. "We... have a hit."

"For Arakovic?"

Zhia nodded.

"Are you serious?"

"As death. Three MIAs too. Maybe more. It's sending them to Simmons urgently."

"Adan," Ellen barked into the comm. "Get Simmons online. Wake him up if need be—he's going to want to see this."

She was still holding Kael's head. She supposed Jenny needed a nurse, but this seemed a little like a waste of her abilities. She moved behind him so he could lean on her stomach, freeing her hands for something else. Like her multi.

As she shifted, the squirming of something white caught her eye.

"Zhia!" Ellen shouted.

Too late. A massive white tentacle shot out and grabbed Zhia by the leg, throwing her down belly-first.

Nova charged in behind her as Ellen fired. But damn it—lasers and bullets hadn't worked on the last one, why did she think a stun would do a thing? She threw the rifle strap over her head and reached for her knife. "Blades, blades!"

In those precious seconds, the body of the Puritan operative had disappeared, and a repulsive pale creature rose up in its place, one tentacle pinning Zhia to the ground by the leg while another wrapped around her throat.

SONGBIRD. We should have known you would come. Mother has a message.

Ellen glared up at the white mass, now towering a few feet above her. She crouched, searching for a target. "Oh, yeah?"

She's coming for you.

"Well, me first," Ellen growled. Then she leapt at the creature, driving the blade into the soft upper half first. Nova followed a few seconds later, hacking at the tentacle that had closed around Zhia's windpipe. Ellen drove the knife deeper, hitting the hard carapace, pulling out, and then plunging back in for more.

Nova's tentacle came free, and she rounded on the creature, diving to dig the blade deep into its back.

Black blood like oil spurted out at them, and Ellen dodged. Who knew what that blood could do?

One of the arachnid legs took that moment to sweep her off her feet, but now Zhia joined in at Nova's side, slashing off another tentacle before digging her knife into the soft upper back—and yanking down. The creature listed to one side and then collapsed to the ground between them.

For a moment, they also stood panting and staring at each other. Black blood dripped from Ellen's blade, and she shuddered.

Nova wiped a splatter of black off her visor and then grinned at them. "You know, of all weapons, sometimes simple is best. Nothing like a knife."

Zhia snorted. "Don't tell that to your precious Stella."

Nova grinned wider. "She gets plenty of play."

"He's stable now," Jenny said. "We should get him out of here."

"I couldn't find his armor," Nova said, face falling.

"It's crap anyway," Ellen said, not hiding her smile. "Let's blow this ice cream stand."

CHAPTER FIFTEEN

ELLEN SWALLOWED AS SHE WAITED, hands clasped behind her back, for Simmons's picture to appear on screen.

"Commander Ryu! We've gotten so much information from Upsilon—I can't wait to show you—"

"This isn't about that, sir." She took a deep breath.

He frowned, waiting silently.

"Simmons, I've developed… personal feelings for the passenger I took onboard."

He raised his eyebrows, then looked at a sheet of paper off to the side of his desk. "I believe you called him… let me see here, a fine, perfect, efficient specimen of manhood?"

She blushed. "What the hell, Doug. Do you transcribe every meeting we have?"

"You called me Doug! This is progress!" He grinned. "I only transcribe the entertaining things."

"Damn it." She rubbed the bridge of her nose between her eyes.

"I have a scrapbook of things here that prove you're human and not an android."

"What?"

"I'm kidding. Mostly. But seriously, congratulations. Does he dig you back? Do you want to try to recruit him?"

She blinked. "I was planning on offering my resignation."

"What?" He sat forward, alarmed.

"It's irresponsible of me to get involved. It's distracting to the mission, and—"

"Nonsense. Dr. Taylor thinks the mutual human support would improve your ability to handle stress and help you make better decisions."

"She... talked to you about that? Wait, you already knew? I have no problem handling stress, sir."

"I didn't mean to imply you did. But you're in an extremely stressful situation regularly, and indefinitely, Commander. Dr. Levereaux continues to have some reservations about his Theroki status, but Dr. Dremer fiercely argued in favor of his addition to the team, especially for his weapons and language skills. She's been lobbying me heavily."

"His weapons skills. Right. I've also got a blackhole with a beach view I could see you if you're interested, Simmons."

His eyes twinkled. "Thanks, but I've already got a beach view. Obviously Dremer would like to reverse engineer him, too. But she pointed out he's been instrumental in defending your ship twice and on several missions."

"Everyone seems pretty aligned on this. Why don't you all just recruit him yourselves?"

Simmons smirked. "I suggested that, but I believe they thought you'd be the most persuasive in his eyes."

She blushed harder. "Are you sure this is a good idea, sir?"

He frowned at her more seriously. "You know, you deserve to live your life too, Ellen. You go around helping people and taking nothing for yourself, you'll burn yourself out. It's not sustainable."

"It's fraternization. It's dangerous. It's—"

"This isn't the military," Simmons snapped, for once sounding almost angry. Ellen's eyes widened. "You can run it like that if it suits you, but most military positions run through rotations for a reason.

People need family. People need home. I thought you were planning to spend the rest of your life on the *Audacity*."

The way he put that brought unexpected wetness to her eyes. She blinked it away viciously. The *Audacity* was her home, her ship. The first real place she'd ever felt she belonged. "I *was*, sir. I mean, I am."

"So you're gonna spend the next ninety-plus years alone? Please. Listen, he seems a good addition to the team. This isn't the Union SF anymore, and you don't have to act like it is. I mean, I might have preferred him to be female, but then maybe that wouldn't have tickled your pickle."

She couldn't hold back a snort. "Not everyone can be as perfect as Dr. Taylor, sir."

"So have I convinced you not to resign? And to recruit this..." He glanced down. "Kael Sidassian?"

"Have your people checked him out, sir?"

"Uh-uh," he said, waggling a finger. "I asked first."

"You have convinced me not to resign."

"I checked him out. He comes from a tough situation, but everything you'd recorded in his file checks out as true. Didn't find any land mines in his past. In fact, he seems to have told you pretty much everything. Bared his soul to you, if you will." He grinned.

She only winced in reply.

"Relax. There was one thing, which is that he was accused of murdering someone on his home planet. Looks like how he was forced into the Theroki."

Her eyes widened. "Sir, that's—"

"Before you get too caught up about it, the local coroner protested the charge as there was literally no evidence. But on Faros planets, the local magistrates have pretty much complete power. He's about as likely to have actually murdered the girl as not, but my nose says not. And my nose can smell faked information from a mile away."

"Girl?" Ellen's heart leapt into her throat. "That sounds... bad, Doug."

He grinned, though. "Look at you! Keep that up, Ellen. Much better than sir. Listen, take a look at this picture and what you know about

Kael Sidassian and tell me if the idea that he killed her doesn't make much sense." He flipped up an image of a woman, a girl really, of fifteen with long black hair, delicate features. She was pretty, if dressed in rags—and had a full, pregnant belly.

"Jesus. How... old was he?" she said softly.

"Another good point. Seventeen, I think? He had also filed for a marriage license."

His words drifted back to her. *They killed her. The gangs didn't agree.* "Oh, Lord. He did tell me about this, didn't he? When he told me about trying to get away from the gangs and—"

"Yes," Simmons said. "I also checked back to Xi's recordings of that conversation. She feels confident he was telling the truth."

"You... watched that?" She winced.

"I had Xi pull up just his necessary phrases. Wasn't trying to invade your privacy, but knowing his background while he's on the ship is part of security."

She didn't entirely believe he hadn't listened to the whole thing. Knowing if your commander was compromised by a rage-charged, telekinetic maniac, as Simmons had once called Kael, was also part of security. She took a deep breath. "You're serious? You think we should recruit him."

"Yes. Dead serious."

"We will make an enemy of the Theroki for harboring a rogue," she pointed out cautiously, hoping it had already occurred to him.

An amused, almost excited smile crossed Simmons's face. "You get him to agree, and I'll take care of that."

She hesitated. Perhaps she shouldn't be so standoffish with Simmons. Perhaps she should try... chatting more. It felt odd with a superior, especially from the shadowy Foundation, but hadn't he been suggesting she be more sociable all along? "You'll take care of it...? Or your people... Doug?"

"I don't have any 'people,' Ellen. I do have a staff of very talented programs I've written. We make an excellent team. One of them even makes me coffee." As if to illustrate, he took a sip from a mug that looked to have a nebula printed across it.

"Do your programs chat with you, sir?"

"Not very well, no. They're practically as business-minded as you. I have to rely on Dremer most of the time."

"And you two have so much in common." She couldn't imagine a twenty-seven-year-old billionaire had much to chat about with a sixty-year-old surgeon.

"Not exactly." He grinned. "But I'm a determined chatter."

"I will try to hold up my end of the bargain better then."

"See to it that you do, Commander," he said, laughter in his eyes.

———

KAEL WOKE up in sick bay, surrounded by Jenny, Levereaux, and Dremer, who'd all been leaning over him, waiting for him to wake up. "How the hell did I get here?" he croaked, his voice rough.

"We dragged you back," Jenny said, grinning. "You're lucky our armor triples our strength."

He snorted. "Where... Are we on the *Audacity*?"

Dremer nodded. "In sick bay."

He looked further around the room. "Where's the commander?"

Dremer glanced at Jenny, smiling. "In her office, I believe."

The comm clicked on. "Kael, if you're feeling up to it, can I speak with you in my cabin, please?"

Dremer grinned. "Speak of the devil, there she is."

Hmm. He wanted to feel excited about that, but her tone was stiffly formal. She was probably going to tell him just exactly which rock they'd be kicking him off on and when. "I'll be right there, ma'am. Assuming I can walk."

With Jenny's and Levereaux's help, he made it to his feet and was remarkably steady, considering the bandages and glue covering his wrists and ankles. And neck too. He shook his head at the memory, then paused.

"Where..." he started slowly. Huh. He felt no oath program running. "Where's the capsule?"

"It's in my lab," said Levereaux. "It needed a bigger containment unit, so we had to oblige."

He blinked. "I don't feel... anything."

Dremer raised her chin with a smug little smile. "While you were out, I may have... tried to make your life a little easier, Mr. Sidassian."

He raised his eyebrows.

But Dremer shooed him toward the door. "Best not keep the commander waiting."

When he arrived, she wasn't alone. Was that the cause for her formal tone? On a vid screen, a young man with blond spiked hair and thin wire glasses waited. He had a deadly serious look on his face, which was undercut by a ridiculous navy-blue shirt patterned with orange and yellow sunsets and surfing cats. Kael wouldn't have been caught dead wearing the thing.

"Yes, Commander?" He glanced from her to the man and back again.

"Sidassian, this is Doug Simmons. Simmons, you've already heard about our Theroki friend here."

"I think I lost the *ki* when we left Desori. If we left Desori?"

"Yes, we're in transit away from there now."

"I'll probably be considered rogue if I don't go back soon. If I'm not already."

"Are you interested in going back?" Simmons asked flatly.

Kael hesitated. Why was he asking? "Not particularly, sir."

"How attached are you to your last name?" Simmons cocked his head sideways.

"Excuse me, sir?" he said.

"Sorry, I'm getting ahead of myself."

"Would you like me to leave, sir?" Ellen offered.

Sir? She just called Simmons "sir." That was hard to believe because the young man didn't look like he had a military bone in his body, but he was apparently above her in her chain of command. Kael hadn't been certain she *had* a chain of command above her. Who was this kid in their hierarchy? One of their "private donors"?

"No way. Clearly I'm not any more talented at accurate communication than *you* are."

"Why, thank you, sir," she said, a wry smile twisting one corner of her mouth.

Simmons sighed, looking even younger for a moment. "Why don't you just tell him? I suck at this."

"Because it's not mine to tell, Patron," she said gently.

Patron? Kael froze. He'd only heard of *one* organization that called anyone within it Patrons. A chill went through him, the pieces flying together at breakneck speed.

"You work for the Foundation?" he said to Ellen alone. "Your private donors—this is them? I mean, him?"

"See, look how well you did that," said Simmons. "Much more understandable than my ramblings."

"Thank you, sir." She met Kael's gaze, eyes denying nothing, but she said no more.

Simmons was grinning. "Yes, Mr. Sidassian, you've guessed correctly. Commander Ryu works for the Foundation. All right, let's see here. Let's dust off that old elevator pitch, shall we?"

"Dusting? Elevators? Excuse me, sir?"

"And we're off to a rousing start. Never mind. This ship is a military outpost of the Orlay-Rockel-Nyelon Foundation. Commander Ryu is the leader of this cell, and I'm its liaison with Foundation leadership and scientists, as well as one of them myself. While we are sincere in our running of humanitarian efforts in the region—efforts that include looking for troubled passengers in need of transportation, such as yourself, I might point out—that is not the primary mission of this cell."

"I... gathered that," Kael said slowly. "Wait, troubled passengers?" He glanced at Ellen, and she gave him a nod.

"It was Simmons's idea to post passenger listings at various ports."

"You'd never guess what the cat drags in," snickered Simmons, mostly to himself.

"You mentioned a primary mission," Kael said. "We've been attacking Enhancer laboratories."

"We are not targeting Enhancers specifically. Our mission is defending people from unscrupulous scientists. Recently, it's mostly been rogue researchers who kidnap and torture people with illegal biological experiments. Or do their experiments where there are no laws at all. It can be anything scientific and unethical, but the bio folks sure have been active lately."

"I gathered that too, sir. Ellen—Commander Ryu—assured me this was not a faction-specific mission. But who determines if something's unethical?" Between every black and white were many shades of gray.

"We do," Simmons said coldly, without a hint of hesitation. "In your region—well, in a lot of regions—Enhancers are most likely to run afoul of ethical experimentation standards. But that's a tactical point. What I'm trying my best to explain is that the Foundation is determined to prevent the abuse of science in any space we can reach. Or limit its abuse, anyway. But unfortunately, that's not the extent of it. Striking back at scientific breaches of ethics may become more of a short-term project because we've had some reports of a much more dangerous enemy on our radars. Metaphorically, speaking. Um, that probably didn't make any sense."

"A more dangerous enemy?"

Simmons nodded, grave now. "The commander tells me you've encountered several at this point."

"The creatures on Desori. The white spider tentacle things," Ellen chimed in.

"We're still gathering information on them, but they may be a newly arrived alien race. You should know that they appear to be targeting men with extreme prejudice. That is the real reason I've asked Commander Ryu to put together this mostly female ship."

"I should know this? Why are you telling me this, Mr. Simmons?" Kael said slowly, choosing the civilian designation to see the young man's reaction. Simmons didn't notice. Kael probably could have called him Doug. He might even have preferred that.

"I'll be straight with you, Sidassian. I've heard a lot of good things about you, and I'd like to offer you the chance to join this cell as a member of the team. A job. If you're interested."

Kael's heartbeat jumped to double time. That he had not expected. "Heard good things? From the commander?" He glanced at Ellen.

Simmons smirked suddenly, a crack in his seriousness, and Kael had an inkling that the man was not at all oblivious to the fact that they might have flirted with more than a professional relationship. "As a matter of fact, not from the commander. She mutters things from time to time that she thinks I don't hear, but—"

"Simmons," she hissed.

"All right, all right. I'm pretty clear on where she stands, though. But no, actually Dremer has been your strongest proponent. Lieutenant Verakov and Sergeant Morales have also each reached out to me independently to recommend your recruitment."

Ellen's eyes widened a little at that. She hadn't known about that, had she?

"Isn't that... a little out of the chain of command, sir?" Kael said.

Simmons shrugged. "I don't think praise is usually limited in its distribution, is it? Besides, we only run a *mostly* military organization around here." His sunset cat shirt certainly drove that point home as he grinned.

"So I've heard."

"So, you want a job?" Simmons said, fidgeting with excitement. "I mean, there's some pay and benefits and stuff. We could talk about that if you want, or I can just send you an email."

Kael snorted, but he eyed Ellen. She wasn't meeting his gaze.

"Are you okay with this, Commander?" he said softly. If she was, why hadn't she asked him herself? He would have liked something along the lines of crawling into his bed in the dark and whispering the offer in his ear.

That was pretty much never happening.

Did she even agree with this idea?

She held her gaze on Simmons, who had raised his eyebrows expectantly, but finally her eyes darted toward him. She froze. Fear crept into her eyes, just as it had in those moments of confessing how scared she was, how she couldn't imagine taking a risk and screwing up so bad again.

He waited.

"Simmons would not do anything against my guidance," she said eventually. "Would you, Simmons?"

"*Of course* I checked with the commander before I considered making this offer. After I talked her out of resigning—"

"Resigning?" Kael snapped. "What the hell, Ellen?" Simmons's face lit up with amusement. Good thing *someone* was enjoying himself. "You said this was the most important thing you've ever done. Why the hell— I— You can't give it up, damn it."

"She's not giving it up," said Simmons. "And you said that, Commander? I'm so touched."

She glared at the vid feed. "Don't get cocky, I can still change my mind and tell you all to piss off," she snapped. "And I would simply prefer that this particular personnel decision be made without my input. So get on with it." She took her eyes off both of them and stared into the distance.

Ah, so that was it. Of course. After what had happened with the *Mirror's Light*, she wanted to prove to herself that she hadn't biased this situation. That he would be here because other people wanted him here too. That way she'd be able to live with herself if anything in the future went wrong.

Maybe.

He straightened, bracing himself for the next part. This was too good to be true. He might as well burst the bubble before he got used to this feeling of maybe not being screwed over by the universe for once. "Sirs, there's probably something you should know. I was..." He gritted his teeth. No matter how many times he had to explain it, it never got easier to say. "I do have a criminal record. I was wrongly accused of murder on Faros IV. Conscription to the Theroki was my sentence. If you have any problems employing felons, that might be an issue for you."

Simmons laced his fingers together in front of his chin. "Oh, we know."

Kael blinked. Then his gaze darted to Ellen, who was still staring off into nothingness. "You know?" he said to Doug but looking at Ellen.

"You think I would divulge the innermost secrets of the Foundation to you if I hadn't already cleared you to take the job?"

No one had ever cleared him for anything. He blinked again, retraining his eyes on Doug. "I'm sorry, what?"

"Cleared you for the job. Soon those fabricated charges won't matter. Although I can clear them, if you want?"

"Yes, sir," he stumbled awkwardly. "I *do* want. But how—"

"I may be a liaison, Kael, but I'm part of this mission too. Information is my business. I find it, I edit it, I keep it. On occasion I create it. Sometimes it's even true. Others… not so much." He grinned, the first predatory expression Kael had seen on him. He immediately liked the man more for it. "To be clear, the false charges are not an issue for us. The offer was extended with full knowledge of them."

Kael took a deep breath, trying to cover how stunned he was. "Email me your details. Assuming things check out, I accept," he said quickly.

"Excellent. I'll be in touch."

"Thank you, uh… what do I call you?"

Simmons winced, his shoulders scrunching self-consciously. "Technically the title is Patron. But it's really not my style. I think they call me that to torture me. Simmons is fine. Just complete the missions, and I really don't give a shit."

"You know, for a shadowy organization of rich scientists, you're not very shadowy."

At that, Simmons grinned. "Thank you. I'll take that as a compliment. I may be the exception, though. Not sure the Founders themselves would give you the same impression. Oh, that reminds me." He snapped his fingers and pointed at Kael through the screen. "Your last name—attached to it?"

Kael frowned. "Why?"

"I can't have Therokis hunting down rogues on my ship."

"Your ship? I thought it was *her* ship."

"He bought it," Ellen said simply, still staring into space.

"And recruited our dear commander, I might add." But then Simmons grinned. "But then I gave it to her. So yes, it *is* her ship."

"What does that have to do with my last name?"

"I need to finish up the programming on your new chip. Assuming you want it, of course."

"My... new... what?"

"Dremer and I have put together a new chip with Foundation firmware that should let you keep your Theroki abilities without any... unwanted side effects, if you catch my drift. Emotional regulation and hormonal stimulation levels will return to relatively normal levels. Should be a little faster too. Hardware is upgraded. Interface connections will identify you as an average citizen of somewhere neutral, I haven't decided where yet. I'll be editing your files in the Theroki databases to record an honorable discharge but also establishing a new identity, with your permission, of course. And of course, deleting those old charges."

"*Editing* Theroki databases? Those are fairly hard to—"

"You infiltrate labs, I infiltrate databases. Or networks, more specifically. Leave it to me, Sidassian, I know what I'm doing."

"He's the one who made the universal translator," Ellen put in.

"Ah" was all Kael could think to say.

"We all have our areas of expertise." Simmons cracked his knuckles and then licked his lips, staring off to the side of the screen as if eager to get to work. "So what do you think?"

"I, uh, I'm not attached to my last name at all, sir," he said eventually. "Or anything about my past. Edit away."

"Great, I love a clean slate. I'll shoot you a message about your new past life too." Simmons clapped his hands together and rubbed them with excitement. "This should be fun. Welcome to the team."

———

THE VID SCREEN flipped off and left Ellen alone, staring terrified into space, Kael still just inside the door of her cabin.

She should... say something, at least. Or rush over to him and throw him against the wall. But something rooted her in place, her eyes transfixed on a meaningless piece of wall.

"Will that be all, Commander?" he said, his voice flat and a touch cold.

Far from it, she wanted to say. But she could barely force her eyes to focus, then turn and meet his. His expression was unreadable. His eyes seemed to gauge hers just as she sought to measure him, and neither of them could understand the other. They were too busy glowering to figure the other out. What was there for him to see? She felt... numb. Dazed. Surprised.

It had all kind of worked out. Except this last little piece. The piece that she needed to do, the chasm that only she could cross.

Did she have it in her to make a grand gesture? To somehow apologize?

"We have a lot of details to work out," she said softly.

"Oh?" he replied, raising an eyebrow.

"Nova is going to be pissed when you outrank her."

He smiled. "You've picked a rank, then?"

"I delegated the task to Lieutenant Verakov, who'd like you to lead the other drop team."

He frowned, not understanding.

"Her recommendation is her rank. Lieutenant."

His mouth fell open, but she didn't miss him straightening just a bit. "Don't you think that's a little high, Commander? I'm not officer material."

She shrugged. "Not my decision. If you disagree, you'll have to take it up with Zhia." Damn, it felt good to say that. She was glad she could lob that one into someone else's court. "But you know, between you and me, I think she just wants someone who'll let her slack more, and none of these ladies wants a promotion. I haven't recruited the most ambitious bunch. So you're stuck with the responsibility, I guess."

He said nothing, still looking stunned, and a silence settled between them, more awkward this time. She searched for the words but found nothing. Nothing seemed enough to make up for her indecision. There were no simple sounds she could utter to simply make it up to him. She needed time to think; he deserved more than just a hasty "I'm sorry" and passionate tumbling into the sheets.

She looked down at her boots, admitting defeat. "That will be all, Kael."

His face showed nothing, but she could have sworn she felt something sink in him. He nodded crisply and turned on his heel without hesitation.

"For now," she whispered.

He strode out, not reacting to the words if he heard them. The hatch slipped open and shut again around him, and he was gone.

———

HE LAY AWAKE that night in the darkness. Footsteps would wander past his cabin, but they'd pass right on by. Voices would amble past, headed to dinner. He ate a ration bar and read network articles about the Foundation, anything he could find. Half of it was almost certainly untrue. More voices ambled past again—Fern and Nova this time, judging from the laughter. The night cycle began its peaceful slumber. There was no sign of Ellen.

For a ship that wanted him aboard, he felt peculiarly alone.

The chip that Simmons and Dremer had designed sounded life changing, but perhaps he should have them keep some of those old emotion-altering bits. Could he live with Ellen and not have her? Would it be torture? Exquisite torture, maybe.

He shook his head. He'd get used to it. He'd find someone else, and eventually that tension would fade. Maybe Josana wasn't too young after all, or maybe in six months she'd seem less so. Mo had an attractive face, sexy and sharp when staring down the barrel of her rifle, and Jenny was of course gorgeous in her cigars-and-shotguns sort of way, both sweet and ballsy.

He sighed. He could have just as easily listed that his Theroki mentors had had great musculature, or that Vala had had blond hair. They were facts, nothing more. Not a bit of it moved him.

Ellen's words drifted back into his mind. *The most audacious thing you can do is giving a shit.* How right she was. If only she gave half as many shits about him as she did about her mission. But then, that was what he loved about her, her bravery, her devotion, her sense of what was right. Her calm resoluteness to actually do something about it.

The chime of an email from Doug—he had decided he would have to get used to calling Patron Simmons that, one way or another—saved him from his thoughts. He already knew he was going to sign. There were next to no other ways that he could escape his Theroki contract, and the few that might have existed wouldn't be half as clean and would haunt him the rest of his days. There was literally no other way that would ever be this good to take control of his life, finally, for the first time.

And no other way would keep him on a ship near Ellen, in case she someday changed her mind.

He snorted as he tapped to open the message. He'd never learn.

Surprisingly, the deal was great. He'd never been paid so much, even on his best commissions. In fact, it was exactly double his previous base pay. He frowned at that, wondering if it was by design. Combat bonuses came on top of that, which looked like they'd be basically continuous with the way the ship had operated so far. So three times as much, and lots of equipment and room and board included. The contract was up for renewal every six months, with clauses for injury, health, family issues. Beyond fair.

He could find nothing that said he had to drink blood or sell his soul to Simmons's grandmother or something, so he signed away and shipped the file back to Doug, feeling a lot more wanted, if still alone. At least the kid techno genius billionaire seemed earnest about having him here. He shouldn't call him a kid, as they were probably about the same age, but Doug was just so green. And so cheerful.

He drifted off to sleep and woke to a pounding on his hatch, then a chime.

"Hey. Theroki. Wake up. C'mon, Xi, let me in."

Ellen's voice set his heart pounding.

"Kael has given specific instructions as to his cabin security, Commander Ryu."

"I'm the commanding officer of this ship, Xi. *His* commanding officer now."

"Would you like to issue your override codes, Commander?"

"No," she grumbled. She pounded on the metal again. "Wake up, Theroki, damn it."

"If you would not like to issue your override codes, Commander, perhaps you should let Kael sleep." Was the AI getting a protective streak now? Surely she knew he was now awake, but she wasn't tattling. At least not yet. She'd also clearly registered that he could have answered but hadn't. "His sleep cycle only began a few hours ago. For optimum crew performance, I recommend you postpone a mission if it is not time-sensitive. It is very early in the morning, Commander." She almost sounded affronted on his behalf.

Kael snorted. Way to tell her I was up all night thinking about her, he thought to himself. Hopefully Ellen wouldn't put two and two together.

"Theroki—you partying without me?" She pounded again.

He sighed. Like she wanted to party *with* him. If she did, all she had to do was show up. But she would be his superior now. He should probably answer the door.

He sat up in his bunk and rubbed his face. He glanced around for his shirt. It was nowhere to be found. Well, she was the one waking him up in his cabin. There was no dress code in Doug's amusing organizational training packet. She'd just have to deal with skin and ink. Or more likely, she could order him to put on a shirt if she didn't like staring at his chest.

Which she almost certainly didn't.

"It's okay, Xi, I'm awake now. Open sesame."

The hatch slid open just as Ellen was raising a fist to pound again. Unperturbed, she stepped one foot inside the hatch, as if she was concerned Xi would shut her out again, but she stopped, straddling the doorway. She wore her red light armor, an external helmet propped on the hip that faced the hallway.

"Up late regretting your life choices?" she said. Her face was oddly bright, her eyes twinkling, a rare smile revealing a glimpse of straight, white teeth.

"Some of them," he said, smiling back, to his chagrin. "You're finally gonna have to break that habit of calling me Theroki now, you know."

"I suppose. Patron Simmons tells me you signed his paperwork, so you're mine for at least six months. That right?" She pursed her lips. He shook his head at how much he liked the sound of that.

Mine. Hers. He wished. "Yes, ma'am. Something I can kill or maim for you this early in the morning?"

"Not exactly." She actually grinned now, and he leaned back, a little concerned. Was that excitement, or was she baring her teeth at him? "We're going shopping."

"What? When?"

"Now. Well, take fifteen to get some clothes on, and meet me at the hatch."

He spread his hands innocently. "I didn't get the memo that shirts were required for missions. There's nothing in this HR packet."

"Doug would love it if you told him that. It'd give him proof someone actually read it."

"But then I'd know for sure if I'd have to put a shirt on." He grinned at her mock-defiantly and hoped she knew he was joking.

She narrowed her eyes, but it seemed playful. He hoped. "You might want a jacket as well. It's a bit chilly on Entrill V."

She stepped out, palmed the hatch shut, and was gone.

"What do you think that's all about, Xi?" he mused. Talking to the air made him feel a little less alone. He kicked around the clothes on the floor. There had to be *a* shirt in here somewhere, right? "Is it chilly on Entrill V?"

"Extremely. The external temperature is six degrees Celsius. As to 'what that's all about,' I could tell you. I am privy to the commander's research history and files, as well as flight plans. But I believe the commander would be angry with me."

"Oh? We certainly wouldn't want that."

"Do you think she will forgive me for not letting her open the door? I hypothesized you might not want to see her, as you did not say anything."

He paused for a moment in putting on a sock, caught somewhere between touched and freaked out. "You're concerned about forgiveness now, Xi?" And you're accurately projecting awkward situations between... what were they? Former lovers? Not exactly.

"I continue to expand my relational models."

"What?" The words were muffled by the shirt he was pulling over his head, but the AI caught them just fine.

"My relational models are concepts constructed to diagram the patterns and structures of inter-human relationships and interactions. Isa and I are working on them together. Forgiveness has been a subject as of late. I do not do that many things needing of forgiveness, but I seem to run into them a lot with the commander."

"You're not the only one. I'd bet the commander has probably already forgotten. I wouldn't worry." He dug his foot into his first boot.

"Worry is one model I intend not to employ unless absolutely necessary."

"Good idea. It's not healthy anyway."

He headed to the hatch in the hold. Sounds in the ship were hushed, still wrapped in the cocoon of sleep. Even his boots seemed loud against the grating. He was glad she hadn't suggested he wear armor. He didn't want to feel like a Theroki today. Just boots and jeans and being an ordinary person for once, if a scarred one. He did have his helmet and his multi slung on his back, though.

She was leaning against the cargo hold wall, turned away from him, her lovely form particularly striking in the way the armor hugged her, the red bright against the dull, dark charcoal of the hull. He let himself appreciate it for just a moment longer, given she wasn't facing him. Chances to admire her openly were few and far between. Her hips started to swivel—hips that had enchanted him since the first day he'd walked onboard that ship, looking to hitch a ride—and he tore his eyes up, hoping she didn't suspect him of his... admiration.

"Ready?" she said, smiling even now.

"I, uh, don't own a jacket, it seems."

"We can fix that." She gestured toward the nearby hoverbike he hadn't noticed with all his staring at her hips. "But good, you have a nonarmor helmet. Bike and breather rated? This is supposed to be a fairly clean planet, but you never know."

"It's both. Only stylish way to avoid getting your genes edited without armor, if you ask me. Breathers are for wimps and Capital types."

She snorted and lowered the helmet over her head. He followed suit. She opened a comm channel as she swung her leg over the bike and settled in. "Get on. Time's a-wasting."

She was almost… chatty. He finished engaging the locks and rubber seals around his neck before answering over the new channel. "My, you're chipper. Does that only happen early in the morning, or are we buying something fun? Laser rail gun for the ship?"

"That *would* be fun, but no. You'll see. Let's go."

He didn't quite believe this was actually happening until he was straddled behind her on the hoverbike. He held on, arms circled around her waist and far closer than he'd been to her since that ill-fated mission. He couldn't help but savor it; it likely wouldn't last long.

But as she dropped the hatch and gunned it, something occurred to him. "Don't we have a couple hoverbikes?" It felt good to say "we" and actually deserve it this time. "I can drive too, if you want."

"Uncomfortable back there, Sidassian?" Her voice was hard to read, distant.

"Not at all," he said, maybe a little too casually.

"I've got some additional shopping trips for others."

"Ah," he said, irrationally disappointed.

"Also, then where we're going wouldn't be a surprise."

He raised an eyebrow no one could see. "A surprise?"

"Yes. Because then I'd have to tell you the address."

"Well, we wouldn't want that, now would we." He eyed the low, grassy hills of sand as they raced past them, and if it was cold outside, it was doubly cold on a hoverbike. But he could tolerate it for some length of time. And maybe their first stop could get him a jacket.

Or a parka.

"How often have you ever been surprised, Kael?" she said casually. "I mean, in a good way and not in an I'm-gonna-die sort of way."

"So this is a good surprise?"

"Answer your commanding officer," she said, more amusement than edge in her voice.

"Not very often." He thought about mentioning the baby. That had been a good surprise, at least to him. It shouldn't have been. That had been irrational too. But at the time it had seemed like a purpose, a light in a life that was a rough sea of gunshots, bribes, and yellow powder. It would have been hard, sure, but it would have been something to live for.

He said nothing. He didn't think he could manage it, still, even though he gathered that maybe she already knew. Doug certainly must know. Man seemed to know everything.

She seemed to sense the darkening of his mood. "Trust me, it's a good surprise."

They rode in silence for a while, the low hills rolling past almost hypnotically uniform in their rise and fall, rise and fall, grass waving in a cold wind.

"So... does 'mostly military' mean you can listen to music while you ride?" he said.

Her body straightened slightly, giving away some surprise, but tones of a languid acoustic guitar started up. He smiled. It was the same kind chords that had been drifting around *Audacity*'s hull when he'd first met her.

"No music in a war zone," she said. "But Entrill V isn't a war zone. Or any kind of combat zone."

"What is it?"

"Mostly a trading post."

He saw the truth of that as the city appeared on the hilly horizon. Well, it was more like a town. A low gathering of one- and two-story buildings, houses stretching off into the distance. She slowed as she turned down a street lined with shops. He glanced around as she pulled off along a street and the bike lowered. She was parking.

Next to him a sign proclaimed Capital Arms: Armory & Repair Shop. To its left was a flower shop, to the right an ammo store, then a pet groomer, then a restaurant. He eyed the armor shop wistfully but then tore his gaze away, not wanting her to notice.

"Here's our stop," she said cheerily. "Get on in there, Sidassian. I'm gonna go buy some coffee first, then I'll join you. You want some?"

"Anything to defrost me would be great. You're right, it's chilly. What do you need me to get, ma'am?" he said as he climbed off the bike. He regretted the distance between them immediately.

She snorted. "Some damn armor that won't wake the dead. And nothing that was styled to look like it was run over by a tank made of chainsaws, please."

"New armor?" he blurted. "Are you serious, Commander?"

"Serious as a duck."

"A *duck*?"

She shrugged. "The old beat-up noisy shit took a beating anyway, on Desori." The part of it that clearly labeled him a Theroki didn't need to be spoken out loud. "Not sure it's worth repairing."

"I'm sure the case is auto-repairing it…"

"We may have different definitions of what 'repaired' looks like."

"It… does have its weaknesses," he muttered, barely paying attention to his words as he stared up at the signs.

"We use a lot of knockout grenades when Theroki are involved. Can't have you ending up flat on your back again, now can we?"

He looked back at her sharply. She was grinning through her unsilvered helmet visor. "Very funny, Commander. I can't believe I didn't guess sooner."

"You had a lot on your mind."

He paused, looking up at the sign, then back down at her. "Thank you, Ellen."

"Thank Simmons, it's his money." But her face said something else entirely. She glowed, if only with vicarious pleasure.

"Not for the armor. For everything. You could have said you didn't want me onboard. Given... you know, everything that's happened. I appreciate you looking past all that."

Her bright expression faltered for a moment, and he thought he saw a brief flash of panic. Why panic? He was being extremely civil, he thought.

"Sorry, I shouldn't have brought it up."

By then, the stoic if surly mask had returned. "No, no. You're welcome. Now get in there before the shop closes."

He glanced at his helmet clock. "Is it even open yet?"

"It's been open for three minutes."

"Yes, ma'am." He gave her a salute, only partly mocking.

"Top-of-the-line, now, Sidassian. Have no fears, it takes a lot to injure Simmons's bank account enough for him to groan."

"Is that the goal?"

"Oh, yes. I think he likes it."

———

THE COFFEE WAS DELICIOUS, wonderfully dark and rich, and so was the armor. Walking in and asking for top-of-the-line wasn't something he really knew how to do, or had ever been able to do, so he was still staring wide-eyed at the different models when she slipped the hot cup into his hand.

"There's like three here that all say they are the best." His eyes flicked from one to the other.

"Best is a matter of situation." She smiled, and for once it was a real smile. It warmed him more than the coffee. "And preference."

"Which line of armor do you have?" he asked before taking a sip.

"Technically, I have all of them." She grinned. "But I think you should go for this one." She pointed at the farthest to the right. The heaviest and taller than the others by a good six inches. "We've got fast folks and good shots. We should play to your strengths."

He eyed her dubiously. "My strengths?"

"Yes. And your resemblance to a boulder."

He practically choked on his coffee as she waved down the

armored man behind a half wall in the back. Guess if you owned an armor store, you should show off the wares? Or was it because if someone tried to *rob* the armor store, you should be prepared?

"Does that one look good?" she said to Kael as the man approached, quieter than Kael would have thought he could.

It *did* look good. His natural proclivity was definitely toward something with a lot of protection and a lot of power behind it. But he wasn't sure if that'd make him the odd man out among the women and all their sleek armor. "Dane's isn't even that big."

She snorted. "Dane doesn't love smashing into things like you do."

"Point taken."

"C'mon—do you want to try that one or not?" She and the shop-keep looked at him expectantly.

He took a deep breath. "Yes, ma'am, I do. Hold my coffee?"

She downright grinned as he followed the armored shopkeep's gesture toward the back.

———

THEY DIDN'T LEAVE with the armor—*his* armor, he still found it hard to believe. He didn't deserve such a beautiful suit. And if he thought the pay was good, the suit was worth more than his whole six-month contract, even if he counted hazard pay.

They were even customizing it some to his measurements, so it wouldn't arrive back at the ship until later in the day. A new jacket and a few other essentials had been acquired, and he'd tried not to feel homeless all over again in the process. He hadn't even brought a real gun on this mission. So unprepared. Luckily, he'd brought skills. And soon, he was back in his happy place, hanging on to Ellen as the hover-bike raced off again back to the ship.

Except she didn't go back to the ship.

They went out the other side of town, the lazy guitar still strumming, sort of sad, sort of peaceful. The sand dunes grew larger and then smaller again. An odd planet. Why was there so much sand if there wasn't a desert? And he'd never seen so many tufts of grass growing in a desert before, so it couldn't be that.

"We going somewhere else, Commander?" he said, when she didn't offer an explanation.

"Just one more stop. Don't worry, the armor won't beat us back."

Finally, she pulled into a small lot where a few cars and bikes were parked amid the pale sand dunes. The lot seemed like it was just in the middle of nowhere, although tall, odd trees he didn't recognize swayed in a ragged copse stretching off to the right on the other side of the dunes, so something must be over there.

He got off, and she did too, and he followed her up the dune. Now that they were stopped, an odd rushing and roaring sound met his ears.

Cresting the dune, he stopped short. The trees were scattered across the last stretch of sand in front of them. Beyond the trees and sand, a massive expanse of water stretched out, slipping away before swelling back to crash against the beach with a roar.

He tried to take another step forward but stumbled. He wasn't paying attention. Her armored hand caught his arm.

"C'mon." She headed toward the copse of trees, and he followed, his mouth hanging open. They sank to a seat, backs leaning against the narrow trunks of the tall, waving trees.

Recovering himself a little, he looked at her. Hard. What did this mean? This kindness... was it just that? Was it more than that? She smiled back at him for a brief moment before turning her dark eyes at the waves again.

"Couldn't let a chance like this go to waste," she said softly. "Not every planet has spaceports near oceans, you know."

He swallowed. "This mean you're going to get me killed, Commander?" he said slowly, hoping it was a joke.

"I sure hope not."

"Well, it's a before-you-die thing I wanted. You know?"

"I remember."

"I'd think you were taking me out here to put me down, regretting your job offer, if you hadn't just spent so much on that suit."

She snorted. But then she met his eye with an earnestness that surprised him. "I'd never do that to you, Kael."

He gazed back out at the water, unable to stare back at such intensity.

He watched the ocean for several long minutes, breathing it in, before he risked a quick glance back. She was still smiling, almost peacefully now, staring out at the water. He'd never seen her smile so much. He wanted to touch her, put his hand on her knee, something. He held still and trained his eyes on the sea instead. This was a gift of some kind, one that he didn't understand yet. But he would, he hoped, someday.

"You seem... different, Commander," he said slowly.

"Inshallah, Kael," she said gently. She hoped she was different? Why? He didn't understand it. "Inshallah."

But he didn't say any of that. He just let his shoulder lean against hers, listened to the roar of this dark ocean, and took a deep breath. For now, it was much more than enough.

AFTERWORD

Thank you so much for reading! I hope you enjoyed.

The next book in this series, *Capital Games,* is planned for later this year. If you'd like to be notified when it comes out, sign up for my mailing list. I share upcoming book news and occasional free bonuses, like maps and character interviews, rarely more than once a month.

If you're feeling froggy, consider leaving a review. Reviews help readers discover their next favorite book—and avoid ones that aren't for them! Whether it's five stars or one, I truly love hearing from readers and appreciate your honest feedback.

ALSO BY R. K. THORNE

The Enslaved Chronicles

Mage Slave

Mage Strike

Star Mage

Audacity Saga

The Empress Capsule

Capital Games (Coming 2018)

ABOUT THE AUTHOR

R. K. Thorne is an independent science fiction and fantasy author whose addiction to notebooks, role-playing games, coffee, and red wine have resulted in this book.

She has read speculative fiction since before she was probably much too young to be doing so and encourages you to do the same.

She lives in the green hills of Pennsylvania with her family and two gray cats that may or may not pull her chariot in their spare time.

For more information:
rkthorne.com

 facebook.com/ThorneBooks

 twitter.com/rk_thorne

 instagram.com/rk_thorne